John Forster

Collection of british authors: The Life of Charles Dickens

Volume V.

John Forster

Collection of british authors: The Life of Charles Dickens
Volume V.

ISBN/EAN: 9783742830890

Manufactured in Europe, USA, Canada, Australia, Japa

Cover: Foto ©Andreas Hilbeck / pixelio.de

Manufactured and distributed by brebook publishing software
(www.brebook.com)

John Forster

Collection of british authors: The Life of Charles Dickens

COLLECTION

OF

BRITISH AUTHORS

TAUCHNITZ EDITION.

VOL. 1391.

THE LIFE OF CHARLES DICKENS BY J. FORSTER.

VOL. V.

THE LIFE

OF

CHARLES DICKENS.

BY

JOHN FORSTER.

VOL. V.

LEIPZIG

BERNHARD TAUCHNITZ

1874.

TABLE OF CONTENTS.

CHAPTER XLVIII. 1853, 1854, and 1856.
Pages 93-118.

THREE SUMMERS AT BOULOGNE. ÆT. 41, 42, 44.

CHAPTER XLIX. 1855, 1856.
Pages 119-153.

RESIDENCE IN PARIS. ÆT. 43-44.

8 TABLE OF CONTENTS.

CHAPTER L. 1855-1857.
Pages 153-171.
LITTLE DORRIT, AND A LAZY TOUR. ÆT. 43-45.

CHAPTER LIII. 1858-1869.
Pages 221-236.
FIRST PAID READINGS. ÆT. 46-47.

CHAPTER LIV. 1859-1861.
Pages 237-252.
ALL THE YEAR ROUND AND THE UNCOMMERCIAL TRAVELLER. ÆT. 47-49.

ILLUSTRATIONS.

THE

LIFE OF CHARLES DICKENS.

***

CHAPTER XLV.

DAVID COPPERFIELD AND BLEAK HOUSE.

1850-1853.

Dickens never stood so high in reputation as at the completion of *Copperfield*. The popularity it obtained at the outset increased to a degree not approached by any previous book excepting *Pickwick*. "You gratify me more than I can tell "you," he wrote to Bulwer Lytton (July 1850), "by what you say about *Copperfield*, because I "hope myself that some heretofore deficient quali- "ties are there." If the power was not greater than in *Chuzzlewit*, the subject had more attrac- tiveness; there was more variety of incident, with a freer play of character; and there was withal a suspicion, which though general and vague had sharpened interest not a little, that underneath the fiction lay something of the author's life. How much, was not known by the world until he had passed away.

To be acquainted with English literature is to know, that, into its most famous prose fiction,

London: 1850.

Interest of *Copperfield*.

London:
1850.

autobiography has entered largely in disguise, and that the characters most familiar to us in the English novel had originals in actual life. Smollett never wrote a story that was not in some degree a recollection of his own adventures; and Fielding, who put something of his wife into all his heroines, had been as fortunate in finding, not Trulliber only, but Parson Adams himself, among his living experiences. To come later down, there was hardly any one ever known to Scott of whom his memory had not treasured up something to give minuter reality to the people of his fancy; and we know exactly whom to look for in Dandie Dinmont and Jonathan Oldbuck, in the office of Alan Fairford and the sick room of Crystal Croftangry. We are to observe also that it is never anything complete that is thus taken from life by a genuine writer, but only leading traits, or such as may give greater finish; that the fine artist will embody in his portraiture of one person his experiences of fifty; and that this would have been Fielding's answer to Trulliber if he had objected to the pigstye, and to Adams if he had sought to make a case of scandal out of the affair in Mrs. Slipslop's bedroom. Such questioning befell Dickens repeatedly in the course of his writings, where he freely followed, as we have seen, the method thus common to the masters in his art; but there was an instance of alleged wrong in the course of *Copperfield* where he felt his vindication to be hardly complete, and what he did thereupon was characteristic.

"I have had the queerest adventure this morn-

Real people
in novels.

Scott,
Smollett, and
Fielding.

A complaint.

"ing," he wrote (28th of December 1849) on LONDON: 1850.
the eve of his tenth number, "the receipt of
"the enclosed from Miss Moucher! It is serio-
"comic, but there is no doubt one is wrong
"in being tempted to such a use of power."
Thinking a grotesque little oddity among his
acquaintance to be safe from recognition, he had
done what Smollett did sometimes, but never
Fielding, and given way, in the first outburst of
fun·that had broken out around the fancy, to the
temptation of copying too closely peculiarities of
figure and face amounting in effect to deformity.
He was shocked at discovering the pain he had Too close to the Real.
given, and a copy is before me of the assurances
by way of reply which he at once sent to the
complainant. That he was grieved and surprised
beyond measure. That he had not intended her
altogether. That all his characters, being made
up out of many people, were composite, and never
individual. That the chair (for table) and other
matters were undoubtedly from her, but that other
traits were not hers at all; and that in Miss
Moucher's "Ain't I volatile" his friends had quite
correctly recognized the favourite utterance of a
different person. That he felt nevertheless he
had done wrong, and would now do anything to
repair it. That he had intended to employ the
character in an unpleasant way, but he would, Confession and atone-ment.
whatever the risk or inconvenience, change it all,
so that nothing but an agreeable impression
should be left. The reader will remember how
this was managed, and that the thirty-second chapter
went far to undo what the twenty-second had done.

LONDON:
1850.
A much earlier instance is the only one known
to me where a character in one of his books
intended to be odious was copied wholly from a
living original. The use of such material, never
without danger, might have been justifiable here
if anywhere, and he had himself a satisfaction in
always admitting the identity of Mr. Fang in
Oliver Twist with Mr. Laing of Hatton-garden.
But the avowal of his purpose in that case, and
Earlier and his mode of setting about it, mark strongly a
later methods. difference of procedure from that which, following
great examples, he adopted in his later books.
An allusion to a common friend in one of his
letters of the present date—"A dreadful thought
"occurs to me! how brilliant in a book!"—expresses both the continued strength of his temptations and the dread he had brought himself to
feel of immediately yielding to them; but he had
no such misgivings in the days of *Oliver Twist*.
A want for Wanting an insolent and harsh police-magistrate,
Oliver Twist. he bethought him of an original ready to his
hand in one of the London offices; and instead
of pursuing his later method of giving a personal
appearance that should in some sort render difficult the identification of mental peculiarities, he
was only eager to get in the whole man complete upon his page, figure and face as well as
manners and mind.

He wrote accordingly (from Doughty-street on
the 3rd of June 1837) to Mr. Haines,* a gentleman who then had general supervision over the

* This letter is now in the possession of S. R. Goodman, Esq. of
Brighton.

police reports for the daily papers. "In my next LONDON: 1850.
"number of *Oliver Twist* I must have a magis-
"trate; and, casting about for a magistrate whose Mr. Laing for Mr. Fang.
"harshness and insolence would render him a fit
"subject to be *shown up*, I have as a necessary
"consequence stumbled upon Mr. Laing of Hatton-
"garden celebrity. I know the man's character
"perfectly well; but as it would be necessary to
"describe his personal appearance also, I ought
"to have seen him, which (fortunately or unfor-
"tunately as the case may be) I have never done.
"In this dilemma it occurred to me that perhaps I
"might under your auspices be smuggled into the
"Hatton-garden office for a few moments some
"morning. If you can further my object I shall
"be really very greatly obliged to you." The oppor- Dickens at Hatton-gar-den (1837).
tunity was found; the magistrate was brought up
before the novelist; and shortly after, on some
fresh outbreak of intolerable temper, the home-
secretary found it an easy and popular step to
remove Mr. Laing from the bench.

This was a comfort to everybody, saving only
the principal person; but the instance was highly
exceptional, and it rarely indeed happens that to
the individual objection natural in every such
case some consideration should not be paid. In
the book that followed *Copperfield*, two characters
appeared having resemblances in manner and
speech to two distinguished writers too vivid to
be mistaken by their personal friends. To Law- Originals of Boythorn and Skimpole.
rence Boythorn, under whom Landor figured, no
objection was made; but Harold Skimpole, re-
cognizable for Leigh Hunt, led to much remark;

2*

London:
1850.

the difference being, that ludicrous traits were employed in the first to enrich without impairing an attractive person in the tale, whereas to the last was assigned a part in the plot which no fascinating foibles or gaieties of speech could redeem from contempt. Though a want of consideration was thus shown to the friend whom the character would be likely to recall to many readers, it is nevertheless very certain that the intention of Dickens was not at first, or at any time, an unkind one. He erred from thoughtlessness only. What led him to the subject at all, he has himself stated. Hunt's philosophy of moneyed obligations, always, though loudly, half jocosely proclaimed, and his ostentatious wilfulness in the humouring of that or any other theme on which he cared for the time to expatiate,*

Sayings from
Hunt's Tatler.

Last glimpse
of Leigh Hunt
(1859).

* Here are two passages taken from Hunt's writing in the *Tatler* (a charming little paper which it was one of the first ventures of the young firm of Chapman and Hall to attempt to establish for Hunt in 1830), to which accident had unluckily attracted Dickens's notice:— "Supposing us to be in want of patronage, and in possession of talent "enough to make it an honour to notice us, we would much rather have "some great and comparatively private friend, rich enough to assist us, "and amiable enough to render obligation delightful, than become the "public property of any man, or of any government. . . . . If a divinity "had given us our choice we should have said—make us La Fontaine. "who goes and lives twenty years with some rich friend, as innocent of "any harm in it as a child, and who writes what he thinks charming "verses, sitting all day under a tree." Such sayings will not bear to be deliberately read and thought over, but any kind of extravagance or oddity came from Hunt's lips with a curious fascination. There was surely never a man of so sunny a nature, who could draw so much pleasure from common things, or to whom books were a world so real, so exhaustless, so delightful. I was only seventeen when I derived from him the tastes which have been the solace of all subsequent years, and I well remember the last time I saw him at Hammersmith, not long before his death in 1859, when, with his delicate, worn, but keenly intellectual face, his large luminous eyes, his thick shock of wiry grey hair, and a little cape of faded black silk over his shoulders, he looked like an old French abbé. He was buoyant and pleasant as ever; and was busy upon a vindication of Chaucer and Spenser from Cardinal Wiseman, who had attacked them for alleged sensuous and voluptuous qualities.

had so often seemed to Dickens to be whimsical and attractive that, wanting an "airy quality" for the man he invented, this of Hunt occurred to him; and "partly for that reason, and partly, he "has since often grieved to think, for the pleasure "it afforded to find a delightful manner repro- "ducing itself under his hand, he yielded to the "temptation of too often making the character "speak like his old friend." This apology was made * after Hunt's death, and mentioned a re- vision of the first sketch, so as to render it less like, at the suggestion of two other friends of Hunt. The friends were Procter (Barry Cornwall) and myself; the feeling having been mine from the first that the likeness was too like. Procter did not immediately think so, but a little reflec- tion brought him to that opinion. "You will see "from the enclosed," Dickens wrote (17th of March 1852), "that Procter is much of my mind. I will "nevertheless go through the character again in "the course of the afternoon, and soften down "words here and there." But before the day closed Procter had again written to him, and next morning this was the result. "I have again gone "over every part of it very carefully, and I think "I have made it much less like. I have also "changed Leonard to Harold. I have no right "to give Hunt pain, and I am so bent upon not "doing it that I wish you would look at all the "proof once more, and indicate any particular "place in which you feel it particularly like. "Whereupon I will alter that place."

*In a paper in *All the Year Round*.

Yielding to temptation.

Friends consulted.

Changes made in Skimpole.

Upon the whole the alterations were considerable, but the radical wrong remained. The pleasant sparkling airy talk, which could not be
mistaken, identified with odious qualities a friend
only known to the writer by attractive ones; and

for this there was no excuse. Perhaps the only
person acquainted with the original who failed to
recognize the copy, was the original himself (a
common case); but good-natured friends in time
told Hunt everything, and painful explanations
followed, where nothing was possible to Dickens
but what amounted to a friendly evasion of the
points really at issue. The time for redress had
gone. I yet well remember with what eager
earnestness, on one of these occasions, he strove

to set Hunt up again in his own esteem. "Sepa-
"rate in your own mind," he said to him,
"what you see of yourself from what other people
"tell you that they see. As it has given you so
"much pain, I take it at its worst, and say I am
"deeply sorry, and that I feel I did wrong in
"doing it. I should otherwise have taken it at
"its best, and ridden off upon what I strongly
"feel to be the truth, that there is nothing in it
"that *should* have given you pain. Every one in
"writing must speak from points of his experience,
"and so I of mine with you: but when I have felt
"it was going too close I stopped myself, and the

"most blotted parts of my MS. are those in which
"I have been striving hard to make the impres-
"sion I was writing from, *un*like you. The diary-
"writing I took from Haydon, not from you. I
"now first learn from yourself that you ever set

"anything to music, and I could not have copied LONDON: 1850.
"*that* from you. The character is not you, for
"there are traits in it common to fifty thousand
"people besides, and I did not fancy you would
"ever recognize it. Under similar disguises my Relatives put into books.
"own father and mother are in my books, and
"you might as well see your likeness in Micawber."
The distinction is that the foibles of Mr. Micawber
and of Mrs. Nickleby, however laughable, make
neither of them in speech or character less love-
able; and that this is not to be said of Skimpole's.
The kindly or unkindly impression makes all the
difference where liberties are taken with a friend;
and even this entirely favourable condition will
not excuse the practice to many, where near relatives are concerned.

For what formerly was said of the Micawber
resemblances, Dickens has been sharply criticized;
and in like manner it was thought objectionable
in Scott that for the closing scenes of Crystal Scott and his father.
Croftangry he should have found the original of
his fretful patient at the death-bed of his own
father. Lockhart, who tells us this, adds with a
sad significance that he himself lived to see the
curtain fall at Abbotsford upon even such another
scene. But to no purpose will such objections
still be made. All great novelists will continue
to use their experiences of nature and fact,
whencesoever derivable; and a remark made to
Lockhart by Scott himself suggests their vindica- Scott to Lockhart.
tion. "If a man will paint from nature, he will
"be most likely to interest and amuse those who
"are daily looking at it."

LONDON:
1850.
The Micawber offence otherwise was not grave. We have seen in what way Dickens was moved or inspired by the rough lessons of his boyhood, and the groundwork of the character was then undoubtedly laid; but the rhetorical exuberance impressed itself upon him later, and from this, as it expanded and developed in a thousand amusing ways, the full-length figure took its great charm. Better illustration of it could not perhaps be given than by passages from
Dickens and his father. letters of Dickens, written long before Micawber was thought of, in which this peculiarity of his father found frequent and always agreeable expression. Several such have been given in this work from time to time, and one or two more may here be added. It is proper to preface them by saying that no one could know the elder Dickens without secretly liking him the better for these flourishes of speech, which adapted themselves so readily to his gloom as well as to his cheerfulness, that it was difficult not to fancy they had helped him considerably in both, and had rendered more tolerable to him, if also more possible, the shade and sunshine of his chequered
Flourishes of speech. life. "If you should have an opportunity *pendente* "*lite*, as my father would observe—indeed did on "some memorable ancient occasions when he in-"formed me that the ban-dogs would shortly have "him at bay"—Dickens wrote in December 1847. "I have a letter from my father" (May 1841) "lamenting the fine weather, invoking congenial "tempests, and informing me that it will not be
I. 231. "possible for him to stay more than another year

"in Devonshire, as he must then proceed to Paris
"to consolidate Augustus's French." "There has ————
"arrived," he writes from the Peschiere in September 1844, "a characteristic letter for Kate
"from my father. He dates it Manchester, and
"says he has reason to believe that he will be in
"town with the pheasants, on or about the first
"of October. He has been with Fanny in the
"Isle of Man for nearly two months: finding
"there, as he goes on to observe, troops of friends, Micawber
"and every description of continental luxury at a flights.
"cheap rate." Describing in the same year the
departure from Genoa of an English physician
and acquaintance, he adds: "We are very sorry
"to lose the benefit of his advice—or, as my
"father would say, to be deprived, to a certain
"extent, of the concomitant advantages, whatever
"they may be, resulting from his medical skill,
"such as it is, and his professional attendance, in
"so far as it may be so considered." Thus also
it delighted Dickens to remember that it was of
one of his connections his father wrote a cele- Sayings of
brated sentence; "And I must express my tendency John
"to believe that his longevity is (to say the least Dickens.
"of it) extremely problematical:" and that it was
to another, who had been insisting somewhat ob-
trusively on dissenting and nonconformist supe-
riorities, he addressed words which deserve to be
no less celebrated; "The Supreme Being must be
"an entirely different individual from what I have
"every reason to believe him to be, if He would
"care in the least for the society of your rela-
"tions." There was a laugh in the enjoyment of

London:
1850.
Humouring
a foible.

all this, no doubt, but with it much personal fondness; and the ·feeling of the creator of Micawber as he thus humoured and remembered the foibles of his original, found its counterpart in that of his readers for the creation itself, as its part was played out in the story. Nobody likes Micawber less for his follies; and Dickens liked his father more, the more he recalled his whim‑sical qualities. "The longer I live, the better man "I think him," he exclaimed afterwards. The fact and the fancy had united whatever was most grateful to him in both.

No harm
done.

It is a tribute to the generally healthful and manly tone of the story of *Copperfield* that such should be the outcome of the eccentricities of this leading personage in it; and the superiority in this respect of Micawber over Skimpole is one of many indications of the inferiority of *Bleak House* to its predecessor. With leading resem‑blances that make it difficult to say which cha‑racter best represents the principle or no principle of impecuniosity, there cannot be any doubt which has the advantage in moral and intellectual de‑velopment. It is genuine humour against personal satire. Between. the worldly circumstances of the two, there is nothing to choose; but as to every‑thing else it is the difference between shabbiness and greatness. Skimpole's sunny talk might be expected to please as much as Micawber's gorgeous speech, the design of both being to take the edge off poverty. But in the ‑one we have no relief from attendant meanness or distress, and we drop down from the airiest fancies into sordidness and

Resem‑
blances and
differences.

pain; whereas in the other nothing pitiful or merely selfish ever touches us. At its lowest depth of what is worst, we never doubt that something better must turn up; and of a man who sells his bedstead that he may entertain his friend, we altogether refuse to think nothing but badly. This is throughout the free and cheery style of *Copperfield.* The masterpieces of Dickens's humour are not in it; but he has nowhere given such variety of play to his invention, and the book is unapproached among his writings for its completeness of effect and uniform pleasantness of tone.

London: 1850.
Skimpole and Micawber.

What has to be said hereafter of those writings generally, will properly restrict what is said here, as in previous instances, mainly to personal illustration. The *Copperfield* disclosures formerly made will for ever connect the book with the author's individual story; but too much has been assumed, from those revelations, of a full identity of Dickens with his hero, and of a supposed intention that his own character as well as parts of his career should be expressed in the narrative. It is right to warn the reader as to this. He can judge for himself how far the childish experiences are likely to have given the turn to Dickens's genius; whether their bitterness had so burnt into his nature, as, in the hatred of oppression, the revolt against abuse of power, and the war with injustice under every form displayed in his earliest books, to have reproduced itself only; and to what extent mere compassion for his own childhood may account for the strange fascination al-

Dickens and David.

Outcome of early trials.

LONDON:
1850.

ways exerted over him by child - suffering and sorrow. But, many as are the resemblances in Copperfield's adventures to portions of those of Dickens, and often as reflections occur to David which no one intimate with Dickens could fail to recognize as but the reproduction of his, it would

Self-por-
traiture not
attempted.

be the greatest mistake to imagine anything like a complete identity of the fictitious novelist with the real one, beyond the Hungerford scenes; or to suppose that the youth, who then received his first harsh schooling in life, came out of it as little harmed or hardened as David did. The language of the fiction reflects only faintly the narrative of

Compare
l. 60-85.
with 11th
chapter of
Copperfield.

the actual fact; and the man whose character it helped to form was expressed not less faintly in the impulsive impressionable youth, incapable of resisting the leading of others, and only disciplined into self-control by the later griefs of his entrance into manhood. Here was but another proof how thoroughly Dickens understood his calling, and that to weave fact with fiction unskilfully would be only to make truth less true.

The character of the hero of the novel finds indeed his right place in the story he is supposed to tell, rather by unlikeness than by likeness to Dickens, even where intentional resemblance might

The auto-
biographic
form.

seem to be prominent. Take autobiography as a design to show that any man's life may be as a mirror of existence to all men, and the individual career becomes altogether secondary to the variety of experiences received and rendered back in it. This particular form in imaginative literature has too often led to the indulgence of mental analysis,

metaphysics, and sentiment, all in excess: but London: 1850. Its dangers avoided.
Dickens was carried safely over these allurements
by a healthy judgment and sleepless creative
fancy; and even the method of his narrative is
more simple here than it generally is in his books.
His imaginative growths have less luxuriance of
underwood, and the crowds of external images
always rising so vividly before him are more
within control.

Consider Copperfield thus in his proper place
in the story, and sequence as well as connection
will be given to the varieties of its childish adventure. The first warm nest of love in which
his vain fond mother, and her quaint kind servant,
cherish him; the quick-following contrast of hard
dependence and servile treatment; the escape from Consistent drawing.
that premature and dwarfed maturity by natural
relapse into a more perfect childhood; the then
leisurely growth of emotions and faculties into
manhood; these are component parts of a character consistently drawn. The sum of its achievement is to be a successful cultivation of letters;
and often as such imaginary discipline has been
the theme of fiction, there are not many happier
conceptions of ·it. The ideal and real parts of
the boy's nature receive development in the proportions which contribute best to the end desired;
the readiness for impulsive attachments that had
put him into the leading of others, has underneath
it a base of truthfulness on which at last he rests
in safety; the practical man is the outcome of the
fanciful youth; and a more than equivalent for Design of David's character.
the graces of his visionary days, is found in the

active sympathies that life has opened to him. Many experiences have come within its range, and his heart has had room for all. Our interest in him cannot but be increased by knowing how much he expresses of what the author had himself gone through; but David includes far less than this, and infinitely more.

That the incidents arise easily, and to the very end connect themselves naturally and unobtrusively with the characters of which they are a part, is to be said perhaps more truly of this than of any other of Dickens's novels. There is a profusion of distinct and distinguishable people, and a prodigal wealth of detail; but unity of drift or purpose is apparent always, and the tone is uniformly right. By the course of the events we learn the value of self-denial and patience, quiet endurance of unavoidable ills, strenuous effort against ills remediable; and everything in the fortunes of the actors warns us, to strengthen our generous emotions and to guard the purities of home. It is easy thus to account for the supreme popularity of *Copperfield*, without the addition that it can hardly have had a reader, man or lad, who did not discover that he was something of a Copperfield himself. Childhood and youth live again for all of us in its marvellous boy-experiences. Mr. Micawber's presence must not prevent my saying that it does not take the lead of the other novels in humorous creation; but in the use of humour to bring out prominently the ludicrous in any object or incident without excluding or weakening its most enchanting senti-

Tone of the novel.

Its boy-life.

Humour and sentiment.

ment, it stands decidedly first. It is the perfection London: 1850.
of English mirth. We are apt to resent the ex-
hibition of too much goodness, but it is here so
qualified by oddity as to become not merely
palatable but attractive; and even pathos is
heightened by what in other hands would only
make it comical. That there are also faults in
the book is certain, but none that are incom-
patible with the most masterly qualities; and a book Why books continue.
becomes everlasting by the fact, not that faults
are not in it, but that genius nevertheless is
there.

Of its method, and its author's generally, in
the delineation of character, something will have
to be said on a later page. The author's own
favourite people in it, I think, were the Peggotty
group; and perhaps he was not far wrong. It
has been their fate, as with all the leading figures
of his invention, to pass their names into the lan- The Peggottys.
guage, and become types; and he has nowhere
given happier embodiment to that purity of
homely goodness, which, by the kindly and all-
reconciling influences of humour, may exalt into
comeliness and even grandeur the clumsiest forms
of humanity. What has been indicated in the
style of the book as its greatest charm is here felt
most strongly. The ludicrous so helps the pathos,
and the humour so uplifts and refines the sentiment, that mere rude affection and simple man-
liness in these Yarmouth boatmen, passed through
the fires of unmerited suffering and heroic endurance, take forms half-chivalrous half-sublime. It
is one of the cants of critical superiority to make

supercilious mention of the serious passages in this great writer; but the storm and shipwreck at the close of *Copperfield*, when the body of the seducer is flung dead upon the shore amid the ruins of the home he has wasted and by the side of the man whose heart he has broken, the one as unconscious of what he had failed to reach as the other of what he has perished to save, is a description that may compare with the most impressive in the language. There are other people drawn into this catastrophe who are among the failures of natural delineation in the book.

Miss Dartle. But though Miss Dartle is curiously unpleasant, there are some natural traits in her (which Dickens's least life-like people are never without); and it was from one of his lady friends, very familiar to him indeed, he copied her peculiarity of never saying anything outright, but hinting it merely, and making more of it that way. Of Mrs. Steerforth it may also be worth remembering that Thackeray had something of a fondness for her.

Mrs. Steer-forth. "I knew how it would be when I began," says a pleasant letter all about himself written immediately after she appeared in the story. "My "letters to my mother are like this, but then she "likes 'em—like Mrs. Steerforth: don't you like "Mrs. Steerforth?"

Turning to another group there is another elderly lady to be liked without a shadow of misgiving; abrupt, angular, extravagant, but the very soul of magnanimity and rectitude; a character thoroughly made out in all its parts; a gnarled and knotted piece of female timber, sound to

the core; a woman Captain Shandy would have
loved for her startling oddities, and who is linked
to the gentlest of her sex by perfect womanhood.
Dickens has done nothing better, for solidness
and truth all round, than Betsey Trotwood. It is
one of her oddities to have a fool for a companion; but this is one of them that has also
most pertinence and wisdom. By a line thrown
out in *Wilhelm Meister*, that the true way of
treating the insane was, in all respects possible,
to act to them as if they were sane, Goethe anticipated what it took a century to apply to the
most terrible disorder of humanity; and what Mrs.
Trotwood does for Mr. Dick goes a step farther,
by showing how often asylums might be dis-
pensed with, and how large might be the number
of deficient intellects manageable with patience in
their own homes.   Characters hardly less distinguishable for truth as well as oddity are the
kind old nurse and her husband the carrier,
whose vicissitudes alike of love and of mortality
are condensed into the three words since become
part of universal speech, *Barkis is willin'*. There
is wholesome satire of much utility in the conversion
of the brutal schoolmaster of the earlier scenes
into the tender Middlesex magistrate at the close.
Nor is the humour anywhere more subtle than
in the country undertaker, who makes up in fullness
of heart for scantness of breath, and has so little
of the vampire propensity of the town undertaker
in *Chuzzlewit*, that he dares not even inquire
after friends who are ill for fear of unkindly mis-
construction. The test of a master in creative

London:
1850.

Betsey
Trotwood.

Wise hint of
Goethe's.

Truths in
oddities.

A country
undertaker.

fiction, according to Hazlitt, is less in contrasting characters that are unlike than in distinguishing those that are like; and to many examples of the art in Dickens, such as the Shepherd and Chadband, Creakle and Squeers, Charley Bates and the Dodger, the Guppys and the Wemmicks, Mr. Jaggers and Mr. Vholes, Sampson Brass and Conversation Kenge, Jack Bunsby, Captain Cuttle, and Bill Barley, the Perkers and Pells, the Dodsons and Fogs, Sarah Gamp and Betsy Prig, and a host of others, is to be added the nicety of distinction between those eminent furnishers of funerals, Mr. Mould and Messrs. Omer and Joram. All the mixed mirth and sadness of the story are skilfully drawn into the handling of this portion of it; and, amid wooings and preparations for weddings and church-ringing bells for baptisms, the steadily-going rat-tat of the hammer on the coffin is heard.

Of the heroines who divide so equally between them the impulsive, easily swayed, not disloyal but sorely distracted affections of the hero, the spoilt foolishness and tenderness of the loving little child-wife, Dora, is more attractive than the too unfailing wisdom and self-sacrificing goodness of the angel-wife, Agnes. The scenes of the courtship and housekeeping are matchless; and the glimpses of Doctors' Commons, opening those views, by Mr. Spenlow, of man's vanity of expectation and inconsistency of conduct in neglecting the sacred duty of making a will, on which he largely moralizes the day before he dies intestate, form a background highly appropriate

to face p. 35.   DEVONSHIRE-T

C-TETI: 29th October 1840.

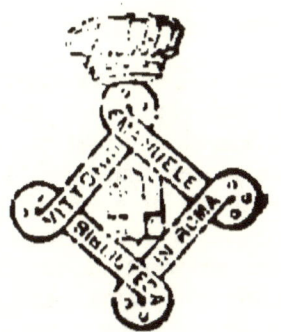

to David's domesticities. This was among the re-productions of personal experience in the book; but it was a sadder knowledge that came with the conviction some years later, that David's contrasts in his earliest married life between his happiness enjoyed and his happiness once anticipated, the "vague unhappy loss or want of something" of which he so frequently complains, reflected also a personal experience which had not been supplied in fact so successfully as in fiction. (A closing word may perhaps be allowed, to connect with Devonshire-terrace the last book written there. On the page opposite is engraved a drawing by Maclise of the house where so many of Dickens's masterpieces were composed, done on the first anniversary of the day when his daughter Kate was born.)

Lo**n**don: 1853.

Bleak House followed *Copperfield*, which in some respects it copied in the autobiographical form by means of extracts from the personal relation of its heroine. But the distinction between the narrative of David and the diary of Esther, like that between Micawber and Skimpole, marks the superiority of the first to its successor. To represent a storyteller as giving the most surprising vividness to manners, motives, and characters of which we are to believe her, all the time, as artlessly unconscious, as she is also entirely ignorant of the good qualities in herself she is naïvely revealing in the story, was a difficult enterprise, full of hazard in any case, not worth success, and certainly not successful. Ingenuity is more apparent than freshness, the invention is

Contrast of Father and David.

Risks not worth running.

3*

neither easy nor unstrained, and though the old
marvellous power over the real is again abun-
dantly manifest, there is some alloy of the artifi-
cial. Nor can this be said of Esther's relation
without some general application to the book of
which it forms so large a part. The novel is
nevertheless, in the very important particular of
construction, perhaps the best thing done by
Dickens.

In his later writings he had been assiduously
cultivating this essential of his art, and here he
brought it very nearly to perfection. Of the
tendency of composing a story piecemeal to induce greater concern for the part than for the
whole, he had been always conscious; but I remember a remark also made by him to the effect
that to read a story in parts had no less a tendency to prevent the reader's noticing how
thoroughly a work so presented might be calcu-
lated for perusal as a whole. Look back from the
last to the first page of the present novel, and
not even in the highest examples of this kind of
elaborate care will it be found, that event leads
more closely to event, or that the separate incidents have been planned with a more studied
consideration of the bearing they are severally to
have on the general result. Nothing is introduced
at random, everything tends to the catastrophe,
the various lines of the plot converge and fit to
its centre, and to the larger interest all the rest is
irresistibly drawn. The heart of the story is a
Chancery suit. On this the plot hinges, and on
incidents connected with it, trivial or important,

the passion and suffering turn exclusively. Chance LONDON: 1853.
words, or the deeds of chance people, to appear-
ance irrelevant, are found everywhere influencing *Constructive art.*
the course taken by a train of incidents of which
the issue is life or death, happiness or misery, to
men and women perfectly unknown to them, and
to whom they are unknown. Attorneys of all possible grades, law clerks of every conceivable kind,
the copyist, the law stationer, the usurer, all sorts
of money lenders, suitors of every description,
haunters of the Chancery court and their victims,
are for ever moving round about the lives of the
chief persons in the tale, and drawing them on
insensibly, but very certainly, to the issues that
await them. Even the fits of the little law- *Incidents and persons interwoven.*
stationer's servant help directly in the chain of
small things that lead indirectly to Lady Dedlock's death. One strong chain of interest holds
together Chesney Wold and its inmates, Bleak
House and the Jarndyce group, Chancery with its
sorry and sordid neighbourhood. The characters
multiply as the tale advances, but in each the
drift is the same. "There's no great odds betwixt
"my noble and learned brother and myself," says
the grotesque proprietor of the rag and bottle
shop under the wall of Lincoln's-inn, "they call *Two Chancery shops.*
"me Lord Chancellor and my shop Chancery,
"and we both of us grub on in a muddle." *Edax
rerum* the motto of both, but with a difference.
Out of the lumber of the shop emerge slowly
some fragments of evidence by which the chief
actors in the story are sensibly affected, and to
which Chancery itself might have succumbed if

LONDON:
1853.
Shells of
the oyster.
its devouring capacities had been less complete. But by the time there is found among the lumber the will which puts all to rights in the Jarndyce suit, it is found to be too late to put anything to rights. The costs have swallowed up the estate, and there is an end of the matter.

What in one sense is a merit however may in others be a defect, and this book has suffered by the very completeness with which its Chancery moral is worked out. The didactic in Dickens's earlier novels derived its strength from being merely incidental to interest of a higher and more permanent kind, and not in a small degree from the playful sportiveness and fancy that lighted up Defects of
Bleak House. its graver illustrations. Here it is of sterner stuff, too little relieved, and all-pervading. The fog so marvellously painted in the opening chapter has hardly cleared away when there arises, in *Jarndyce v. Jarndyce*, as bad an atmosphere to breathe in; and thenceforward to the end, clinging round the people of the story as they come or go, in dreary mist or in heavy cloud, it is rarely absent. Dickens has himself described his purpose to have been to dwell on the romantic side of familiar things. But it is the romance of discontent and misery, with a very restless dissatisfied moral, and is too much brought about by agencies disagreeable and sordid. The Guppys, Weevles, Snagsbys, Chadbands, Krooks, and Smallweeds, even the Kenges, Vholeses, and Too little
relief. Tulkinghorns, are much too real to be pleasant; and the necessity becomes urgent for the reliefs and contrasts of a finer humanity. These last are

not wanting; yet it must be said that we hardly London, 1853.
escape, even with them, into the old freedom and
freshness of the author's imaginative worlds, and
that the too conscious unconsciousness of Esther
flings something of a shade on the radiant goodness of John Jarndyce himself. Nevertheless there
are very fine delineations in the story. The crazed Set-off.
little Chancery lunatic, Miss Flite; the loud-voiced
tender-souled Chancery victim, Gridley; the poor
good-hearted youth Richard, broken up in life
and character by the suspense of the Chancery
suit on whose success he is to "begin the world,"
believing himself to be saving money when he is
stopped from squandering it, and thinking that
having saved it he is entitled to fling it away;
trooper George, with the Bagnets and their house- Successes in character.
hold, where the most ludicrous points are more
forcible for the pathetic touches underlying them;
the Jellyby interior, and its philanthropic strong-
minded mistress, placid and smiling amid a
household muddle out-muddling Chancery itself;
the model of deportment, Turveydrop the elder,
whose relations to the young people, whom he so
superbly patronizes by being dependent on them
for everything, touch delightfully some subtle
points of truth; the inscrutable Tulkinghorn, and
the immortal Bucket; all these, and especially the
last, have been added by this book to the list of
people more intimately and permanently known
to us than the scores of actual familiar acquaintance whom we see around us living and
dying.

But how do we know them? There are plenty

London:
1853.
Praise with
a grudge. to tell us that it is by vividness of external observation rather than by depth of imaginative insight,
by tricks of manner and phrase rather than by
truth of character, by manifestation outwardly
rather than by what lies behind. Another opportunity will present itself for some remark on this
kind of criticism, which has always had a special
pride in the subtlety of its differences from what
the world may have shown itself prone to admire.
"In my father's library," wrote Landor to Southey's
Value of
critical
judgments. daughter Edith, "was the *Critical Review* from its
"commencement; and it would have taught me, if
"I could not even at a very early age teach my-
"self better, that Fielding, Sterne, and Goldsmith
"were really worth nothing." It is a style. that
will never be without cultivators, and its frequent
application to Dickens will be shown hereafter.
But in speaking of a book in which some want
of all the freshness of his genius first became
apparent, it would be wrong to omit to add that
his method of handling a character is as strongly
impressed on the better portions of it as on the
best of his writings. It is difficult to say when
a peculiarity becomes too grotesque, or an extra-
What Art has
room for. vagance too farcical, to be within the limits of art,
for it is the truth of these as of graver things
that they exist in the world in just the proportions
and degree in which genius can discover them.
But no man had ever so surprising a faculty as
Dickens of becoming himself what he was representing; and of entering into mental phases
and processes so absolutely, in conditions of life
the most varied, as to reproduce them completely

in dialogue without need of an explanatory word. LONDON: 1853.
(He only departed from this method once, with Mastery in
a result which will then be pointed out.) In dialogue.
speaking on a former page of the impression of
reality thus to a singular degree conveyed by
him, it was remarked that where characters so
revealed themselves the author's part in them was
done; and in the book under notice there is none,
not excepting those least attractive which apparently present only prominent or salient qualities, in
which it will not be found that the characteristic *Handling of*
feature embodied, or the main idea personified, *character.*
contains as certainly also some human truth
universally applicable. To expound or discuss
his creations, to lay them psychologically bare, to
analyse their organisms, to subject to minute
demonstration their fibrous and other tissues, was
not at all Dickens's way. His genius was his
fellow feeling with his race; his mere personality
was never the bound or limit to his perceptions,
however strongly sometimes it might colour them;
he never stopped to dissect or anatomize his own
work; but no man could better adjust the outward
and visible oddities in a delineation to its inner
and unchangeable veracities. The rough estimates
we form of character, if we have any truth of
perception, are on the whole correct: but men *The contact*
touch and interfere with one another by the *of extremes.*
contact of their extremes, and it may very often
become necessarily the main business of a novelist
to display the salient points, the sharp angles, or
the prominences merely.

The pathetic parts of *Bleak House* do not live

largely in remembrance, but the deaths of Richard
and of Gridley, the wandering fancies of Miss
Flite, and the extremely touching way in which
the gentleman-nature of the pompous old baronet,
Dedlock, asserts itself under suffering, belong to
a high order of writing.   There is another most
affecting example, taking the lead of the rest, in
the poor street-sweeper Jo; which has made perhaps as deep an impression as anything in
Dickens.   "We have been reading *Bleak House*
"aloud," the good Dean Ramsay wrote to me
very shortly before his death.   "Surely it is one
"of his most powerful and successful!   What a
"triumph is Jo!   Uncultured nature is *there* indeed;
"the intimations of true heartfeeling, the glimmer-
"ings of higher feeling, all are there; but every-
"thing still consistent and in harmony.   Wonderful
"is the genius that can show all this, yet keep it
"only and really part of the character itself, low
"or common as it may be, and use no morbid or
"fictitious colouring.   To my mind, nothing in
"the field of fiction is to be found in English
"literature surpassing the death of Jo!"   What
occurs at and after the inquest is as worth remembering.   Jo's evidence is rejected because he
cannot exactly say what will be done to him
after he is dead if he should tell a lie;* but he

* "O!   Here's the boy, gentlemen!   Here he is, very muddy, very
"hoarse, very ragged.   Now, boy!—But stop a minute.   Caution.   This
"boy must be put through a few preliminary paces.   Name, Jo.   No-
"thing else that he knows on.   Don't know that everybody has two
"names.   Never heerd of sich a think.   Don't know that Jo is short for
"a longer name.   Thinks it long enough for *him*.   *He* don't find no fault
"with it.   Spell it?   No.   *He* can't spell it.   No father, no mother, no
"friends.   Never been to school.   What's home?   Knows a broom's a
"broom, and knows it's wicked to tell a lie.   Don't recollect who told

manages to say afterwards very exactly what the London:
·1853.
deceased while he lived did to him. That one
cold winter night, when he was shivering in a
doorway near his crossing, a man turned to look What Jo
cannot say
exactly.
at him, and came back, and, having questioned
him and found he had not a friend in the world,
said "Neither have I. Not one!" and gave him
the price of a supper and a night's lodging.
That the man had often spoken to him since,
and asked him if he slept of a night, and how
he bore cold and hunger, or if he ever wished to
die; and would say in passing "I am as poor as
"you to-day, Jo" when he had no money, but What he
remembers
very exactly.
when he had any would always give some. "He
"wos wery good to me," says the boy, wiping his
eyes with his wretched sleeve. "Wen I see him
"a-layin' so stritched out just now, I wished he
"could have heerd me tell him so. He wos werry
"good to me, he wos!" The inquest over, the
body is flung into a pestiferous churchyard in
the next street, houses overlooking it on every
side, and a reeking little tunnel of a court giving
access to its iron gate. "With the night, comes Town graves.
"a slouching figure through the tunnel-court, to
"the outside of the iron gate. It holds the gate
"with its hands, and looks in within the bars;
"stands looking in, for a little while. It then,

"him about the broom, or about the lie, but knows both. Can't exactly
"say what'll be done to him arter he's dead if he tells a lie to the gentle-
"man here, but believes it'll be something wery bad to punish him, and
"serve him right—and so he'll tell the truth. 'This won't do, gentle-
"'men,' says the coroner, with a melancholy shake of the head. . . .
"'Can't exactly say won't do, you know. . . . It's terrible depravity.
"'Put the boy aside.' Boy put aside; to the great edification of the
"audience;—especially of Little Swills, the Comic Vocalist."

LONDON:
1853.

One last
friend.

"with an old broom it carries, softly sweeps the "step, and makes the archway clean.   It does so, "very busily, and trimly; looks in again, a little "while; and so departs."   These are among the things in Dickens that cannot be forgotten; and if *Bleak House* had many more faults than have been found in it, such salt and savour as this might freshen it for some generations.

The first intention was to have made Jo more prominent in the story, and its earliest title was taken from the tumbling tenements in Chancery, "Tom-all-Alone's," where he finds his wretched habitation; but this was abandoned.   On the other hand, Dickens was encouraged and strengthened in his design of assailing Chancery abuses and delays by receiving, a few days after the appear-

Originals of
Chancery
abuses.

ance of his first number, a striking pamphlet on the subject containing details so apposite that he took from them, without change in any material point, the memorable case related in his fifteenth chapter.   Any one who examines the tract* will see how exactly true is the reference to it made by Dickens in his preface.   "The case of Gridley "is in no essential altered from one of actual oc- "currence, made public by a disinterested person

The truth of
Gridley's
case.

"who was professionally acquainted with the "whole of the monstrous wrong from beginning "to end."   The suit, of which all particulars are given, affected a single farm, in value not more

---

* By W. Challinor Esq. of Leek in Staffordshire, by whom it has been obligingly sent to me, with a copy of Dickens's letter acknowledging the receipt of it from the author on the 11th of March 1852. On the first of that month the first number of *Bleak House* had appeared, but two numbers of it were then already written.

than £1200, but all that its owner possessed in the world, against which a bill had been filed for a £300 legacy left in the will bequeathing the farm. In reality there was only one defendant, but in the bill, by the rule of the Court, there were seventeen; and, after two years had been occupied over the seventeen answers, everything had to begin over again because an eighteenth had been accidentally omitted. "What a mockery "of justice this is," says Mr. Challinor, "the facts An actual "speak for themselves, and I can personally vouch occurrence. "for their accuracy. The costs already incurred "in reference to this £300 legacy are not less "than from £800 to £900, and the parties are "no forwarder. Already near five years have "passed by, and the plaintiff would be glad to "give up his chance of the legacy if he could "escape from his liability to costs, while the de- "fendants, who own the little farm left by the "testator, have scarce any other prospect before "them than ruin."

CHAPTER XLVI.

HOME INCIDENTS AND HARD TIMES.

1853—1851—1853.

LONDON:
1852.

DAVID COPPERFIELD had been written in Devonshire-terrace for the most part, between the
opening of 1849 and October 1850, its publication covering that time; and its sale, which has
since taken the lead of all his books but *Pickwick*, never then exceeding twenty-five thousand.
But though it remained thus steady for the time,
the popularity of the book added largely to the
sale of its successor. *Bleak House* was begun in
his new abode of Tavistock House at the end of
November 1851; was carried on, amid the excitements of the Guild performances, through the
following year; was finished at Boulogne in the
August of 1853; and was dedicated to "his
"friends and companions in the Guild of Litera-
"ture and Art."

-In March 1852 the first number appeared,*

*Bleak
House sale,
IV. 247.*

*Completion.
Aug. 1853.*

Proposed
titles.

* I subjoin the dozen titles successively proposed for *Bleak House.*
1. "Tom-all-Alone's. The Ruined House;" 2. "Tom-all-Alone's. The
"Solitary House that was always shut up;" 3. "Bleak House Academy;"
4. "The East Wind;" 5. "Tom-all-Alone's. The Ruined [House,
"Building, Factory, Mill] that got into Chancery and never got out;"
6. "Tom-all-Alone's. The Solitary House where the Grass grew;"
7. "Tom-all-Alone's. The Solitary House that was always shut up
"and never Lighted;" 8. "Tom-all-Alone's. The Ruined Mill, that got
"into Chancery and never got out;" 9. "Tom-all-Alone's. The Solitary
"House where the Wind howled;" 10. "Tom-all-Alone's. The Ruined
"House that got into Chancery and never got out;" 11. "Bleak House
"and the East Wind. How they both got into Chancery and never got
"out;" 12. "Bleak House."

and its sale was mentioned in the same letter London:
1852.
from Tavistock House (7th of March) which told ————
of his troubles in the story at its outset, and of
other anxieties incident to the common lot and
inseparable equally from its joys and sorrows,
through which his life was passing at the time.
"My Highgate journey yesterday was a sad one. Grave at
"Sad to think how all journeys tend that way. I Highgate,
IV. 277.
"went up to the cemetery to look for a piece of
"ground. In no hope of a Government bill,* and
"in a foolish dislike to leaving the little child
"shut up in a vault there, I think of pitching a
"tent under the sky. . . Nothing has taken place
"here: but I believe, every hour, that it must next
"hour. Wild ideas are upon me of going to
"Paris — Rouen — Switzerland — somewhere — and Restless.
"writing the remaining two-thirds of the next No.
"aloft in some queer inn room. I have been
"hanging over it, and have got restless. Want a
"change I think. Stupid. We were at 30,000 Sale of his
novel.
"when I last heard. . . I am sorry to say that
"after all kinds of evasions, I am obliged to dine
"at Lansdowne House to-morrow. But maybe
"the affair will come off to-night and give me an
"excuse! I enclose proofs of No. 2. Browne has Skimpole
portrait.
"done Skimpole, and helped to make him singu-
"larly unlike the great original. Look it over,
"and say what occurs to you. . . Don't you think
"Mrs. Gaskell charming? With one ill-considered
"thing that looks like a want of natural percep-

---

* He was greatly interested in the movement for closing town and
city graves (see the close of the 11th chapter of *Bleak House*), and providing places of burial under State supervision.

"tion, I think it masterly."   His last allusion is

TAVISTOCK
HOUSE.

to the story by a delightful writer then appearing
in *Household Words;* and of the others it only

needs to say that the family affair which might
have excused his absence at the Lansdowne dinner did not come off until four days later. On
the 13th of March his last child was born; and
the boy, his seventh son, bears his godfather's
distinguished name, Edward Bulwer Lytton.

The inability to "grind sparks out of his dull
"blade," as he characterized his present labour at
Bleak House, still fretting him, he struck out a
scheme for Paris. "I could not get to Switzer-
"land very well at this time of year. The Jura
"would be covered with snow. And if I went to
"Geneva I don't know where I might *not* go to."
It ended at last in a flight to Dover; but he
found time before he left, amid many occupations
and some anxieties, for a good-natured journey
to Walworth to see a youth rehearse who was
supposed to have talents for the stage, and he
was able to gladden Mr. Toole's friends by
thinking favourably of his chances of success.
"I remember what I once myself wanted in that
"way," he said, "and I should like to serve him."

At one of the last dinners in Tavistock House
before his departure, Mr. Watson of Rockingham
was present; and he was hardly settled in Cam-
den-crescent, Dover, when he had news of the
death of that excellent friend. "Poor dear Wat-
"son! It was this day two weeks when you rode
"with us and, he dined with us. We all remarked
"after he had gone how happy he seemed to
"have got over his election troubles, and how
"cheerful he was. He was full of Christmas plans
"for Rockingham, and was very anxious that we

"should get up a little French piece I had been
"telling him the plot of. He went abroad next
"day to join Mrs. Watson and the children at
"Homburg, and then go to Lausanne, where they
"had taken a house for a month. He was seized
"at Homburg with violent internal inflammation,
"and died—without much pain—in four days.
". . . I was so fond of him that I am sorry
"you didn't know him better. I believe he was
"as thoroughly good and true a man as ever
"lived; and I am sure I can have felt no greater
"affection for him than he felt for me. When I
"think of that bright house, and his fine simple
"honest heart, both so open to me, the blank and
"loss are like a dream." Other deaths followed.

"Poor d'Orsay!" he wrote after only seven days
(8th of August). "It is a tremendous considera-
"tion that friends should fall around us in such
"awful numbers as we attain middle life. What
"a field of battle it is!" Nor had another month
quite passed before he lost, in Mrs. Macready, a
very dear family friend. "Ah me! ah me!" he

wrote. "This tremendous sickle certainly does
"cut deep into the surrounding corn, when one's
"own small blade has ripened. But *this* is all a
"Dream, may be, and death will wake us."

Able at last to settle to his work, he stayed
in Dover three months; and early in October,
sending home his family caravan, crossed to

Boulogne to try it as a resort for seaside holiday.
"I never saw a better instance of our countrymen
"than this place. Because it is accessible it is
"genteel to say it is of no character, quite Eng-

"lish, nothing continental about it, and so forth. Boulogne: 1852.
"It is as quaint, picturesque, good a place as I Liking for Boulogne.
"know; the boatmen and fishing-people quite a
"race apart, and some of their villages as good
"as the fishing-villages on the Mediterranean.
"The Haute Ville, with a walk all round it on
"the ramparts, charming. The country walks,
"delightful. It is the best mixture of town and
"country (with sea air into the bargain) I ever
"saw; everything cheap, everything good; and
"please God I shall be writing on those said
"ramparts next July!"

Before the year closed, the time to which his Publishing Agreements iii. 90-1.
publishing arrangements with Messrs. Bradbury
and Evans were limited had expired, but at his
suggestion the fourth share in such books as he
might write, which they had now received for
eight years, was continued to them on the understanding that the publishers' per-centage should
no longer be charged in the partnership accounts,
and with a power reserved to himself to withdraw
when he pleased. In the new year his first ad- Birmingham: 1853.
venture was an ovation in Birmingham, where a
silver-gilt salver and a diamond ring were presented to him, as well for eloquent service specially
rendered to the Institution, as in general testimony
of "varied literary acquirements, genial philosophy,
"and high moral teaching." A great banquet A banquet and a promise.
followed on Twelfth Night, made memorable by
an offer* to give a couple of readings from his

* The promise was formally conveyed next morning in a letter to C. D. to Mr.
one who took the lead then and since in all good work for Birmingham, Hyland.
Mr. Arthur Ryland. The reading would, he said in this letter (7th of
Jan. 1853), "take about two hours, with a pause of ten minutes half

books at the following Christmas, in aid of the new Midland Institute. It might seem to have been drawn from him as a grateful return for the enthusiastic greeting of his entertainers, but it was in his mind before he left London. It was his first formal undertaking to read in public.

His eldest son had now left Eton, and, the boy's wishes pointing at the time to a mercantile career, he was sent to Leipzig for completion of his education.* At this date it seemed to me that the overstrain of attempting too much, brought upon him by the necessities of his weekly periodical, became first apparent in Dickens. Not unfrequently a complaint strange upon his lips fell from him. "Hypochondriacal whisperings tell "me that I am rather overworked. The spring "does not seem to fly back again directly, as it "always did when I put my own work aside, and "had nothing else to do. Yet I have everything "to keep me going with a brave heart, Heaven "knows!" Courage and hopefulness he might well derive from the increasing sale of *Bleak House*, which had risen to nearly forty thousand; but he could no longer bear easily what he carried so lightly of old, and enjoyments with work were

"way through. There would be some novelty in the thing, as I have "never done it in public, though I have in private, and (if I may say so) "with a great effect on the hearers."
* Baron Tauchnitz, describing to me his long and uninterrupted friendly intercourse with Dickens, has this remark: "I give also a passage from one of his letters written at the time when he sent his son "Charles, through my mediation, to Leipzig. He says in it what he "desires for his son. 'I want him to have all interest in, and to acquire "'a knowledge of, the life around him, and to he treated like a gentle-"'man though pampered in nothing. By punctuality in all things, great "'or small, I set great store.'"

too much for him. "What with *Bleak House*, and   LONDON:
1853.
Over-
doing it.
"*Household Words*, and *Child's History*" (he
dictated from week to week the papers which
formed that little book, and cannot be said to
have quite hit the mark. with it), "and Miss
"Coutts's Home, and the invitations to feasts and
"festivals, I really feel as if my head would split
"like a fired shell if I remained here." He tried
Brighton first, but did not find it answer, and
returned.* A few days of unalloyed enjoyment
were afterwards given to the visit of his excellent
American friend Felton; and on the 13th of June
he was again in Boulogne, thanking heaven for
escape from a breakdown. "If I had substituted
"anybody's knowledge of myself for my own, and
"lingered in London, I never could have got
"through."

What befell him in Boulogne will be given,   BOULOGNE:
1853.
with the incidents of his second and third summer
visits to the place, on a later page. He completed, by the third week of August, his novel of
Bleak House; and it was resolved to celebrate the

---

* From one of his letters while there I take a passage of observation
full of character. "Great excitement here about a wretched woman who
" has murdered her child. Apropos of which I observed a curious thing
" last night. The newspaper offices (local journals) had placards like
" this outside :

"CHILD MURDER IN BRIGHTON.

"INQUEST.

"COMMITTAL OF THE MURDERESS.

" I saw so many common people stand profoundly staring at these lines   Seeing is
believing.
" for half-an-hour together—and even go back to stare again—that I feel
" quite certain they had not the power of thinking about the thing at all
" connectedly or continuously, without having something about it before
" their sense of sight. Having got that, they were considering the case,
" wondering how the devil they had come into that power. I saw one
" man in a smock frock lose the said power the moment he turned away,
" and bring his hob-nails back again."

event by a two months' trip to Italy, in company
with Mr. Wilkie Collins and Mr. Augustus Egg.
The start was to be made from Boulogne in the
middle of October, when he would send his family
home; and he described the intervening weeks as
a fearful "reaction and prostration of laziness"·
only broken by the *Child's History*. At the end
of September he wrote: "I finished the little
"*History* yesterday, and am trying to think of
"something for the Christmas number. After
"which I shall knock off; having had quite enough
"to do, small as it would have seemed to me at
"any other time, since I finished *Bleak House*."
He added, a week before his departure: "I get·
"letters from Genoa and Lausanne as if I were
"going to stay in each place at least a month.
"If I were to measure my deserts by people's re-
"membrance of me, I should be a prodigy of
"intolerability. Have recovered my Italian, which
"I had all but forgotten, and am one entire and
"perfect chrysolite of idleness."

From this trip, of which the incidents have an
interest independent of my ordinary narrative,
Dickens was home again in the middle of December 1853, and kept his promise to his Birmingham friends by reading in their Town Hall his
Christmas Carol on the 27th, * and his *Cricket on
the Hearth* on the 29th. The enthusiasm was
great, and he consented to read his *Carol* a
second time, on Friday the 30th, if seats were
reserved for working men at prices within their

* The reading occupied nearly three hours: double the time devoted
to it in the later years.

means. The result was an addition of between
four and five hundred pounds to the funds for
establishment of the new Institute; and a prettily
worked flower-basket in silver, presented to Mrs.
Dickens, commemorated these first public readings "to nearly six thousand people," and the
design they had generously helped. Other applications then followed to such extent that limits
to compliance had to be put; and a letter of the
16th of May 1854 is one of many that express Desire to
become a
public reader:
III.188, IV.45.
both the difficulty in which he found himself, and
his much desired expedient for solving it. "The
"objection you suggest to paid public lecturing
"does not strike me at all. It is worth considera-
"tion, but I do not think there is anything in it.
"On the contrary, if the lecturing would have any
"motive power at all (like my poor father this, in
"the sound!) I believe it would tend the other
"way. In the Colchester matter I had already Promises
made.
"received a letter from a Colchester magnate; to
"whom I had honestly replied that I stood pledged
"to Christmas readings at Bradford * and at Read-
"ing, and could in no kind of reason do more in
"the public way." The promise to the people of
Reading was for Talfourd's sake; the other was
given after the Birmingham nights, when an institute in Bradford asked similar help, and offered
a fee of fifty pounds. At first this was enter- Argument
against paid
Readings.
tained; but was abandoned, with some reluctance,

* "After correspondence with all parts of England, and every kind
"of refusal and evasion on my part, I am now obliged to decide this Offer from
Bradford.
"question—whether I shall read two nights at Bradford for a hundred
"pounds. If I do, I may take as many hundred pounds as I choose."
27th of Jan. 1854.

upon the argument that to become publicly a reader must alter without improving his position publicly as a writer, and that it was a change to be justified only when the higher calling should have failed of the old success. Thus yielding for the time, he nevertheless soon found the question rising again with the same importunity; his own position to it being always that of a man assenting against his will that it should rest in abeyance. But nothing farther was resolved on yet. The readings mentioned came off as promised, in aid of public objects;* and besides others two years later for the family of a friend, he had given the like liberal help to institutes in Folkestone, Chatham, and again in Birmingham, Peterborough, Sheffield, Coventry, and Edinburgh, before the question settled itself finally in the announcement for paid public readings issued by him in 1858.

Children's
theatricals.

Carrying memory back to his home in the first half of 1854, there are few things that rise more pleasantly in connection with it than the children's theatricals. These began with the first

Gratuitous
Readings.

* On the 28th of Dec. 1854 he wrote from Bradford: "The hall is "enormous, and they expect to seat 3700 people to-night! Notwith- "standing which, it seems to me a tolerably easy place—except that the "width of the platform is so very great to the eye at first." From Folke- stone, on his way to Paris, he wrote in the autumn of 1855: "16th of "Sept. I am going to read for them here, on the 5th of next month, and "have answered in the last fortnight thirty applications to do the like "all over England, Ireland, and Scotland. Fancy my having to come "from Paris in December, to do this, at Peterborough, Birmingham, "and Sheffield—old promises." Again: 23rd of Sept. "I am going to "read here, next Friday week. There are (as there are everywhere) a "Literary Institution and a Working Men's Institution, which have not "the slightest sympathy or connexion. The stalls are five shillings, but "I have made them fix the working men's admission at threepence, and "I hope it may bring them together. The event comes off in a car- "penter's shop, as the biggest place that can be got." In 1857, at Pax- ton's request, he read his *Carol* at Coventry for the Institute.

Twelfth Night at Tavistock House, and were renewed until the principal actors ceased to be children. The best of the performances were *Tom Thumb* and *Fortunio*, in '54 and '55; Dickens now joining first in the revel, and Mr. Mark Lemon bringing into it his own clever children and a very mountain of child-pleasing fun in himself. Dickens had become very intimate with him, and his merry genial ways had given him unbounded popularity with the "young 'uns," who had no such favourite as "Uncle Mark." In Fielding's burlesque he was the giantess Glumdalca, and Dickens was the ghost of Gaffer Thumb; the names by which they respectively appeared being the Infant Phenomenon and the Modern Garrick. But the younger actors carried off the palm. There was a Lord Grizzle, at whose ballad of Miss Villikins, introduced by desire, Thackeray rolled off his seat in a burst of laughter that became absurdly contagious. Yet even this, with hardly less fun from the Noodles, Doodles, and King Arthurs, was not so good as the pretty, fantastic, comic grace of Dollalolla, Huncamunca, and Tom. The girls wore steadily the grave airs irresistible when put on by little children; and an actor not out of his fourth year, who went through the comic songs and the tragic exploits without a wrong note or a victim unslain, represented the small helmeted hero. He was in the bills as Mr. H——, but bore in fact the name of the illustrious author whose conception he embodied; and who certainly would have hugged him for Tom's opening song, delivered in the arms of Hunca-

LONDON:
1855.
munca, if he could have forgiven the later master in his own craft for having composed it afresh to the air of a ditty then wildly popular at the "Coal Hole." *   The encores were frequent, and for the most part the little fellow responded to them; but the misplaced enthusiasm that took similar form at the heroic intensity with which he stabbed Dollalolla, he rebuked by going gravely

Acting of Fortunio.

on to the close.   His Fortunio, the next Twelfth Night, was not so great; yet when, as a prelude to getting the better of the Dragon, he adulterated his drink (Mr. Lemon played the Dragon) with sherry, the sly relish with which he watched the demoralization, by this means, of his formidable adversary into a helpless imbecility, was perfect. Here Dickens played the testy old Baron, and

Dickens and the Czar.

took advantage of the excitement against the Czar raging in 1855 to denounce him (in a song) as no other than own cousin to the very Bear that Fortunio had gone forth to subdue.   He depicted him, in his desolation of autocracy, as the Robinson Crusoe of absolute state, who had at his court many a show-day and many a high-day, but hadn't in all his dominions a Friday.**   The

* My name it is Tom Thumb,
Small my size,
Small my size,
My name it is Tom Thumb,
Small my size.
Yet though I am so small

I have kill'd the giants tall:
And now I'm paid for all,
Small my size,
Small my size:
And now I'm paid for all,
Small my size.

** This finds mention, I observe, in a pleasant description of "Mr. "Dickens's Amateur Theatricals," which appeared in *Macmillan's Magazine* two years ago, by one who had been a member of the Juvenile Company.   I quote a passage, recommending the whole paper as very agreeably written, with some shrewd criticism.   "Mr. Planché had in "one portion of the extravaganza put into the mouth of one of the cha- "racters for the moment a few lines of burlesque upon Macbeth, and we "remember Mr. Dickens's unsuccessful attempts to teach the performer

bill, which attributed these interpolations to "the
"Dramatic Poet of the Establishment," deserves
also mention for the fun of the six large-lettered
announcements which stood at the head of it,
and could not have been bettered by Mr. Crummles
himself. "Re-engagement of that irresistible "come-
"dian" (the performer of Lord Grizzle) "Mr.
"Ainger!" "Reappearance of Mr. H. who created
"so powerful an impression last year!" "Re-
"turn of Mr. Charles Dickens Junior from his
"German engagements!" "Engagement of Miss
"Kate, who declined the munificent offers of the
"Management last season!" "Mr. Passé, Mr. Mud-
"period, Mr. Measly Servile, and Mr. Wilkini Col-
"lini!" "First appearance on any stage of Mr.
"Plornishmaroontigoonter (who has been kept out
"of bed at a vast expense)." The last performer
mentioned * was yet at some distance from the
third year of his age. Dickens was Mr. Passé.

LONDON:
1855.

Mr. Crummles.

Smallest of
the come-
dians.

"how to imitate Macready, whom he (the performer) had never seen!
"And after the performance, when we were restored to our evening-
"party costumes, and the school-room was cleared for dancing, still a
"stray 'property' or two had escaped the vigilant eye of the property-
"man, for Douglas Jerrold had picked up the horse's head (Fortunio's
"faithful steed *Comrade*), and was holding it up before the greatest liv-
"ing animal painter, who had been one of the audience, with 'Looks as
"'if it knew *you*, Edwin!'"

* He went with the rest to Boulogne in the summer, and an anecdote transmitted in one of his father's letters will show that he maintained the reputation as a comedian which his early debut had awakened.
"ORIGINAL ANECDOTE OF THE PLORNISHGHENTER. This distinguished
"wit, being at Boulogne with his family, made a close acquaintance
"with his landlord, whose name was M. Beaucourt—the only French
"word with which he was at that time acquainted. It happened that
"one day he was left unusually long in a bathing-machine when the
"tide was making, accompanied by his two young brothers and little
"English nurse, without being drawn to land. The little nurse, being
"frightened, cried 'M'soo! M'soo!' The two young brothers being
"frightened, cried 'Ici! Ici!' Our wit, at once perceiving that his
"English was of no use to him under the foreign circumstances, im-
"mediately fell to bawling 'Beau-court!' which he continued to shout

From a
Boulogne
jest-book.

LONDON:
1854.

Gravities were mixed with these gaieties. "I "wish you would look" (20th of January 1854) "at "the enclosed titles for the *H. IV.* story, between "this and two o'clock or so, when I will call. It is "my usual day, you observe, on which I have "jotted them down—Friday! It seems to me that "there are three very good ones among them. I "should like to know whether you hit upon the "same." On the paper enclosed was written: 1. According to Cocker. 2. Prove it. 3. Stubborn Things. 4. Mr. Gradgrind's Facts. 5. The Grindstone. 6. Hard Times. 7. Two and Two are Four. 8. Something Tangible. 9. Our Hardheaded Friend. 10. Rust and Dust. 11. Simple Arithmetic. 12. A Matter of Calculation. 13. A Mere Question of Figures. 14. The Gradgrind Philosophy.* The three selected by me were 2, 6, and 11; the three that were his own favourites were 6, 13, and 14; and as 6 had been chosen by both, that title was taken.

Titles for a
new story.

"Hard
"Times"
chosen.

It was the first story written by him for *Household Words;* and in the course of it the old troubles of the *Clock* came back, with the difference that the greater brevity of the weekly portions made it easier to write them up to time, but much more difficult to get sufficient interest into each. "The difficulty of the space," he wrote after a few weeks' trial, "is CRUSHING. Nobody "can have an idea of it who has not had an ex-

i. 255.

Difficulties
of weekly
publication.

"at the utmost pitch of his voice and with great gravity, until rescued.
"—*New Boulogne Jest Book*, page 578."
　* To show the pains he took in such matters I will give other titles also thought of for this tale. 1. Fact: 2. Hard-headed Gradgrind: 3. Hard Heads and Soft Hearts; 4. Heads and Tales; 5. Black and White.

"perience of patient fiction-writing with some London: 1854.
"elbow-room always, and open places in per-
"spective. In this form, with any kind of regard
"to the current number, there is absolutely no
"such thing." He went on, however; and, of the What was proposed and what was done.
two designs he started with, accomplished one
very perfectly and the other at least partially.
He more than doubled the circulation of his
journal; and he wrote a story which, though not
among his best, contains things as characteristic
as any he has written. I may not go as far as
Mr. Ruskin in giving it a high place; but to anything falling from that writer, however one may
differ from it, great respect is due, and every
word here said of Dickens's intention is in the
most strict sense just.* "The essential value and
"truth of Dickens's writings," he says, "have been Unto this End: note to First Essay, 14-15.
"unwisely lost sight of by many thoughtful per-
"sons, merely because he presents his truth with
"some colour of caricature. Unwisely, because
"Dickens's caricature, though often gross, is never
"mistaken. Allowing for his manner of telling
"them, the things he tells us are always true. I
"wish that he could think it right to limit his
"brilliant exaggeration to works written only for
"public amusement; and when he takes up a sub-

---

* It is well to remember, too, what he wrote about the story to Dickens to Charles Knight. It had no design, he said, to damage the really useful truths of Political Economy, but was wholly directed against "those "who see figures and averages, and nothing else; who would take the "average of cold in the Crimea during twelve months as a reason for "clothing a soldier in nankeen on a night when he would be frozen to "death in fur; and who would comfort the labourer in travelling twelve "miles a day to and from his work, by telling him that the average dis- "tance of one inhabited place from another, on the whole area of Eng- "land, is not more than four miles."

"ject of high national importance, such as that
"which he handled in *Hard Times*, that he would
"use severer and more accurate analysis. The
"usefulness of that work (to my mind, in several
"respects, the greatest he has written) is with
"many persons seriously diminished, because Mr.
"Bounderby is a dramatic monster, instead of a
"characteristic example of a worldly master; and
"Stephen Blackpool a dramatic perfection, instead

"of a characteristic example of an honest work-
"man. But let us not lose the use of Dickens's
"wit and insight, because he chooses to speak in
"a circle of stage fire. He is entirely right in his
"main drift and purpose in every book he has
"written; and all of them, but especially *Hard
"Times*, should be studied with close and earnest
"care by persons interested in social questions.
"They will find much that is partial, and, because
"partial, apparently unjust; but if they examine
"all the evidence on the other side, which Dickens
"seems to overlook, it will appear, after all their
"trouble, that his view was the finally right one,
"grossly and sharply told." *   The best points in

* It is curious that with as strong a view in the opposite direction,
and with an equally mistaken exaltation, above the writer's ordinary
level, of a book which on the whole was undoubtedly below it, Mr.
Taine speaks of *Hard Times* as that one of Dickens's romances which

is a summary of all the rest: exalting instinct above reason, and the in-
tuitions of the heart above practical knowledge; attacking all education
based on statistic figures and facts; heaping sorrow and ridicule on the
practical mercantile people; fighting against the pride, hardness, and
selfishness of the merchant and noble; cursing the manufacturing towns
for imprisoning bodies in smoke and mud, and souls in falsehood and
factitiousness;—while it contrasts, with that satire of social oppression,
lofty eulogy of the oppressed; and searches out poor workmen, jugglers,
foundlings, and circus people, for types of good sense, sweetness of disposition, generosity, delicacy, and courage, to perpetual confusion of the
pretended knowledge, pretended happiness, pretended virtue, of the rich

it, out of the circle of stage fire (an expression
of wider application to this part of Dickens's life
than its inventor supposed it to be), were the
sketches of the riding-circus people and the
Bounderby household; but it is a wise hint of
Mr. Ruskin's that there may be, in the drift of a
story, truths of sufficient importance to set against
defects of workmanship; and here they challenged
wide attention. You cannot train any one properly,
unless you cultivate the fancy, and allow fair scope
to the affections. You cannot govern men on a
principle of averages; and to buy in the cheapest
and sell in the dearest market is not the *summum
bonum* of life. You cannot treat the working man
fairly unless, in dealing with his wrongs and his
delusions, you take equally into account the simplicity and tenacity of [his nature, arising partly
from limited knowledge, but more from honesty
and singleness of intention. Fiction cannot prove
a case, but it can express forcibly a righteous
sentiment; and this is here done unsparingly upon
matters of universal concern. The book was
finished at Boulogne in the middle of July,* and
is inscribed to Carlyle.

and powerful who trample upon them! This is a fair specimen of the
exaggerations with which exaggeration is rebuked, in Mr. Taine's and
much similar criticism.

    * Here is a note at the close. "Tavistock House. Look at that!
"Boulogne, of course. Friday, 14th of July, 1854. I am three parts
"mad, and the fourth delirious, with perpetual rushing at *Hard Times*.
"I have done what I hope is a good thing with Stephen, taking his
"story as a whole; and hope to be over in town with the end of the
"book on Wednesday night. . . I have been looking forward through
"so many weeks and sides of paper to this Stephen business, that now
"—as usual—it being over. I feel as if nothing in the world, in the way
"of intense and violent rushing hither and thither, could quite restore
"my balance."

BOULOGNE:
1854.

An American admirer accounted for the viva-
city of the circus-scenes by declaring that Dickens
had "arranged with the master of Astley's Circus
Horse-riding
scenes.
"to spend many hours behind the scenes with
"the riders and among the horses;" a thing just
as likely as that he went into training as a stroller
to qualify for Mr. Crummles in *Nickleby*.   Such
successes belonged to the experiences of his youth;
he had nothing to add to what his marvellous
observation had made familiar from almost childish
days; and the glimpses we get of them in the
Sketches by Boz are in these points as perfect as
anything his later experience could supply.   There
was one thing nevertheless which the choice of
his subject made him anxious to verify while
Hard Times was in hand; and this was a strike
in a manufacturing town.   He went to Preston to
see one at the end of January, and was somewhat
disappointed.   "I am afraid I shall not be able
"to get much here.   Except the crowds at the
"street-corners reading the placards pro and con;
"and the cold absence of smoke from the mill-
"chimneys; there is very little in the streets to
"make the town remarkable.   I am told that the
"people 'sit at home and mope.'   The delegates
"with the money from the neighbouring places
"come in to-day to report the amounts they bring;
"and to-morrow the people are paid.   When I
"have seen both these ceremonies, I shall return.
"It is a nasty place (I thought it was a model
"town); and I am in the Bull Hotel, before which
"some time ago the people assembled supposing
"the masters to be here, and on demanding to

PRESTON.

Manufac-
turing town
on strike.

"have them out were remonstrated with by the PRESTON: 1854.
"landlady in person.   I saw the account in an
"Italian paper, in which it was stated that 'the
"'populace then environed the Palazzo Bull, until Palazzo Bull.
"'the padrona of the Palazzo heroically appeared
"'at one of the upper windows and addressed
"'them!'   One can hardly conceive anything less
"likely to be represented to an Italian mind by
"this description, than the old, grubby, 'smoky,
"mean, intensely formal red brick house with a
"narrow gateway and a dingy yard, to which it
"applies.   At the theatre last night I saw *Hamlet*, Hamlet at Preston.
"and should have done better to 'sit at home
"'and mope' like the idle workmen.   In the last
"scene, Laertes on being asked how it was with
"him replied (verbatim) 'Why, like a woodcock
"'—on account of my treachery.'"   (29th Jan.)

The home incidents of the summer and autumn LONDON: 1855.
of 1855 may be mentioned briefly.   It was a year
of much unsettled discontent with him, and upon
return from a short trip to Paris with Mr. Wilkie
Collins, he flung himself rather hotly into agitation with the administrative reformers,* and spoke
at one of the great meetings in Drury-lane Theatre. Speaking at Drury-lane.
In the following month (April) he took occasion,
even from the chair of the General Theatrical
Fund, to give renewed expression to political dis-

---

* "I have hope of Mr. Morley—whom one cannot see without
"knowing to be a straightforward, earnest man.   Travers, too, I think Adminis-
"a man of the Anti-corn-law-league order.   I also think Higgins will trative re-
"materially help them.   Generally I quite agree with you that they formers.
"hardly know what to be at; but it is an immensely difficult subject to
"start, and they must have every allowance.   At any rate, it is not by
"leaving them alone and giving them no help, that they can be urged
"on to success."   29th of March 1855.

London:
1855.
satisfactions.*   In the summer he threw open to many friends his Tavistock House Theatre, having secured for its "lessee and manager Mr. Crum- "mles;" for its poet Mr. Wilkie Collins, in "an en- "tirely new and original domestic melodrama;" and for its scene-painter "Mr. Stanfield, R.A."**

Tavistock
House
theatricals.
The Lighthouse, by Mr. Wilkie Collins, was then produced, its actors being Mr. Crummles the ma- nager (Dickens in other words), the Author of the play, Mr. Lemon, and Mr. Egg, and the manager's sister-in-law and eldest daughter. It was followed

IV. 171.
by the Guild farce of *Mr. Nightingale's Diary*, in which besides the performers named, and Dickens in his old personation part, the manager's youngest daughter and Mr. Frank Stone assisted. The success was wonderful; and in the three de- lighted audiences who crowded to what the bills described as "the smallest theatre in the world,"

Tavern-
keeper and
toast-master.
* "The Government hit took immensely, but I'm afraid to look at "the report, these things are so ill done. It came into my head as I "was walking about at Hampstead yesterday ', . . . On coming away "I told B. we must have a toastmaster in future less given to constant "drinking while the speeches are going on. B. replied 'Yes sir, you are "' quite right sir, he has no head whatever sir, look at him now sir '— "Toastmaster was weakly contemplating the coats and hats—' do you "' not find it difficult to keep your hands off him sir, he ought to have "' his head knocked against the wall sir,—and he should sir, I assure "' you sir, if he was not in too debased a condition to be aware of it "' sir.'"   April 3rd 1855.

Clarkson
Stanfield,
R. A.
** For the scene of the Eddystone Lighthouse at this little play, afterwards placed in a frame in the hall at Gadshill, a thousand guineas was given at the Dickens sale. It occupied the great painter only one or two mornings, and Dickens will tell how it originated. Walking on Hampstead Heath to think over his Theatrical Fund speech, he met Mr. Lemon, and they went together to Stanfield. "He has been very "ill, and he told us that large pictures are too much for him, and he "must confine himself to small ones. But I would not have this, I de- "clared he must paint bigger ones than ever, and what would he think "of beginning upon an act-drop for a proposed vast theatre at Tavistock "House? He laughed and caught at this, we cheered him up very much, "and he said he was quite a man again."   April 1855.

were not a few of the notabilities of London. Mr.
Carlyle compared' Dickens's wild picturesqueness
in the old lighthouse keeper to the famous figure
in Nicholas Poussin's bacchanalian dance in the
National Gallery; and at one of the joyous suppers
that followed on each night of the play, Lord
Campbell told the company that he had much
rather have written *Pickwick* than be Chief Justice
of England and a peer of parliament.*

Then came the beginning of *Nobody's Fault*,
as *Little Dorrit* continued to be called by him
up to the eve of its publication; a flight to Folkestone to help his sluggish fancy; and his return
to London in October to preside at a dinner to
Thackeray on his going to lecture in America. It
was a muster of more than sixty admiring entertainers, and Dickens's speech gave happy expression to the spirit that animated all, telling Thackeray
not alone how much his friendship was prized by
those present, and how proud they were of his
genius, but offering him in the name of the tens
of thousands absent who had never touched his
hand or seen his face, life-long thanks for the
treasures of mirth, wit, and wisdom within the
yellow-covered numbers of *Pendennis* and *Vanity
Fair*. Peter Cunningham, one of the sons of

* Sitting at Nisi Prius not long before, the Chief Justice, with the
same eccentric liking for literature, had committed what was called at the
time a breach of judicial decorum. (Such indecorums were less uncom-
mon in the great days of the Bench.) "The name," he said, "of the il-
' lustrious Charles Dickens has been called on the jury, but he has not an-
"swered. If his great Chancery suit had been still going on, I certainly
"would have excused him, but, as that is over, he might have done us
"the honour of attending here, that he might have seen how we went on
"at common law."

Allan, was secretary to the banquet; and for many
pleasures given to the subject of this memoir, who
had a hearty regard for him, should have a few
words to his memory.

His presence was always welcome to Dickens,
and indeed to all who knew him, for his relish of
social life was great, and something of his keen
enjoyment could not but be shared by his company. His geniality would have carried with it a
pleasurable glow even if it had stood alone, and
it was invigorated by very considerable acquirements. He had some knowledge of the works of
eminent authors and artists; and he had an eager
interest in their lives and haunts, which he had
made the subject of minute and novel enquiry.
This store of knowledge gave substance to his
talk, yet never interrupted his buoyancy and plea-
santry, because only introduced when called for,
and not made matter of parade or display. But
the happy combination of qualities that rendered
him a favourite companion, and won him many
friends, proved in the end injurious to himself.
He had done much while young in certain lines
of investigation which he had made almost his
own, and there was every promise that, in the department of biographical and literary research, he
would have produced much weightier works with
advancing years. This however was not to be.
The fascinations of good fellowship encroached
more and more upon literary pursuits, until he
nearly abandoned his former favourite studies,
and sacrificed all the deeper purposes of his life
to the present temptation of a festive hour. Then

*Peter
Cunningham.*

A life wasted.

his health gave way, and he became lost to friends
as well as to literature. But the impression of the
bright and amiable intercourse of his better time
survived, and his old associates never ceased to
think of Peter Cunningham with regret and kindness.

Dickens went to Paris early in October, and
at its close was brought again to London by the
sudden death of a friend, much deplored by himself, and still more so by a distinguished lady
who had his loyal service at all times. An incident before his return to France is worth brief
relation. He had sallied out for one of his night
walks, full of thoughts of his story, one wintery
rainy evening (the 8th of November), and "pulled
himself up," outside the door of Whitechapel Work-
house, at a strange sight which arrested him there.
Against the dreary enclosure of the house were
leaning, in the midst of the downpouring rain and
storm, what seemed to be seven heaps of rags:
"dumb, wet, silent horrors" he described them,
"sphinxes set up against that dead wall, and no
"one likely to be at the pains of solving them until
"the General Overthrow." He sent in his card
to the Master. Against him there was no ground
of complaint; he gave prompt personal attention;
but the casual ward was full, and there was no
help. The rag-heaps were all girls, and Dickens
gave each a shilling. One girl, "twenty or so,"
had been without food a day and night. "Look
"at me," she said, as she clutched the shilling,
and without thanks shuffled off. So with the rest.
There was not a single "thank you." A crowd

meanwhile, only less poor than these objects of misery, had gathered round the scene; but though they saw the seven shillings given away they asked for no relief to themselves, they recognized in their sad wild way the other greater wretchedness, and made room in silence for Dickens to walk on.

Not more tolerant of the way in which laws meant to be most humane are too often administered in England, he left in a day or two to resume his *Little Dorrit* in Paris. But before his life there is described, some sketches from his holiday trip to Italy with Mr. Wilkie Collins and Mr. Augustus Egg, and from his three summer visits to Boulogne, claim to themselves two intervening chapters.

#

CHAPTER XLVII.

SWITZERLAND AND ITALY REVISITED.

1853.

THE first news of the three travellers was CHAMOUNIX:
1853.
from Chamounix, on the 20th of October; and
in it there was little made of the fatigue, and
much of the enjoyment, of their Swiss travel.
Great attention and cleanliness at the inns, very
small windows and very bleak passages, doors
opening to wintery blasts, overhanging eaves and
external galleries, plenty of milk, honey, cows,
and goats, much singing towards sunset on mountain sides, mountains almost too solemn to look
at—that was the picture of it, with the country
everywhere in one of its finest aspects, as winter
began to close in. They had started from Ge- Swiss people.
neva the previous morning at four, and in their
day's travel Dickens had again noticed what he
spoke of formerly, the ill-favoured look of the
people in the valleys owing to their hard and
stern climate. "All the women were like used-
"up men, and all the men like a sort of fagged
"dogs. But the good, genuine, grateful Swiss re-
"cognition of the commonest kind word—not too
"often thrown to them by our countrymen—made
"them quite radiant. I walked the greater part
"of the way, which was like going up the Monu-

CHAMOUNIX: "ment." On the day the letter was written they
1853. had been up to the Mer de Glace, finding it not so
beautiful in colour as in summer, but grander in its
desolation; the green ice, like the greater part of
the ascent, being covered with snow. "We were
"alarmingly near to a very dismal accident. We
"were a train of four mules and two guides,
"going along an immense height like a chimney-
"piece, with sheer precipice below, when there
"came rolling from above, with fearful velocity, a
Narrow "block of stone about the size of one of the
escape. "fountains in Trafalgar-square, which Egg, the last
"of the party, had preceded by not a yard, when it
"swept over the ledge, breaking away a tree, and
"rolled and tumbled down into the valley. It had
"been loosened by the heavy rains, or by some
"woodcutters afterwards reported to be above."
Berne. The only place new to Dickens was Berne: "a
"surprisingly picturesque old town, with a view
"of the Alps from the outside of it singularly
"beautiful in the morning light." Everything else
was familiar to him: though at that winter season,
when the inns were shutting up, and all who
could afford it were off to Geneva, most things
in the valley struck him with a new aspect. From
such of his old friends as he found at Lausanne,
where a day or two's rest was taken, he had the
Lausanne. gladdest of greetings; "and the wonderful manner
"in which they turned out in the wettest morning
"ever beheld for a Godspeed down the Lake was
"really quite pathetic."

He had found time to see again the deaf,
dumb, and blind youth at Mr. Haldimand's Insti-

tution who had aroused so deep an interest in
him seven years before, but, in his brief present
visit, the old associations would not reawaken.
"Tremendous efforts were made by Hertzel to
"impress him with an idea of me, and the asso-
"ciations belonging to me; but it seemed in my
"eyes quite a failure, and I much doubt if he
"had the least perception of his old acquaintance.
"According to his custom, he went on muttering
"strange eager sounds like Town and Down and
"Mown, but nothing more. I left ten francs to
"be spent in cigars for my old friend. If I had
"taken one with me, I think I could, more suc-
"cessfully than his master, have established my
"identity." The child similarly afflicted, the little
girl whom he saw at the same old time, had been
after some trial discharged as an idiot.

Before October closed, the travellers had
reached Genoa, having been thirty-one consecu-
tive hours on the road from Milan. They arrived
in somewhat damaged condition, and took up
their lodging in the top rooms of the Croce di
Malta, "overlooking the port and sea pleasantly
"and airily enough, but it was no joke to get so
"high, and the apartment is rather vast and
"faded." The warmth of personal greeting that
here awaited Dickens was given no less to the
friends who accompanied him, and though the
reader may not share in such private confidences
as would show the sensation created by his reappearance, and the jovial hours that were passed
among old associates, he will perhaps be interested to know how far the intervening years had

Genoa:
1853.
changed the aspect of things and places made
pleasantly familiar to us in his former letters. He
wrote to his sister-in-law that the old walks were
pretty much the same as ever except that there
had been building behind the Peschiere up the
San Bartolomeo hill, and the whole town towards
San Pietro d'Arena had been quite changed. The
Bisagno looked just the same, stony just then,
having very little water in it; the vicoli were
Old and new places. fragrant with the same old flavour of "very rotten
"cheese kept in very hot blankets;" and every-
where he saw the mezzaro as of yore. The Je-
suits' College in the Strada Nuova was become,
under the changed government, the Hôtel de
Ville, and a splendid caffè with a terrace-garden
had arisen between it and Palaviccini's old palace.
Owner of the Peschiere. "Pal himself has gone to the dogs." Another
new and handsome caffè had been built in the
Piazza Carlo Felice, between the old one of the
Bei Arti and the Strada Carlo Felice; and the
Teatro Diurno had now stone galleries and seats,
like an ancient amphitheatre. "The beastly gate
"and guardhouse in the Albaro road are still in
"their dear old beastly state; and the whole of
"that road is just as it was. The man without
"legs is still in the Strada Nuova; but the beggars
"in general are all cleared off, and our old one-
"arm'd Belisario made a sudden evaporation a
Peschiere revisited. III. 148-150. "year or two ago. I am going to the Peschiere
"to-day." To myself he described his former
favourite abode as converted into a girls' college;
all the paintings of gods and goddesses canvassed
over, and the gardens gone to ruin; "but O! what

"a wonderful place!"   He observed an extraordinary increase everywhere else, since he was last
in the splendid city, of "life, growth, and enter-
"prise;" and he declared his old conviction to
be confirmed that for picturesque beauty and
character there was nothing in Italy, Venice ex-
cepted, "near brilliant old Genoa."

The voyage thence to Naples, written from the
latter place, is too capital a description to be
lost.   The steamer in which they embarked was
"the new express English ship," but they found
her to be already more than full of passengers
from Marseilles (among them an old friend, Sir
Emerson Tennent, with his family), and everything in confusion.   There were no places at the
captain's table, dinner had to be taken on deck,
no berth or sleeping accommodation was available, and heavy first-class fares had to be paid.
Thus they made their way to Leghorn, where
worse awaited them.   The authorities proved to
be not favourable to the "crack" English-officered
vessel (she had just been started for the India
mail); and her papers not being examined in
time, it was too late to steam away again that
day, and she had to lie all night long off the
lighthouse.   "The scene on board beggars de-
"scription. Ladies on the tables; gentlemen under
"the tables; bed-room appliances not usually be-
"held in public airing themselves in positions
"where soup-tureens had been lately developing
"themselves; and ladies and gentlemen lying in-
"discriminately on the open deck, arranged like
"spoons on a sideboard.   No mattresses, no

"blankets, nothing. Towards midnight attempts
"were made, by means of awning and flags, to
"make this latter scene remotely approach an
"Australian encampment; and we three (Collins,
"Egg, and self) lay together on the bare planks
"covered with our coats. We were all gradually
"dozing off, when a perfectly tropical rain fell,
"and in a moment drowned the whole ship. The
"rest of the night we passed upon the stairs, with
"an immense jumble of men and women. When
"anybody came up for any purpose we all fell
"down, and when anybody came down we all
"fell up again. Still, the good-humour in the
"English part of the passengers was quite extra-
"ordinary. . . There were excellent officers aboard,
"and, in the morning, the first mate lent me his
"cabin to wash in—which I afterwards lent to
"Egg and Collins. Then we, the Emerson Ten-
"nents, the captain, the doctor, and the second
"officer, went off on a jaunt together to Pisa, as
"the ship was to lie all day at Leghorn. The
"captain was a capital fellow, but I led him,
"facetiously, such a life the whole day, that I got
"most things altered at night. Emerson Ten-
"nent's son, with the greatest amiability, insisted
"on turning out of his state-room for me, and I
"got a good bed there. The store-room down
"by the hold was opened for Collins and Egg;
"and they slept with the moist sugar, the cheese
"in cut, the spices, the cruets, the apples and
"pears, in a perfect chandler's shop—in company
"with what a friend of ours would call a hold
"gent, who had been so horribly wet through

"over night that his condition frightened the au-
"thorities; a cat; and the steward, who dozed in
"an arm-chair, and all-night-long fell head fore-
"most, once every five minutes, on Egg, who
"slept on the counter or dresser. Last night, I
"had the steward's own cabin, opening on deck,
"all to myself. It had been previously occupied
"by some desolate lady who went ashore at
"Civita Vecchia. There was little or no sea,
"thank Heaven, all the trip; but the rain was
"heavier than any I have ever seen, and the
"lightning very constant and vivid. We were,
"with the crew, some 200 people—provided with
"boats, at the utmost stretch, for one hundred
"perhaps. I could not help thinking what would
"happen if we met with any accident: the crew
"being chiefly Maltese, and evidently fellows who
"would cut off alone in the largest boat, on the
"least alarm; the speed very high; and the run-
"ning, thro' all the narrow rocky channels. Thank
"God, however, here we are."

A whimsical postscript closed the amusing
narrative. "We towed from Civita Vecchia the
"entire Greek navy, I believe; consisting of a
"little brig of war with no guns, fitted as a
"steamer, but disabled by having burnt the bot-
"toms of her boilers out, in her first run. She
"was just big enough to carry the captain and a
"crew of six or so: but the captain was so covered
"with buttons and gold that there never would
"have been room for him on board to put those
"valuables away, if he hadn't worn them—which
"he consequently did, all night. Whenever any-

Naples:
1853.

"thing was wanted to be done, as slackening the "tow-rope or anything of that sort, our officers "roared at this miserable potentate, in violent "English, through a speaking trumpet; of which "he couldn't have understood a word in the most "favourable circumstances. So he did all the "wrong things first, and the right thing always "last. The absence of any knowledge of any-

English officers and stewards.

"thing but English on the part of the officers and "stewards was most ridiculous. I met an Italian "gentleman on the cabin steps yesterday morning, "vainly endeavouring to explain that he wanted "a cup of tea for his sick wife. And when we "were coming out of the harbour at Genoa, and "it was necessary to order away that boat of music "you remember, the chief officer (called 'aft' for

English Italian.

"the purpose, as 'knowing something of Italian') "delivered himself in this explicit and clear Italian "to the principal performer—'Now Signora, if you "'don't sheer off you'll be run down, so you had "'better trice up that guitar of yours and put about.'"

At Naples some days were passed very merrily; going up Vesuvius and into the buried cities, with Layard who had joined them, and with the Tennents. Here a small adventure befell Dickens specially, in itself extremely unimportant, but told by him with delightful humour in a letter to his sister-in-law. The old idle Frenchman, to whom all things are possible, with his snuff-box and dusty umbrella, and all the delicate and kindly observation, would have enchanted Leigh Hunt, and made his way to the heart of Charles Lamb. After mentioning Mr. Lowther, then Eng-

lish chargé d'affaires in Naples, as a very agree- NAPLES:
1853.
able fellow who had been at the Rockingham
play, he alludes to a meeting at his house. "We IV. 263.
"had an exceedingly pleasant dinner of eight,
"preparatory to which I was near having the
"ridiculous adventure of not being able to find
"the house and coming back dinnerless. I went
"in an open carriage from the hotel in all state,
"and the coachman to my surprise pulled up at
"the end of the Chiaja. 'Behold the house,' says Going out to
dinner.
"he, 'of Il Signor Larthoor!'—at the same time
"pointing with his whip into the seventh heaven
"where the early stars were shining. 'But the
"'Signor Larthoor,' says I, 'lives at Pausilippo.'
"'It is true,' says the coachman (still pointing to
"the evening star), 'but he lives high up the
"'Salita Sant' Antonio where no carriage ever yet
"'ascended, and that is the house' (evening star
"as aforesaid), 'and one must go on foot. Behold
"'the Salita Sant' Antonio!' I went up it, a mile Difficult
road.
"and a half I should think. I got into the strangest
"places among the wildest Neapolitans; kitchens,
"washing-places, archways, stables, vineyards; was
"baited by dogs, and answered, in profoundly
"unintelligible language, from behind lonely
"locked doors in cracked female voices, quaking
"with fear; but could hear of no such English-
"man, nor any Englishman. Bye and bye, I came
"upon a polenta-shop in the clouds, where an
"old Frenchman with an umbrella like a faded Old Frenchman at the
polenta-shop.
"tropical leaf (it had not rained in Naples for six
"weeks) was staring at nothing at all, with a snuff-
"box in his hand. To him I appealed, con-

"cerning the Signor Larthoor. 'Sir,' said he, with
"the sweetest politeness, ' can you speak French?'
" 'Sir,' said I, 'a little.' 'Sir,' said he, 'I presume
"'the Signor Loothere'—you will observe that he
"changed the name according to the custom of
"his country—'is an Englishman?' I admitted
"that he was the victim of circumstances and had
"that misfortune. 'Sir,' said he, 'one word more.
"'*Has* he a servant with a wooden leg?' 'Great
"'heaven, sir,' said I, 'how do I know? I should
"'think not, but it is possible.' 'It is always,'
"said the Frenchman, 'possible. Almost all the

"'things of the world are always possible.' 'Sir,'
"said I—you may imagine my condition and
"dismal sense of my own absurdity, by this
"time—'that is true.' He then took an immense
"pinch of snuff, wiped the dust off his umbrella,
"led me to an arch commanding a wonderful
"view of the Bay of Naples, and pointed deep
"into the earth from which I had mounted.
"'Below there, near the lamp, one finds an Eng-
"'lishman with a servant with a wooden leg. It
"'is always possible that he is the Signor Loothere.'
"I had been asked at six o'clock, and it was now
"getting on for seven. I went back in a state of
"perspiration and misery not to be described,
"and without the faintest hope of finding the spot.
"But as I was going farther down to the lamp,
"I saw the strangest staircase up a dark corner,

"with a man in a white waistcoat (evidently
"hired) standing on the top of it fuming. I
"dashed in at a venture, found it was the house,
"made the most of the whole story, and achieved

"much popularity. The best of it was that as NAPLES:
"nobody ever did find the place, Lowther had —————— 1853.
"put a servant at the bottom of the Salita to wait
"'for an English gentleman;' but the servant (as
"he presently pleaded), deceived by the moustache,
"challenged."

From Naples they went to Rome, where they
found Lockhart, "fearfully weak and broken, yet
"hopeful of himself too" (he died the following
year); smoked and drank punch with David
Roberts, then painting every day with Louis Haghe
in St. Peter's; and took the old walks. The
Coliseum, Appian Way, and Streets of Tombs,
seemed desolate and grand as ever; but generally,
Dickens adds, "I discovered the Roman anti-
"quities to be *smaller* than my imagination in
"nine years had made them. The Electric Tele-
"graph now goes like a sunbeam through the
"thing to think about, I fancied. The Pantheon
"I thought even nobler than of yore." The
amusements were of course an attraction; and
nothing at the Opera amused the party of three
English more, than another party of four Americans who sat behind them in the pit. "All the
"seats are numbered arm-chairs, and you buy
"your number at the pay-place, and go to it with
"the easiest direction on the ticket itself. We
"were early, and the four places of the Americans
"were on the next row behind us—all together.
"After looking about them for some time, and
"seeing the greater part of the seats empty (be-

"cause the audience generally wait in a caffè
"which is part of the theatre), one of them said
"'Waal I dunno—I expect we aint no call to set
"'so nigh to one another neither—will you scatter
"'Kernel, will you scatter sir?—' Upon this the

"Kernel 'scattered' some twenty benches off;
"and they distributed themselves (for no earthly
"reason apparently but to get rid of one another)
"all over the pit. As soon as the overture began,
"in came the audience in a mass. Then the
"people who had got the numbers into which
"they had 'scattered,' had to get them out; and
"as they understood nothing that was said to
"them, and could make no reply but 'A-mericani,'
"you may imagine the number of cocked hats it
"took to dislodge them. At last they were all
"got back into their right places, except one.·
"About an hour afterwards when Moses (*Moses
"in Egypt* was the opera) was invoking the dark-
"ness, and there was a dead silence all over the
"house, unwonted sounds of disturbance broke
"out from a distant corner of the pit, and here
"and there a beard got up to look. 'What is it
"'neow sir?' said one of the Americans to an-
"other;—'some person seems to be getting along,

"'again, streem.' 'Waal sir' he replied 'I dunno.
"'But I xpect 'tis the Kernel sir, a holdin on.' So
"it was. The Kernel was ignominiously escorted
"back to his right place, not in the least discon-
"certed, and in perfectly good spirits and temper."
The opera was excellently done, and the price
of the stalls one and threepence English. At
Milan, on the other hand, the Scala was fallen

from its old estate, dirty, gloomy, dull, and the Rome: 1853. performance execrable.

Another theatre of the smallest pretension Dickens sought out with avidity in Rome, and eagerly enjoyed. He had heard it said in his old time in Genoa that the finest Marionetti were here; and now, after great difficulty, he discovered the company in a sort of stable attached to a decayed palace. "It was a wet night, and there "was no audience but a party of French officers "and ourselves. We all sat together. I never Performance of puppets. "saw anything more amazing than the performance "—altogether only an hour long, but managed "by as many as ten people, for we saw them all "go behind, at the ringing of a bell. The saving "of a young lady by a good fairy from the "machinations of an enchanter, coupled with the "comic business of her servant Pulcinella (the "Roman Punch) formed the plot of the first piece. "A scolding old peasant woman, who always "leaned forward to scold and put her hands in "the pockets of her apron, was incredibly natural. "Pulcinella, so airy, so merry, so life-like, so "graceful, he was irresistible. To see him carry-"ing an umbrella over his mistress's head in a Pulcinella, giant, and pony. "storm, talking to a prodigious giant whom he "met in the forest, and going to bed with a pony, "were things never to be forgotten. And so "delicate are the hands of the people who move "them, that every puppet was an Italian, and did "exactly what an Italian does. If he pointed at "any object, if he saluted anybody, if he laughed, "if he cried, he did it as never Englishman did

6*

Rome:
1853.

"it since Britain first at Heaven's command arose
"—arose—arose, &c.   There was a ballet after-
"wards, on the same scale, and we really came
"away quite enchanted with the delicate drollery
"of the thing.   French officers more than ditto."

Of the great enemy to the health of the now
capital of the kingdom of Italy, Dickens remarked
in the same letter.   "I have been led into some
"curious speculations by the existence and pro-
"gress of the Malaria about Rome.   Isn't it very
"extraordinary to think of its encroaching and
"encroaching on the Eternal City as if it were
"commissioned to swallow it up.   This year it
"has been extremely bad, and has long outstayed

Malaria.

"its usual time.   Rome has been very unhealthy,
"and is not free now.   Few people care to be
"out at the bad times of sunset and sunrise, and
"the streets are like a desert at night.   There is a
"church, a very little way outside the walls, de-
"stroyed by fire some 16 or 18 years ago, and
"now restored and re-created at an enormous
"expense.   It stands in a wilderness.   For any
"human creature who goes near it, or can sleep
"near it, after nightfall, it might as well be at the
"bottom of the uppermost cataract of the Nile.
"Along the whole extent of the Pontine Marshes
"(which we came across the other day), no crea-

Desolation.

"ture in Adam's likeness lives, except the sallow
"people at the lonely posting-stations.   I walk
"out from the Coliseum through the Street of
"Tombs to the ruins of the old Appian Way—
"pass no human being, and see no human habi-
"tation but ruined houses from which the people

"have fled, and where it is Death to sleep: these Rome:
1853.
"houses being three miles outside a gate of Rome
"at its farthest extent. Leaving Rome by the
"opposite side, we travel for many many hours
"over the dreary Campagna, shunned and avoided
"by all but the wretched shepherds. Thirteen
"hours' good posting brings us to Bolsena (I slept At Bolsena.
"there once before), on the margin of a stagnant
"lake whence the workpeople fly as the sun goes
"down—where it is a risk to go; where from a
"distance we saw a mist hang on the place; where,
"in the inconceivably wretched inn, no window
"can be opened; where our dinner was a pale
"ghost of a fish with an oily omelette, and we
"slept in great mouldering rooms tainted with
"ruined arches and heaps of dung—and coming Plague-
"from which we saw no colour in the cheek of smitten tract.
"man, woman, or child for another twenty miles.
"Imagine this phantom knocking at the gates of
"Rome; passing them; creeping along the streets;
"haunting the aisles and pillars of the churches;
"year by year more encroaching, and more im-
"possible of avoidance."

From Rome they posted to Florence, reaching Venice:
it in three days and a half, on the morning of November.
the 20th of November; having then been out six
weeks, with only three days' rain; and in another
week they were at Venice. "The fine weather
"has accompanied us here," Dickens wrote on
the 28th of November, "the place of all others
"where it is necessary, and the city has been a
"blaze of sunlight and blue sky (with an extremely
"clear cold air) ever since we have been in it.

Venice: 1853. iii. 176.
"If you could see it at this moment you would
"never forget it. We live in the same house that
"I lived in nine years ago, and have the same
"sitting-room—close to the Bridge of Sighs and
"the Palace of the Doges. The room is at the
"corner of the house, and there is a narrow street
"of water running round the side: so that we
"have the Grand Canal before the two front
"windows, and this wild little street at the corner
" window: into which, too, our three bedrooms

Gondola hired.

"look. We established a gondola as soon as we
"arrived, and we slide out of the hall on to the
"water twenty times a day. The gondoliers have
"queer old customs that belong to their class,
"and some are sufficiently disconcerting. . . It is
"a point of honour with them, while they are
"engaged, to be always at your disposal. Hence
"it is no use telling them they may go home for
"an hour or two—for they won't go. They roll
"themselves in shaggy capuccins, great coats with
"hoods, and lie down on the stone or marble

Habits of gondoliers.

"pavement until they are wanted again. So that
"when I come in or go out, on foot—which can
"be done from this house for some miles, over
"little bridges and by narrow ways—I usually
"walk over the principal of my vassals, whose
"custom it is to snore immediately across the
"doorway. Conceive the oddity of the most
"familiar things in this place, from one instance:
"Last night we go downstairs at half-past eight,
"step into the gondola, slide away on the black
"water, ripple and plash swiftly along for a mile
"or two, land at a broad flight of steps, and in-

"stantly walk into the most brilliant and beautiful VENICE: 1853.
"theatre conceivable—all silver and blue, and
"precious little fringes made of glittering prisms
"of glass. There we sit until half-past eleven, At the theatre.
"come out again (gondolier asleep outside the
"box-door), and in a moment are on the black
"silent water, floating away as if there were no
"dry building in the world. It stops, and in a
"moment we are out again, upon the broad solid
"Piazza of St. Mark, brilliantly lighted with gas,
"very like the Palais Royal at Paris, only far
"more handsome, and shining with no end of
"caffès. The two old pillars and the enormous
"bell-tower are as gruff and solid against the ex-
"quisite starlight as if they were a thousand miles
"from the sea or any undermining water; and the
"front of the cathedral, overlaid with golden
"mosaics and beautiful colours, is like a thousand
"rainbows even in the night."

His formerly expressed notions as to art and III. 179-182.
pictures in Italy received confirmation at this visit.
"I am more than ever confirmed in my conviction
"that one of the great uses of travelling is to en-
"courage a man to think for himself, to be bold
"enough always to declare without offence that
"he *does* think for himself, and to overcome the
"villainous meanness of professing what other
"people have professed when he knows (if he
"has capacity to originate an opinion) that his Uses of travel.
"profession is untrue. The intolerable nonsense
"against which genteel taste and subserviency
"are afraid to rise, in connection with art, is
"astounding. Egg's honest amazement and con-

Venice:
1853.
A painter
among
paintings.

"sternation when he saw some of the most
"trumpeted things was what the Americans call 'a
"'caution.' In the very same hour and minute
"there were scores of people falling into con-
"ventional raptures with that very poor Apollo,
"and passing over the most beautiful little figures
"and heads in the whole Vatican because they
"were not expressly set up to be worshipped. So

Tintoretto.

"in this place. There are pictures by Tintoretto
"in Venice, more delightful and masterly than it
"is possible sufficiently to express. His Assembly
"of the Blest I do believe to be, take it all in all,
"the most wonderful and charming picture ever
"painted. Your guide-book writer, represent-
"ing the general swarming of humbugs, rather
"patronizes Tintoretto as a man of some sort of

Conventional
praises.

"merit; and (bound to follow Eustace, Forsyth, and
"all the rest of them) directs you, on pain of
"being broke for want of gentility in appreciation,
"to go into ecstacies with things that have neither
"imagination, nature, proportion, possibility, nor
"anything else in them. You immediately obey,
"and tell your son to obey. He tells his son, and
"he tells his, and so the world gets at three-
"fourths of its frauds and miseries."

Turin:
December.

The last place visited was Turin, where the
travellers arrived on the 5th of December, finding
it, with a brightly shining sun, intensely cold and
freezing hard. "There are double windows to all
"the rooms, but the Alpine air comes down and
"numbs my feet as I write (in a cap and shawl)
"within six feet of the fire." There was yet
something better than this to report of that bracing

Alpine air. To Dickens's remarks on the Sardinian race, and to what he says of the exile of the noblest Italians, the momentous events of the few following years gave striking comment; nor could better proof be afforded of the judgment he brought to the observation of what passed before him. The letter had in all respects much interest and attractiveness. "This is a remarkably agree-"able place. A beautiful town, prosperous, thriv-"ing, growing prodigiously, as Genoa is; crowded "with busy inhabitants; full of noble streets and "squares. The Alps, now covered deep with snow, "are close upon it, and here and there seem al-"most ready to tumble into the houses. The "contrast this part of Italy presents to the rest, is "amazing. Beautifully made railroads, admirably "managed; cheerful, active people; spirit, energy, "life, progress. In Milan, in every street, the "noble palace of some exile is a barrack, and "dirty soldiers are lolling out of the magnificent "windows—it seems as if the whole place were "being gradually absorbed into soldiers. In Naples, "something like a hundred thousand troops. 'I "'knew,' I said to a certain Neapolitan Marchese "there whom I had known before, and who came "to see me the night after I arrived, 'I knew a "'very remarkable gentleman when I was last "'here; who had never been out of his own "'country, but was perfectly acquainted with "'English literature, and had taught himself to "'speak English in that wonderful manner that "'no one could have known him for a foreigner; "'I am very anxious to see him again, but I for-

"'get his name.'—He named him, and his face
"fell directly. 'Dead?' said I.—'In exile.'—'O
"'dear me!' said I, 'I had looked forward to see-
"'ing him again, more than any one I was ac-
"'quainted with in the country!'—'What would
"'you have!' says the Marchese in a low voice.
"'He was a remarkable man—full of knowledge,
"'full of spirit, full of generosity. Where should
"'he be but in exile? .Where could he be!' We
"said not another word about it, but I shall al-
"ways remember the short dialogue."

On the other hand there were incidents of
the Austrian occupation as to which Dickens
thought the ordinary style of comment unfair;
and his closing remark on their police is well
worth preserving. "I am strongly inclined to
"think that our countrymen are to blame in the
"matter of the Austrian vexations to travellers

"that have been complained of. Their manner
"is so very bad, they are so extraordinarily sus-
"picious, so determined to be done by everybody,
"and give so much offence. Now, the Austrian
"police are very strict, but they really know how
"to do business, and they do it. And if you treat
"them like gentlemen, they will always respond.
"When we first crossed the Austrian frontier, and
"were ushered into the police office, I took off

"my hat. The officer immediately took off his,
"and was as polite—still doing his duty, without
"any compromise—as it was possible to be.
"When we came to Venice, the arrangements
"were very strict, but were so business-like that
"the smallest possible amount of inconvenience

"consistent with strictness ensued. Here is the
"scene. A soldier has come into the railway car-
"riage (a saloon on the American plan) some
"miles off, has touched his hat, and asked for my
"passport. I have given it. Soldier has touched
"his hat again, and retired as from the presence
"of superior officer. Alighted from carriage, we
"pass into a place like a banking-house, lighted up
"with gas. Nobody bullies us or drives us there,
"but we must go, because the road ends there.
"Several soldierly clerks. One very sharp chief.
"My passport is brought out of an inner room,
"certified to be en règle. Very sharp chief takes
"it, looks at it (it is rather longer, now, than
"*Hamlet*), calls out—'Signor Carlo Dickens!'
"'Here I am, sir.' 'Do you intend remaining
"'long in Venice sir?' 'Probably four days sir!'
"'Italian is known to you sir. You have been
"'in Venice before?' 'Once before sir.' 'Per-
"'haps you remained longer then sir?' 'No in-
"'deed; I merely came to see, and went as I
"'came.' 'Truly sir? Do I infer that you are
"'going by Trieste?' 'No. I am going to Parma,
"'and Turin, and by Paris home.' 'A cold jour-
"'ney sir, I hope it may be a pleasant one.'
"'Thank you.'—He gives me one very sharp look
"all over, and wishes me a very happy night. I
"wish *him* a very happy night and it's done. The
"thing being done at all, could not be better
"done, or more politely—though I dare say if I
"had been sucking a gentish cane all the time,
"or talking in English to my compatriots, it might
"not unnaturally have been different. At Turin

"and at Genoa there are no such stoppages at
"all; but in any other part of Italy, give me an
"Austrian in preference to a native functionary.
"At Naples it is done in a beggarly, shambling,
"bungling, tardy, vulgar way; but I am strength-
"ened in my old impression that Naples is one
"of the most odious places on the face of the
"earth. The general degradation oppresses me
"like foul air."

CHAPTER XLVIII.

THREE SUMMERS AT BOULOGNE.

1853, 1854, AND 1856.

DICKENS was in Boulogne, in 1853, from the BOULOGNE:
1853. middle of June to the end of September, and for the next three months, as we have seen, was in Switzerland and Italy. In the following year he went again to Boulogne in June, and stayed, after finishing *Hard Times*, until far into October. In February of 1855 he was for a fortnight in Paris with Mr. Wilkie Collins; not taking up his Visit to
France. more prolonged residence there until the winter. From November 1855 to the end of April 1856 he made the French capital his home, working at *Little Dorrit* during all those months. Then, after a month's interval in Dover and London, he took up his third summer residence in Boulogne, whither his younger children had gone direct from Paris; and stayed until September, finishing *Little Dorrit* in London in the spring of 1857.

Of the first of these visits, a few lively notes of humour and character out of his letters will tell the story sufficiently. The second and third had points of more attractiveness. Those were the years of the French-English alliance, of the great exposition of English paintings, of the return of the troops from the Crimea, and of the visit of the Prince Consort to the Emperor; such interest as Dickens took in these several matters appearing in his letters with the usual vividness, and the story of his continental life coming out with amusing distinctness in the successive pictures they paint with so much warmth and colour. Another chapter will be given to Paris. This deals only with Boulogne.

His first residence.
For his first summer residence, in June 1853, he had taken a house on the high ground near the Calais road; an odd French place with the strangest little rooms and halls, but standing in the midst of a large garden, with wood and water-fall, a conservatory opening on a great bank of roses, and paths and gates on one side to the ramparts, on the other to the sea. Above all there was a capital proprietor and landlord, by whom the cost of keeping up gardens and wood The "forest." (which he called a forest) was defrayed, while he gave his tenant the whole range of both and all the flowers for nothing, sold him the garden pro-duce as it was wanted, and kept a cow on the estate to supply the family milk. "If this were "but 300 miles farther off," wrote Dickens, "how "the English would rave about it! I do assure "you that there are picturesque people, and town, "and country, about this place, that quite fill up "the eye and fancy. As to the fishing people Fisherman's quarter. "(whose dress can have changed neither in colour "nor in form for many many years), and their "quarter of the town cobweb-hung with great "brown nets across the narrow up-hill streets,

"they are as good as Naples, every bit." His description both of house and landlord, of which I tested the exactness when I visited him, was in the old pleasant vein; requiring no connection with himself to give it interest, but, by the charm and ease with which everything picturesque or characteristic was disclosed, placed in the domain of art.

"O the rain here yesterday!" (26th of June.) "A great sea-fog rolling in, a strong wind blow- "ing, and the rain coming down in torrents all "day long. . . This house is on a great hill- "side, backed up by woods of young trees. It "faces the Haute Ville with the ramparts and the "unfinished cathedral—which capital object is "exactly opposite the windows. On the slope in "front, going steep down to the right, all Bou- "logne is piled and jumbled about in a very "picturesque manner. The view is charming— "closed in at last by the tops of swelling hills; "and the door is within ten minutes of the post- "office, and within quarter of an hour of the sea. "The garden is made in terraces up the hill-side, "like an Italian garden; the top walks being in "the before-mentioned woods. The best part of "it begins at the level of the house, and goes up "at the back, a couple of hundred feet perhaps. "There are at present thousands of roses all "about the house, and no end of other flowers. "There are five great summer-houses, and (I think) "fifteen fountains—not one of which (according "to the invariable French custom) ever plays. "The house is a doll's house of many rooms. It

A doll's
house.

Rooms.

Offices.

"is one story high, with eight and thirty steps up
"and down—tribune wise—to the front door: the
"noblest French demonstration I have ever seen
"I think. It is a double house; and as there are
"only four windows and a pigeon-hole to be be-
"held in front, you would suppose it to contain
"about four rooms. Being built on the hill-side,
"the top story of the house at the back—there
"are two stories there—opens on the level of
"another garden. On the ground floor there is
"a very pretty hall, almost all glass; a little
"dining-room opening on a beautiful conservatory,
"which is also looked into through a great
"transparent glass in a mirror-frame over the
"chimney-piece, just as in Paxton's room at
"Chatsworth; a spare bed-room, two little draw-
"ing-rooms opening into one another, the family
"bed-rooms, a bath-room, a glass corridor, an
"open yard, and a kind of kitchen with a
"machinery of stoves and boilers. Above, there
"are eight tiny bed-rooms all opening on one
"great room in the roof, originally intended for
"a billiard-room. In the basement there is an
"admirable kitchen with every conceivable re-
"quisite in it, a noble cellar, first-rate man's room
"and pantry; coach-house, stable, coal-store and
"wood-store; and in the garden is a pavilion,
"containing an excellent spare bed-room on the
"ground floor. The getting-up of these places,
"the looking-glasses, clocks, little stoves, all man-
"ner of fittings, must be seen to be appreciated.
"The conservatory is full of choice flowers and
"perfectly beautiful."

Then came the charm of the letter, his de- BOULOGNE:
1853.
Landlord.
scription of his landlord, lightly sketched by him
in print as M. Loyal-Devasseur, but here filled in
with the most attractive touches his loving hand
could give. "But the landlord—M. Beaucourt—
"is wonderful. Everybody here has two sur-
"names (I cannot conceive why), and M. Beau- Wife's name
and his own.
"court, as he is always called, is by rights M.
"Beaucourt-Mutuel. He is a portly jolly fellow
"with a fine open face; lives on the hill behind,
"just outside the top of the garden; and was a
"linen draper in the town, where he still has a
"shop, but is supposed to have mortgaged his
"business and to be in difficulties—all along of
"this place, which he has planted with his own
"hands; which he cultivates all day; and which
"he never on any consideration speaks of but as
"'the Property.' He is extraordinarily popular in
"Boulogne (the people in the shops invariably Bon garçon.
"brightening up at the mention of his name, and
"congratulating us on being his tenants), and
"really seems to deserve it. He is such a liberal
"fellow that I can't bear to ask him for anything,
"since he instantly supplies it whatever it is.
"The things he has done in respect of unreason-
"able bedsteads and washing-stands, I blush to
"think of. I observed the other day in one of
"the side gardens—there are gardens at each
"side of the house too—a place where I thought
"the Comic Countryman" (a name he was giving I. 226.
III. 272.
IV. 60.
just then to his youngest boy) "must infallibly
"trip over, and make a little descent of a dozen
"feet. So I said, 'M. Beaucourt'—who instantly

"pulled off his cap and stood bareheaded—
"'there are some spare pieces of wood lying by
"'the cow-house, if you would have the kindness
"'to have one laid across here I think it would
"'be safer.' 'Ah, mon dieu sir,' said M. Beau-
"court, 'it must be iron.   This is not a portion
"'of the property where you would like to see
"'wood.' 'But iron is so expensive,' said I, 'and
"'it really is not worth while——' 'Sir, pardon
"'me a thousand times,' said M. Beaucourt, 'it
"'shall be iron. Assuredly and perfectly it shall
"'be iron.' 'Then M. Beaucourt,' said I, 'I shall
"'be glad to pay a moiety of the cost.' 'Sir,'
"said M. Beaucourt, 'Never!'   Then to change
"the subject, he slided from his firmness and
"gravity into a graceful conversational tone,
"and said, 'In the moonlight last night, the
"'flowers on the property appeared, O Heaven,
"'to be *bathing themselves in the sky*. You like
"'the property?' 'M. Beaucourt,' said I, 'I am
"'enchanted with it; I am more than satisfied
"'with everything.' 'And I sir,' said M. Beau-
"court, laying his cap upon his breast, and
"kissing his hand—'I equally!' Yesterday two
"blacksmiths came for a day's work, and put up
"a good solid handsome bit of iron-railing, mor-
"ticed into the stone parapet. . . If the extra-
"ordinary things in the house defy description,
"the amazing phenomena in the gardens never
"could have been dreamed of by anybody but a
"Frenchman bent upon one idea. Besides a
"portrait of the house in the dining-room, there
"is a plan of the property in the hall. It looks

"about the size of Ireland; and to every one of
"the extraordinary objects, there is a reference
"with some portentous name. There are fifty-
"one such references, including the Cottage of
"Tom Thumb, the Bridge of Austerlitz, the Bridge
"of Jena, the Hermitage, the Bower of the Old
"Guard, the Labyrinth (I have no idea which is
"which); and there is guidance to every room in
"the house, as if it were a place on that stupendous
"scale that without such a clue you must in-
"fallibly lose your way, and perhaps perish of
"starvation between bedroom and bedroom."*

On the 3rd of July there came a fresh trait of
the good fellow of a landlord. "Fancy what
"Beaucourt told me last night. When he 'con-
"'ceived the inspiration' of planting the property
"ten years ago, he went over to England to buy
"the trees, took a small cottage in the market-
"gardens at. Putney, lived there three months,
"held a symposium every night attended by the
"principal gardeners of Fulham, Putney, Kew,
"and Hammersmith (which he calls Hamsterdam),
"and wound up with a supper at which the market-
"gardeners rose, clinked their glasses, and ex-
"claimed with one accord (I quote him exactly)
"VIVE BEAUCOURT! He was a captain in the

Marginal notes:
BOULOGNE:
1853.

Making the
most of it.

Beaucourt's
visit to
England.

Among the
Putney
market-
gardeners.

---

* Prices are reported in one of the letters; and, considering what
they have been since, the touch of disappointment hinted at may raise a
smile. "Provisions are scarcely as cheap as I expected, though very
"different from London: besides which, a pound weight here, is a pound
"and a quarter English. So that meat at 7d. a pound, is actually a
"fourth less. A capital dish of asparagus costs us about fivepence; a
"fowl, one and threepence; a duck, a few halfpence more; a dish of
"fish, about a shilling. The very best wine at tenpence that I ever
"drank—I used to get it very good for the same money in Genoa, but not
"so good. The common people very engaging and obliging."   Prices.

"National Guard, and Cavaignac his general.
"Brave Capitaine Beaucourt! said Cavaignac, you
"must receive a decoration. My General, said
"Beaucourt, No! It is enough for me that I have
"done my duty. I go to lay the first stone of a
"house upon a Property I have—that house shall
"be my decoration. (Regard that house!)" Addition to the picture came in a letter of the 24th
of July: with a droll glimpse of Shakespeare at
the theatre, and of the Saturday's pig-market.

"I may mention that the great Beaucourt daily
"changes the orthography of this place. He has
"now fixed it, by having painted up outside the
"garden gate, 'Entrée particulière de la Villa des
"'Moulineaux.' On another gate a little higher
"up, he has had painted 'Entrée des Ecuries de
"'la Villa des Moulineaux.' On another gate a
"little lower down (applicable to one of the in-
"numerable buildings in the garden), 'Entrée du
"'Tom Pouce.' On the highest gate of the lot,
"leading to his own house, 'Entrée du Château
"'Napoléonienne.' All of which inscriptions you
"will behold in black and white when you come.
"I see little of him now, as, all things being
"'bien arrangées,' he is delicate of appearing.
"His wife has been making a trip in the country
"during the last three weeks, but (as he men-
"tioned to me with his hat in his hand) it was
"necessary that he should remain here, to be
"continually at the disposition of the tenant of
"the Property. (The better to do this, he has
"had roaring dinner parties of fifteen daily; and
"the old woman who milks the cows has been

"fainting up the hill under vast burdens of cham-
"pagne.)

"We went to the theatre last night, to see the
"*Midsummer Night's Dream*—of the Opera Co-
"mique. It is a beautiful little theatre now, with
"a very good company; and the nonsense of the
"piece was done with a sense quite confounding
"in that connexion. Willy Am Shay Kes Peer;
"Sirzhon Foll Stayffe; Lor Lattimeer; and that
"celebrated Maid of Honour to Queen Elizabeth,
"Meees Oleevecir—were the principal characters.

"Outside the old town, an army of workmen
"are (and have been for a week or so, already)
"employed upon an immense building which I
"supposed might be a Fort, or a Monastery, or a
"Barrack, or other something designed to last for
"ages. I find it is for the annual fair, which
"begins on the fifth of August and lasts a fort-
"night. Almost every Sunday we have a fête,
"where there is dancing in the open air, and
"where immense men with prodigious beards
"revolve on little wooden horses like Italian irons,
"in what we islanders call a roundabout, by the
"hour together. But really the good humour and
"cheerfulness are very delightful. Among the
"other sights of the place, there is a pig-market
"every Saturday, perfectly insupportable in its
"absurdity. An excited French peasant, male or
"female, with a determined young pig, is the most
"amazing spectacle. I saw a little Drama enacted
"yesterday week, the drollery of which was per-
"fect. *Dram. Pers.* 1. A pretty young woman
"with short petticoats and trim blue stockings,

"riding a donkey with two baskets and a pig in
"each. 2. An ancient farmer in a blouse, driving
"four pigs, his four in hand, with an enormous
"whip—and being drawn against walls and into
"smoking shops by any one of the four. 3. A
"cart, with an old pig (manacled) looking out of
"it, and terrifying six hundred and fifty young
"pigs in the market by his terrific grunts. 4. Col-
"lector of Octroi in an immense cocked hat, with
"a stream of young pigs running, night and day,
"between his military boots· and rendering ac-
"counts impossible. 5. Inimitable, confronted by
"a radiation of elderly pigs, fastened each by one
"leg to a bunch of stakes in the ground. 6. John
"Edmund Reade, poet, expressing eternal devo-
"tion to and admiration of Landor, unconscious
"of approaching pig recently escaped from barrow.
"7. Priests, peasants, soldiers, &c. &c."

He had meanwhile gathered friendly faces
round him. Frank Stone went over with his
family to a house taken for him on the St. Omer
road by Dickens, who was joined in the chateau
by Mr. and Mrs. Leech and Mr. Wilkie Collins.
"Leech says that when he stepped from the boat
"after their stormy passage, he was received by
"the congregated spectators with a distinct round
"of applause as by far the most intensely and
"unutterably miserable looking object that had
"yet appeared. The laughter was tumultuous,
"and he wishes his friends to know that alto-
"gether he made an immense hit." So passed
·the summer months: excursions with these friends
to Amiens and Beauvais relieving the work upon

his novel, and the trip to Italy, already described,
following on its completion.

In June, 1854, M. Beaucourt had again re- ceived his famous tenant, but in another cottage or chateau (to him convertible terms) on the much cherished property, placed on the very summit of the hill with a private road leading out to the Column, a really pretty place, rooms larger than in the other house, a noble sea view, everywhere nice prospects, good garden, and plenty of sloping turf.* It was called the Villa du Camp de Droite, and here Dickens stayed, as I have intimated, until the eve of his winter residence in Paris.

The formation of the Northern Camp at Bou-logne began the week after he had finished *Hard* *Times*, and he watched its progress, as it increased and extended itself along the cliffs towards Calais, with the liveliest amusement. At first he was startled by the suddenness with which soldiers overran the roads, became billeted in every house, made the bridges red with their trowsers, and "sprang upon the pier like fantastic mustard and "cress when boats were expected, many of them "never having seen the sea before." But the good behaviour of the men had a reconciling effect, and their ingenuity delighted him. The quickness with which they raised whole streets of

---

* Besides the old friends before named, Thackeray and his family were here in the early weeks, living "in a melancholy but very good "chateau on the Paris road, where their landlord (a Baron) has supplied "them, T. tells me, with one milk-jug as the entire crockery of the estab-"lishment." Our friend soon tired of this, going off to Spa, and on his return, after ascending the hill to smoke a farewell cigar with Dickens, left for London and Scotland in October.

mud-huts, less picturesque than the tents,* but (like most unpicturesque things) more comfortable, was like an Arabian Nights' tale. "Each little "street holds 144 men, and every corner-door has "the number of the street upon it as soon as it is "put up; and the postmen can fall to work as "easily as in the Rue de Rivoli at Paris." His patience was again a little tried when he found baggage-wagons ploughing up his favourite walks, and trumpeters in twos and threes teaching newly-recruited trumpeters in all the sylvan places, and making the echoes hideous. But this had its amusement too. "I met to-day a weazen sun-"burnt youth from the south with such an im-
"mense regimental shako on, that he looked like "a sort of lucifer match-box, evidently blowing "his life rapidly out, under the auspices of two "magnificent creatures all hair and lungs, of "such breadth across the shoulders that I couldn't "see their breast-buttons when I stood in front of "them."

The interest culminated as the visit of the Prince Consort approached with its attendant glories of illuminations and reviews. Beaucourt's excitement became intense. The Villa du Camp de Droite was to be a blaze of triumph on the night of the arrival; Dickens, who had carried over with him the meteor flag of England and set it streaming over a haystack in his field,** now

---

* Another of his letters questioned even the picturesqueness a little, for he discovered that on a sunny day the white tents, seen from a distance, looked exactly like an immense washing establishment with all the linen put out to dry.
** "Whence it can be seen for miles and miles, to the glory of Eng-"land and the joy of Beaucourt."

hoisted the French colours over the British Jack
in honour of the national alliance; the Emperor
was to subside to the station of a general officer,
so that all the rejoicings should be in honour of
the Prince; and there was to be a review in the
open country near Wimereux, when "at one stage
"of the maneuvres (I am too excited to spell the
"word but you know what I mean)" the whole
hundred thousand men in the camp of the North
were to be placed before the Prince's eyes, to
show him what a division of the French army
might be. "I believe everything I hear," said
Dickens. It was the state of mind of Hood's
country gentleman after the fire at the Houses of
Parliament. "Beaucourt, as one of the town
"council, receives summonses to turn out and
"debate about something, or receive somebody,
"every five minutes. Whenever I look out of
"window, or go to the door, I see an immense
"black object at Beaucourt's porch like a boat set
"up on end in the air with a pair of white trow-
"sers below it. This is the cocked hat of an of-
"ficial Huissier, newly arrived with a summons,
"whose head is thrown back as he is in the act
"of drinking Beaucourt's wine." The day came
at last, and all Boulogne turned out for its holiday; "but I" Dickens wrote, "had by this cooled
"down a little, and, reserving myself for the
"illuminations, I abandoned the great men and
"set off upon my usual country walk. See my re-
"ward. Coming home by the Calais road, cov-
"ered with dust, I suddenly find myself face to
"face with Albert and Napoleon, jogging along in

"the pleasantest way, a little in front, talking ex-
"tremely loud about the view, and attended by a
"brilliant staff of some sixty or seventy horsemen,
"with a couple of our royal grooms with their red
"coats riding oddly enough in the midst of the

"magnates. I took off my wide-awake without
"stopping to stare, whereupon the Emperor pulled
"off his cocked hat; and Albert (seeing, I suppose,
"that it was an Englishman) pulled off his. Then
"we went our several ways. The Emperor is
"broader across the chest than in the old times
"when we used to see him so often at Gore-
"House, and stoops more in the shoulders. In-
"deed his carriage thereabouts is like Fon-
"blanque's." *   The town he described as "one
"great flag" for the rest of the visit; and to the
success of the illuminations he contributed largely
himself by leading off splendidly with a hundred

and twenty wax candles blazing in his seventeen
front windows, and visible from that great height
over all the place. "On the first eruption Beau-
"court *danced and screamed* on the grass before
"the door; and when he was more composed, set
"off with Madame Beaucourt to look at the house
"from every possible quarter, and, he said, collect
"the suffrages of his compatriots."

Their suffrages seem to have gone, however,

* The picture had changed drearily in less than a year and a half,
when (17th of Feb. 1856) Dickens thus wrote from Paris. "I suppose
"mortal man out of bed never looked so ill and worn as the Emperor
"does just now. He passed close by me on horseback, as I was coming
"in at the door on Friday, and I never saw so haggard a face. Some
"English saluted him, and he lifted his hand to his hat as slowly, pain-
"fully, and laboriously, as if his arm were made of lead. I think he
"*must* be in pain."

mainly in another direction. "It was wonderful,"
Dickens wrote, "to behold about the streets the
"small French soldiers of the line seizing our
"Guards by the hand and embracing them. It
"was wonderful, too, to behold the English sailors
"in the town, shaking hands with everybody and
"generally patronizing everything. When the
"people could not get hold of either a soldier or
"a sailor, they rejoiced in the royal grooms, and
"embraced *them*. I don't think the Boulogne people
"were surprised by anything so much, as by the
"three cheers the crew of the yacht gave when
"the Emperor went aboard to lunch. The pro-
"digious volume of them, and the precision, and
"the circumstance that no man was left straggling
"on his own account either before or afterwards,
"seemed to strike the general mind with amaze-
"ment. Beaucourt said it was *like boxing*." That
was written on the 10th of September; but in a
very few days Dickens was unwillingly convinced
that whatever the friendly disposition to England
might be, the war with Russia was decidedly un-
popular. He was present when the false report
of the taking of Sebastopol reached the Emperor
and Empress. "I was at the Review" (8th of October) "yesterday week, very near the Emperor
"and Empress, when the taking of Sebastopol was
"announced. It was a magnificent show on a
"magnificent day; and if any circumstance could
"make it special, the arrival of the telegraphic
"despatch would be the culminating point one
"might suppose. It quite disturbed and mortified
"me to find how faintly, feebly, miserably, the

BOULOGNE:
1854.
"men responded to the call of the officers to
"cheer, as each regiment passed by. Fifty ex-
"cited Englishmen would make a greater sign
"and sound than a thousand of these men do...
"The Empress was very pretty, and her slight
"figure sat capitally on her grey horse. When
"the Emperor gave her the despatch to read, she
"flushed and fired up in a very pleasant way, and
"kissed it with as natural an impulse as one could
"desire to see."

A play at
the Camp.
On the night of that day Dickens went up to
see a play acted at a café at the camp, and found
himself one of an audience composed wholly of
officers and men, with only four ladies among
them, officers' wives. The steady, working, sensible faces all about him told their own story;
"and as to kindness and consideration towards
"the poor actors, it was real benevolence." Another attraction at the camp was a conjuror, who
had been called to exhibit twice before the im-
A French
conjuror.
perial party, and whom Dickens always afterwards
referred to as the most consummate master of
legerdemain he had seen. Nor was he a mean
authority as to this, being himself, with his tools
at hand, a capital conjuror;* but the Frenchman

---

* I permit myself to quote from the bill of one of his entertainments
in the old merry days at Bonchurch (IV. 202—15), of course drawn up
by himself, whom it describes as "The Unparalleled Necromancer RHIA
"RHAMA RHOOS, educated cabalistically in the Orange Groves of Sala-
"manca and the Ocean Caves of Alum Bay," some of, whose proposed
wonders it thus prefigures:

THE LEAPING CARD
WONDER.

Two Cards being drawn from

the Pack by two of the company,
and placed, with the Pack, in the
Necromancer's box, will leap forth
at the command of any lady of not

scorned help, stood among the company without

less than eight, or more than eighty, years of age.

⁎ *This wonder is the result of nine years' seclusion in the mines of Russia.*

THE PYRAMID WONDER.

A shilling being lent to the Necromancer by any gentleman of not less than twelve months, or more than one hundred years, of age, and carefully marked by the said gentleman, ⁎ will disappear from within a brazen box at the word of command, and pass through the hearts of an infinity of boxes, which will afterwards build themselves into pyramids and sink into a small mahogany box, at the Necromancer's bidding.

⁎ *Five thousand guineas were paid for the acquisition of this wonder, to a Chinese Mandarin, who died of grief immediately after parting with the secret.*

THE CONFLAGRATION WONDER.

A Card being drawn from the Pack by any lady, not under a direct and positive promise of marriage, will be immediately named by the Necromancer, destroyed by fire, and reproduced from its own ashes.

⁎ *An annuity of one thousand pounds has been offered to the Necromancer by the Directors of the Sun Fire Office for the secret of this wonder—and refused!!!*

THE LOAF OF BREAD WONDER.

The watch of any truly prepossessing lady, of any age, single or married, being locked by the Necromancer in a strong box, will fly at the word of command from within that box into the heart of an ordinary half-quartern loaf, whence it shall be cut out in the presence of the whole company, whose cries of astonishment will be audible at a distance of some miles.

⁎ *Ten years in the Plains of Tartary were devoted to the study of this wonder.*

THE TRAVELLING DOLL WONDER.

The travelling doll is composed of solid wood throughout, but, by putting on a travelling dress of the simplest construction, becomes invisible, performs enormous journeys in half a minute, and passes from visibility to invisibility with an expedition so astonishing that no eye can follow its transformations.

⁎ *The Necromancer's attendant usually faints on beholding this wonder, and is only to be revived by the administration of brandy and water.*

THE PUDDING WONDER.

The company having agreed among themselves to offer to the Necromancer, by way of loan, the hat of any gentleman whose head has arrived at maturity of size, the Necromancer, without removing that hat for an instant from before the eyes of the delighted company, will light a fire in it, make a plum-pudding in his magic saucepan, boil it over the said fire, produce it in two minutes, thoroughly done, cut it, and dispense it in portions to the whole company, for their consumption then and there; returning the hat at last, wholly uninjured by fire, to its lawful owner.

⁎ *The extreme liberality of this wonder awakening the jealousy of the beneficent Austrian Government, when exhibited in Milan, the Necromancer had the honour to be seized, and confined for five years in the fortress of that city.*

BOULOGNE:
1854.
any sort of apparatus, and, by the mere force of sleight of hand and an astonishing memory, performed feats having no likeness to anything Dickens had ever seen done, and totally inex- Legerdemain in perfection. plicable to his most vigilant reflection. "So far "as I know, a perfectly original genius, and that "puts any sort of knowledge of legerdemain, such "as I supposed that I possessed, at utter defiance." The account he gave dealt with two exploits only, the easiest to describe, and, not being with cards, not the most remarkable; for he would also say Making demons of cards. of this Frenchman that he transformed cards into very demons. He never saw a human hand touch them in the same way, fling them about so amazingly, or change them in his, one's own, or another's hand, with a skill so impossible to follow.

"You are to observe that he was *with the* "*company,* not in the least removed from them; "and that we occupied the front row. He brought "in some writing paper with him when he entered, "and a black-lead pencil; and he wrote some "words on half-sheets of paper. One of these "half-sheets he folded into two, and gave to "Catherine to hold. Madame, he says aloud, will "you think of any class of objects? I have done Examples of a conjuror's art. "so.—Of what class, Madame? Animals.—Will "you think of a particular animal, Madame? I "have done so.—Of what animal? The Lion.— "Will you think of another class of objects, Ma- "dame? I have done so.—Of what class? Flowers. "—The particular flower? The Rose.—Will you "open the paper you hold in your hand? She "opened it, and there was neatly and plainly written

"in pencil—*The Lion. The Rose.* Nothing what-
"ever had led up to these words, and they were
"the most distant conceivable from Catherine's
"thoughts when she entered the room.   He had
"several common school-slates about a foot square.
"He took one of these to a field-officer from the
"camp, decoré and what not, who sat about six
"from us, with a grave saturnine friend next him.
"My General, says he, will you write a name on
"this slate, after your friend has done so?   Don't
"show it to me.   The friend wrote a name, and
"the General wrote a name.   The conjuror took
"the slate rapidly from the officer, threw it violently
"down on the ground with its written side to the
"floor, and asked the officer to put his foot upon
"it and keep it there: which he did.   The con-
"juror considered for about a minute, looking
"devilish hard at the General.—My General, says
"he, your friend wrote Dagobert, upon the slate
"under your foot.   The friend admits it.—And
"you, my General, wrote Nicholas.   General ad-
"mits it, and everybody laughs and applauds.—
"My General, will you excuse me, if I change
"that name into a name expressive of the power
"of a great nation, which, in happy alliance with
"the gallantry and spirit of France will shake that
"name to its centre?   Certainly I will excuse it.
"—My General, take up the slate and read.   Ge-
"neral reads: DAGOBERT, VICTORIA.   The first in
"his friend's writing; the second in a new hand.
"I never saw anything in the least like this; or at
"all approaching to the absolute certainty, the
"familiarity, quickness, absence of all machinery,

"and actual face-to-face, hand-to-hand fairness "between the conjuror and the audience, with "which it was done. I have not the slightest "idea of the secret.—One more. He was blinded "with several table napkins, and then a great cloth "was bodily thrown over them and his head too, "so that his voice sounded as if he were under a "bed. Perhaps half a dozen dates were written "on a slate. He takes the slate in his hand, and "throws it violently down on the floor as before, "remains silent a minute, seems to become agitated,

and sees London in 1666.
"and bursts out thus: 'What is this I see? A "'great city, but of narrow streets and old-fash- "'ioned houses, many of which are of wood, re- "'solving itself into ruins! How is it falling into "'ruins? Hark! I hear the crackling of a great "'conflagration, and, looking up, I behold a vast "'cloud of flame and smoke. The ground is "'covered with hot cinders too, and people are "'flying into the fields and endeavouring to save "'their goods. This great fire, this great wind, "'this roaring noise! This is the great fire of "'London, and the first date upon the slate must "'be one, six, six, six—the year in which it hap- "'pened!' And so on with all the other dates. "There! Now, if you will take a cab and impart "these mysteries to Rogers, I shall be very glad "to have his opinion of them." Rogers had taxed our credulity with some wonderful clair- voyant experiences of his own in Paris to which here was a parallel at last!

June 1856.
When leaving Paris for his third visit to Boulogne, at the beginning of June 1856, he had

not written a word of the ninth number of his
new book, and did not expect for another month
to "see land from the running sea of *Little Dorrit*."
He had resumed the house he first occupied, the
cottage or villa "des Moulineaux," and after dawd-
ling about his garden for a few days with surprising industry in a French farmer garb of blue
blouse, leathern belt, and military cap, which he
had mounted as "the only one for complete com-
"fort," he wrote to me that he was getting "Now
"to work again—to work! The story lies before
"me, I hope, strong and clear. Not to be easily
"told; but nothing of that sort is to be easily done
"that *I* know of." At work it became his habit
to sit late, and then, putting off his usual walk
until night, to lie down among the roses reading
until after tea ("middle-aged Love in a blouse
"and belt"), when he went down to the pier.
"The said pier at evening is a phase of the place
"we never see, and which I hardly knew. But I
"never did behold such specimens of the youth
"of my country, male and female, as pervade that
"place. They are really, in their vulgarity and
"insolence, quite disheartening. One is so fear-
"fully ashamed of them, and they contrast so very
"unfavourably with the natives." Mr. Wilkie
Collins was again his companion in the summer
weeks, and the presence of Jerrold for the greater
part of the time added much to his enjoyment.

The last of the camp was now at hand. It
had only a battalion of men in it, and a few
days would see them out. At first there was horrible weather, "storms of wind, rushes of rain,

"heavy squalls, cold airs, sea fogs, banging shutters,
"flapping doors, and beaten down rose-trees by
"the hundred;" but then came a delightful week
among the corn fields and bean fields, and afterwards the end. "It looks very singular and very
"miserable. The soil being sand, and the grass
"having been trodden away these two years, the
"wind from the sea carries the sand into the
"chinks and ledges of all the doors and windows,
"and chokes them;—just as if they belonged to
"Arab huts in the desert. A number of the non-
"commissioned officers made turf-couches outside
"their huts, and there were turf orchestras for the
"bands to play in; all of which are fast getting
"sanded over in a most Egyptian manner. The
"Fair is on, under the walls of the haute ville

"over the way. At one popular show, the Mala-
"khoff is taken every half-hour between 4 and 11.
"Bouncing explosions announce every triumph of
"the French arms (the English have nothing to

"do with it); and in the intervals a man outside
"blows a railway whistle—straight into the dining-
"room. Do you know that the French soldiers
"call the English medal 'The Salvage Medal'—
"meaning that they got it for saving the English
"army? I don't suppose there are a thousand
"people in all France who believe that we did
"anything but get rescued by the French. And
"I am confident that the no-result of our precious
"Chelsea enquiry has wonderfully strengthened
"this conviction. Nobody at home has yet any
"adequate idea, I am deplorably sure, of what
"the Barnacles and the Circumlocution Office

"have done for us. But whenever we get into
"war again, the people will begin to find out."

His own household had got into a small war A house-
already, of which the commander-in-chief was hold war.
his man-servant "French," the bulk of the forces
engaged being his children, and the invaders two
cats. Business brought him to London on the
hostilities breaking out, and on his return after a
few days the story of the war was told. "Dick," "Dick" in
it should be said, was a canary very dear both to danger.
Dickens and his eldest daughter, who had so
tamed to her loving hand its wild little heart that
it was become the most docile of companions.*
"The only thing new in this garden is that war
"is raging against two particularly tigerish and
"fearful cats (from the mill, I suppose), which are
"always glaring in dark corners, after our wonder-
"ful little Dick. Keeping the house open at all
"points, it is impossible to shut them out, and The two
"they hide themselves in the most terrific manner: invaders.
"hanging themselves up behind draperies, like
"bats, and tumbling out in the dead of night with
"frightful caterwaulings. Hereupon, French bor- Feline foes.
"rows Beaucourt's gun, loads the same to the
"muzzle, discharges it twice in vain and throws
"himself over with the recoil, exactly like a clown.
"But at last (while I was in town) he aims at the
"more amiable cat of the two, and shoots that
"animal dead. Insufferably elated by this victory,
"he is now engaged from morning to night in
"hiding behind bushes to get aim at the other.

---

* Dick died at Gadshill in 1866, in the sixteenth year of his age,
and was honoured with a small tomb and epitaph.

"He does nothing else whatever. All the boys "encourage him and watch for the enemy—on "whose appearance they give an alarm which im-"mediately serves as a warning to the creature, "who runs away. They are at this moment (ready "dressed for church) all lying on their stomachs "in various parts of the garden. Horrible whistles "give notice to the gun what point it is to "approach. I am afraid to go out, lest I should "be shot. Mr. Plornish says his prayers at night "in a whisper, lest the cat should overhear him "and take offence. The tradesmen cry out as "they come up the avenue, 'Me voici! C'est moi "'—boulanger—ne tirez pas, Monsieur Franche!' "It is like living in a state of siege; and the won-"derful manner in which the cat preserves the "character of being the only person not much "put out by the intensity of this monomania, is "most ridiculous." (6th of July.) . . . "About "four pounds of powder and half a ton of shot "have been (13th of July) fired off at the cat (and "the public in general) during the week. The "finest thing is that immediately after I have heard "the noble sportsman blazing away at her in the "garden in front, I look out of my room door "into the drawing-room, and am pretty sure to "see her coming in after the birds, in the calmest "manner, by the back window. Intelligence has "been brought to me from a source on which I "can rely, that French has newly conceived the "atrocious project of tempting her into the coach-"house by meat and kindness, and there, from an "elevated portmanteau, blowing her head off.

"This I mean sternly to interdict, and to do so
"to-day as a work of piety."

Besides the graver work which Mr. Wilkie Preparing for
Collins and himself were busy with, in these Christmas.
months, and by which *Household Words* mainly
was to profit, some lighter matters occupied the
leisure of both. There were to be, at Christmas,
theatricals again at Tavistock House; in which
the children, with the help of their father and
other friends, were to follow up the success of
the *Lighthouse* by again acquitting themselves as
grown-up actors; and Mr. Collins was busy preparing for them a new drama to be called *The
Frozen Deep*, while Dickens was sketching a farce
for Mr. Lemon to fill in. But this pleasant employment had sudden and sad interruption.

An epidemic broke out in the town, affecting *Deaths in
the children of several families known to Dickens, the town.*
among them that of his friend Mr. Gilbert A'Becket;
who, upon arriving from Paris, and finding a
favourite little son stricken dangerously, sank himself under an illness from which he had been
suffering, and died two days after the boy. "He *Gilbert
"had for three days shown symptoms of rallying, A'Becket.*
"and we had some hope of his recovery; but he
"sank and died, and never even knew that the
"child had gone before him. A sad, sad story."
Dickens meanwhile had sent his own children
home with his wife, and the rest soon followed.
Poor M. Beaucourt was inconsolable. "The de-
"solation of the place is wretched. When Mamey
"and Katey went, Beaucourt came in and wept.
"He really is almost broken-hearted about it. He *Leaving for
England.*

Boulogne:
1856.

"had planted all manner of flowers for next month,
"and has thrown down the spade and left off
"weeding the garden, so that it looks something
"like a dreary bird-cage with all manner of grasses
"and chickweeds sticking through the bars and
M. Beau-
court's grief.
"lying in the sand. 'Such a loss too,' he says,
"'for Monsieur Dickens!' Then he looks in at
"the kitchen window (which seems to be his only
"relief), and sighs himself up the hill home."*

The interval of residence in Paris between
these two last visits to Boulogne is now to be
described.

The goodness
of M. Beau-
court.
* I cannot take leave of M. Beaucourt without saying that I am necessarily silent as to the most touching traits recorded of him by Dickens, because they refer to the generosity shown by him to an English family in
occupation of another of his houses, in connection with whom his losses
must have been considerable, but for whom he had nothing but help and
sympathy. Replying to some questions about them, put by Dickens one
day, he had only enlarged on their sacrifices and self-denials. "Ah that
"family unfortunate! 'And you, Monsieur Beaucourt,' I said to him,
"'you are unfortunate too, God knows!' Upon which he said in the
pleasantest way in the world, Ah, Monsieur Dickens, thank you, don't
"speak of it!--And backed himself down the avenue with his cap in his
"hand, as if he were going to back himself straight into the evening
"star, without the ceremony of dying first. I never did see such a gentle,
"kind heart."

CHAPTER XLIX.

RESIDENCE IN PARIS.

1855-1856.

IN Paris Dickens's life was passed among
artists, and in the exercise of his own art. His
associates were writers, painters, actors, or musi-
cians, and when he wanted relief from any strain
of work he found it at the theatre. The years
since his last residence in the great city had made
him better known, and the increased attentions
pleased him. He had to help in preparing for a
translation of his books into French; and this,
with continued labour at the story he had in
hand, occupied him as long as he remained. It
will be all best told by extracts from his letters;
in which the people he met, the theatres he visited,
and the incidents, public or private, that seemed
to him worthy of mention, reappear with the old
force and liveliness.

Nor is anything better worth preserving from
them than choice bits of description of an actor
or a drama, for this perishable enjoyment has
only so much as may survive out of such recol-
lections to witness for itself to another generation;
and an unusually high place may be challenged
for the subtlety and delicacy of what is said in
these letters of things theatrical, when the writer

PARIS:
1855-6.

Actors and
dramas.

Paris:
1855-6.
Ante, 93.
was especially attracted by a performer or a play.
Frédéric Lemaitre has never had a higher tribute than Dickens paid to him during his few
days' earlier stay at Paris in the spring.

"Incomparably the finest acting I ever saw, I
"saw last night at the Ambigu. They have revived
"that old piece, once immensely popular in Lon-
"don under the name of *Thirty Years of a*
"*Gambler's Life*. Old Lemaitre plays his famous
"character, * and never did I see anything, in
"art, so exaltedly horrible and awful. In the earlier
"acts he was so well made up, and so light and
"active, that he really looked sufficiently young.
"But in the last two, when he had grown old and
Criticism of
Frédéric
Lemaitre.
"miserable, he did the finest things, I really be-
"lieve, that are within the power of acting. Two
"or three times, a great cry of horror went all
"round the house. When he met, in the inn
"yard, the traveller whom he murders, and first
"saw his money, the manner in which the crime
"came into his head—and eyes—was as truthful
"as it was terrific. This traveller, being a good
"fellow, gives him wine. You should see the
"dim remembrance of his better days that comes
"over him as he takes the glass, and in a strange
"dazed way makes as if he were going to touch
"the other man's, or do some airy thing with it;
"and then stops and flings the contents down his
"hot throat, as if he were pouring it into a lime-
"kiln. But this was nothing to what follows after

---

* Twenty-one years before this date, in this same part, Lemaitre
had made a deep impression in London; and now, eighteen years later,
he is appearing in one of the revivals of Victor Hugo in Paris. (1873.)

"he has done the murder, and comes home, with
"a basket of provisions, a ragged pocket full of
"money, and a badly-washed bloody right hand
"—which his little girl finds out. After the child
"asked him if he had hurt his hand, his going
"aside, turning himself round, and looking over
"all his clothes for spots, was so inexpressibly
"dreadful that it really scared one. He called
"for wine, and the sickness that came upon him
"when he saw the colour, was one of the things
"that brought out the curious cry I have spoken
"of, from the audience. Then he fell into a sort
"of bloody mist, and went on to the end groping
"about, with no mind for anything, except mak-
"ing his fortune by staking this money, and a
"faint dull kind of love for the child. It is quite
"impossible to satisfy one's-self by saying enough
"of such a magnificent performance. I have
"never seen him come near its finest points, in
"anything else. He said two things in a way
"that alone would put him far apart from all
"other actors. One to his wife, when he has ex-
"ultingly shewn her the money and she has
"asked him how he got it—'I found it'—and the
"other to his old companion and tempter, when
"he charged him with having killed that traveller,
"and he suddenly went headlong mad and took
"him by the throat and howled out, 'It wasn't
"'I who murdered him—it was Misery!' And
"such a dress; such a face; and, above all,
"such an extraordinary guilty wicked thing as
"he made of a knotted branch of a tree which
"was his walking-stick, from the moment when

Paris: 1855-6.

Last scene in the Dumbler's Life described.

Paris:
1855-6.

"the idea of the murder came into his head!
"I could write pages about him. It is an im-
"pression quite ineffaceable. He got half-boast-
"ful of that walking-staff to himself, and half-
"afraid of it; and didn't know whether to be
"grimly pleased that it had the jagged end, or to
"hate it and be horrified at it. He sat at a little
"table in the inn-yard, drinking with the traveller;
"and this horrible stick got between them like
"the Devil, while he counted on his fingers the
"uses he could put the money to."

That was at the close of February. In October, Dickens's longer residence began. He be-
took himself with his family, after two unsuccessful attempts in the new region of the Rue Balzac
and Rue Lord Byron, to an apartment in the
Avenue des Champs Elysées. Over him was an
English bachelor with an establishment consisting of an English groom and five English horses.

Bachelor
"Six."

"The concierge and his wife told us that his
"name was *Six*, which drove me nearly mad un-
"til we discovered it to be *Sykes*." The situation
was a good one, very cheerful for himself and
with amusement for his children. It was a quarter
of a mile above Franconi's on the other side of
the way, and within a door or two of the Jardin
d'Hiver. The Exposition was just below; the Barrière de l'Etoile from a quarter to half a mile below; and all Paris, including Emperor and Empress coming from and returning to St. Cloud,
thronged past the windows in open carriages or

Increase of
celebrity.

on horseback, all day long. Now it was he found
himself more of a celebrity than when he had

ton of the *Moniteur* was filled daily with a translation of *Chuzzlewit;* and he had soon to consider
the proposal I have named, to publish in French
his collected novels and tales.* Before he had
been a week in his new abode, Ary Scheffer, "a
frank and noble fellow," had made his acquaint-

Margin notes: Paris: 1855-6. Ary Scheffer.

* "It is surprising what a change nine years have made in my no-
"toriety here. So many of the rising French generation now read Eng-
"lish (and *Chuzzlewit* is now being translated daily in the *Moniteur*),
"that I can't go into a shop and give my card without being acknow-
"ledged in the pleasantest way possible. A curiosity-dealer brought
"home some little knick-knacks I had bought, the other night, and knew
"all about my books from beginning to end of 'em. There is much of
"the personal friendliness in my readers, here, that is so delightful at
"home; and I have been greatly surprised and pleased by the unex-
"pected discovery." To this I may add a line from one of his letters six
years later. "I see my books in French at every railway station great
"and small."--13th of Oct. 1862.

Margin note: Personal attentions.

* "I forget whether" (6th of Jan. 1856) "I have already told you
"that I have received a proposal from a responsible bookselling house
"here, for a complete edition, authorized by myself, of a French trans-
"lation of all my books. The terms involve questions of space and
"amount of matter; but I should say, at a rough calculation, that I shall
"get about £300 by it—perhaps £50 more." "I have arranged" (30th
of Jan.) "with the French bookselling house to receive, by monthly
"payments of £40, the sum of £440 for the right to translate all my
"books: that is, what they call my Romances, and what I call my
"Stories. This does not include the Christmas Books, *American Notes*,
"*Pictures from Italy*, or the *Sketches;* but they are to have the right
"to translate them for extra payments if they choose. In consideration
"of this venture as to the unprotected property, I cede them the right
"of translating all future Romances at a thousand francs (£40) each.
"Considering that I get so much for what is otherwise worth nothing,
"and get my books before so clever and important a people, I think
"this is not a bad move!" The first friend with whom he advised about
it, I should mention, was the famous Leipzig publisher, M. Tauchnitz,
in whose judgment, as well as in his honour and good faith, he had im-
plicit reliance, and who thought the offer fair. On the 17th of April he
wrote: "On Monday I am going to dine with all my translators at Ha-
"chette's, the bookseller who has made the bargain for the complete
"edition, and who began this week to pay his monthly £40 for a year.
"I don't mean to go out any more. Please to imagine me in the midst
"of my French dressers." He wrote an address for the Edition in which
he praised the liberality of his publishers and expressed his pride in
being so presented to the French people whom he sincerely loved and
honoured. Another word may be added. "It is rather appropriate that
"the French translation edition will pay my rent for the whole year,
"and travelling charges to boot."—24th of Feb. 1856.

Margin notes: French translation of Dickens. M. von Tauchnitz.

Paris:
1855-6.

Daniel
Manin.

English
friends.
IV. 202-3.

ance; introduced him to several distinguished Frenchmen; and expressed the wish to paint him. To Scheffer was also due an advantage obtained for my friend's two little daughters of which they may always keep the memory with pride. "Mamey "and Katey are learning Italian, and their master "is Manin of Venetian fame, the best and the noblest "of those unhappy gentlemen. He came here "with a wife and a beloved daughter, and they "are both dead. Scheffer made him known to "me, and has been, I understand, wonderfully "generous and good to him." Nor may I omit to state the enjoyment afforded him, not only by the presence in Paris during the winter of Mr. Wilkie Collins and of Mr. and Mrs. White of Bonchurch, but by the many friends from England whom the Art Exposition brought over. Sir Alexander Cockburn was one of these; Edwin Landseer, Charles Robert Leslie, and William Boxall, were others. Macready left his retreat at Sherborne to make him a visit of several days. Thackeray went to and fro all the time between London and his mother's house, also in the Champs Elysées, where his daughters were. And Paris for the time was the home of Robert Lytton, who belonged to the Embassy, of the Sartorises, of the Brownings, and of others whom Dickens liked and cared for.

At the first play he went to, the performance was stopped while the news of the last Crimean engagement, just issued in a supplement to the *Moniteur*, was read from the stage. "It made not "the faintest effect upon the audience; and even

"the hired claqueurs, who had been absurdly loud
"during the piece, seemed to consider the war
"not at all within their contract, and were as stag-
"nant as ditch-water. The theatre was full. It is
"quite impossible to see such apathy, and sup-
"pose the war to be popular, whatever may be
"asserted to the contrary." The day before, he
had met the Emperor and the King of Sardinia
in the streets, "and, as usual, no man touching
"his hat, and very very few so much as looking
"round."

The success of a most agreeable little piece
by our old friend Regnier took him next to the
Français, where Plessy's acting enchanted him.
"Of course the interest of it turns upon a flawed
"piece of living china (*that* seems to be positively
"essential), but, as in most of these cases, if you
"will accept the position in which you find the
"people, you have nothing more to bother your
"morality about." The theatre in the Rue Riche-
lieu, however, was not generally his favourite resort. He used to talk of it whimsically as a
kind of tomb, where you went, as the Eastern
people did in the stories, to think of your unsuccessful loves and dead relations. "There is a
"dreary classicality at that establishment cal-
"culated to freeze the marrow. Between our-
"selves, even one's best friends there are at times
"very aggravating. One tires of seeing a man,
"through any number of acts, remembering every-
"thing by patting his forehead with the flat of
"his hand, jerking out sentences by shaking him-
"self, and piling them up in pyramids over his

"head with his right forefinger. And they have a
"generic small comedy-piece, where you see two
"sofas and three little tables, to which a man
"enters with his hat on, to talk to another man—
"and in respect of which you know exactly when
"he will get up from one sofa to sit on the other,
"and take his hat off one table to put it upon the
"other—which strikes one quite as ludicrously as
"a good farce.*   ... There seems to be a good
"piece at the Vaudeville, on the idea of the
"*Town and Country Mouse.* It is too respectable
"and inoffensive for me to-night, but I hope to
"see it before I leave...I have a horrible idea of
"making friends with Franconi, and sauntering
"when I am at work into their sawdust green-
"room."

At a theatre of a yet heavier school than the
Français he had a drearier experience. "On
"Wednesday we went to the Odéon to see a new

"piece, in four acts and in verse, called *Michel
"Cervantes.* I suppose such an infernal dose of
"ditch-water never was concocted. But there
"were certain passages, describing the suppression
"of public opinion in Madrid, which were received
"with a shout of savage application to France
"that made one stare again! And once more,
"here again, at every pause, steady, compact,
"regular as military drums, the Ça Ira!" On an-

---

* He wrote a short and very comical account of one of these stock
performances at the Français, in which he brought out into strong relief
all their conventionalities and formal habits, their regular surprises surprising nobody, and their mysterious disclosures of immense secrets
known to everybody beforehand, which he meant for *Household Words;*
but it occurred to him that it might give pain to Regnier, and he destroyed it.

other night, even at the Porte St. Martin, drawn
there doubtless by the attraction of repulsion, he
supped full with the horrors of classicality at a
performance of *Orestes* versified by Alexandre
Dumas. "Nothing have I ever seen so weighty
"and so ridiculous. If I had not already learnt
"to tremble at the sight of classic drapery on the
"human form, I should have plumbed the utmost
"depths of terrified boredom in this achievement.
"The chorus is not preserved otherwise than that
"bits of it are taken out for characters to speak.
"It is really so bad as to be almost good. Some
"of the Frenchified classical anguish struck me
"as so unspeakably ridiculous that it puts me on
"the broad grin as I write."

At the same theatre, in the early spring, he
had a somewhat livelier entertainment. "I was at
"the Porte St. Martin last night, where there is a
"rather good melodrama called *Sang Melt*, in
"which one of the characters is an English Lord
"—Lord William Falkland—who is called through-
"out the piece Milor Williams Fack Lorn, and is
"a hundred times described by others and de-
"scribed by himself as Williams. He is admirably
"played; but two English travelling ladies are be-
"yond expression ridiculous, and there is some-
"thing positively vicious in their utter want of
"truth. One 'set,' where the action of a whole
"act is supposed to take place in the great
"wooden verandah of a Swiss hotel overhanging
"a mountain ravine, is the best piece of stage
"carpentering I have seen in France. Next week
"we are to have at the Ambigu *Paradise Lost*,

"with the murder of Abel, and the Deluge. The
"wildest rumours are afloat as to the un-dressing
"of our first parents." Anticipation far outdoes
a reality of this kind; and at the fever-pitch to
which rumours raised it here, Dickens might
vainly have attempted to get admission on the first
night, if Mr. Webster, the English manager and
comedian, had not obtained a ticket for him. He
went with Mr. Wilkie Collins. "We were rung
"in (out of the café below the Ambigu) at 8, and
"the play was over at half-past 1: the waits be-
"tween the acts being very much longer than the
"acts themselves. The house was crammed to ex-
"cess in every part, and the galleries awful with
"Blouses, who again, during the whole of the
"waits, beat with the regularity of military drums
"the revolutionary tune of famous memory—Ça
"Ira! The play is a compound of *Paradise Lost*
"and Byron's *Cain;* and some of the controver-
"sies between the archangel and the devil, when
"the celestial power argues with the infernal in
"conversational French, as 'Eh bien! Satan, crois-
"'tu donc que notre Seigneur t'aurait exposé aux
"'tourments que tu endures à présent, sans avoir
"'prévu,' &c. &c. are very ridiculous. All the
"supernatural personages are alarmingly natural
"(as theatre nature goes), and walk about in the
"stupidest way. Which has occasioned Collins
"and myself to institute a perquisition whether
"the French ever have shown any kind of idea
"of the supernatural; and to decide this rather in
"the negative. The people are very well dressed,
"and Eve very modestly. All Paris and the pro-

"vinces had been ransacked for a woman who Paris: 1855-6.
"had brown hair that would fall to the calves of
"her legs—and she was found at last at the
"Odéon. There was nothing attractive until the
"4th act, when there was a pretty good scene of the
"children of Cain dancing in, and desecrating, a
"temple, while Ábel and his family were ham-
"mering hard at the Ark, outside, in all the
"pauses of the revel. The Deluge in the fifth act Profane nonsense.
"was up to about the mark of a drowning scene
"at the Adelphi; but it had one new feature.
"When the rain ceased, and the ark drove in on
"the great expanse of water, then lying waveless
"as the mists cleared and the sun broke out,
"numbers of bodies drifted up and down. These
"were all real men and boys, each separate, on a
"new kind of horizontal sloat. They looked hor-
"rible and real. Altogether, a merely dull busi-
"ness; but I dare say it will go for a long
"while."

A piece of honest farce is a relief from these
profane absurdities. "An uncommonly droll
"piece with an original comic idea in it has been
"in course of representation here. It is called
"*Les Cheveux de ma Femme.* A man who is dot-
"ingly fond of his wife, and who wishes to know
"whether she loved anybody else before they
"were married, cuts off a lock of her hair by
"stealth, and takes it to a great mesmeriser, who Good farce.
"submits it to a clairvoyante who never was
"wrong. It is discovered that the owner of this
"hair has been up to the most frightful dissipa-
"tions, insomuch that the clairvoyante can't men-

The Life of Charles Dickens. I'.   9

"tion half of them. The distracted husband goes "home to reproach his wife, and she then reveals "that she wears a wig, and takes it off."

The last piece he went to see before leaving Paris was a French version of *As You Like It;* but he found two acts of it to be more than enough. "In *Comme il vous Plaira* nobody had "anything to do but to sit down as often as "possible on as many stones and trunks of trees "as possible. When I had seen Jacques seat him- "self on 17 roots of trees, and 25 grey stones, "which was at the end of the second act, I came "away." Only one more sketch taken in a theatre, and perhaps the best, I will give from these letters. It simply tells us what is necessary to understand a particular "tag" to a play, but it is related so prettily that the thing it celebrates could not have a nicer effect than is produced by this account of it. The play in question, *Mémoires du Diable,* and another piece of enchanting interest, the *Médecin des Enfants,** were his favourites among all he saw at this time. "As I have no news, I

* Before he saw this he wrote: "That piece you spoke of (the " *Médecin des Enfants*) is one of the very best melodramas I have ever "read. Situations, admirable. I will send it to you by Landseer. I am "very curious indeed to go and see it; and it is an instance to me of the "powerful emotions from which art is shut out in England by the con- "ventionalities." After seeing it he writes: "The low cry of excitement "and expectation that goes round the house when any one of the "great situations is felt to be coming, is very remarkable indeed. I "suppose there has not been so great a success of the genuine and "worthy kind (for the authors have really taken the French dramatic "bull by the horns, and put the adulterous wife in the right position), "for many years. When you come over and see it, you will say you never "saw anything so admirably done. There is one actor, Bignon (M. De- "lormel), who has a good deal of Macready in him; sometimes looks "very like him; and who seems to me the perfection of manly good "sense." 17th of April 1856.

"may as well tell you about the tag that I thought
"so pretty to the *Mémoires du Diable;* in which
"piece by the way, there is a most admirable
"part, most admirably played, in which a man
"says merely 'Yes' or 'No' all through the piece,
"until the last scene. A certain M. Robin has
"got hold of the papers of a deceased lawyer,
"concerning a certain estate which has been
"swindled away from its rightful owner, a Baron's
"widow, into other hands. They disclose so much
"roguery that he binds them up into a volume
"lettered 'Mémoires du Diable.' The knowledge Story of a
"he derives from these papers not only enables French drama.
"him to unmask the hypocrites all through the
"piece (in an excellent manner), but induces him
"to propose to the Baroness that if he restores to
"her her estate and good name—for even her
"marriage to the deceased Baron is denied—she
"shall give him her daughter in marriage. The
"daughter herself, on hearing the offer, accepts
"it; and a part of the plot is, her going to a
"masked ball, to which he goes as the Devil, to
"see how she likes him (when she finds, of course,
"that she likes him very much). The country
"people about the Château in dispute, suppose
"him to be really the Devil, because of his strange
"knowledge, and his strange comings and goings;
"and he, being with this girl in one of its old
"rooms, in the beginning of the 3rd act, shews
"her a little coffer on the table with a bell in it. *Mémoires*
"'They suppose,' he tells her, 'that whenever this *du Diable.*
"'bell is rung, I appear and obey the summons.
"'Very ignorant, isn't it? But, if you ever want

9*

"'me particularly—very particularly—ring the
"'little bell and try.' The plot proceeds to its
"development. The wrong-doers are exposed;
"the missing document, proving the marriage, is
"found; everything is finished; they are all on
"the stage; and M. Robin hands the paper to the
"Baroness. 'You are reinstated in your rights,
"'Madame; you are happy; I will not hold you
"'to a compact made when you didn't know me;
"'I release you and your fair daughter; the pleasure
"'of doing what I have done, is my sufficient
"'reward; I kiss your hand and take my leave.
"'Farewell!' He backs himself courteously out;
"the piece seems concluded, everybody wonders,
"the girl (little Mdlle. Luther) stands amazed;
"when she suddenly remembers the little bell. In
"the prettiest way possible, she runs to the coffer
"on the table, takes out the little bell, rings it,
"and he comes rushing back and folds her to his
"heart. I never saw a prettier thing in my life.
"It made me laugh in that most delightful of
"ways, with the tears in my eyes; so that I
"can never forget it, and must go and see it
"again."

Delightful
close to a
play.

But great as was the pleasure thus derived
from the theatre, he was, in the matter of social
intercourse, even more indebted to distinguished
men connected with it by authorship or acting.
At Scribe's he was entertained frequently; and
"very handsome and pleasant" was his account
of the dinners, as of all the belongings, of the
prolific dramatist—a charming place in Paris, a
fine estate in the country, capital carriage, hand-

At M.
Scribe's.

some pair of horses, "all made, as he says, by his
pen." One of the guests the first evening was
Auber, "a stolid little elderly man, rather petulant
"in manner," who told Dickens he had once lived
"at Stock Noonton" (Stoke Newington) to study
English, but had forgotten it all. "Louis Philippe
"had invited him to meet the Queen of England,
"and when L. P. presented him, the Queen said
"'We are such old acquaintances through M.
"'Auber's works, that an introduction is quite
"'unnecessary.'" They met again a few nights
later, with the author of the *History of the Giron-
dins*, at the hospitable table of M. Pichot, to whom
Lamartine had expressed a strong desire again to
meet Dickens as "un des grands amis de son
"imagination." "He continues to be precisely
"as we formerly knew him, both in appearance
"and manner; highly prepossessing, and with a
"sort of calm passion about him, very taking
"indeed. We talked of De Foe* and Richardson,

Margin notes:
Paris: 1855-6.
Auber and Queen Victoria.
Lamartine.
IV. 50.

---

* I subjoin from another of these French letters of later date a remark on *Robinson Crusoe*. "You remember my saying to you some time
"ago how curious I thought it that *Robinson Crusoe* should be the only
"instance of an universally popular book that could make no one laugh
"and could make no one cry. I have been reading it again just now, in
"the course of my numerous refreshings at those English wells, and I
"will venture to say that there is not in literature a more surprising in-
"stance of an utter want of tenderness and sentiment, than the death
"of Friday. It is as heartless as *Gil Blas*, in a very different and far
"more serious way. But the second part altogether will not bear en-
"quiry. In the second part of *Don Quixote* are some of the finest things.
"But the second part of *Robinson Crusoe* is perfectly contemptible, in
"the glaring defect that it exhibits the man who was 30 years on that
"desert island with no visible effect made on his character by that ex-
"perience. De Foe's women too—Robinson Crusoe's wife for instance
"—are terrible dull commonplace fellows without breeches; and I have
"no doubt he was a precious dry and disagreeable article himself—I
"mean De Foe: not Robinson. Poor dear Goldsmith (I remember as I
"write) derived the same impression."

Margin notes:
Robinson Crusoe.

Paris:
1855-6.
"and of that wonderful genius for the minutest
"details in a narrative, which has given them so
"much fame in France. I found him frank and
"unaffected, and full of curious knowledge of the
"French common people. He informed the com-
"pany at dinner that he had rarely met a foreigner
"who spoke French so easily as your inimitable cor-
A compliment
and its result. "respondent, whereat your correspondent blushed
"modestly, and almost immediately afterwards
"so nearly choked himself with the bone of a
"fowl (which is still in his throat), that he sat in
"torture for ten minutes with a strong apprehen-
"sion that he was going to make the good Pichot
"famous by dying like the little Hunchback at
"his table. Scribe and his wife were of the party,
Scribe's
author-
anxieties. "but had to go away at the ice-time because it
"was the first representation at the Opéra Comique
"of a new opera by Auber and himself, of which
"very great expectations have been formed.   It
"was very curious to see him—the author of 400
"pieces—getting nervous as the time approached,
"and pulling out his watch every minute. At last
"he dashed out as if he were going into what a
"friend of mine calls a plunge-bath.   Whereat
"she rose and followed. She is the most extra-
"ordinary woman I ever beheld; for her eldest
"son must be thirty, and she has the figure of
"five-and-twenty, and is strikingly handsome. So
Madame
Scribe. "graceful too, that her manner of rising, curt-
"seying, laughing, and going out after him, was
"pleasanter than the pleasantest thing I have ever
"seen done on the stage."   The opera Dickens
himself saw a week later, and wrote of it as "most

"charming. Delightful music, an excellent story,
"immense stage tact, capital scenic arrangements,
"and the most delightful little prima donna ever
"seen or heard, in the person of Marie Cabel. It
"is called *Manon Lescaut*—from the old romance
"—and is charming throughout. She sings a
"laughing song in it which is received with mad-
"ness, and which is the only real laughing song
"that ever was written. Auber told me that when
"it was first rehearsed, it made a great effect upon
"the orchestra; and that he could not have had
"a better compliment upon its freshness than the
"musical director paid him, in coming and clap-
"ping him on the shoulder with 'Bravo, jeune
"'homme! Cela promet bien!'"

At dinner at Regnier's he met M. Legouvet,
in whose tragedy Rachel, after its acceptance,
had refused to act Medea; a caprice which had
led not only to her condemnation in costs of so
much a night until she did act it, but to a quasi
rivalry against her by Ristori, who was now on
her way to Paris to play it in Italian. To this
performance Dickens and Macready subsequently
went together, and pronounced it to be hopelessly
bad. "In the day entertainments, and little
"melodrama theatres, of Italy, I have seen the
"same thing fifty times, only not at once so
"conventional and so exaggerated. The papers
"have all been in fits respecting the sublimity
"of the performance, and the genuineness of the
"applause—particularly of the bouquets; which
"were thrown on at the most preposterous times

Paris:
1855-6.
"in the midst of agonizing scenes, so that the
"characters had to pick their way among them,
"and a certain stout gentleman who played King
"Creon was obliged to keep a wary eye, all night,
"on the proscenium boxes, and dodge them as
"they came down. Now Scribe, who dined here
"next day (and who follows on the Ristori side,
"being offended, as everybody has been, by the
"insolence of Rachel), could not resist the temp-
"tation of telling us, that, going round at the
Serviceablo
bouquets.
"end of the first act to offer his congratulations,
"he met all the bouquets coming back in men's
"arms to be thrown on again in the second act.
". . . By the bye, I see a fine actor lost in
"Scribe. In all his pieces he has everything done
"in his own way; and on that same night he was
An actor lost
in Scribe.
"showing what Rachel did not do, and wouldn't
"do, in the last scene of Adrienne Lecouvreur,
"with extraordinary force and intensity."

At the house of another great artist, Madame
Viardot,* the sister of Malibran, Dickens dined

* When in Paris six years later Dickens saw this fine singer in an
opera by Gluck, and the reader will not be sorry to have his description
of it. "Last night I saw Madame Viardot do Gluck's Orphée. It is a
"most extraordinary performance—pathetic in the highest degree, and
"full of quite sublime acting. Though it is unapproachably fine from
"first to last, the beginning of it, at the tomb of Eurydice, is a thing
"that I cannot remember at this moment of writing, without emotion.
"It is the finest presentation of grief that I can imagine. And when she
"has received hope from the Gods, and encouragement to go into the
"other world and seek Eurydice, Viardot's manner of taking the relin-
"quished lyre from the tomb and becoming radiant again, is most noble.
"Also she recognizes Eurydice's touch, when at length the hand is put
Viardot in
Orphée.
"in hers from behind, like a most transcendant genius. And when,
"yielding to Eurydice's entreaties she has turned round and slain her
"with a look, her despair over the body is grand in the extreme. It is
"worth a journey to Paris to see, for there is no such Art to be other-
"wise looked upon. Her husband stumbled over me by mere chance,
"and took me to her dressing-room. Nothing could have happened

to meet Georges Sand, that lady having appointed
the day and hour for the interesting festival,
which came off duly on the 10th of January. "I
"suppose it to be impossible to imagine anybody
"more unlike my preconceptions than the illus-
"trious Sand. Just the kind of woman in appear-
"ance whom you might suppose to be the Queen's
"monthly nurse. Chubby, matronly, swarthy,
"black-eyed. Nothing of the blue-stocking about
"her, except a little final way of settling all your
"opinions with hers, which I take to have been
"acquired in the country where she lives, and in
"the domination of a small circle. A singularly
"ordinary woman in appearance and manner.
"The dinner was very good and remarkably un-
"pretending. Ourselves, Madame and her son,
"the Scheffers, the Sartorises, and some Lady
"somebody (from the Crimea last) who wore a
"species of paletot, and smoked. The Viardots
"have a house away in the new part of Paris, which
"looks exactly as if they had moved into it last
"week and were going away next. Notwithstand-
"ing which, they have lived in it eight years. The
"opera the very last thing on earth you would
"associate with the family. Piano not even
"opened. Her husband is an extremely good
"fellow, and she is as natural as it is possible to
"be."

Dickens was hardly the man to take fair measure of Madame Dudevant in meeting her thus.
He was not familiar with her writings, and had

,PARIS:
1855-6.
Meets
Georges
Sand.

Madame
Dudevant at
the Viardots.

"better as a genuine homage to the performance, for I was disfigured
"with crying."—30th of November 1862.

Paris:
1855-6.

Banquet at
Girardin's.

Dining-room.

Kitchen.

Truffles.

no very special liking for such of them as he
knew. But no disappointment, nothing but amazement, awaited him at a dinner that followed soon
after. Emile de Girardin gave a banquet in his
honour. His description of it, which he declares
to be strictly prosaic, sounds a little Oriental, but
not inappropriately so. "No man unacquainted
"with my determination never to embellish or
"fancify such accounts, could believe in the de-
"scription I shall let off when we meet of dining
"at Emile Girardin's—of the three gorgeous
"drawing rooms with ten thousand wax candles
"in golden sconces, terminating in a dining-room
"of urprecedented magnificence with two enor-
"mous transparent plate-glass doors in it, looking
"(across an ante-chamber full of clean plates)
"straight into the kitchen, with the cooks in their
"white paper caps dishing the dinner. From his
"seat in the midst of the table, the host (like a
"Giant in a Fairy story) beholds the kitchen, and
"the snow-white tables, and the profound order
"and silence there prevailing. Forth from the
"plate-glass doors issues the Banquet—the most
"wonderful feast ever tasted by mortal: at the pre-
"sent price of Truffles, that article alone costing
"(for eight people) at least five pounds. On the
"table are ground glass jugs of peculiar construc-
"tion, laden with the finest growth of Champagne
"and the coolest ice. With the third course is
"issued Port Wine (previously unheard of in a
"good state on this continent), which would fetch
"two guineas a bottle at any sale. The dinner
"done, Oriental flowers in vases of golden cob-

"web are placed upon the board. With the ice Paris: 1855-6. Dessert.
"is issued Brandy, buried for 100 years. To that
"succeeds Coffee, brought by the brother of one
"of the convives from the remotest East, in ex-
"change for an equal quantity of Californian gold
"dust. The company being returned to the
"drawing-room—tables roll in by unseen agency,
"laden with Cigarettes from the Hareem of the Cigarettes.
"Sultan, and with cool drinks in which the
"flavour of the Lemon arrived yesterday from
"Algeria, struggles voluptuously with the delicate
"Orange arrived this morning from Lisbon. That
"period past, and the guests reposing on Divans
"worked with many-coloured blossoms, big table
"rolls in, heavy with massive furniture of silver,
"and breathing incense in the form of a little
"present of Tea direct from China—table and
"all, I believe; but cannot swear to it, and am
"resolved to be prosaic. All this time the host What the host thought of the dinner.
"perpetually repeats 'Ce petit diner-ci n'est que
"'pour faire la connaissance de Monsieur Dickens;
"'il ne compte pas; ce n'est rien.' And even
"now I have forgotten to set down half of it—
"in particular the item of a far larger plum pud-
"ding than ever was seen in England at Christ-
"mas time, served with a celestial sauce in colour
"like the orange blossom, and in substance like
"the blossom powdered and bathed in dew, and
"called in the carte (carte in a gold frame like a
"little fish-slice to be handed about) 'Hommage National and personal compliment.
"'à l'illustre écrivain d'Angleterre.' That illus-
"trious man staggered out at the last drawing-
"room door, speechless with wonder, finally; and

Paris 1855-6.

"even at that moment his host, holding to his "lips a chalice set with precious stones and con-"taining nectar distilled from the air that blew "over the fields of beans in bloom for fifteen "summers, remarked 'Le dîner que nous avons "'eu, mon cher, n'est rien—il ne compte pas—il "'a été tout-à-fait en famille—il faut dîner (en

Au revoir.

"'vérité, dîner) bientôt. Au plaisir! Au revoir! "'Au dîner!'"

The second dinner came, wonderful as the first; among the company were Regnier, Jules Sandeau, and the new Director of the Français; and his host again played Lucullus in the same

Second banquet.

style, with success even more consummate. The only absolutely new incident however was that "After dinner he asked me if I would come into "another room and smoke a cigar? and on my "saying Yes, coolly opened a drawer, containing "about 5000 inestimable cigars in prodigious "bundles—just as the Captain of the Robbers in "*Ali Baba* might have gone to a corner of the "cave for bales of brocade. A little man dined "who was blacking shoes 8 years ago, and is now

One of the guests.

"enormously rich—the richest man in Paris—"having ascended with rapidity up the usual lad-"der of the Bourse. By merely observing that "perhaps he might come down again, I clouded "so many faces as to render it very clear to me "that *everybody present* was at the same game for "some stake or other!" He returned to that sub-ject in a letter a few days later. "If you were to

The Bourse and its victims.

"see the steps of the Bourse at about 4 in the "afternoon, and the crowd of blouses and patches

"among the speculators there assembled, all howl-
"ing and haggard with speculation, you would
"stand aghast at the consideration of what must
"be going on. Concierges and people like that
"perpetually blow their brains out, or fly into the
"Seine, 'à cause des pertes sur la Bourse.' I
"hardly ever take up a French paper without
"lighting on such a paragraph. On the other
"hand, thoroughbred horses without end, and
"red velvet carriages with white kid harness on
"jet black horses, go by here all day long; and
"the pedestrians who turn to look at them, laugh,
"and say 'C'est la Bourse!' Such crashes must
"be staved off every week as have not been seen
"since Law's time."

Another picture connects itself with this, and
throws light on the speculation thus raging. The
French loans connected with the war, so much
puffed and praised in England at the time for the
supposed spirit in which they were taken up, had
in fact only ministered to the commonest and
lowest gambling; and the war had never in the
least been popular. "Emile Girardin," wrote
Dickens on the 23rd of March, "was here yester-
"day, and he says that Peace is to be formally
"announced at Paris to-morrow amid general
"apathy." But the French are never wholly
apathetic to their own exploits; and a display
with a touch of excitement in it had been witnessed a couple of months before on the entry
of the troops from the Crimea,* when the Zouaves,

* Here is another picture of Regiments in the Streets of which the
date is the 30th of January. "It was cold this afternoon, as bright as

as they marched past, pleased Dickens most. "A
"remarkable body of men," he wrote, "wild,
"dangerous, and picturesque. Close-cropped head,
"red skull cap, Greek jacket, full red petticoat
"trowsers trimmed with yellow, and high white
"gaiters—the most sensible things for the purpose
"I know, and coming into use in the line. A man
"with such things on his legs is always free there,
"and ready for a muddy march; and might flounder
"through roads two feet deep in mud, and, simply
"by changing his gaiters (he has another pair in
"his haversack), be clean and comfortable and
"wholesome again, directly. Plenty of beard and
"moustache, and the musket carried reverse-wise
"with the stock over the shoulder, make up the

"sunburnt Zouave. He strides like Bobadil, smok-
"ing as he goes; and when he laughs (they were
"under my window for half-an-hour or so), plunges
"backward in the wildest way, as if he were going
"to throw a sommersault.   They have a black
"dog belonging to the regiment, and, when they
"now marched along with their medals, this dog
"marched after the one non-commissioned officer

" Italy, and these Elysian Fields crowded with carriages, riders, and
" foot passengers. All the fountains were playing, all the Heavens shin-
" ing. Just as I went out at 4 o'clock, several regiments that had passed
" out at the Barrière in the morning to exercise in the country, came
" marching back, in the straggling French manner, which is far more
" picturesque and real than anything you can imagine in that way. Al-
" ternately great storms of drums played, and then the most delicious
" and skilful hands, 'Trovatore' music, 'Barber of Seville' music, all
" sorts of music with well-marked melody and time. All bloused Paris
" (led by the Inimitable, and a poor cripple who works himself up and
" down all day in a big-wheeled car) went at quick march down the
" avenue, in a sort of hilarious dance. If the colours with the golden
" eagle on the top had only been unfurled, we should have followed them
" anywhere, in any cause—much as the children follow Punches in the
" better cause of Comedy. Napoleon on the top of the Column seemed
" up to the whole thing, I thought."

"he invariably follows with a profound conviction PARIS:
"that he was decorated. I couldn't see whether 1855-6.
"he had a medal, his hair being long; but he was Dog of the regiment.
"perfectly up to what had befallen his regiment;
"and I never saw anything so capital as his way
"of regarding the public. Whatever the regiment
"does, he is always in his place; and it was im-
"possible to mistake the air of modest triumph
"which was now upon him. A small dog, cor-
"poreally, but of a great mind." * On that night
there was an illumination in honour of the army,
when the "whole of Paris, bye streets and lanes
"and all sorts of out of the way places, was most
"brilliantly illuminated. It looked in the dark Paris illu-
"like Venice and Genoa rolled into one, and split minated.
"up through the middle by the Corso at Rome
"in the carnival time. The French people cer-
"tainly do know how to honour their own
"countrymen, in a most marvellous way." It was
the festival time of the New Year, and Dickens
was fairly lost in a mystery of amazement at
where the money could come from that everybody
was spending on the étrennes they were giving to
everybody else. All the famous shops on the
Boulevards had been blockaded for more than a
week. "There is now a line of wooden stalls, Streets on
"three miles long, on each side of that immense New Year's Day.
"thoroughfare; and wherever a retiring house or
"two admits of a double line, there it is. All
"sorts of objects from shoes and sabots, through

* Apropos of this, I may mention that the little shaggy white ter-
rier who came with him from America, so long a favourite in his household, had died of old age a few weeks before (5th of Oct. 1855) in
Boulogne. Timber's death. III. 21.

"porcelain and crystal, up to live fowls and
"rabbits which are played for at a sort of dwarf
"skittles (to their immense disturbance, as the ball
"rolls under them and shakes them off their shelves
"and perches whenever it is delivered by a vigorous
"hand), are on sale in this great Fair. And what
"you may get in the way of ornament for twopence,
"is astounding." Unhappily there came dark and
rainy weather, and one of the improvements of
the Empire ended, as so many others did, in
slush and misery.*

Some sketches connected with the Art Exposition in the winter of 1855, and with the fulfilment of Ary Scheffer's design to paint the portrait
of Dickens, may close these Paris pictures. He
did not think that English art showed to advantage beside the French. It seemed to him
small, shrunken, insignificant, "niggling." He
thought the general absence of ideas horribly

* "We have wet weather here—and dark too for these latitudes—
"and oceans of mud. Although numbers of men are perpetually scoop-
"ing and sweeping it away in this thoroughfare, it accumulates under
"the windows so fast, and in such sludgy masses, that to get across the
"road is to get half over one's shoes in the first outset of a walk." . . .
"It is difficult," he added (20th of Jan.) "to picture the change made
"in this place by the removal of the paving stones (too ready for bar-
"ricades), and macadamization. It suits neither the climate nor the
"soil. We are again in a sea of mud. One cannot cross the road of the
"Champs Elysées here, without being half over one's boots" A few
more days brought a welcome change. "Three days ago the weather
"changed here in an hour, and we have had bright weather and hard
"frost ever since. All the mud disappeared with marvellous rapidity,
"and the sky became Italian. Taking advantage of such a happy
"change, I started off yesterday morning (for exercise and meditation)
"on a scheme I have taken into my head, to walk round the walls of
"Paris. It is a very odd walk, and will make a good description. Yester-
"day I turned to the right when I got outside the Barrière de l'Etoile,
"walked round the wall till I came to the river, and then entered
"Paris beyond the site of the Bastille. To-day I mean to turn to the
"left when I get outside the Barrière, and see what comes of that."

apparent; "and even when one comes to Mul-
"ready, and sees two old men talking over a
"much-too-prominent table-cloth, and reads the
"French explanation of their proceedings, 'La
"'discussion sur les principes de Docteur Whiston,'
"one is dissatisfied. Somehow or other they don't
"tell. Even Leslie's Sancho wants go, and Stanny
"is too much like a set-scene. It is of no use
"disguising the fact that what we know to be
"wanting in the men is wanting in their works—
"character, fire, purpose, and the power of using
"the vehicle and the model as mere means to an
"end. There is a horrible respectability about
"most of the best of them—a little, finite,
"systematic routine in them, strangely expressive
"to me of the state of England itself. As a mere
"fact, Frith, Ward, and Egg, come out the best
"in such pictures as are here, and attract to the
"greatest extent. The first, in the picture from
"the Good-natured Man; the second, in the Royal
"Family in the Temple; the third, in the Peter
"the Great first seeing Catherine—which I always
"thought a good picture, and in which foreigners
"evidently descry a sudden dramatic touch that
"pleases them. There are no end of bad pictures
"among the French, but, Lord! the goodness
"also!—the fearlessness of them; the bold draw-
"ing; the dashing conception; the passion and
"action in them!* The Belgian department is

PARIS:
1855-6.

English and
French art.

Popular Eng-
lish pictures.

The Emperor
and Edwin
Landseer.

* This was much the tone of Edwin Landseer also, whose praise of
Horace Vernet was nothing short of rapture: and how well I remember
the humour of his description of the Emperor on the day when the prizes
were given, and, as his old friend the great painter came up, the comical
expression in his face that said plainly "What a devilish odd thing this

"full of merit. It has the best landscape in it,
"the best portrait, and the best scene of homely
"life, to be found in the building.   Don't think
"it a part of my despondency about public affairs,
"and my fear that our national glory is on the
"decline, when I say that mere form and con-
"ventionalities usurp, in English art, as in English
"government and social relations, the place of
"living force and truth.   I tried to resist the im-
"pression yesterday, and went to the English
"gallery first, and praised and admired with great
"diligence; but it was of no use.   I could not
"make anything better of it than what I tell you.
"Of course this is between ourselves.   Friendship
"is better than criticism, and I shall steadily hold
"my tongue.   Discussion is worse than useless
"when you cannot agree about what you are

"going to discuss."   French nature is all wrong,
said the English artists whom Dickens talked to;
but surely not because it is French, was his reply.
The English point of view is not the only one
to take men and women from.   The French pictures are "theatrical," was the rejoinder.   But the
French themselves are a demonstrative and
gesticulating people, was Dickens's retort; and
what thus is rendered by their artists is the truth
through an immense part of the world.   "I never
"saw anything so strange.   They seem to me to

" is altogether, isn't it?" composing itself to gravity as he took Edwin
by the hand, and said in cordial English "I am very glad to see you."
He stood, Landseer told us, in a recess so arranged as to produce a
clear echo of every word he said, and this had a startling effect. In the
evening of that day Dickens, Landseer, Boxall, Leslie "and three
"others" dined together in the Palais Royal.

"have got a fixed idea that there is no natural PARIS: 1855-6.
"manner but the English manner (in itself so
"exceptional that it is a thing apart, in all coun-
"tries); and that unless a Frenchman—represent̀ed
"as going to the guillotine for example—is as
"calm as Clapham, or as respectable as Richmond-
"hill, he cannot be right."

To the sittings at Ary Scheffer's some troubles Sitting to Ary Scheffer;
as well as many pleasures were incident, and both
had mention in his letters. "You may faintly
"imagine what I have suffered from sitting to
"Scheffer every day since I came back. He is a
"most noble fellow, and I have the greatest plea-
"sure in his society, and have made all sorts of
"acquaintances at his house; but I can scarcely
"express how uneasy and unsettled it makes me
"to have to sit, sit, sit, with *Little Dorrit* on my
"mind, and the Christmas business too—though
"that is now happily dismissed. On, Monday
"afternoon, *and all day on Wednesday*, I am going
"to sit again. And the crowning feature is, that and to Henri Scheffer.
"I do not discern the slightest resemblance, either
"in his portrait or his brother's! They both peg
"away at me at the same time." The sittings
were varied by a special entertainment, when
Scheffer received some sixty people in his "long
"atelier"—"including a lot of French who *say*
"(but I don't believe it) that they know English"
—to whom Dickens, by special entreaty, read his A Reading in Scheffer's studio.
Cricket on the Hearth.

That was at the close of November. January
came, and the end of the sittings was supposed
to be at hand. "The nightmare portrait is nearly

"done; and Scheffer promises that an interminable "sitting next Saturday, beginning at 10 o'clock in "the morning, shall finish it. It is a fine spirited "head, painted at his very best, and with a very "easy and natural appearance in it. But it does "not look to me at all like, nor does it strike me "that if I saw it in a gallery I should suppose "myself to be the original. It is always possible "that I don't know my own face. It is going to "be engraved here, in two sizes and ways—the "mere head and the whole thing." A fortnight later, the interminable sitting came. "Imagine "me if you please with No. 5 on my head and "hands, sitting to Scheffer yesterday four hours! "At this stage of a story, no one can conceive "how it distresses me." Still this was not the last. March had come before the portrait was done. "Scheffer finished yesterday; and Collins, who has "a good eye for pictures, says that there is no "man living who could do the painting about the "eyes. As a work of art I see in it spirit "combined with perfect ease, and yet I don't see "myself. So I come to the conclusion that I "never *do* see myself. I shall be very curious to "know the effect of it upon you." March had then begun; and at its close Dickens, who had meanwhile been in England, thus wrote: "I have "not seen Scheffer since I came back, but he told "Catherine a few days ago that he was not satisfied "with the likeness after all, and thought he must "do more to it. My own impression of it, you "remember?" In these few words he anticipated the impression made upon myself. I was not

Doubts of
the likeness.

More sittings.
January.

Scheffer's
own opinion.

satisfied with it. The picture had much merit,
but not as a portrait. From its very resemblance
in the eyes and mouth one derived the sense of
a general unlikeness. But the work of the artist's
brother, Henri Scheffer, painted from the same
sittings, was in all ways greatly inferior.

Before Dickens left Paris in May he had sent
over two descriptions that the reader most anxious
to follow him to a new scene would perhaps be
sorry to lose. A Duchess was murdered in the
Champs Elysées. "The murder over the way (the
"third or fourth event of that nature in the
"Champs Elysées since we have been here) seems
"to disclose the strangest state of things. The
"Duchess who is murdered lived alone in a great
"house which was always shut up, and passed
"her time entirely in the dark. In a little lodge
"outside lived a coachman (the murderer), and
"there had been a long succession of coachmen
"who had been unable to stay there, and upon
"whom, whenever they asked for their wages, she
"plunged out with an immense knife, by way of
"an immediate settlement. The coachman never
"had anything to do, for the coach hadn't been
"driven out for years; neither would she ever
"allow the horses to be taken out for exercise.
"Between the lodge and the house, is a miserable
"bit of garden, all overgrown with long rank
"grass, weeds, and nettles; and in this, the horses
"used to be taken out to swim—in a dead green
"vegetable sea, up to their haunches. On the
"day of the murder, there was a great crowd, of
"course; and in the midst of it up comes the

"Duke her husband (from whom she was separated), "and rings at the gate. The police open the "grate. 'C'est vrai donc,' says the Duke, 'que "'Madame la Duchesse n'est plus?'—'C'est trop "'vrai, Monseigneur.'—'Tant mieux,' says the "Duke, and walks off deliberately, to the great "satisfaction of the assemblage."

The second description relates an occurrence in England of only three years previous date, be-
longing to that wildly improbable class of realities which Dickens always held, with Fielding, to be (properly) closed to fiction. Only, he would add, critics should not be so eager to assume that what had never happened to themselves could not, by any human possibility, ever be supposed to have happened to anybody else. "B. was with me the "other day, and, among other things that he told "me, described an extraordinary adventure in his "life, at a place not a thousand miles from my "'property' at Gadshill, three years ago. He
"lived at the tavern and was sketching one day "when an open carriage came by with a gentle- "man and lady in it. He was sitting in the same "place working at the same sketch, next day, "when it came by again. So, another day, when "the gentleman got out and introduced himself. "Fond of art; lived at the great house yonder, "which perhaps he knew; was an Oxford man "and a Devonshire squire, but not resident on "his estate, for domestic reasons; would be glad
"to see him to dinner to-morrow. He went, and "found among other things a very fine library. "'At your disposition,' said the Squire, to whom

"he had now described himself and his pursuits.
"'Use it for your writing and drawing. Nobody
"'else uses it.' He stayed in the house *six*
"*months.* The lady was a mistress, aged five-and-
"twenty, and very beautiful, drinking her life
"away. The Squire was drunken, and utterly
"depraved and wicked; but an excellent scholar,
"an admirable linguist, and a great theologian.
"Two other mad visitors stayed the six months.
"One, a man well known in Paris here, who goes
"about the world with a crimson silk stocking in
"his breast pocket, containing a tooth-brush and
"an immense quantity of ready money. The other,
"a college chum of the Squire's, now ruined; with
"an insatiate thirst for drink; who constantly got
"up in the middle of the night, crept down to
"the dining-room and emptied all the decanters...
"B. stayed on in the place, under a sort of de-
"vilish fascination to discover what might come
"of it... Tea or coffee never seen in the house,
"and very seldom water. Beer, champagne, and
"brandy, were the three drinkables. Breakfast:
"leg of mutton, champagne, beer and brandy.
"Lunch: shoulder of mutton, champagne, beer,
"and brandy. Dinner: every conceivable dish
"(Squire's income, £7,000 a-year), champagne,
"beer, and brandy. The Squire had married a
"woman of the town from whom he was now
"separated, but by whom he had a daughter.
"The mother, to spite the father, had bred the
"daughter in every conceivable vice. , Daughter,
"then 13, came from school once a month. In-
"tensely coarse in talk, and always drunk. As

"they drove about the country in two open car-
"riages the drunken mistress would be perpetually
"tumbling out of one, and the drunken daughter
"perpetually tumbling out of the other. At last
"the drunken mistress drank her stomach away,
"and began to die on the sofa. Got worse and
"worse, and was always raving about Somebody's
"where she had once been a lodger, and perpe-
"tually shrieking that she would cut somebody
"else's heart out. At last she died on the sofa,
"and, after the funeral, the party broke up. A
"few months ago, B. met the man with the crimson
"silk stocking at Brighton, who told him that the
"Squire was dead 'of a broken heart'; that the
"chum was dead of delirium tremens; and that
"the daughter was heiress to the fortune. He told
"me all this, which I fully believe to be true,
"without any embellishment—just in the off-hand
"way in which I have told it to you."

Dickens left Paris at the end of April, and,
after the summer in Boulogne which has been
described, passed the winter in London, giving to
his theatrical enterprise nearly all the time that
Little Dorrit did not claim from him. His book
was finished in the following spring; was inscribed to Clarkson Stanfield; and now claims to
have something said about it.

CHAPTER L.

LITTLE DORRIT, AND A LAZY TOUR.

1855-1857.

BETWEEN *Hard Times* and *Little Dorrit*, Dickens's principal literary work had been the contribution to *Household Words* of two tales for Christmas (1854 and 1855) which his readings afterwards made widely popular, the Story of Richard Doubledick,* and Boots at the Holly-Tree Inn. In the latter was related, with a charming naturalness and spirit, the elopement, to get married at Gretna Green, of two little children of the mature respective ages of eight and seven. At Christmas 1855 came out the first number of *Little Dorrit*, and in April 1857 the last.

The book took its origin from the notion he had of a leading man for a story who should

LONDON:
1855-7.

Christmas tales.

---

* The framework for this sketch was a graphic description, also done by Dickens, of the celebrated Charity at Rochester founded in the sixteenth century by Richard Watts, "for six poor travellers, who, not "being Rogues or Proctors, may receive gratis for one night, lodging, "entertainment, and fourpence each." A quaint monument to Watts is the most prominent object on the wall of the south-west transept of the cathedral, and underneath it is now placed a brass thus inscribed: "CHARLES DICKENS. Born at Portsmouth, seventh of February 1812. "Died at Gadshill Place by Rochester, ninth of June 1870. Buried in "Westminster Abbey. To connect his memory with the scenes in which "his earliest and his latest years were passed, and with the associations "of Rochester Cathedral and its neighbourhood which extended over all "his life, this Tablet, with the sanction of the Dean and Chapter, is "placed by his Executors."

Brass tablet to Dickens in Rochester Cathedral.

bring about all the mischief in it, lay it all on
Providence, and say at every fresh calamity, "Well
"it's a mercy, however, nobody was to blame you
"know!" The title first chosen, out of many
suggested, was *Nobody's Fault;* and four numbers
had been written, of which the first was on the
eve of appearance, before this was changed.
When about to fall to work he excused himself
from an engagement he should have kept because
"the story is breaking out all round me, and I
"am going off down the railroad to humour it."
The humouring was a little difficult, however;
and such indications of a droop in his invention

as presented themselves in portions of *Bleak
House*, were noticeable again. "As to the story
"I am in the second number, and last-night and
"this morning had half a mind to begin again,
"and work in what I have done, afterwards."

It had occurred to him, that, by making the fellow-
travellers at once known to each other, as the
opening of the story stands, he had missed an
effect. "It struck me that it would be a new
"thing to show people coming together, in a
"chance way, as fellow-travellers, and being in
"the same place, ignorant of one another, as

"happens in life; and to connect them afterwards,
"and to make the waiting for that connection a
"part of the interest." The change was not made;
but the mention of it was one of several intimations to me of the altered conditions under which
he was writing, and that the old, unstinted, irrepressible flow of fancy had received temporary
check. In this view I have found it very inter-

esting to compare the original notes, which as
usual he prepared for each number of the tale,
and which with the rest are in my possession,
with those of *Chuzzlewit* or *Copperfield;* observing
in the former the labour and pains, and in the
latter the lightness and confidence of handling.*
"I am just now getting to work on number
"three: sometimes enthusiastic, more often dull
"enough.   There is an enormous outlay in the
"Father of the Marshalsea chapter, in the way of
"getting a great lot of matter into a small space.
"I am not quite resolved, but I have a great idea
"of overwhelming that family with wealth.   Their
"condition would be very curious.   I can make
"Dorrit very strong in the story, I hope."   The
Marshalsea part of the tale undoubtedly was excellent, and there was masterly treatment of character in the contrasts of the brothers Dorrit; but
of the family generally it may be said that its
least important members had most of his genius
in them. The younger of the brothers, the scape-
grace son, and "Fanny dear," are perfectly real
people in what makes them unattractive; but what
is meant for attractiveness in the heroine becomes
often tiresome by want of reality.

The first number appeared in December 1855,
and on the 2nd there was an exultant note. "*Little*
"*Dorrit* has beaten even *Bleak House* out of the
"field.   It is a most tremendous start, and I am
"overjoyed at it;" to which he added, writing

---

* So curious a contrast, taking *Copperfield* for the purpose, I have
thought worth giving in fac-simile; and can assure the reader that the
examples taken express very fairly the general character of the Notes to
the two books respectively.

LONDON:
1856-7.
Sale of the
book.

from Paris on the 6th of the month following,
"You know that they had sold 35,000 of number
"two on new year's day." He was still in Paris
on the day of the appearance of that portion of
the tale by which it will always be most vividly
remembered, and thus wrote on the 30th of
January 1856: "I have a grim pleasure upon me
"to-night in thinking that the Circumlocution

Circumlocu-
tion Office.

"Office sees the light, and in wondering ,what
"effect it will make. But my head really stings
"with the visions of the book, and I am going,
"as we French say, to disembarrass it by plunging
"out into some of the strange places I glide into
"of nights in these latitudes." The Circumlocution heroes led to the Society scenes, the Hampton-

Satirical
scenes:

court dowager-sketches, and Mr. Gowan; all parts
of one satire levelled against prevailing political
and social vices. Aim had been taken, in the
course of it, at some living originals, disguised
sufficiently from recognition to enable him to
make his thrust more sure; but there was one
exception self-revealed. "I had the general idea,"
he wrote while engaged on the sixth number,
"of the Society business before the Sadleir affair,
"but I shaped Mr. Merdle himself out of that

Parts of
general
design.

"precious rascality. Society, the Circumlocution
"Office, and Mr. Gowan, are of course three parts
"of one idea and design. Mr. Merdle's complaint,
"which you will find in the end to be fraud and
"forgery, came into my mind as the last drop in
"the silver cream-jug on Hampstead-heath. I
"shall beg, when you have read the present num-
"ber, to enquire whether you consider 'Bar' an

"instance, in reference to K F, of a suggested London: 1856-7.
"likeness in not many touches?"   The likeness
no one could mistake; and, though that particular From the life.
Bar has since been moved into a higher and
happier sphere, Westminster-hall is in no danger
of losing "the insinuating Jury-droop, and per-
"suasive double-eyeglass," by which this keen
observer could express a type of character in half
a dozen words.

Of the other portions of the book that had a
strong personal interest for him I have spoken I. 114-17.
on a former page, and I will now only add an April 7th. 1856.
allusion of his own.   "There are some things in
"Flora in number seven that seem to me to be
"extraordinarily droll, with something serious at
"the bottom of them after all.   Ah, well! was
"there *not* something very serious in it once?   I
"am glad to think of being in the country with
"the long summer mornings as I approach num-
"ber ten, where I have finally resolved to make
"Dorrit rich.   It should be a very fine point in
"the story . . . Nothing in Flora made me laugh
"so much as the confusion of ideas between gout
"flying upwards, and its soaring with Mr. F——
"to another sphere."   He had himself no incon-
siderable enjoyment also of Mr. F.'s aunt; and in
the old rascal of a patriarch, the smooth-surfaced Flora and her surroundings.
Casby, and other surroundings of poor Flora,
there was fun enough to float an argosy of
second-rates, assuming such to have formed the
staple of the tale.   It would be far from fair to
say they did.   The defect in the book was less
the absence of excellent character or keen ob-

London:
1856-7.

Weak points
in the book.

Characters
good but not
essential.

Episodes in
novels.

servation, than the want of ease and coherence among the figures of the story, and of a central interest in the plan of it.   The agencies that bring about its catastrophe, too, are less agreeable even than in *Bleak House;* and, most unlike that well-constructed story, some of the most deeply considered things that occur in it have really little to do with the tale itself.   The surface-painting of both Miss Wade and Tattycoram, to take an instance, is anything but attractive, yet there is under it a rare force of likeness in the unlikeness between the two which has much subtlety of intention; and they must both have had, as well as Mr. Gowan himself, a striking effect in the novel, if they had been made to contribute in a more essential way to its interest or development.   The failure nevertheless had not been for want of care and study, as well of his own design as of models by masters in his art.   A happier hint of apology, for example, could hardly be given for Fielding's introduction of such an episode as the Man of the Hill between the youth and manhood of Blifil and Tom Jones, than is suggested by what Dickens wrote of the least interesting part of *Little Dorrit.*   In the mere form, Fielding of course was only following the lead of Cervantes and Le Sage; but Dickens rightly judged his purpose also to have been, to supply a kind of connection between the episode and the story.   "I don't see the prac-"ticability of making the History of a Self-Tor-"mentor, with which I took great pains, a written "narrative.   But I do see the possibility" (he saw

the other practicability before the number was London: 1856-7.
published) "of making it a chapter by itself,
"which might enable me to dispense with the
"necessity of the turned commas.   Do you think
"that would be better?   I have no doubt that a
"great part of Fielding's reason for the intro-
"duced story, and Smollett's also, was, that it is
"sometimes really impossible to present, in a full
"book, the idea it contains (which yet it may be
"on all accounts desirable to present), without
"supposing the reader to be possessed of almost
"as much romantic allowance as would put him
"on a level with the writer.   In Miss Wade I had
"an idea, which I thought a new one, of making
"the introduced story so fit into surroundings im-
"possible of separation from the main story, as to Miss Wade's narrative.
"make the blood of the book circulate through
"both.   But I can only suppose, from what
"you say, that I have not exactly succeeded in
"this."

Shortly after the date of his letter he was in
London on business connected with the purchase
of Gadshill Place, and he went over to the
Borough to see what traces were left of the prison Coming to the close.
of which his first impression was taken in his
boyhood, which had played so important a part
in this latest novel, and every brick and stone of
which he had been able to rebuild in his book
by the mere vividness of his marvellous memory.
"Went to the Borough yesterday morning before Remains of Marshalsea visited.
"going to Gadshill, to see if I could find any
"ruins of the Marshalsea.   Found a great part of
"the original building—now 'Marshalsea Place.'

London:
1850-7.
"Found the rooms that have been in my mind's
"eye in the story. Found, nursing a very big
"boy, a very small boy, who, seeing me standing
"on the Marshalsea pavement, looking about,
"told me how it all used to be. God knows how
"he learned it (for he was a world too young to
"know anything about it), but he was right
"enough. . . . There is a room there—still stand-

A scene of his
boy trials.
I. 78-80.
"ing, to my amazement—that I think of taking!
"It is the room through which the ever-memor-
"able signers of Captain Porter's petition filed off
"in my boyhood. The spikes are gone, and the
"wall is lowered, and anybody can go out now
"who likes to go, and is not bedridden; and I
"said to the boy 'Who lives there?' and he said,
"'Jack Pithick.' 'Who is Jack Pithick?' I asked
"him. And he said, 'Joe Pithick's uncle.'"

Mention was made of this visit in the preface
that appeared with the last number; and all it is
necessary to add of the completed book will be,
that, though in the humour and satire of its finer
parts not unworthy of him, and though it had the
clear design, worthy of him in an especial degree, of contrasting, both in private and in public
life, and in poverty equally as in wealth, duty
done and duty not done, it made no material

Reception of
the novel.
addition to his reputation. His public, however,
showed no falling-off in its enormous numbers;
and what is said in one of his letters, noticeable
for this touch of character, illustrates his anxiety
to avoid any set-off from the disquiet that critical
discourtesies might give. "I was ludicrously foiled
"here the other night in a resolution I have kept

"for twenty years not to know of any attack upon
"myself, by stumbling, before I could pick myself—
"up, on a short extract in the *Globe* from *Black-*
"*wood's Magazine*, informing me that *Little Dorrit*
"is 'Twaddle.' I was sufficiently put out by it to
"be angry with myself for being such a fool, and
"then pleased with myself for having so long
"been constant to a good resolution." There was
a scene that made itself part of history not four
months after his death, which, if he could have
lived to hear of it, might have more than consoled him. It was the meeting of Bismarck and
Jules Favre under the walls of Paris. The Prus-
sian was waiting to open fire on the city; the
Frenchman was engaged in the arduous task of
showing the wisdom of not doing it; and "we
"learn," say the papers of the day, "that while
"the two eminent statesmen were trying to find a
"basis of negotiation, Von Moltke was seated in
"a corner reading *Little Dorrit*." Who will
doubt that the chapter on HOW NOT TO DO IT
was then absorbing the old soldier's attention?

London:
1856-7.

Criticism and
its set-off.

Pall Mall
Gazette of 3rd
of Oct. Paris
letter of 29th
of Sept. 1870.

Preparations for the private play had gone on
incessantly up to Christmas, and, in turning the
schoolroom into a theatre, sawing and hammering
worthy of Babel continued for weeks. The priceless help of Stanfield had again been secured, and
I remember finding him one day at Tavistock
House in the act of upsetting some elaborate arrangements by Dickens, with a proscenium before
him made up of chairs, and the scenery planned

Christmas
theatricals
preparing.

out with walking-sticks. But Dickens's art in a
matter of this kind was to know how to take advice; and no suggestion came to him that he was
not ready to act upon, if it presented the remotest
likelihood. In one of his great difficulties of ob-
taining more space, for audience as well as actors,

he was told that Mr. Cooke of Astley's was a man
of much resource in that way; and to Mr. Cooke
he applied, with the following result. "One of
"the finest things" (18th of October 1856) "I have
"ever seen in my life of that kind was the arrival
"of my friend Mr. Cooke one morning this week,
"in an open phaeton drawn by two white ponies
"with black spots all over them (evidently sten-
"cilled), who came in at the gate with a little jolt
"and a rattle, exactly as they come into the Ring
"when they draw anything, and went round and
"round the centre bed of the front court, ap-

"parently looking for the clown. A multitude of
"boys who felt them to be no common ponies
"rushed up in a breathless state—twined them-
"selves like ivy about the railings—and were only
"deterred from storming the enclosure by the glare
"of the Inimitable's eye. Some of these boys had
"evidently followed from Astley's. I grieve to
"add that my friend, being taken to the point of
"difficulty, had no sort of suggestion in him; no
"gleam of an idea; and might just as well have
"been the popular minister from the Tabernacle
"in Tottenham Court Road. All he could say

"was—answering me, posed in the garden, pre-
"cisely as if I were the clown asking him a riddle
"at night—that two of their stable tents would be

"home in November, and that they were '20 foot
"square,' and I was heartily welcome to 'em. Also,
"he said, 'You might have half a dozen of my
"'trapezes, or my middle-distance-tables, but they're
"'all 6 foot and all too low sir.' Since then, I
"have arranged to do it in my own way, and
"with my own carpenter. You will be surprised *Theatre-*
"by the look of the place. It is no more like the *making.*
"schoolroom than it is like the sign of the Saluta-
"tion Inn at Ambleside in Westmoreland. The
"sounds in the house remind me, as to the present
"time, of Chatham Dockyard—as to a remote
"epoch, of the building of Noah's ark. Joiners
"are never out of the house, and the carpenter
"appears to be unsettled (or settled) for life."

Of course time did not mend matters, and as
Christmas approached the house was in a state of
siege. "All day long, a labourer heats size over
"the fire in a great crucible. We eat it, drink it,
"breathe it, and smell it. Seventy paint-pots (which
"came in a van) adorn the stage; and thereon
"may be beheld, Stanny, and three Dansons (from *Scene-*
"the Surrey Zoological Gardens), all painting at *painting.*
"once!! Meanwhile, Telbin, in a secluded bower
"in Brewer-street, Golden-square, plies *his* part
"of the little undertaking." How worthily it turned
out in the end, the excellence of the performances
and the delight of the audiences, became known
to all London; and the pressure for admittance at
last took the form of a tragi-comedy, composed
of ludicrous makeshifts and gloomy disappoint-
ments, with which even Dickens's resources could
not deal. "My audience is now 93," he wrote *Rush for*
places.

11*

one day in despair, "and at least 10 will neither
"hear nor see." There was nothing for it but to
increase the number of nights; and it was not
until the 20th of January he described "the
"workmen smashing the last atoms of the theatre."

His book was finished soon after at Gadshill
Place, to be presently described, which he had
purchased the previous year, and taken possession of in February; subscribing himself, in the
letter announcing the fact, as "the Kentish Free-
"holder on his native heath, his name Protection."*
The new abode occupied him in various ways in
the early part of the summer; and Hans Andersen
the Dane had just arrived upon a visit to him
there, when Douglas Jerrold's unexpected death
befell. It was a shock to every one, and an
especial grief to Dickens. Jerrold's wit, and the
bright shrewd intellect that had so many triumphs,
need no celebration from me; but the keenest of
satirists was one of the kindliest of men, and
Dickens had a fondness for Jerrold as genuine as
his admiration for him. "I chance to know a
"good deal about the poor fellow's illness, for I
"was with him on the last day he was out. It
"was ten days ago, when we dined at a dinner
"given by Russell at Greenwich. He was com-
"plaining much when we met, said he had been
"sick three days, and attributed it to the inhaling
"of white paint from his study window. I did

---

* In the same letter was an illustration of the ruling passion in
death, which, even in so undignified a subject, might have interested
Pope. "You remember little Wieland who did grotesque demons so
"well. Did you ever hear how he died? He lay very still in bed
"with the life fading out of him—suddenly spring out of it, threw what
"is professionally called a flip-flap, and fell dead on the floor."

"not think much of it at the moment, as we were
"very social; but while we walked through Lei-
"cester-square he suddenly fell into a white, hot,
"sick perspiration, and had to lean against the
"railings. Then, at my urgent request, he was to
"let me put him in a cab and send him home;
"but he rallied a little after that, and, on our
"meeting Russell, determined to come with us.
"We three went down by steamboat that we might
"see the great ship, and then got an open fly and
"rode about Blackheath: poor Jerrold mightily
"enjoying the air, and constantly saying that it
"set him up. He was rather quiet at dinner—sat
"next Delane—but was very humorous and good,
"and in spirits, though he took hardly anything.
"We parted with references to coming down here"
(Gadshill) "and I never saw him again. Next
"morning he was taken very ill when he tried to
"get up. On the Wednesday and Thursday he
"was very bad, but rallied on the Friday, and was
"quite confident of getting well. On the Sunday
"he was very ill again, and on the Monday fore-
"noon died; 'at peace with all the world' he said,
"and asking to be remembered to friends. He
"had become indistinct and insensible, until for
"but a few minutes at the end. I knew nothing
"about it, except that he had been ill and was
"better, until, going up by railway yesterday morn-
"ing, I heard a man in the carriage, unfolding his
"'newspaper, say to another 'Douglas Jerrold is
"'dead.' I immediately went up there, and then
"to Whitefriars . . . I propose that there shall be
"a night at a theatre when the actors (with old

"Cooke) shall play the *Rent Day* and *Black-ey'd*
"*Susan;* another night elsewhere, with a lecture
"from Thackeray; a day reading by me; a night
"reading by me; a lecture by Russell; and a sub-
"scription performance of the *Frozen Deep*, as at
"Tavistock House. I don't mean to do it beg-
"gingly; but merely to announce the whole series,
"the day after the funeral, 'In memory of the late
"'Mr. Douglas Jerrold,' or some such phrase. I
"have got hold of Arthur Smith as the best man
"of business I know, and go to work with him
"to-morrow morning—inquiries being made in
"the meantime as to the likeliest places to be had
"for these various purposes. My confident hope
"is that we shall get close upon two thousand
"pounds."

The friendly enterprise was carried to the
close with a vigour, promptitude, and success,
that well corresponded with this opening. In
addition to the performances named, there were
others in the country also organized by Dickens,
in which he took active personal part; and the
result did not fall short of his expectations. The
sum was invested ultimately for our friend's un-
married daughter, who still receives the income
from myself, the last surviving trustee.

So passed the greater part of the summer,*

* One of its incidents made such an impression on him that it will
be worth while to preserve his description of it. "I have been (by mere
"accident) seeing the serpents fed to-day, with the live birds, rabbits,
"and guinea pigs—a sight so very horrible that I cannot get rid of the
"impression, and am, at this present, imagining serpents coming up the
"legs of the table, with their infernal flat heads, and their tongues like
"the Devil's tail (evidently taken from that model, in the magic lanterns
"and other such popular representations), elongated for dinner. I saw
"one small serpent, whose father was asleep, go up to a guinea pig

and when the country performances were over at
the end of August I had this intimation. "I
"have arranged with Collins that he and I will
"start next Monday on a ten or twelve days' ex-
"pedition to out-of-the-way places, to do (in inns
"and coast-corners) a little tour in search of an
"article and in avoidance of railroads. I must
"get a good name for it, and I propose it in five
"articles, one for the beginning of every number
"in the October part." Next day: "Our decision
"is for a foray upon the fells of Cumberland; I
"having discovered in the books some promising
"moors and bleak places thereabout." Into the
lake-country they went accordingly; and The Lazy
Tour of Two Idle Apprentices, contributed to
Household Words, was a narrative of the trip. But
his letters had descriptive touches, and some
whimsical personal experiences, not in the published account.

　　Looking over the *Beauties of England and*

London:
1856-7.

Lazy Tour
projected.

Scene chosen.

"(white and yellow, and with a gentle eye—every hair upon him erect
" with horror); corkscrew himself on the tip of his tail; open a mouth
" which couldn't have swallowed the guinea pig's nose; dilate a throat
" which wouldn't have made him a stocking; and show him what his
" father meant to do with him when he came out of that ill-looking
" Hookah into which he had resolved himself. The guinea pig backed
" against the side of the cage said 'I know it, I know it!' and his
" eye glared and his coat turned wiry, as he made the remark. Five
" small sparrows crouching together in a little trench at the back of the
" cage, peeped over the brim of it, all the time; and when they saw the
" guinea pig give it up, and the young serpent go away looking at him
" over about two yards and a quarter of shoulder, struggled which should
" get into the innermost angle and be seized last. Everyone of them
" then hid his eyes in another's breast, and then they all shook together
" like dry leaves—as I daresay they may be doing now, for old Hookah
" was as dull as laudanum . . . . Please to imagine two small
" serpents, one beginning on the tail of a white mouse, and one on the
" head, and each pulling his own way, and the mouse very much alive
" all the time, with the middle of him madly writhing."

At the
Zoological
Gardens.

Wales before he left London, his ambition was fired by mention of Carrick Fell, "a gloomy old "mountain 1500 feet high," which he secretly resolved to go up. "We came straight to it yester-"day" (9th of September). "Nobody goes up. "Guides have forgotten it. Master of a little inn, "excellent north-countryman, volunteered. Went

"up, in a tremendous rain. C. D. beat Mr. Porter "(name of landlord) in half a mile. Mr. P. done "up in no time. Three nevertheless went on. Mr. "P. again leading; C. D. and C." (Mr. Wilkie Collins) "following. Rain terrific, black mists, "darkness of night. Mr. P. agitated. C. D. con-"fident. C. (a long way down in perspective) sub-"missive. All wet through. No poles. Not so

"much as a walking-stick in the party. Reach the "summit, at about one in the day. Dead dark-"ness as of night. Mr. P. (excellent fellow to the "last) uneasy. C. D. produces compass from "pocket. Mr. P. reassured. Farm-house where dog-"cart was left, N. N. W. Mr. P. complimentary. "Descent commenced. C. D. with compass triumph-"ant, until compass, with the heat and wet of "C. D.'s pocket, breaks. Mr. P. (who never had "a compass), inconsolable, confesses he has not "been on Carrick Fell for twenty years, and he "don't know the way down. Darker and darker. "Nobody discernible, two yards off, by the other

"two. Mr. P. makes suggestions, but no way. It "becomes clear to C. D. and to C. that Mr. P. is "going round and round the mountain, and never "coming down. Mr. P. sits on angular granite, "and says he is 'just fairly doon.' C. D. revives

"Mr. P. with laughter, the only restorative in the
"company. Mr. P. again complimentary. Descent
"tried once more. Mr. P. worse and worse. Council
"of war. Proposals from C. D. to go 'slap down,'
"Seconded by C. Mr. P. objects, on account of
"precipice called The Black Arches, and terror of
"the country-side. More wandering. Mr. P. ter-
"ror-stricken, but game. Watercourse, thundering
"and roaring, reached. C. D. suggests that it
"must run to the river, and had best be followed,
"subject to all gymnastic hazards. Mr. P. opposes,
"but gives in. Watercourse followed accordingly.
"Leaps, splashes, and tumbles, for two hours. C.
"lost. C. D. whoops. Cries for assistance from
"behind. C. D. returns. C. with horribly sprained
"ankle, lying in rivulet!"

(margin note: CUMBER-LAND: 1857.)

(margin note: Accident to Wilkie Collins.)

All the danger was over when Dickens sent
his description; but great had been the trouble in
binding up the sufferer's ankle and getting him
painfully on, shoving, shouldering, carrying alternately, till terra firma was reached. "We got
"down at last in the wildest place, preposterously
"out of the course; and, propping up C. against
"stones, sent Mr. P. to the other side of Cumber-
"land for dog-cart, so got back to his inn, and
"changed. Shoe or stocking on the bad foot, out
"of the question. Foot tumbled up in a flannel
"waistcoat. C. D. carrying C. melo-dramatically
"(Wardour to the life!)* everywhere; into and out
"of carriages; up and down stairs; to bed; every

(margin note: Down at last.)

* There was a situation in the *Frozen Deep* where Richard Wardour,
played by Dickens, had thus to carry about Frank Aldersley in the person of Wilkie Collins.

"step. And so to Wigton, got doctor, and here
"we are!!   A pretty business, we flatter our-
"selves!"

Wigton, Dickens described as a place of little
houses all in half-mourning, yellow stone or white
stone and black, with the wonderful peculiarity
that though it had no population, no business,
and no streets to speak of, it had five linen-
drapers within range of their single window, one
linendraper's next door, and five more linen-
drapers round the corner. "I ordered a night
"light in my bed-room. A queer little old woman
"brought me one of the common Child's night
"lights, and, seeming to think that I looked at it
"with interest, said, 'It's joost a vara keeyourious
"'thing, sir, and joost new coom oop. It'll burn
"'awt hoors a' end, and no gootther, nor no waste,
"'nor ony sike a thing, if you can creedit what
"'I say, seein' the airticle.'"   In these primitive
quarters there befell a difficulty about letters,
which Dickens solved in a fashion especially his
own. "The day after Carrick there was a mess
"about our letters, through our not going to a
"place called Mayport. So, while the landlord
"was planning how to get them (they were only
"twelve miles off), I walked off, to his great as-
"tonishment, and brought them over." The night
after leaving Wigton they were at the Ship-hotel
in Allonby.

Allonby his letters presented as a small un-
tidy outlandish place; rough stone houses in half
mourning, a few coarse yellow-stone lodging
houses with black roofs (bills in all the windows),

five bathing-machines, five girls in straw hats, five CUMBER-LANDS 1857. men in straw hats (wishing they had not come); very much what Broadstairs would have been if it had been born Irish, and had not inherited a cliff. "But this is a capital little homely inn, "looking out upon the sea; with the coast of Scot- "land, mountainous and romantic, over against "the windows; and though I can just stand up- "right in my bedroom, we are really well lodged. "It is a clean nice place in a rough wild country, "and we have a very obliging and comfortable "landlady." He had found indeed, in the latter, an acquaintance of old date. "The landlady at An old ac-quaintance. "the little inn at Allonby, lived at Greta-Bridge "in Yorkshire when I went down there before "*Nickleby;* and was smuggled into the room to "see me, after I was secretly found out. She is "an immensely fat woman now. 'But I could "'tuck my arm round her waist then, Mr. Dickens,' "the landlord said when she told me the story as "I was going to bed the night before last. 'And "'can't you do it now?' I said. 'You insensible "'dog! Look at me! Here's a picture!' Accord- A picture. "ingly I got round as much of her as I could; and "this gallant action was the most successful I have "ever performed, on the whole."

On their way home the friends were at Don- At Doncaster. caster, and this was Dickens's first experience of the St. Leger and its saturnalia. His companion had by this time so far recovered as to be able, doubled-up, to walk with a thick stick; in which condition, "being exactly like the gouty admiral "in a comedy I have given him that name." The

impressions received from the race-week were not
favourable.   It was noise and turmoil all day
long, and a gathering of vagabonds from all parts
of the racing earth. Every bad face that had ever
caught wickedness from an innocent horse had
its representative in the streets; and as Dickens,
like Gulliver looking down upon his fellow-men
after coming from the horse-country, looked down
into Doncaster High-street from his inn-window,
he seemed to see everywhere a then notorious
personage who had just poisoned his betting-
companion.   "Everywhere I see the late Mr.
"Palmer with his betting-book in his hand.   Mr.
"Palmer sits next me at the theatre; Mr. Palmer
"goes before me down the street; Mr. Palmer
"follows me into the chemist's shop where I go
"to buy rose water after breakfast, and says to
"the chemist 'Give us soom sal volatile or soom
"'damned thing o' that soort, in wather—my
"'head's bad!' And I look at the back of his
"bad head repeated in long, long lines on the
"race course, and in the betting stand and out-
"side the betting rooms in the town, and I vow
"to God that I can see nothing in it but cruelty,
"covetousness, calculation, insensibility, and low
"wickedness."

The race-
week.

Jotting men.

Racing
prophecy
by Dickens!
Even a half-appalling kind of luck was not
absent from my friend's experiences at the race
course, when, what he called a "wonderful, para-
"lysing, coincidence" befell him.   He bought the
card; facetiously wrote down three names for the
winners of the three chief races (never in his life
having heard or thought of any of the horses, ex-

cept that the winner of the Derby, who proved to
be nowhere, had been mentioned to him); "and,
"if you can believe it without your hair standing
"on end, those three races were won, one after
"another, by those three horses!!!" That was the
St. Leger-day, of which he also thought it noticeable, that, though the losses were enormous, nobody had won, for there was nothing but grind-
ing of teeth and blaspheming of ill-luck.   Nor
had matters mended on the Cup-day, after which
celebration "a groaning phantom" lay in the doorway of his bed-room and howled all night.   The
landlord came up in the morning to apologise,
"and said it was a gentleman who had lost £1500
"or £2000; and he had drunk a deal afterwards;
"and then they put him to bed, and then he—
"took the 'orrors, and got up, and yelled till
"morning."*   Dickens might well believe, as he
declared at the end of his letter, that if a boy
with any good in him, but with a dawning propensity to sporting and betting, were but brought
to the Doncaster races soon enough, it would
cure him.

Doncaster:
1857.

The
"horrors."

* The mention of a performance of Lord Lytton's *Money* at the
theatre will supply the farce to this tragedy.   "I have rarely seen any-
"thing finer than Lord Glossmore, a chorus-singer in bluchers, drab
"trowsers, and a brown sack; and Dudley Smooth, in somebody else's
"wig, hindside before. Stout also, in anything he could lay hold of. The
"waiter at the club had an immense moustache, white trowsers, and a
"striped jacket; and he brought everybody who came in, a vinegar-
"cruet.   The man who read the will began thus: ' I so-and-so, being
"'of unsound mind but firm in body. .'   In spite of all this, however,
"the real character, humour, wit, and good writing of the comedy, made
"themselves apparent; and the applause was loud and repeated, and
"really seemed genuine.   Its capital things were not lost altogether.   It
"was succeeded by a Jockey Dance by five ladies, who put their whips
"in their mouths and worked imaginary winners up to the float— an im-
"mense success."

A perform-
ance of
Money.

CHAPTER LI.

WHAT HAPPENED AT THIS TIME.

1857-1858.

An unsettled feeling greatly in excess of what was usual with Dickens, more or less observable since his first residence at Boulogne, became at this time almost habitual, and the satisfactions which home should have supplied, and which indeed were essential requirements of his nature, he had failed to find in his home. He had not the alternative that under this disappointment some can discover in what is called society. It did not suit him, and he set no store by it. No man was better fitted to adorn any circle he entered, but beyond that of friends and equals he rarely passed. He would take as much pains to keep out of the houses of the great as others take to get into them. Not always wisely, it may be admitted. Mere contempt for toadyism and flunkeyism was not at all times the prevailing motive with him which he supposed it to be. Beneath his horror of those vices of Englishmen in his own rank of life, there was a still stronger resentment at the social inequalities that engender them, of which he was not so conscious and to which he owned less freely. Not the less it served secretly to justify what he might otherwise have

had no mind to. To say he was not a gentleman would be as true as to say he was not a
writer; but if any one should assert his occasional
preference for what was even beneath his level
over that which was above it, this would be difficult of disproof. It was among those defects of
temperament for which his early trials and his
early successes were accountable in perhaps equal
measure. He was sensitive in a passionate degree
to praise and blame, which yet he made it for
the most part a point of pride to assume indiffer-
ence to; the inequalities of rank which he secretly
resented took more galling as well as glaring
prominence from the contrast of the necessities
he had gone through with the fame that had
come to him; and when the forces he most affected
to despise assumed the form of barriers he could
not easily overleap, he was led to appear frequently intolerant (for he very seldom was really
so) in opinions and language. His early suffer-
ings brought with them the healing powers of
energy, will, and persistence, and taught him the
inexpressible value of determined resolve to live
down difficulties; but the habit, in small as in
great things, of renunciation and self-sacrifice,
they did not teach; and, by his sudden leap into
a world-wide popularity and influence, he became
master of everything that might seem to be at-
tainable in life, before he had mastered what
a man must undergo to be equal to its hardest
trials.

Nothing of all this has yet presented itself to
notice, except in occasional forms of restlessness

London: 1857.

What wo soom and aro.

Contrasted influences.

LONDON:
1857.

and desire of change of place, which were themselves, when his books were in progress, so incident as well to the active requirements of his
fancy as to call, thus far, for no other explanation.
Up to the date of the completion of *Copperfield*
he had felt himself to be in possession of an all-
sufficient resource. Against whatever might befall
he had a set-off in his imaginative creations, a
compensation derived from his art that never
failed him, because there he was supreme. It
was the world he could bend to his will, and
make subserve to all his desires. He had otherwise, underneath his exterior of a singular precision, method, and strictly orderly arrangement
in all things, and notwithstanding a temperament
to which home and home interests were really a
necessity, something in common with those eager,
impetuous, somewhat overbearing natures, that
rush at existence without heeding the cost of it,
and are not more ready to accept and make the
most of its enjoyments than to be easily and
quickly overthrown by its burdens.* But the
world he had called into being had thus far borne

Compensa-
tions of art.

Hidden
perils.

---

* Anything more completely opposed to the Micawber type could
hardly be conceived, and yet there were moments (really and truly only
moments) when the fancy would arise that if the conditions of his life
had been reversed, something of a vagabond existence (using the word
in Goldsmith's meaning) might have supervened. It would have been an
unspeakable misery to him, but it might have come nevertheless. The
question of hereditary transmission had a curious attraction for him, and
considerations connected with it were frequently present to his mind.
Of a youth who had fallen into a father's weaknesses without the possibility of having himself observed them for imitation, he thus wrote on
one occasion : "It suggests the strangest consideration as to which of our
"own failings we are really responsible, and as to which of them we can-
"not quite reasonably hold ourselves to be so. What A. evidently de-
"rived from his father cannot in his case be derived from association and
"observation, but must be in the very principles of his individuality as a
"living creature."

Hereditary
transmission.

him safely through these perils. He had his own
creations always by his side. They were living,
speaking companions. With them only he was
everywhere thoroughly identified. He laughed
and wept with them; was as much elated by their
fun as cast down by their grief; and brought to
the consideration of them a belief in their reality
as well as in the influences they were meant to
exercise, which in every circumstance sustained
him.

 It was during the composition of *Little Dorrit* Misgivings.
that I think he first felt a certain strain upon his
invention which brought with it other misgivings.
In a modified form this was present during the
later portions of *Bleak House*, of which not a few
of the defects might be traced to the acting excitements amid which it was written; but the suc-
ceeding book made it plainer to him; and it is
remarkable that in the interval between them he
resorted for the first and only time in his life to
a practice, which he abandoned at the close of
his next and last story published in the twenty-
number form, of putting down written "Memo-
randa" of suggestions for characters or incidents by Written
way of resource to him in his writing. Never before suggestions
had his teeming fancy seemed to want such help; the for stories.
need being less to contribute to its fullness than to
check its overflowing; but it is another proof that
he had been secretly bringing before himself, at
least, the possibility that what had ever been his
great support might some day desert him. It was
strange that he should have had such doubt, and
he would hardly have confessed it openly; but

LONDON:
1857.

apart from that wonderful world of his books, the range of his thoughts was not always proportioned to the width and largeness of his nature. His ordinary circle of activity, whether in likings or thinkings, was full of such surprising animation, that one was apt to believe it more comprehensive than it really was; and again and again, when a wide horizon might seem to be ahead of him, he would pull up suddenly and stop short, as though nothing lay beyond. For the time, though each had its term and change, he was very much a man of one idea, each having its turn of absolute predominance; and this was one of the secrets of the thoroughness with which everything he took in hand was done. As to the matter of his writings, the actual truth was that his creative genius never really failed him. Not a few of his inventions of character and humour, up to the very close of his life, his Marigolds, Lirripers, Gargerys, Pips, Sapseas and many others, were as fresh and fine as in his greatest day. He had however lost the free and fertile method of the earlier time. He could no longer fill a wide-spread canvas with the same facility and certainty as of old; and he had frequently a quite unfounded apprehension of some possible break-down, of which the end might be at any moment beginning. There came accordingly, from time to time, intervals of unusual impatience and restlessness, strange to me in connection with his home; his old pursuits were too often laid aside for other excitements and occupations; he joined a public political agitation, set on foot by administrative reformers; he got up various quasi-public private theatricals, in which he took the leading place; and though it was but part of his always generous devotion in any friendly duty to organize the series of performances on his friend Jerrold's death, yet the eagerness with which he flung himself into them, so arranging them as to assume an amount of labour in acting and travelling that might have appalled an experienced comedian, and carrying them on week after week unceasingly in London and the provinces, expressed but the craving which still had possession of him to get by some means at some change that should make existence easier. What was highest in his nature had ceased for the time to be highest in his life, and he had put himself at the mercy of lower accidents and conditions. The mere effect of the strolling wandering ways into which this acting led him could not be other than unfavourable. But remonstrance as yet was unavailing.

London: 1857.
Restlessness and impatience.
Jerrold performances.

To one very earnestly made in the early autumn of 1857, in which opportunity was taken to compare his recent rush up Carrick Fell to his rush into other difficulties, here was the reply. "Too late to say, put the curb on, and don't rush "at hills—the wrong man to say it to. I have "now no relief but in action. I am become in-"capable of rest. I am quite confident I should "rust, break, and die, if I spared myself. Much "better to die, doing. What I am in that way, "nature made me first, and my way of life has of "late, alas! confirmed. I must accept the draw-"back—since it is one—with the powers I have;

Reply to a remonstrance.

12*

"and I must hold upon the tenure prescribed to "me." Something of the same sad feeling, it is right to say, had been expressed from time to time, in connection also with home dissatisfactions and misgivings, through the three years preceding; but I attributed it to other causes, and gave little attention to it. During his absences abroad for the greater part of 1854, '55, and '56, while the elder of his children were growing out of childhood, and his books were less easy to him than in his earlier manhood, evidences presented themselves in his letters of the old "unhappy loss "or want of something" to which he had given a pervading prominence in *Copperfield*. In the first of those years he made express allusion to the kind of experience which had been one of his descriptions in that favourite book, and, mentioning the drawbacks of his present life, had first identified it with his own: "the so happy and yet "so unhappy existence which seeks its realities in "unrealities, and finds its dangerous comfort in "a perpetual escape from the disappointment of "heart around it."

Later in the same year he thus wrote from Boulogne: "I have had dreadful thoughts of get-"ting away somewhere altogether by myself. If I "could have managed it, I think possibly I might "have gone to the Pyreennees (you know what I "mean that word for, so I won't re-write it) for "six months! I have put the idea into the per-"spective of six months, but have not abandoned "it. I have visions of living for half a year or "so, in all sorts of inaccessible places, and open-

LONDON:
1857.

"ing a new book therein. A floating idea of
"going up above the snow-line in Switzerland,
"and living in some astonishing convent, hovers
"about me. If *Household Words* could be got into
"a good train, in short, I don't know in what
"strange place, or at what remote elevation above
"the level of the sea, I might fall to work next.
"*Restlessness*, you will say. Whatever it is, it is
"always driving me, and I cannot help it. I have
"rested nine or ten weeks, and sometimes feel as
"if it had been a year—though I had the strangest
"nervous miseries before I stopped. If I couldn't
"walk fast and far, I should just explode and
"perish." Again, four months later he wrote:
"You will hear of me in Paris, probably next
"Sunday, and I *may* go on to Bordeaux. Have
"general ideas of emigrating in the summer to
"the mountain-ground between France and Spain.
"Am altogether in a dishevelled state of mind—
"motes of new books in the dirty air, miseries
"of older growth threatening to close upon me.
"Why is it, that as with poor David, a sense
"comes always crushing on me now, when I fall
"into low spirits, as of one happiness I have
"missed in life, and one friend and companion I
"have never made?"

One happi-
ness missed.

Early in 1856 (20th of January) the notion
revisited him of writing a book in solitude.
"Again I am beset by my former notions of a
"book whereof the whole story shall be on the
"top of the Great St. Bernard. As I accept and
"reject ideas for *Little Dorrit*, it perpetually
"comes back to me. Two or three years hence,

More book
projects.

LONDON:
1857.
"perhaps you'll find me living with the Monks
"and the Dogs a whole winter—among the blind-
"ing snows that fall about that monastery. I have
"a serious idea that I shall do it, if I live." He
was at this date in Paris; and during the visit
to him of Macready in the following April, the
self-revelations were resumed. The great actor
was then living in retirement at Sherborne, to
which he had gone on quitting the stage; and
Dickens gave favourable report of his enjoyment
of the change to his little holiday at Paris. Then,
after recurring to his own old notion of having
some slight idea of going to settle in Australia,
only he could not do it until he should have
An old friend
retired.
finished *Little Dorrit*, he went on to say that
perhaps Macready, if he could get into harness
again, would not be the worse for some such
troubles as were worrying himself. "It fills me
"with pity to think of him away in that lonely
"Sherborne place. I have always 'felt' of myself
"that I must, please God, die in harness, but I
"have never felt it more strongly than in looking
"at, and thinking of, him. However strange it is
"to be never at rest, and never satisfied, and ever
Homily on
life.
"trying after something that is never reached, and
"to be always laden with plot and plan and care
"and worry, how clear it is that it must be, and
"that one is driven by an irresistible might until
"the journey is worked out! It is much better to
"go on and fret, than to stop and fret. As to
"repose—for some men there's no such thing in
"this life. The foregoing has the appearance of
"a small sermon; but it is so often in my head in

"these days that it cannot help coming out. The London;
1857.
Fruitless'
aspirations.
"old days—the old days! Shall I ever, I wonder,
"get the frame of mind back as it used to be
"then? Something of it perhaps—but never quite
"as it used to be. I find that the skeleton in
"my domestic closet is becoming a pretty big
"one."

It would be unjust and uncandid not to admit that these and other similar passages in the
letters that extended over the years while he
lived abroad, had served in some degree as a
preparation for what came after his return to
England in the following year. It came with a
great shock nevertheless; because it told plainly
what before had never been avowed, but only
hinted at more or less obscurely. The opening What lay
behind.
reference is to the reply which had been made
to a previous expression of his wish for some
confidences as in the old time. I give only what
is strictly necessary to account for what followed,
and even this with deep reluctance. "Your letter
"of yesterday was so kind and hearty, and
"sounded so gently the many chords we have
"touched together, that I cannot leave it unan-
"swered, though I have not much (to any pur-
"pose) to say. My reference to 'confidences' Confidences.
"was merely to the relief of saying a word of
"what has long been pent up in my mind. Poor
"Catherine and I are not made for each other,
"and there is no help for it. It is not only that
"she makes me uneasy and unhappy, but that I
"make her so too—and much more so. She is
"exactly what you know, in the way of being

London:
1857.
"amiable and complying; but we are strangely
"ill-assorted for the bond there is between us.
"God knows she would have been a thousand
"times happier if she had married another kind
"of man, and that her avoidance of this destiny
"would have been at least equally good for us
"both. I am often cut to the heart by thinking
"what a pity it is, for her own sake, that I ever
"fell in her way; and if I were sick or disabled
"to-morrow, I know how sorry she would be, and
"how deeply grieved myself, to think how we
"had lost each other. But exactly the same in-
"compatibility would arise, the moment I was
"well again; and nothing on earth could make
"her understand me, or suit us to each other.
"Her temperament will not go with mine. It
"mattered not so much when we had only our-
"selves to consider, but reasons have been grow-
"ing since which make it all but hopeless that
"we should even try to struggle on. What is
"now befalling me I have seen steadily coming,
"ever since the days you remember when Mary
"was born; and I know too well that you can-
"not, and no one can, help me. Why I have
"even written I hardly know; but it is a miserable
"sort of comfort that you should be clearly aware
"how matters stand. The mere mention of the
"fact, without any complaint or blame of any
"sort, is a relief to my present state of spirits—
"and I can get this only from you, because I
"I can speak of it to no one else." In the same
tone was his rejoinder to my reply. "To the
"most part of what you say—Amen! You are

Sorrowful convictions.

Hopeless of help.

Rejoinder to a reply.

"not so tolerant as perhaps you might be of the
"wayward and unsettled feeling which is part (I——
"suppose) of the tenure on which one holds an
"imaginative life, and which I have, as you ought
"to know well, often only kept down by riding
"over it like a dragoon—but let that go by. I
"make no maudlin complaint. I agree with you
"as to the very possible incidents, even not less
"bearable than mine, that might and must often
"occur to the married condition when it is en-
"tered into very young. I am always deeply
"sensible of the wonderful exercise I have of life
"and its highest sensations, and have said to
"myself for years, and have honestly and truly
"felt, This is the drawback to such a career, and
"is not to be complained of. I say it and feel it
"now as strongly as ever I did; and, as I told
"you in my last, I do not with that view put all
"this forward. But the years have not made it
"easier to bear for either of us; and, for her
"sake as well as mine, the wish will force itself
"upon me that something might be done. I
"know too well it is impossible. There is the
"fact, and that is all one can say. Nor are you
"to suppose that I disguise from myself what
• "might be urged on the other side. I claim no
"immunity from blame. There is plenty of fault
"on my side, I dare say, in the way of a thou-
"sand uncertainties, caprices, and difficulties of
"disposition; but only one thing will alter all
"that, and that is, the end which alters every-
"thing."

It will not seem to most people that there

was anything here which in happier circumstances might not have been susceptible of considerate adjustment; but all the circumstances were unfavourable, and the moderate middle course which the admissions in that letter might wisely have prompted and wholly justified, was unfortunately not taken. Compare what before was said of his temperament, with what is there said by himself of its defects, and the explanation will not be difficult. Every counteracting influence against the one idea which now predominated over him had been so weakened as to be almost powerless. His elder children were no longer children; his books had lost for the time the importance they formerly had over every other consideration in his life; and he had not in himself the resource that such a man, judging him from the surface, might be expected to have had. Not his genius only, but his whole nature, was too exclusively made up of sympathy for, and with, the real in its most intense form, to be sufficiently provided against failure in the realities around him. There was for him no "city of the mind" against outward ills, for inner consolation and shelter. It was in and from the actual he still stretched forward to find the freedom and satisfactions of an ideal, and by his very attempts to escape the world he was driven back into the thick of it. But what he would have sought there, it supplies to none; and to get the infinite out of anything so finite, has broken many a stout heart.

At the close of that last letter from Gadshill (5th of September) was this question—"What do

"you think of my paying for this place, by reviv- LONDON: 1857-8.
"ing that old idea of some Readings from my ——————
"books. I am very strongly tempted. Think of Old project revived.
"it." The reasons against it had great force, and
took, in my judgment, greater from the time at
which it was again proposed. The old ground Ante, 55.
of opposition remained. It was a substitution of
lower for higher aims; a change to commonplace
from more elevated pursuits; and it had so much
of the character of a public exhibition for money
as to raise, in the question of respect for his
calling as a writer, a question also of respect for Objections to it.
himself as a gentleman. This opinion, now
strongly reiterated, was referred ultimately to two
distinguished ladies of his acquaintance, who
decided against it. * Yet not without such
momentary misgiving in the direction of "the
"stage," as pointed strongly to the danger, which,
by those who took the opposite view, was most

* "You may as well know" (20th of March 1858) "that I went on"
"(I designate the ladies by A and B respectively) "and propounded the
"matter to A, without any preparation. Result.—'I am surprised, and
"'I should have been surprised if I had seen it in the newspaper with-
"'out previous confidence from you. But nothing more. N—no. Cer-
"'tainly not. Nothing more. I don't see that there is anything de-
"'rogatory in it, even now when you ask me that question. I think
"'upon the whole that most people would be glad you should have the
"'money, rather than other people. It might be misunderstood here
"'and there, at first; but I think the thing would very soon express it-
"'self, and that your own power of making it express itself would be very
"'great.' As she wished me to ask B, who was in another room, I did Opinions
"so. She was for a moment tremendously disconcerted, '*under the im*- asked and
"'*pression that it was to lead to the stage*' (!!). Then, without know- given.
"ing anything of A's opinion, closely followed it. That absurd associa-
"tion had never entered my head or yours; but it might enter some
"other heads for all that. Take these two opinions for whatever they
"are worth. A (being very much interested and very anxious to help to
"a right conclusion) proposed to ask a few people of various degrees
"who know what the Readings are, what *they* think—not compromising
"me, but suggesting the project afaroff, as an idea in somebody else's
"mind. I thanked her, and said ' Yes,' of course."

of all thought incident to the particular time of the proposal. It might be a wild exaggeration to fear that he was in danger of being led to adopt the stage as a calling, but he was certainly about to place himself within reach of not a few of its drawbacks and disadvantages. To the full

extent he perhaps did not himself know, how much his eager present wish to become a public reader was but the outcome of the restless domestic discontents of the last four years; and that to indulge it, and the unsettled habits inseparable from it, was to abandon every hope of resettling his disordered home. There is nothing, in its application to so divine a genius as Shakespeare, more affecting than his expressed dislike to a profession, which, in the jealous self-watchfulness of his noble nature, he feared might hurt his mind. * The long subsequent line of

actors admirable in private as in public life, and all the gentle and generous associations of the histrionic art, have not weakened the testimony of its greatest name against its less favourable influences; against the laxity of habits it may encourage; and its public manners, bred of public

---

* Oh! for my sake do you with Fortune chide
   The guilty goddess of my harmful deeds,
That did not better for my life provide
   Than public means which public manners breeds.
Thence comes it that my name receives a brand:
   And almost thence my nature is subdu'd
To what it works in, like the dyer's hand. . .
   Pity me, then, and wish I were renew'd. . .
                    Sonnet cxi.
And in the preceding Sonnet cx.

   Alas, 'tis true I have gone here and there,
   And made myself a motley to the view,
Gor'd mine own thoughts, sold cheap what is most dear. . .

means, not always compatible with home felici- Loxdox: 1857-8.
ties and duties. But, freely open as Dickens was
to counsel in regard of his books, he was, for
reasons formerly stated,* less accessible to it on
points of personal conduct; and when he had
neither self-distrust nor self-denial to hold him
back, he would push persistently forward to whatever object he had in view.

An occurrence of the time hastened the deci- Hospital for sick children. 1858.
sion in this case. An enterprise had been set on
foot for establishment of a hospital for sick
children;** a large old-fashioned mansion in Great
Ormond-street, with spacious garden, had been
fitted up with more than thirty beds; during the
four or five years of its existence, outdoor and
indoor relief had been afforded by it to nearly
fifty thousand children, of whom thirty thousand
were under five years of age; but, want of funds
having threatened to arrest the merciful work, it
was resolved to try a public dinner by way of
charitable appeal, and for president the happy
choice was made of one who had enchanted

* Vol. I. p. 88-9. I repeat from that passage one or two sentences, though it is hardly fair to give them without the modifications that accompany them. "A too great confidence in himself, a sense that every-"thing was possible to the will that would make it so, laid occasionally "upon him self-imposed burdens greater than might be borne by any one "with safety. In that direction there was in him, at such times, some-"thing even hard and aggressive; in his determinations a something that "had almost the tone of fierceness; something in his nature that made "his resolves insuperable, however hasty the opinions on which they had "been formed."

** The Board of Health returns, showing that out of every annual Deaths thousand of deaths in London, the immense proportion of four hundred of little were those of children under four years old, had established the neces- children. sity for such a scheme. Of course the stress of this mortality fell on the children of the poor, "dragged up rather than brought up," as Charles Lamb expressed it, and perishing unhelped by the way.

everybody with the joys and sorrows of little children.   Dickens threw himself into the service heart and soul.   There was a simple pathos in his address from the chair quite startling in its effect at such a meeting; and he probably never moved any audience so much as by the strong personal feeling with which he referred to the

sacrifices made for the Hospital by the very poor themselves: from whom a subscription of fifty pounds, contributed in single pennies, had come to the treasurer during almost every year it had been open.   The whole speech, indeed, is the best of the kind spoken by him; and two little pictures from it, one of the misery he had witnessed, the other of the remedy he had found, should not be absent from the picture of his own life.

"Some years ago, being in Scotland, I went with "one of the most humane members of the most hu- "mane of professions, on a morning tour among "some of the worst lodged inhabitants of the old "town of Edinburgh.   In the closes and wynds of "that picturesque place (I am sorry to remind you "what fast friends picturesqueness and typhus "often are), we saw more poverty and sickness in "an hour than many people would believe in, in "a life.   Our way lay from one to another of the "most wretched dwellings, reeking with horrible "odours; shut out from the sky and from the air, "mere pits and dens.   In a room in one of these "places, where there was an empty porridge-pot "on the cold hearth, a ragged woman and some
"ragged children crouching on the bare ground

"near it,—and, I remember as I speak, where the
"very light, refracted from a high damp-stained
"wall outside, came in trembling, as if the fever
"which had shaken everything else had shaken
"even it,—there lay, in an old egg-box which the
"mother had begged from a shop, a little, feeble,
"wan, sick child.   With his little wasted face,
"and his little hot worn hands folded over his
"breast, and his little bright attentive eyes, I can
"see him now, as I have seen him for several
"years, looking steadily at us.   There he lay in
"his small frail box, which was not at all a bad
"emblem of the small body from which he was
"slowly parting—there he lay, quite quiet, quite
"patient, saying never a word.   He seldom cried,
"the mother said; he seldom complained; 'he lay
"'there, seemin' to woonder what it was a' abool.'
"God knows, I thought, as I stood looking at
"him, he had his reasons for wondering . . . Many
"a poor child, sick and neglected, I have seen
"since that time in London; many have I also
"seen most affectionately tended, in unwholesome
"houses and hard circumstances where recovery
"was impossible: but at all such times I have
"seen my little drooping friend in his egg-box,
"and he has always addressed his dumb wonder
"to me what it meant, and why, in the name of
"a gracious God, such things should be! . . But,
"ladies and gentlemen," Dickens added, "such
"things need NOT be, and will not be, if this
"company, which is a drop of the life-blood of
"the great compassionate public heart, will only
"accept the means of rescue and prevention which

LONDON:
1858.

Hospital
described.

"it is mine to offer. Within a quarter of a mile
"of this place where I speak, stands a once courtly
"old house, where blooming children were born,
"and grew up to be men and women, and married,
"and brought their own blooming children back
"to patter up the old oak staircase which stood
"but the other day and to wonder at the old oak
"carvings on the chimney-pieces. In the airy
"wards into which the old state drawing-rooms
"and family bedchambers of that house are now
"converted, are lodged such small patients that
"the attendant nurses look like reclaimed giant-
"esses, and the kind medical practitioner like an
"amiable Christian ogre. Grouped about the
See Ch. IX.
of Our Mutual
Friend.
"little low tables in the centre of the rooms, are
"such tiny convalescents that they seem to be
"playing at having been ill. On the doll's beds
"are such diminutive creatures that each poor
"sufferer is supplied with its tray of toys: and,
"looking round, you may see how the little tired
"flushed cheek has toppled over half the brute
"creation on its way into the ark; or how one
"little dimpled arm has mowed down (as I saw
"myself) the whole tin soldiery of Europe. On
"the walls of these rooms are graceful, pleasant,
"bright, childish pictures. At the beds' heads,
"hang representations of the figure which is the
"universal embodiment of all mercy and com-
"passion, the figure of Him who was once a child
"Himself, and a poor one. But alas! reckoning
Appeal for
sick children.
"up the number of beds that are there, the visitor
"to this Child's Hospital will find himself perforce
"obliged to stop at very little over thirty; and

"will learn, with sorrow and surprise, that even
"that small number, so forlornly, so miserably
"diminutive compared with this vast London,
"cannot possibly be maintained unless the Hos-
"pital be made better known. I limit myself to
"saying better known, because I will not believe
"that in a Christian community of fathers and
"mothers, and brothers and sisters, it can fail,
"being better known, to be well and richly en-
"dowed." It was a brave and true prediction. The
Child's Hospital has never since known want.
That night alone added greatly more than three
thousand pounds to its funds, and Dickens put
the crown to his good work by reading on its
behalf, shortly afterwards, his *Christmas Carol;*
when the sum realized, and the urgent demand
that followed for a repetition of the pleasure given
by the reading, bore down farther opposition to
the project of his engaging publicly in such readings for himself.

The Child's Hospital night was the 9th of
February, its Reading was appointed for the 15th
of April, and, nearly a month before, renewed
efforts at remonstrance had been made. "Your
"view of the reading matter," Dickens replied,
"I still think is unconsciously taken from your
"own particular point. You don't seem to me to
"get out of yourself in considering it. A word more
"upon it. You are not to think I have made up
"my mind. If I had, why should I not say so?
"I find very great difficulty in doing so because
"of what you urge, because I know the question
"to be a balance of doubts, and because I most

London:
1858.

Reasons for
and against
paid readings.

A proposal
from Mr.
Beale.

"honestly feel in my innermost heart, in this
"matter (as in all others for years and years), the
"honour of the calling by which I have always
"stood most conscientiously. But do you quite
"consider that the public exhibition of oneself
"takes place equally, whosoever may get the
"money? And have you any idea that at this
"moment—this very time—half the public at least
"supposes me to be paid? My dear F, out of
"the twenty or five-and-twenty letters a week that
"I get about Readings, twenty will ask at what
"price, or on what terms, it can be done. The
"only exceptions, in truth, are when the cor-
"respondent is a clergyman, or a banker, or the
"member for the place in question. Why, at this
"very time half Scotland believes that I am paid
"for going to Edinburgh!—Here is Greenock writes
"to me, and asks could it be done for a hundred
"pounds? There is Aberdeen writes, and states
"the capacity of its hall, and says, though far less
"profitable than the very large hall in Edinburgh,
"is it not enough to come on for? W. answers
"such letters continually. (—At this place, enter
"Beale. He called here yesterday morning, and
"then wrote to ask if I would see him to-day. I
"replied 'Yes,' so here he came in. With long
"preface called to know whether it was possible
"to arrange anything in the way of Readings for
"this autumn—say, six months. Large capital at
"command. Could produce partners, in such an
"enterprise, also with large capital. Represented
"such. Returns would be enormous. Would I
"name a sum? a minimum sum that I required

"to have, in any case? Would I look at it as a LONDON: 1856.
"Fortune, and in no other point of view? I shook ————
"my head, and said, my tongue was tied on the
"subject for the present; I might be more com-
"municative at another time.   Exit Beale in con-
"fusion and disappointment.)—You will be happy
"to hear that at one on Friday, the Lord Provost,
"Dean of Guild, Magistrates, and Council of the
"ancient city of Edinburgh will wait (in pro-
"cession) on their brother freeman, at the Music II. 67.
"Hall, to give him hospitable welcome.   Their
"brother freeman has been cursing their stars and
"his own, ever since the receipt of solemn notifica-
"tion to this effect."   But very grateful, when it
came, was the enthusiasm of the greeting, and
welcome the gift of the silver wassail-bowl which
followed the reading of the *Carol*. "I had no Edinburgh
"opportunity of asking any one's advice in Edin- gift.
"burgh," he wrote on his return. "The crowd
"was too enormous, and the excitement in it much
"too great. But my determination is all but taken.
"I must do *something*, or I shall wear my heart
"away.   I can see no better thing to do that is
"half so hopeful in itself, or half so well suited
"to my restless state."

What is pointed at in those last words had Nearer and
been taken as a ground of objection, and thus he nearer.
turned it into an argument the other way. During
all these months many sorrowful misunderstand-
ings had continued in his home, and the relief
sought from the misery had but the effect of
making desperate any hope of a better understanding. "It becomes necessary," he wrote at

13*

Question of
the Plunge.

the end of March, "with a view to the arrange-
"ments that would have to be begun next month
"if I decided on the Readings, to consider and
"settle the question of the Plunge. Quite dismiss
"from your mind any reference whatever to present
"circumstances at home. Nothing can put *them*
"right, until we are all dead and buried and risen.
"It is not, with me, a matter of will, or trial, or
"sufferance, or good humour, or making the best
"of it, or making the worst of it, any longer. It
"is all despairingly over. Have no lingering
"hope of, or for, me in this association. A dismal
"failure has to be borne, and there an end. Will
"you then try to think of this reading project (as
"I do) apart from all personal likings and dis-
"likings, and solely with a view to its effect on
"that peculiar relation (personally affectionate,
"and like no other man's) which subsists between
"me and the public? I want your most careful
"consideration. If you would like, when you
"have gone over it in your mind, to discuss the
"matter with me and Arthur Smith (who would
"manage the whole of the Business, which I
"should never touch); we will make an appoint-
"ment. But I ought to add that Arthur Smith

Doubt and
no doubt.

"plainly says, 'Of the immense return in money,
"'I have no doubt. Of the Dash into the new
"'position, however, I am not so good a judge.'
"I enclose you a rough note* of my project, as
"it stands in my mind."

* Here is the rough note: in which the reader will be interested to
observe the limits originally placed to the proposal. The first Readings
were to comprise only the *Carol*, and for others a new story was to be
written. He had not yet the full confidence in his power or versatility

Mr. Arthur Smith, a man possessed of many
qualities that justified the confidence Dickens
placed in him, might not have been a good judge
of the "Dash" into the new position, but no man
knew better every disadvantage incident to it, or
was less likely to be disconcerted by any. His
exact fitness to manage the scheme successfully,
made him an unsafe counsellor respecting it.
Within a week from this time the reading for the
Charity was to be given. "They have let," Dickens
wrote on the 9th of April, "five hundred stalls for
"the Hospital night; and as people come every
"day for more, and it is out of the question to
"make more, they cannot be restrained at St.
"Martin's Hall from taking down names for other
"Readings." This closed the attempt at further

London:
1858.

Mr. Arthur
Smith.

Child's
Hospital
reading.

as an actor which subsequent experience gave him. "I propose to an-
"nounce in a short and plain advertisement (what is quite true) that I
"cannot so much as answer the numerous applications that are made to
"me to read, and that compliance with ever so few of them is, in any
"reason, impossible. That I have therefore resolved upon a course of
"readings of the *Christmas Carol* both in town and country, and that
"those in London will take place at St. Martin's Hall on certain even-
"ings. Those evenings will be either four or six Thursdays, in May
"and the beginning of June . . . I propose an Autumn Tour, for the
"country, extending through August, September, and October. It would
"comprise the Eastern Counties, the West, Lancashire, Yorkshire, and
"Scotland. I should read from 35 to 40 times in this tour, at the least.
"At each place where there was a great success, I would myself an-
"nounce that I should come back, on the turn of Christmas, to read a
"new Christmas story written for that purpose. This story I should first
"read a certain number of times in London. I have the strongest belief
"that by April in next year, a very large sum of money indeed would
"be gained by these means. Ireland would be still untouched, and I
"conceive America alone (if I could resolve to go there) to be worth Ten
"Thousand Pounds. In all these proceedings, the Business would be
"wholly detached from me, and I should never appear in it. I would
"have an office, belonging to the Readings and to nothing else, opened
"in London; I would have the advertisements emanating from it, and
"also signed by some one belonging to it; and they should always men-
"tion me as a third person—just as the Child's Hospital, for instance, in
"addressing the public, mentions me."

First rough
note as to
readings.

objection. Exactly a fortnight after the reading
for the children's hospital, on Thursday the
29th April, came the first public reading for his
own benefit; and before the next month was over,
this launch into a new life had been followed by
a change in his old home. Thenceforward he

and his wife lived apart. The eldest son went
with his mother, Dickens at once giving effect to
her expressed wish in this respect; and the other
children remained with himself, their intercourse
with Mrs. Dickens being left entirely to themselves. It was thus far an arrangement of a
strictly private nature, and no decent person
could have had excuse for regarding it in any
other light, if public attention had not been unexpectedly invited to it by a printed statement in

Household Words. Dickens was stung into this
by some miserable gossip at which in ordinary
circumstances no man would more determinedly
have been silent; but he had now publicly to
show himself, at stated times, as a public enter-
tainer, and this, with his name even so aspersed,
he found to be impossible. All he would con-
cede to my strenuous resistance against such a
publication, was an offer to suppress it, if, upon
reference to the opinion of a certain distinguished
man (still living), that opinion should prove to be
in agreement with mine. Unhappily it fell in

with his own, and the publication went on. It
was followed by another statement, a letter subscribed with his name, which got into print without his sanction; nothing publicly being known
of it (I was not among those who had read it

privately) until it appeared in the *New York*
Tribune. It had been addressed and given to
Mr. Arthur Smith as an authority for correction
of false rumours and scandals, and Mr. Smith
had given a copy of it, with like intention, to the
Tribune correspondent in London. Its writer
referred to it always afterwards as his "violated
letter."

The course taken by the author of this book
at the time of these occurrences, will not be departed from here. Such illustration of grave defects in Dickens's character as the passage in his
life affords, I have not shrunk from placing side
by side with such excuses in regard to it as he
had unquestionable right to claim should be put
forward also. How far what remained of his What alone
concerned
story took tone or colour from it, and especially the public.
from the altered career on which at the same
time he entered, will thus be sufficiently explained; and with anything else the public have
nothing to do.

CHAPTER LII.

GADSHILL PLACE.

1856-1870.

Gadshill ·
Place:
1856-70.

"I WAS better pleased with Gadshill Place last "Saturday," he wrote to me from Paris on the 13th of February 1856, "on going down there, "even than I had prepared myself to be. The "country, against every disadvantage of season, is "beautiful; and the house is so old fashioned,

First descrip-
tion of it.

"cheerful, and comfortable, that it is really pleasant "to look at. The good old Rector now there, has "lived in it six and twenty years, so I have not "the heart to turn him out. He is to remain till "Lady-Day next year, when I shall go in, please "God; make my alterations; furnish the house; "and keep it for myself that summer." Returning to England through the Kentish country with Mr. Wilkie Collins in July, other advantages occurred to him. "A railroad opened from Rochester to

Expected
advantages.

"Maidstone, which connects Gadshill at once "with the whole sea coast, is certainly an addi-"tion to the place, and an enhancement of its "value. Bye and bye we shall have the London, "Chatham and Dover, too; and that will bring it "within an hour of Canterbury and an hour and "a half of Dover. I am glad to hear of your hav-"ing been in the neighbourhood. There is no

The Porch at Gadshill.

GADSHILL
PLACE:
1856-70.
"healthier (marshes avoided), and none in my. "eyes more beautiful. One of these days I shall "show you some places up the Medway with "which you will be charmed."

The association with his youthful fancy that first made the place attractive to him has been told; and it was with wonder he had heard one day, from his friend and fellow worker at *Household Words*, Mr. W. H. Wills, that not only was Odd chances.
I. 24-7. the house for sale to which he had so often looked wistfully, but that the lady chiefly interested as its owner had been long known and much esteemed by himself. Such curious chances led Dickens to his saying about the smallness of the world; but the close relation often found thus existing between things and persons far apart, I. 16c. suggests not so much the smallness of the world as the possible importance of the least things done in it, and is better explained by the grander teaching of Carlyle, that causes and effects, connecting every man and thing with every other, extend through all space and time.

It was at the close of 1855 the negociation for its purchase began. "They wouldn't," he wrote (25th of November), "take £1700 for the Gads-"hill property, but 'finally' wanted £1800. I Negociations
for purchase. "have finally offered £1750. It will require an "expenditure of about £300 more before yield-"ing £100 a year." The usual discovery of course awaited him that this first estimate would have to be increased threefold. "The changes "absolutely necessary" (9th of February 1856) "will take a thousand pounds; which sum I am

"always resolving to squeeze out of this, grind
"out of that, and wring out of the other; this,
"that, and the other generally all three declining
"to come up to the scratch for the purpose."
"This day,"* he wrote on the 14th of March, "I
"have paid the purchase money for Gadshill
"Place. After drawing the cheque (£1790) I
"turned round to give it to Wills, and said,
"'Now isn't it an extraordinary thing—look at
"'the Day—Friday! I have been nearly drawing
"'it half a dozen times when the lawyers have
"'not been ready, and here it comes round upon
"'a Friday as a matter of course.'" He had no
thought at this time of reserving the place wholly
for himself, or of making it his own residence
except at intervals of summer. He looked upon
it as an investment only. "You will hardly know
"Gadshill again," he wrote in January 1858, "I
"am improving it so much—yet I have no interest
"in the place." But continued ownership brought
increased liking; he took more and more interest
in his own improvements, which were just the
kind of occasional occupation and resource his
life most wanted in its next seven or eight years;
and any farther idea of letting it he soon abandoned altogether. It only once passed out of
his possession thus, for four months in 1859; in
the following year, on the sale of Tavistock
House, he transferred to it his books and pictures and choicer furniture; and thenceforward,

---

* On New Year's Day he had written from Paris. "When in Lon-
"don Coutts's advised me not to sell out the money for Gadshill Place
"(the title of my estate sir, my place down in Kent) until the convey-
"ance was settled and ready."

GADSHILL
PLACE:
1856-70.
Becomes his
home in 1859.
varied only by houses taken from time to time
for the London season, he made it his permanent
family abode.   Now and then, even during those
years, he would talk of selling it; and on his last
return from America, when he had sent the last
of his sons out into the world, he really might
have sold it if he could then have found a house
in London suitable to him, and such as he could
purchase.   But in this he failed; secretly to his
own satisfaction, as I believe; and thereupon, in
that last autumn of his life, he projected and car-
Improve-
ments and
additions.
ried out his most costly addition to Gadshill.   Already of course more money had been spent
upon it than his first intention in buying it would
have justified.   He had so enlarged the accommodation, improved the grounds and offices, and
added to the land, that, taking also into account
this final outlay, the reserved price placed upon
the whole after his death more than quadrupled
what he had given in 1856 for the house, shrubbery, and twenty years' lease of a meadow field.
It was then purchased, and is now inhabited, by
his eldest son.

I. 21-5.
Its position has been described, and one of
the last-century-histories of Rochester quaintly
mentions the principal interest of the locality.
"Near the twenty-seventh stone from London is
"Gadshill, supposed to have been the scene of
Gadshill a
century ago.
"the robbery mentioned by Shakespeare in his
"play of Henry IV; there being reason to think
"also that it was Sir John Fallstaff, of truly comic
"memory, who under the name of Oldcastle in-
"habited Cooling Castle of which the ruins are

"in the neighbourhood. A small distance to the
"left appears on an eminence the Hermitage, the
"seat of the late Sir Francis Head, Bart;* and
"close to the road, on a small ascent, is a neat
"building lately erected by Mr. Day. In descend-
"ing Strood-hill is a fine prospect of Strood,
"Rochester, and Chatham, which three towns form
"a continued street extending above two miles in
"length." It had been supposed** that "the neat
"building lately erected by Mr. Day" was that
which the great novelist made famous; but Gadshill Place had no existence until eight years after
the date of the history. The good rector who so
long lived in it told me, in 1859, that it had
been built eighty years before by a then well-
known character in those parts, one Stevens,
father-in-law of Henslow the Cambridge professor
of botany. Stevens, who could only with much
difficulty manage to write his name, had begun
life as ostler at an inn; had become husband to
the landlord's widow; then a brewer; and finally,
as he subscribed himself on one occasion, "mare"
of Rochester. Afterwards the house was inhabited
by Mr. Lynn (from some of the members of whose
family Dickens made his purchase); and, before
the Rev. Mr. Hindle became its tenant, it was
inhabited by a Macaroni parson named Town-

---

* Two houses now stand on what was Sir Francis Head's estate, the
Great and Little Hermitage, occupied respectively by Mr. Malleson and
Mr. Hulkes, who became intimate with Dickens. Perry of the *Morning
Chronicle*, whose town house was in that court out of Tavistock-square
of which Tavistock House formed part, had occupied the Great Hermi-
tage previously.

** By the obliging correspondent who sent me this *History of Rochester*, 8vo. (Rochester, 1772), p. 302.

Gadshill
Place:
1856-70.
shend, whose horses the Prince Regent bought, throwing into the bargain a box of much desired cigars. Altogether the place had notable associations even apart from those which have connected it with the masterpieces of English humour. "This House, Gadshill Place, stands on the "summit of Shakespeare's Gadshill, ever meGreeting to
visitors."morable for its association with Sir John Falstaff "in his noble fancy. *But, my lads, my lads, to-* "*morrow morning, by four o'clock, early at Gads-* "*hill! there are pilgrims going to Canterbury* "*with rich offerings, and traders riding to London* "*with fat purses: I have vizards for you all; you* "*have horses for yourselves.*" Illuminated by Mr. Owen Jones, and placed in a frame on the first-floor landing, these words were the greeting of the new tenant to his visitors. It was his first act of ownership.

All his improvements, it should perhaps be remarked, were not exclusively matters of choice; and to illustrate by his letters what befell at the beginning of his changes, will show what attended them to the close. His earliest difficulty was very grave. There was only one spring of water for gentlefolk and villagers, and from some of the houses or cottages it was two miles away. "We Deficient
water-supply."are still" (6th of July) "boring for water here, "at the rate of two pounds per day for wages. "The men seem to like it very much, and to be "perfectly comfortable." Another of his earliest experiences (5th of September) was thus expressed: "Hop-picking is going on, and people sleep in "the garden, and breathe in at the keyhole of the

"house door. I have been amazed, before this
"year, by the number of miserable lean wretches,
"hardly able to crawl, who go hop-picking. I
"find it is a superstition that the dust of the
"newly picked hop, falling freshly into the throat,
"is a cure for consumption. So the poor creatures
"drag themselves along the roads, and sleep
"under wet hedges, and get cured soon and
"finally." Towards the close of the same month
(24th of September) he wrote: "Here are six men
"perpetually going up and down the well (I know
"that somebody will be killed), in the course of
"fitting a pump; which is quite a railway ter-
"minus—it is so iron, and so big. The process
"is much more like putting Oxford-street end-
"wise, and laying gas along it, than anything else.
"By the time it is finished, the cost of this water
"will be something absolutely frightful. But of
"course it proportionately increases the value of
"the property, and that's my only comfort... The
"horse has gone lame from a sprain, the big dog
"has run a tenpenny nail into one of his hind
"feet, the bolts have all flown out of the basket-
"carriage, and the gardener says all the fruit
"trees want replacing with new ones." Another
note came in three days. "I have discovered
"that the seven miles between Maidstone and
"Rochester is one of the most beautiful walks in
"England. Five men have been looking atten-
"tively at the pump for a week, and (I should
"hope) may begin to fit it in the course of Octo-
"ber." . .

With even such varying fortune he effected

GADSHILL
PLACE:
1856-70.
other changes.* The exterior remained to the
last much as it was when he used as a boy to
see it first; a plain, old-fashioned, two-story, brick-
built country house, with a bell-turret on the roof,
and over the front door a quaint neat wooden
porch with pillars and seats. But, among his
additions and alterations, was a new drawing-
room built out from the smaller existing one,
both being thrown together ultimately; two good
bedrooms built on a third floor at the back; and
Gradual
additions.
such re-arrangement of the ground floor as, besides its handsome drawing-room, and its dining-
room which he hung with pictures, transformed
its bedroom into a study which he lined with
books and sometimes wrote in, and changed its
breakfast-parlour into a retreat fitted up for
smokers into which he put a small billiard-table.
These several rooms opened from a hall having
in it a series of Hogarth prints, until, after the
artist's death, Stanfield's noble scenes were placed
there, when the Hogarths were moved to his
bedroom; and in this hall, during his last absence in America, a parquet floor was laid down.
Later
changes.
Nor did he omit such changes as might increase
the comfort of his servants. He built entirely
new offices and stables, and replaced a very old
coach-house by a capital servants' hall, trans-
forming the loft above into a commodious school-

---

* "As to the carpenters," he wrote to his daughter in September
1860, "they are absolutely maddening. They are always at work yet
"never seem to do anything. L. was down on Friday, and said
"(with his eye fixed on Maidstone and rubbing his hands to conciliate
"his moody employer) that 'he didn't think there would be very
"'much left to do after Saturday the 29th.' I didn't throw him out of
"window."

room or study for his boys. He made at the
same time an excellent croquet-ground out of a
waste piece of orchard.

Belonging to the house, but unfortunately
placed on the other side of the high road, was a
shrubbery, well wooded though in desolate condition, in which stood two magnificent cedars;
and having obtained, in 1859, the consent of the
local authorities for the necessary underground
work, Dickens constructed a passage beneath the
road* from his front lawn; and in the shrubbery
thus rendered accessible, and which he then laid
out very prettily, he placed afterwards a Swiss
châlet** presented to him by Mr. Fechter, which
arrived from Paris in ninety-four pieces fitting
like the joints of a puzzle, but which proved to
be somewhat costly in setting on its legs by
means of a foundation of brickwork. Once up,
however, it was a great resource in the summer
months, and much of Dickens's work was done
there. "I have put five mirrors in the châlet
"where I write," *** he told an American friend,

---

* A passage in his paper on Tramps embodies very amusingly experience recorded in his letters of this brick-work tunnel and the sinking
of the well; but I can only borrow one sentence. "The current of my
"uncommercial pursuits caused me only last summer to want a little
"body of workmen for a certain spell of work in a pleasant part of the
"country; and I was at one time honoured with the attendance of as
"many as seven-and-twenty, who were looking at six." Bits of wonderful observation are in that paper.

** This was at the beginning of 1865. "The chalet," he wrote to me
on the 7th of January, "is going on excellently, though the ornamental
"part is more slowly put together than the substantial. It will really be
"a very pretty thing; and in the summer (supposing it not to be blown
"away in the spring), the upper room will make a charming study. It
"is much higher than we supposed."

*** As surely, however, as he did any work there, so surely his in-
dispensable little accompaniments of work (III. 263) were carried along
with him; and of these I will quote what was written shortly after his

GADSHILL
PLACE:
1856-70.

"and they reflect and refract, in all kinds of "ways, the leaves that are quivering at the win-"dows, and the great fields of waving corn, and

In the châlet.

"the sail-dotted river. My room is up among "the branches of the trees; and the birds and the "butterflies fly in and out, and the green branches "shoot in at the open windows, and the lights "and shadows of the clouds come and go with "the rest of the company. The scent of the "flowers, and indeed of everything that is grow-"ing for miles and miles, is most delicious." He used to make great boast, too, not only of his crowds of singing birds all day, but of his night-ingales at night.

death by his son-in-law, Mr. Charles Collins, to illustrate a very touching sketch by Mr. Fildes of his writing-desk and vacant chair. "Ranged "in front of, and round about him, were always a variety of objects for "his eye to rest on in the intervals of actual writing, and any one of "which he would have instantly missed had it been removed. There "was a French bronze group representing a duel with swords, fought by "a couple of very fat toads, one of them (characterised by that particular "buoyancy which belongs to corpulence) in the act of making a pro-"digious lunge forward, which the other receives in the very middle of "his digestive apparatus, and under the influence of which it seems "likely that he will satisfy the wounded honour of his opponent by

Dickens's
writing-table.

"promptly expiring. There was another bronze figure which always "stood near the toads, also of French manufacture, and also full of "comic suggestion. It was a statuette of a dog-fancier, such a one as "you used to see on the bridges or quays of Paris, with a profusion of "little dogs stuck under his arms and into his pockets, and everywhere "where little dogs could possibly be insinuated, all for sale, and all, as "even a casual glance at the vendor's exterior would convince the most "unsuspicious person, with some screw loose in their physical constitu-"tions or moral natures, to be discovered immediately after purchase. "There was the long gilt leaf with the rabbit sitting erect upon its "haunches, the huge paper-knife often held in his hand during his "public readings, and the little fresh green cup ornamented with "the leaves and blossoms of the cowslip, in which a few fresh flowers "were always placed every morning—for Dickens invariably worked "with flowers on his writing-table. There was also the register of the "day of the week and of the month, which stood always before him; and "when the room in the châlet in which he wrote his last paragraph was "opened, some time after his death, the first thing to be noticed by "those who entered was this register, set at "Wednesday, June 8"—the "day of his seizure." It remains to this day as it was found.

One or two more extracts from letters having reference to these changes may show something of the interest to him with which Gadshill thus

The Chalet: presented by Mr. Fechter.

grew under his hands. A sun-dial on his back-lawn had a bit of historic interest about it. "One "of the balustrades of the destroyed old Roches-"ter bridge," he wrote to his daughter in June

1859, "has been (very nicely) presented to me
"by the contractors for the works, and has been
"duly stone-masoned and set up on the lawn be-
"hind the house. I have ordered a sun-dial for
"the top of it, and it will be a very good object
"indeed." "When you come down here next
"month," he wrote to me, "we have an idea that
"we shall show you rather a neat house. What
"terrific adventures have been in action; how
"many overladen vans were knocked up at
"Gravesend, and had to be dragged out of
"Chalk-turnpike in the dead of the night by the
"whole equine power of this establishment; shall
"be revealed at another time." That was in the
autumn of 1860, when, on the sale of his London house, its contents were transferred to his
country home. "I shall have an alteration or two
"to show you at Gadshill that greatly improve
"the little property; and when I get the workmen
"out this time, I think I'll leave off." October
1861 had now come, when the new bedrooms
were built; but in the same month of 1863 he
announced his transformation of the old coach-
house. "I shall have a small new improvement
"to show you at Gads, which I think you will
"accept as the crowning ingenuity of the in-
"imitable." But of course it was not over yet.
"My small work and planting," he wrote in the
spring of 1866, "really, truly, and positively the
"last, are nearly at an end in these regions, and
"the result will await summer inspection." No,
nor even yet. He afterwards obtained, by exchange of some land with the trustees of Watts's

Charity, the much coveted meadow at the back
of the house of which heretofore he had the lease
only; and he was then able to plant a number of
young limes and chestnuts and other quick-grow-
ing trees. He had already planted a row of limes
in front. He had no idea, he would say, of
planting only for the benefit of posterity, but
would put into the ground what he might himself enjoy the sight and shade of. He put them
in two or three clumps in the meadow, and in a
belt all round.

Still there were "more last words," for the
limit was only to be set by his last year of life.
On abandoning his notion, after the American
Readings, of exchanging Gadshill for London, a
new staircase was put up from the hall; a parquet
floor laid on the first landing; and a conservatory
built, opening into both drawing-room and dining-
room, "glass and iron," as he described it, "bril-
"liant but expensive, with foundations as of an
"ancient Roman work of horrible solidity." This
last addition had long been an object of desire
with him; though he would hardly even now
have given himself the indulgence but for the
golden shower from America. He saw it first in
a completed state on the Sunday before his death,
when his younger daughter was on a visit to
him. "Well, Katey," he said to her, "now you
"see POSITIVELY the last improvement at Gads-
"hill;" and everyone laughed at the joke against
himself. The success of the new conservatory
was unquestionable. It was the remark of all
around him that he was certainly, from this last
of all improvements, drawing more enjoyment

than from any of its predecessors, when the scene for ever closed.

Of the course of his daily life in the country

House and
conservatory:
from the
meadow.

there is not much to be said. Perhaps there was never a man who changed places so much and habits so little. He was always methodical and regular; and passed his life from day to day, divided for the most part between working and

Course of
daily life.

walking, the same wherever he was. The only
exception was when special or infrequent visitors
were with him. When such friends as Longfellow and his daughters, or Charles Eliot Norton
and his wife, came, or when Mr. Fields brought
his wife and Professor Lowell's daughter, or when
he received other Americans to whom he owed
special courtesy, he would compress into infinitely
few days an enormous amount of sight seeing and
country enjoyment, castles, cathedrals, and fortified
lines, lunches and picnics among cherry orchards
and hop-gardens, excursions to Canterbury or
Maidstone and their beautiful neighbourhoods,
Druid-stone and Blue Bell Hill. "All the neigh-
"bouring country that could be shown in so short
"a time," he wrote of the Longfellow visit, "they
"saw. I turned out a couple of postilions in the
"old red jackets of the old red royal Dover road
"for our ride, and it was like a holiday ride in
"England fifty years ago." For Lord Lytton he
did the same, for the Emerson Tennents, for Mr.
Layard and Mr. Helps, for Lady Molesworth and
the Higginses (Jacob Omnium), and such other
less frequent visitors.

Excepting on such particular occasions however, and not always even then, his mornings
were reserved wholly to himself; and he would
generally preface his morning work (such was
his love of order in everything around him) by
seeing that all was in its place in the several
rooms, visiting also the dogs, stables, and kitchen
garden, and closing, unless the weather was very
bad indeed, with a turn or two round the meadow before settling to his desk. His dogs were

a great enjoyment to him;* and, with his high
road traversed as frequently as any in England
by tramps and wayfarers of a singularly unde-
sirable description, they were also a necessity.

There were always two, of the mastiff kind, but
latterly the number increased. His own favourite
was Turk, a noble animal, full of affection and
intelligence, whose death by a railway-accident,
shortly after the Staplehurst catastrophe, caused
him great grief. Turk's sole companion up to

that date was Linda, puppy of a great St. Bernard brought over by Mr. Albert Smith, and
grown into a superbly beautiful creature. After

Turk there was an interval of an Irish dog, Sultan, given by Mr. Percy Fitzgerald; a cross between a St. Bernard and a bloodhound, built and
coloured like a lioness and of splendid proportions, but of such indomitably aggressive propen-
sities, that, after breaking his kennel-chain and

---

* Dickens's interest in dogs (as in the habits and ways of all animals)
was inexhaustible, and he welcomed with delight any new trait. The
subjoined, told him by a lady friend, was a great acquisition. "I must
"close" (14th of May 1867) " with an odd story of a Newfoundland dog.
"An immense black good-humoured Newfoundland dog. He came from
"Oxford and had lived all his life at a brewery. Instructions were given
"with him that if he were let out every morning alone, he would im-
"mediately find out the river; regularly take a swim; and gravely come
"home again. This he did with the greatest punctuality, but after a
"little while was observed to smell of beer. She was so sure that he
"smelt of beer that she resolved to watch him. Accordingly, he was
"seen to come back from his swim, round the usual corner, and to go up
"a flight of steps into a beer-shop. Being instantly followed, the beer-
"shop-keeper is seen to take down a pot (pewter pot), and is heard to
"say: 'Well, old chap! Come for your beer as usual, have you?'
"Upon which he draws a pint and puts it down, and the dog drinks it.
"Being required to explain how this comes to pass, the man says, 'Yes
"'ma'am. I know he's your dog ma'am, but I didn't when he first
"'come. He looked in ma'am as a Brickmaker might and then he
"'come in—as a Brickmaker might—and he wagged his tail at the pots,
"'and he giv' a sniff round, and conveyed to me as he was used to beer.
"'So I draw'd him a drop, and he drunk it up. Next morning he come
"'agen by the clock and I drawed him a pint, and ever since he has
"'took his pint reglar.'"

waiting Room ? No

" office ? No

" Read ... Town ? Yes

" her from China ? Yes

" drive ? Y/2

" ... ? Y/0

Family and her daughters ?

Working families and their story.

People to meet and part as travellers do, and
carry on ... between them in the story, not ...
other ... but ... worked out as in life —
... if and their not putting of them by
... of others. Details and every time

to face p. 155.

nearly devouring a luckless little sister of one of
the servants, he had to be killed. Dickens always protested that Sultan was a Fenian, for that
no dog, not a secretly sworn member of that
body, would ever have made such a point, muz-
zled as he was, of rushing at and bearing down
with fury anything in scarlet with the remotest
resemblance to a British uniform. Sultan's successor was Don, presented by Mr. Frederic Lehmann, a grand Newfoundland brought over very
young, who with Linda became parent to a
couple of Newfoundlands, that were still gambol-
ling about their master, huge, though hardly out
of puppydom, when they lost him. He had given
to one of them the name of Bumble, from having
observed, as he described it, "a peculiarly pom-
"pous and overbearing manner he had of appear-
"ing to mount guard over the yard when he was
"an absolute infant." Bumble was often in
scrapes. Describing to Mr. Fields a drought in
the summer of 1868, when their poor supply of
ponds and surface wells had become waterless,
he wrote: "I do not let the great dogs swim in
"the canal, because the people have to drink of
"it. But when they get into the Medway, it is
"hard to get them out again. The other day
"Bumble (the son, Newfoundland dog) got into
"difficulties among some floating timber, and be-
"came frightened. Don (the father) was standing
"by me, shaking off the wet and looking on care-
"lessly, when all of a sudden he perceived some-
"thing amiss, and went in with a bound and
"brought Bumble out by the ear. The scientific
"way in which he towed him along was charm-

"ing." The description of his own reception, on his reappearance after America, by Bumble and his brother, by the big and beautiful Linda, and by his daughter Mary's handsome little Pomeranian, may be added from his letters to the same

correspondent. "The two Newfoundland dogs "coming to meet me, with the usual carriage and "the usual driver, and beholding me coming in my "usual dress out at the usual door, it struck me that "their recollection of my having been absent for "any unusual time was at once cancelled. They "behaved (they are both young dogs) exactly in "their usual manner; coming behind the basket "phaeton as we trotted along, and lifting their

"heads to have their ears pulled, a special at- "tention which they receive from no one else. "But when I drove into the stable-yard, Linda "(the St. Bernard) was greatly excited; weeping "profusely, and throwing herself on her back that "she might caress my foot with her great fore- "paws. Mary's little dog too, Mrs. Bouncer,

"barked in the greatest agitation on being called "down and asked by Mary, 'Who is this?' and "tore round and round me like the dog in the "Faust outlines." The father and mother and their two sons, four formidable-looking companions, were with him generally in his later walks.

Round Cobham, skirting the park and village, and passing the Leather Bottle famous in the page of *Pickwick*, was a favourite walk with Dickens. By Rochester and the Medway, to the Chatham Lines, was another. He would turn out of Rochester High-street through The Vines (where some old buildings, from one of which called

Restoration-house he took Satis-house for *Great Expectations*, had a curious attraction for him), would pass round by Fort Pitt, and coming back by Frindsbury would bring himself by some cross fields again into the high road. Or, taking the other side, he would walk through the marshes to Gravesend, return by Chalk Church, and stop always to have greeting with a comical old monk who for some incomprehensible reason sits carved in stone, cross-legged with a jovial pot, over the porch of that sacred edifice. To another drearier churchyard, itself forming part of the marshes beyond the Medway, he often took friends to show them the dozen small tombstones of various sizes adapted to the respective ages of a dozen small children of one family which he made part of his story of *Great Expectations*, though, with the reserves always necessary in copying nature not to overstep her modesty by copying too closely, he makes the number that appalled little Pip not more than half the reality. About the whole of this Cooling churchyard, indeed, and the neighbouring castle ruins, there was a weird strangeness that made it one of his attractive walks in the late year or winter, when from Higham he could get to it across country over the stubble fields; and, for a shorter summer walk, he was not less fond of going round the village of Shorne, and sitting on a hot afternoon in its pretty shaded churchyard. But on the whole, though Maidstone had also much that attracted him to its neighbourhood, the Cobham neighbourhood was certainly that which he had greatest pleasure in; and he would have taken oftener than he did the walk through Cobham park and woods, which was the last he enjoyed before life suddenly closed upon him, but that here he did not like his dogs to follow.

Don now has his home there with Lord Darnley, and Linda lies under one of the cedars at Gadshill.

The Study at Gadshill.

CHAPTER LIII.

FIRST PAID READINGS.

1858-1859.

DICKENS gave his paid public Readings suc-   London:
cessively, with not long intervals, at four several   1858-9.
dates; in 1858—59, in 1861—63, in 1866—67,
and in 1868—70; the first series under Mr.
Arthur Smith's management, the second under
Mr. Headland's, and the third and fourth, in
America as well as before and after it, under
that of Mr. George Dolby, who, excepting in Various
America, acted for the Messrs. Chappell. The manage-
references in the present chapter are to the first   ments.
series only.

It began with sixteen nights at St. Martin's
Hall, the first on the 29th of April, the last on
the 22nd of July, 1858;. and there was afterwards
a provincial tour of 87 readings, beginning at
Clifton on the 2nd of August, ending at Brighton
on the 13th of November, and taking in Ireland First series.
and Scotland as well as the principal English
cities: to which were added, in London, three
Christmas readings, three in January, with two in
the following month; and, in the provinces in
the month of October, fourteen, beginning at
Ipswich and Norwich, taking in Cambridge and
Oxford, and closing with Birmingham and Chel-

tenham.   The series had comprised altogether 125 Readings when it ended on the 27th of October, 1859; and without the touches of character and interest afforded by his letters written while thus employed, the picture of the man would not be complete.

One day's work.
Here was one day's work at the opening which will show something of the fatigue they involved even at their outset. "On Friday we "came from Shrewsbury to Chester; saw all right "for the evening; and then went to Liverpool. "Came back from Liverpool and read at Chester. "Left Chester at 11 at night, after the reading, "and went to London.   Got to Tavistock House "at 5 a.m. on Saturday, left it at a quarter past "10 that morning, and came down here" (Gadshill: 15th of August 1858).

The "greatest personal affection and respect" had greeted him everywhere.   Nothing could have been "more strongly marked or warmly ex-"pressed;" and the readings had "gone" quite wonderfully.   What in this respect had most impressed him, at the outset of his adventures, was
Exeter audience.
Exeter.   "I think they were the finest audience I "ever read to; I don't think I ever read in some "respects so well; and I never beheld anything "like the personal affection which they poured "out upon me at the end.   I shall always look "back upon it with pleasure."   He often lost his voice in these early days, having still to acquire the art of husbanding it; and in the trial to recover it would again waste its power.   "I think

"I sang half the Irish melodies to myself as I Ireland: 1858.
"walked about, to test it."

An audience of two thousand three hundred Liverpool.
people (the largest he had had) greeted him at
Liverpool on his way to Dublin, and, besides the
tickets sold, more than two hundred pounds in
money was taken at the doors. This taxed his
business staff a little. "They turned away hun-
"dreds, sold all the books, rolled on the ground
"of my room knee-deep in checks, and made a
"perfect pantomime of the whole thing." (20th
of August.) He had to repeat the reading
thrice.*

It was the first time he had seen Ireland, and Impressions of Dublin.
Dublin greatly surprised him by appearing to be
so much larger and more populous than he had
supposed. He found it to have altogether an
unexpectedly thriving look, being pretty nigh as
big, he first thought, as Paris; of which some
places in it, such as the quays on the river, re-
minded him. Half the first day he was there, he
took to explore it; walking till tired, and then
taking a car. "Power, dressed for the character
"of Teddy the Tiler, drove me: in a suit of
"patches, and with his hat unbrushed for twenty
"years. Wonderfully pleasant, light, intelligent,
"and careless."** The number of common people

---

* This was the *Carol* and *Pickwick.* "We are reduced some-
"times," he adds, "to a ludicrous state of distress by the quantity of
"silver we have to carry about. Arthur Smith is always accompanied
"by an immense black leather-bag full." Mr. Smith had an illness a
couple of days later, and Dickens whimsically describes his rapid recovery on discovering the state of their balances. "He is now sitting
"opposite to me on a bag of £40 of silver. It must be dreadfully
"hard."

** A letter to his eldest daughter (23rd of Aug.) makes humorous adhe saw in his drive, "also riding about in cars as "hard as they could split," brought to his recollection a more distant scene, and but for the dresses he could have thought himself on the Toledo at Naples.

The audience.

In respect of the number of his audience, and their reception of him, Dublin was one of his marked successes. He came to have some doubt of their capacity of receiving the pathetic, but of their quickness as to the humorous there could be no question, any more than of their heartiness. He got on wonderfully well with the Dublin people.* The Boots at Morrison's expressed the general feeling in a patriotic point of view. "He "was waiting for me at the hotel door last night.

Boots at
Morrison's.

Irish car-
driver.

dition. "The man who drove our jaunting car yesterday hadn't a piece "in his coat as big as a penny roll, and had had his hat on (apparently "without brushing it) ever since he was grown-up. But he was remark-"ably intelligent and agreeable, with something to say about everything. "For instance, when I asked him what a certain building was, he didn't "say 'Courts of Law' and nothing else, but 'Av yer plase Sir, its the foor "'Coorts o' looyers, where Misther O'Connell stood his trial wunst, as "'ye'll remimbir sir, afore I till ye ov it.' When we got into the Phœnix "Park, he looked round him as if it were his own, and said 'That's a "'Park sir, av ye plase!' I complimented it, and he said 'Gintlemen "'tills me as they iv bin, sir, over Europe and never see a Park aqualling "'ov it. Yander's the Vice-regal Lodge, sir; in thim two corners lives "'the two Sicretaries, wishing I was thim sir. There's air here sir, av "'yer plase! There's scenery here sir! There's mountains thim sir! "'Yer coonsider it a Park sir? It is that sir!'"

* The Irish girls outdid the American (ii. 239-40) in one particular. He wrote to his sister-in-law: "Every night, by the bye, since I have been "in Ireland, the ladies have beguiled John out of the bouquet from my "coat; and yesterday morning, as I had showered the leaves from my "geranium in reading Little Dombey, they mounted the platform after "I was gone, and picked them all up as a keepsake." A few days earlier he had written to the same correspondent: "The papers are full of re-"marks upon my white tie, and describe it as being of enormous size, "which is a wonderful delusion; because, as you very well know, it is a "small tie. Generally, I am happy to report, the Emerald press is in "favour of my appearance, and likes my eyes. But one gentleman "comes out with a letter at Cork, wherein he says that although only "46, I look like an old man."

Irish girls.

"'Whaat sart of a hoose sur?' he asked me.
"'Capital.' 'The Lard be praised fur the 'onor
"'o' Dooblin!'" Within the hotel, on getting up
next morning, he had a dialogue with a smaller
resident, landlord's son he supposed, a little boy
of the ripe age of six, which he presented, in his
letter to his sister-in-law, as a colloquy between
Old England and Young Ireland inadequately
reported for want of the "imitation" it required
for its full effect. "I am sitting on the sofa,
"writing, and find him sitting beside me.

"*Old England.* Halloa old chap.

"*Young Ireland.* Hal—loo!

"*Old England* (in his delightful way). What
"a nice old fellow you are. I am very fond of
"little boys.

"*Young Ireland.* Air yes? Ye'r right.

"*Old England.* What do you learn, old
"fellow?

"*Young Ireland* (very intent on Old England,
"and always childish except in his brogue). I
"lairn wureds of three sillibils—and wureds of
"two sillibils—and wureds of one sillibil.

"*Old England* (cheerfully). Get out, you
"humbug! You learn only words of one syl-
"lable.

"*Young Ireland* (laughs heartily). You may
"say that it is mostly wureds of one sillibil.

"*Old England.* Can you write?

"*Young Ireland.* Not yet. Things comes by
"deegrays.

"*Old England.* Can you cipher?

"*Young Ireland* (very quickly). Whaat's that?

"*Old England.* Can you make figures?

"*Young Ireland.* I can make a nought, which "is not asy, being roond.

"*Old England.* I say, old boy! Wasn't it "you I saw on Sunday morning in the Hall, "in a soldier's cap? You know!—In a soldier's "cap?

"*Young Ireland* (cogitating deeply). Was it "a very good cap?

"*Old England.* Yes.

"*Young Ireland.* Did it fit ankommon?

"*Old England.* Yes.

"*Young Ireland.* Dat was me!"

The last night in Dublin was an extraordinary scene. "You can hardly imagine it. All the "way from the hotel to the Rotunda (a mile), I "had to contend against the stream of people who "were turned away. When I got there, they had "broken the glass in the pay-boxes, and were "offering £5 freely for a stall. Half of my plat-"form had to be taken down, and people heaped "in among the ruins. You never saw such a "scene."* But he would not return after his other Irish engagements. "I have positively said "No. The work is too hard. It is not like doing "it in one easy room, and always the same room. "With a different place every night, and a differ-"ent audience with its own peculiarity every night,

"it is a tremendous strain . . . I seem to be always

---

* "They had offered frantic prices for stalls. Eleven bank-notes "were thrust into a payhox at one time for eleven stalls. Our men "were flattened against walls and squeezed against beams. Ladies stood "all night with their chins against my platform. Other ladies sat all "night upon my steps. We turned away people enough to make im-"mense houses for a week." Letter to his eldest daughter.

"either in a railway carriage or reading, or going
"to bed; and I get so knocked up whenever I
"have a minute to remember it, that then I go to
"bed as a matter of course."

Belfast he liked quite as much as Dublin in
another way. "A fine place with a rough people;
"everything looking prosperous; the railway ride
"from Dublin quite amazing in the order, neatness,
"and cleanness of all you see; every cottage look-
"ing as if it had been whitewashed the day be-
"fore; and many with charming gardens, prettily
"kept with bright flowers." The success, too,
was quite as great. "Enormous audiences. We
"turn away half the town.* I think them a better
"audience on the whole than Dublin; and the
"personal affection is something overwhelming. I
"wish you and the dear girls" (he is writing to
his sister-in-law) "could have seen the people look
"at me in the street; or heard them ask me, as I
"hurried to the hotel after the reading last night,
"to 'do me the honor to shake hands Misther
"'Dickens and God bless you sir; not ounly for
"'the light you've been to me this night, but for
"'the light you've been in mee house sir (and
"'God love your face!) this many a year!'"** He
had never seen men "go in to cry so undis-
"guisedly," as they did at the Belfast *Dombey*

---

* "Shillings get into stalls, and half-crowns get into shillings, and
"stalls get nowhere, and there is immense confusion." Letter to his
daughter.
** "I was brought very near to what I sometimes dream may be my
"Fame," he says in a letter of later date to myself from York, "when his Fame.
"a lady whose face I had never seen stopped me yesterday in the street,
"and said to me, *Mr. Dickens, will you let me touch the hand that has
"filled my house with many friends.*" October 1858.

reading; and as to the *Boots* and *Mrs. Gamp* "it "was just one roar with me and them. For they "made me laugh so, that sometimes I *could not* "compose my face to go on." His greatest trial in this way however was a little later at Harrogate—"the queerest place, with the strangest "people in it, leading the oddest lives of dancing, "newspaper-reading, and tables d'hôte"—where he noticed, at the same reading, embodiments respectively of the tears and laughter to which he has moved his fellow creatures so largely. "There "was one gentleman at the *Little Dombey* yesterday

Paul Dombey. "morning" (he is still writing to his sister-in-law) "who exhibited—or rather concealed—the pro- "foundest grief. After crying a good deal without "hiding it, he covered his face with both his "hands, and laid it down on the back of the seat "before him, and really shook with emotion. He "was not in mourning, but I supposed him to "have lost some child in old time . . . There was "a remarkably good fellow too, of thirty or "so, who found something so very ludicrous in "Toots that he *could not* compose himself at all, "but laughed until he sat wiping his eyes with "his handkerchief; and whenever he felt Toots "coming again, he began to laugh and wipe his

Mr. Toots. "eyes afresh; and when Toots came once more, "he gave a kind of cry, as if it were too much "for him. It was uncommonly droll, and made "me laugh heartily."

York. At Harrogate he read twice on one day (a Saturday), and had to engage a special engine to take him back that night to York, which, hav-

ing reached at one o'clock in the morning, he York:
1858.
had to leave, because of Sunday restrictions on
travel, the same morning at half-past four, to
enable him to fulfil a Monday's reading at Scar-
borough. Such fatigues became matters of course;
but their effect, not noted at the time, was grave.
"At York I had a most magnificent audience, and
"might have filled the place for a week. . . . I
"think the audience possessed of a better know-
"ledge of character than any I have seen. But I A knowing
audience.
"recollect Doctor Belcombe to have told me long
"ago that they first found out Charles Mathews's
"father, and to the last understood him (he used
"to say) better than any other people. . . The let
"is enormous for next Saturday at Manchester,
"stalls alone four hundred! I shall soon be able
"to send you the list of places to the 15th of
"November, the end. I shall be, O most heartily Cheering
prospect.
"glad, when that time comes! But I must say
"that the intelligence and warmth of the audiences
"are an immense sustainment, and one that
"always sets me up. Sometimes before I go
"down to read (especially when it is in the day),
"I am so oppressed by having to do it that I feel
"perfectly unequal to the task. But the people
"lift me out of this directly; and I find that I
"have quite forgotten everything but them and
"the book, in a quarter of an hour."
     The reception that awaited him at Manchester MANCHESTER.
had very special warmth in it, occasioned by an
adverse tone taken in the comment of one of the
Manchester daily papers on the letter which by
a breach of confidence had been then recently

MANCHESTER:
1858.
"Violated
"letter."
Ante, 198.
printed. "My violated letter" Dickens always called it. "When I came to Manchester on Sa-"turday I found seven hundred stalls taken! "When I went into the room at night 2500 people "had paid, and more were being turned away "from every door. The welcome they gave me "was astounding in its affectionate recognition of

Affectionate
greeting.
"the late trouble, and fairly for once unmanned "me. I never saw such a sight or heard such a "sound. When they had thoroughly done it, they "settled down to enjoy themselves; and certainly did "enjoy themselves most heartily to the last minute." Nor, for the rest of his English tour, in any of the towns that remained, had he reason to com- plain of any want of hearty greeting. At Sheffield great crowds came in excess of the places. At Leeds the hall overflowed in half an hour. At

Continued
successes.
Hull the vast concourse had to be addressed by Mr. Smith on the gallery stairs, and additional Readings had to be given, day and night, "for "the people out of town and for the people in "town."

The net profit to himself, thus far, had been upwards of three hundred pounds a week;* but

---

* "That is no doubt immense, our expenses being necessarily large, "and the travelling party being always five." Another source of profit was the sale of the copies of the several Readings prepared by himself. "Our people alone sell eight, ten, and twelve dozen a night." A later letter says: "The men with the reading books were sold out, for about "the twentieth time, at Manchester. Eleven dozen of the *Poor Tra-* "*veller, Boots,* and *Gamp* being sold in about ten minutes, they had no "more left; and Manchester became green with the little tracts, in every "bookshop, outside every omnibus, and passing along every street. "The sale of them, apart from us, must be very great." "Did I tell "you," he writes in another letter, "that the agents for our tickets who "are also booksellers, say very generally that the readings decidedly "increase the sale of the books they are taken from? We were "first told of this by a Mr. Parke, a wealthy old gentleman in a

Books of
Readings.

Mr. Parke
of Wolver-
hampton.

this was nothing to the success in Scotland, where Scotland;
1858.
his profit in a week, with all expenses paid, was
five hundred pounds. The pleasure was enhanced,
too, by the presence of his two daughters, who Joined by his
daughters.
had joined him over the Border. At first the look
of Edinburgh was not promising. "We began
"with, for us, a poor room. . . But the effect of
"that reading (it was the *Chimes*) was immense;
"and on the next night, for *Little Dombey*, we had
"a full room. It is our greatest triumph every-
"where. Next night *(Poor Traveller, Boots*, and
"*Gamp)* we turned away hundreds upon hundreds
"of people; and last night, for the *Carol*, in spite
"of advertisements in the morning that the tickets Scene at
Edinburgh.
"were gone, the people had to be got in through
"such a crowd as rendered it a work of the ut-
"most difficulty to keep an alley into the room.
"They were seated about me on the platform, put
"into the doorway of the waiting-room, squeezed
"into every conceivable place, and a multitude
"turned away once more. I think I am better
"pleased with what was done in Edinburgh than
"with what has been done anywhere, almost. It
"was so completely taken by storm, and carried
"in spite of itself. Mary and Katey have been
"infinitely pleased and interested with Edinburgh.
"We are just going to sit down to dinner and
"therefore I cut my missive short. Travelling,
"dinner, reading, and everything else, come crowd- Strange life.
"ing together into this strange life."

"very large way at Wolverhampton, who did all the business for love,
"and would not take a farthing. Since then, we have constantly come
"upon it; and M'Glashin and Gill at Dublin were very strong about it
"indeed."

Then came Dundee: "An odd place," he wrote, "like Wapping with high rugged hills be-"hind it. We had the strangest journey here—"bits of sea, and bits of railroad, alternately;"which carried my mind back to travelling in "America. The room is an immense new one, "belonging to Lord Kinnaird, and Lord Panmure, "and some others of that sort. It looks some-"thing between the Crystal-palace and Westminster-"hall (I can't imagine who wants it in this place), "and has never been tried yet for speaking in. "Quite disinterestedly of course, I hope it will "succeed." The people he thought, in respect of taste and intelligence, below any other of his Scotch audiences; but they woke up surprisingly, and the rest of his Caledonian tour was a succes- sion of triumphs. "At Aberdeen we were crammed "to the street, twice in one day. At Perth (where "I thought when I arrived, there literally could "be nobody to come) the gentlefolk came posting "in from thirty miles round, and the whole town "came besides, and filled an immense hall. They "were as full of perception, fire, and enthusiasm "as any people I have seen. At Glasgow, where "I read three evenings and one morning, we took "the prodigiously large sum of six hundred pounds! "And this at the Manchester prices, which are "lower than St. Martin's Hall. As to the effect—I "wish you could have seen them after Lilian died "in the *Chimes*, or when Scrooge woke in the "*Carol* and talked to the boy outside the window. "And at the end of *Dombey* yesterday afternoon, "in the cold light of day, they all got up, after

"a short pause, gentle and simple, and thundered
"and waved their hats with such astonishing hearti-
"ness and fondness that, for the first time in all
"my public career, they took me completely off
"my legs, and I saw the whole eighteen hundred
"of them reel to one side as if a shock from
"without had shaken the hall. Notwithstanding
"which, I must confess to you, I am very anxious
- "to get to the end of my Readings, and to be at
"home again, and able to sit down and think in
"my own study.   There has been only one thing
"quite without alloy. The dear girls have enjoyed
"themselves immensely, and their trip with me
"has been a great success."

The subjects of his readings during this first
circuit were the *Carol*, the *Chimes*, the *Trial in
Pickwick*, the chapters containing *Paul Dombey*,
Boots at the Holly Tree Inn, the *Poor Traveller*
(Captain Doubledick), and *Mrs. Gamp:* to which
he continued to restrict himself through the supplementary nights that closed in the autumn of
1859.*   Of these the most successful in their
uniform effect upon his audiences were undoubtedly the *Carol*, the *Pickwick* scene, *Mrs. Gamp*,
and the *Dombey*—the quickness, variety, and completeness of his assumption of character, having
greatest scope in these. Here, I think, more than
in the pathos or graver level passages, his strength

---

* The last of them were given immediately after his completion of
the *Tale of Two Cities:* "I am a little tired; but as little, I suspect, as
"any man could be with the work of the last four days, and perhaps the
"change of work was better than subsiding into rest and rust. The
"Norwich people were a noble audience. There, and at Ipswich and
"Bury, we had the demonstrativeness of the great working-towns, and a
"much finer perception."—14th of October 1859.

lay; but this is entitled to no weight other than as an individual opinion, and his audiences gave him many reasons for thinking differently.[*]

The incidents of the period covered by this chapter that had any general interest in them, claim to be mentioned briefly. At the close of 1857 he presided at the fourth anniversary of the Warehousemen and Clerks' Schools, describing and discriminating, with keenest wit and kindliest fun, the sort of schools he liked and he disliked. To the spring and summer of 1858 belongs the first collection of his writings into a succinct library form, each of the larger novels occupying two volumes. In March he paid warm public tribute to Thackeray (who had been induced to take the chair at the General Theatrical Fund) as one for whose genius he entertained the warmest admiration, who did honour to literature, and in whom literature was honoured. In May he presided at the Artists' Benevolent Fund dinner, and made striking appeal for that excellent charity. In July he took earnest part in the opening efforts on be- half of the Royal Dramatic College, which he supplemented later by a speech for the establishment of schools for actors' children; in which he took occasion to declare his belief that there were no institutions in England so socially liberal as its public schools, and that there was nowhere in the country so complete an absence of servility to mere rank, position, or riches. "A boy, there, is

---

[*] Two pleasing little volumes may here be named as devoted to special descriptions of the several Readings: by his friend Mr. Charles Kent in England (*Charles Dickens as a Reader*), and by Miss Kate Field in America (*Pen Photographs*).

"always what his abilities or his personal qualities Loxbox:
1858-9.
On public
schools.
"make him. We may differ about the curriculum
"and other matters, but of the frank, free, manly,
"independent spirit preserved in our public schools,
"I apprehend there can be no kind of question."
In December* he was entertained at a public
dinner in Coventry on the occasion of receiving, At Coventry.
by way of thanks for help rendered to their Institute, a gold repeater of special construction by
the watchmakers of the town; as to which he kept
faithfully his pledge to the givers, that it should
be thenceforward the inseparable companion of
his workings and wanderings, and reckon off the
future labours of his days until he should have
done with the measurement of time. Within a
day from this celebration, he presided at the In-
stitutional Association of Lancashire and Cheshire
in Manchester Free Trade Hall; gave prizes to At Man-
candidates from a hundred and fourteen local chester.

* Let me subjoin his own note of a less important incident of that
month which will show his quick and sure eye for any bit of acting out
of the common. The lady has since justified its closing prediction. Describing an early dinner with Chauncy Townshend, he adds (17th of December 1858): "I escaped at half-past seven and went to the Strand
"Theatre: having taken a stall beforehand, for it is always crammed.
"I really wish you would go, between this and next Thursday, to see
"the *Maid and the Magpie* burlesque there. There is the strangest
"thing in it that ever I have seen on the stage. The boy, Pippo, by
"Miss Wilton. While it is astonishingly impudent (must be, or it couldn't Miss Marie
Wilton as
"Pippo."
"be done at all), it is so stupendously like a boy, and unlike a woman,
"that it is perfect, free from offence. I never have seen such a thing.
"Priscilla Horton, as a boy, not to be thought of beside it. She does an
"imitation of the dancing of the Christy Minstrels—wonderfully clever
" which, in the audacity of its thorough-going, is surprising. A thing
"that you *can not* imagine a woman's doing at all; and yet the manner,
"the appearance, the levity, impulse, and spirits of it, are so exactly
"like a boy that you cannot think of anything like her sex in association
"with it. It begins at 8, and is over by a quarter-past 9. I never have
"seen such a curious thing, and the girl's talent is unchallengeable. I
"call her the cleverest girl I have ever seen on the stage in my time,
"and the most singularly original."

mechanics' institutes affiliated to the Association; described in his most attractive language the gallant toiling fellows by whom the prizes had been won; and ended with the monition he never failed to couple with his eulogies of Knowledge, that it should follow the teaching of the Saviour, and not satisfy the understanding merely. "Know-"ledge has a very limited power when it informs "the head only; but when it informs the heart as "well, it has a power over life and death, the "body and the soul, and dominates the universe."

This too was the year when Mr. Frith completed Dickens's portrait, and it appeared upon the walls of the Academy in the following spring. "I wish," said Edwin Landseer as he stood before it, "he looked less eager and busy, and not "so much out of himself, or beyond himself. I "should like to catch him asleep and quiet now "and then." There is something in the objection, and he also would be envious at times of what he too surely knew could never be his lot. On the other hand who would willingly have lost the fruits of an activity on the whole so healthy and beneficent?

CHAPTER LIV.

ALL THE YEAR ROUND AND THE UNCOMMERCIAL TRAVELLER.

1859-1861.

In the interval before the close of the first circuit of readings, painful personal disputes arising out of the occurrences of the previous year were settled by the discontinuance of *Household Words*, and the establishment in its place of *All the Year Round*. The disputes turned upon matters of feeling exclusively, and involved no charge on either side that would render any detailed reference here other than gravely out of place. The question into which the difference ultimately resolved itself was that of the respective rights of the parties as proprietors of *Household Words;* and this, upon a bill filed in Chancery, was settled by a winding-up order, under which the property was sold. It was bought by Dickens, who, even before the sale, exactly fulfilling a previous announcement of the proposed discontinuance of the existing periodical and establishment of another in its place, precisely similar but under a different title, had started *All the Year Round*. It was to be regretted perhaps that he should have thought it necessary to move at all, but he moved strictly within his rights.

London: 1859-61.

All the Year Round started.

Household Words discontinued.

Ante, 51.

London
1859-61.
To the publishers first associated with his great success in literature, Messrs. Chapman and Hall, he now returned for the issue of the remainder of his books; of which he always in future reserved the copyrights, making each the subject of such arrangement as for the time might seem to him desirable. In this he was met by no difficulty; and indeed it will be only proper to add, that, in any points affecting his relations with those concerned in the production of his books, though his resentments were easily and quickly roused, they were never very lasting. The only fair rule therefore was, in a memoir of his life, to confine the mention of such things to what was strictly necessary to explain its narrative. This accordingly has been done; and, in the several disagreements it has been necessary to advert to, I cannot charge myself with having in a single instance overstepped the rule. Objection has been made to my revival of the early differences with Mr. Bentley. But silence respecting them was incompatible with what absolutely required to be said, if the picture of Dickens in his most interesting time, at the outset of his career in letters, was not to be omitted altogether; and, suppressing everything of mere temper that gathered round the dispute, use was made of those letters only containing the young writer's urgent appeal to be absolved, rightly or wrongly, from engagements he had too precipitately entered into. Wrongly, some might say, because the law was undoubtedly on Mr. Bentley's side; but all subsequent reflection has

Earliest
and latest
publishers.

Differences
with Mr.
Bentley.

Literary
agreements.

confirmed the view I was led strongly to take at
the time, that in the facts there had come to be
involved what the law could not afford to overlook, and that the sale of brain-work can never
be adjusted by agreement with the same exactness and certainty as that of ordinary goods and
chattels.   Quitting the subject once for all with
this remark, it is not less incumbent on me to
say that there was no stage of the dispute in
which Mr. Bentley, holding as strongly the other
view, might not think it to have sufficient justi-
fication; and certainly in later years there was
no absence of friendly feeling on the part of
Dickens to his old publisher.   This already has
been mentioned; and on the occasion of Hans
Andersen's recent visit to Gadshill, Mr. Bentley
was invited to meet the celebrated Dane.   Nor
should I omit to say, that, in the year to which
this narrative has now arrived, his prompt compliance with an intercession made to him for a
common friend pleased Dickens greatly.

At the opening of 1859, bent upon such a
successor to *Household Words* as should carry on
the associations connected with its name, Dickens
was deep in search of a title to give expression
to them.   "My determination to settle the title
"arises out of my knowledge that I shall never
"be able to do anything for the work until it has
"a fixed name; also out of my observation that
"the same odd feeling affects everybody else."
He had proposed to himself a title that, as in
Household Words, might be capable of illustration
by a line from Shakespeare; and alighting upon

London
1859-61.

Friendly
relations of
Dickens and
Mr. Bentley.
IV. 261.

In search of a
name for new
periodical.

London:
1859-61. that wherein poor Henry the Sixth is fain to solace his captivity by the fancy, that, like birds encaged he might soothe himself for loss of liberty "at last by notes of household harmony," he for the time forgot that this might hardly be accepted as a happy comment on the occurrences out of which the supposed necessity had arisen of replacing the old by a new household friend. "Don't you think," he wrote on the 24th of January, "this is a good name and quotation? I "have been quite delighted to get hold of it for "our title.

First title
chosen.

"HOUSEHOLD HARMONY.

"'At last by notes of Household Harmony.'--*Shakespeare*."

He was at first reluctant even to admit the objection when stated to him. "I am afraid we "must not be too particular about the possibility "of personal references and applications: other-"wise it is manifest that I never can write an-"other book. I could not invent a story of any "sort, it is quite plain, incapable of being twisted "into some such nonsensical shape. It would be "wholly impossible to turn one through half a "dozen chapters." Of course he yielded, never-theless; and much consideration followed over sundry other titles submitted. Reviving none of those formerly rejected, here were a few of these now rejected in their turn. THE HEARTH. THE FORGE. THE CRUCIBLE. THE ANVIL OF THE TIME. CHARLES DICKENS'S OWN. SEASONABLE LEAVES. EVERGREEN LEAVES. HOME. HOME-MUSIC. CHANGE. TIME AND TIDE. TWOPENCE.

Reply to a
doubt.

Other titles
suggested.

English Bells. Weekly Bells. The Rocket. London: 1859-61.
Good Humour. Still the great want was the
line adaptable from Shakespeare, which at last
exultingly he sent on the 28th of January. "I
"am dining early, before reading, and write
"literally with my mouth full. But I have just
"hit upon a name that I think really an ad-
"mirable one—especially with the quotation be-
"fore it, in the place where our, present *H. W.*
"quotation stands.

"'The story of our lives, from year to year.'—*Shakespeare.*" "

"All The Year Round. Title found.
"A weekly journal conducted by Charles
"Dickens."

With the same resolution and energy other
things necessary to the adventure were as
promptly done. "I have taken the new office,"
he wrote from Tavistock House on the 21st of
February; "have got workmen in; have ordered
"the paper; settled with the printer; and am
"getting an immense system of advertising ready.'
"Blow to be struck on the 12th of March. ..
"Meantime I cannot please myself with the open-
"ing of my story" (the *Tale of Two Cities*, which Opening a
All the Year Round was to start with), "and can- story.
"not in the least settle at it or take to it. .. I
"wish you would come and look at what I flatter
"myself is a rather ingenious account to which I
"have turned 'the Stanfield scenery here." He Ante, 66, 161.
had placed the *Lighthouse* scene in a single
frame; had divided the scene of the *Frozen Deep*

The Life of Charles Dickens. V.   16

into two subjects, a British man-of-war and an
Arctic sea, which he had also framed; and the
school-room that had been the theatre was now
hung with sea-pieces by a great painter of the
sea.   To believe them to have been but the
amusement of a few mornings was difficult indeed.   Seen from the due distance there was
nothing wanting to the most masterly and elaborate art.

The first number of *All the Year Round* appeared on the 30th of April, and the result of
the first quarter's accounts of the sale will tell
everything that needs to be said of a success that
went on without intermission to the close.   "A
"word before I go back to Gadshill," he wrote
from Tavistock House in July, "which I know
"you will be glad to receive.   So well has *All*
"*the Year Round* gone that it was yesterday able
"to repay me, with five per cent interest, all the
"money I advanced for its establishment (paper,
"print &c. all paid, down to the last number),
"and yet to leave a good £500 balance at the
"banker's!"   Beside the opening of his *Tale of
Two Cities* its first number had contained another piece of his writing, the "Poor Man and
"his Beer;" as to which an interesting note has
been sent me.   The Rev. T. B. Lawes, of
Rothamsted, St. Alban's, had been associated
upon a sanitary commission with Mr. Henry
Austin, Dickens's brother-in-law and counsellor
in regard to all such matters in his own houses,
or in the houses of the poor; and this connection
led to Dickens's knowledge of a club that Mr.

Lawes had established at Rothamsted, which he became eager to recommend as an example to other country neighbourhoods. The club had been set on foot* to enable the agricultural labourers of the parish to have their beer and pipes independent of the public-house; and the description of it, says Mr. Lawes, "was the oc-"cupation of a drive between this place (Rotham-"sted) and London, 25 miles, Mr. Dickens re-"fusing the offer of a bed, and saying that he "could arrange his ideas on the journey. In the "course of our conversation I mentioned that the "labourers were very jealous of the small trades-"men, blacksmiths and others, holding allotment-"gardens; but that the latter did so indirectly by "paying higher rents to the labourers for a share. "This circumstance is not forgotten in the verses "on the Blacksmith in the same number, com-"posed by Mr. Dickens and repeated to me while "he was walking about, and which close the men-"tion of his gains with allusion to

LONDON: 1859-61. Beer without the public-house.

Verses in first number.

> "A share (concealed) in the poor man's field,
> "Which adds to the poor man's store."

The periodical thus established was in all respects, save one, so exactly the counterpart of what it replaced, that a mention of this point of difference is the only description of it called for. Besides his own three-volume stories of *The Tale of Two Cities* and *Great Expectations*, Dickens admitted into it other stories of the same length by writers of character and name, of which the

---

* It is pleasant to have to state that it was still flourishing when I received Mr. Lawes's letter, on the 18th of December 1871.

16*

London:
1859-61.
Difference
between
*Household
Words* and
*All the Year
Round.*

authorship was avowed. It published tales of
varied merit and success by Mr. Edmund Yates,
Mr. Percy Fitzgerald, and Mr. Charles Lever.
Mr. Wilkie Collins contributed to it his *Woman
in White*, *No Name*, and *Moonstone*, the first of
which had a pre-eminent success; Mr. Reade his
Hard Cash; and Lord Lytton his *Strange Story*.
Conferring about the latter Dickens passed a week
at Knebworth, accompanied by his daughter and
sister-in-law, in the summer of 1861, as soon as
he had closed *Great Expectations;* and there met
Mr. Arthur Helps, with whom and Lord Orford
he visited the so-called "Hermit" near Stevenage,
whom he described as Mr. Mopes in *Tom Tiddler's
Ground*. With his great brother-artist he thoroughly
enjoyed himself, as he invariably did; and reported him · as "in better health and spirits than
"I have seen him in, in all these years,—a little
"weird occasionally regarding magic and spirits,
"but always fair and frank under opposition. He

"was brilliantly talkative, anecdotical, and droll;
"looked young and well; laughed heartily; and
"enjoyed with great zest some games we played.
"In his artist-character and talk, he was full of
"interest and matter, saying the subtlest and finest
"things—but that he never fails in. I enjoyed
"myself immensely, as we all did." *

* From the same letter, dated 1st of July 1861, I take what follows.
"Poor Lord Campbell's seems to me as easy and good a death as one
"could desire. There must be a sweep of these men very soon, ·and
"one feels as if it must fall out like the breaking of an arch—one stone
"goes from a prominent place, and then the rest begin to drop. So,
"one looks, not without satisfaction (in our sadness) at lives so rounded
"and complete, towards Brougham, and Lyndhurst, and Pollock" . . .
Yet, of Dickens's own death, Pollock lived to write to me as the death
of "one of the most distinguished and honoured men England has ever

In *All the Year Round*, as in its predecessor, LONDON: 1859-61. the tales for Christmas were of course continued, but with a surprisingly increased popularity; and Dickens never had such sale for any of his writings as for his Christmas pieces in the later periodical. It had reached, before he died, to Sale of Christmas numbers. nearly three hundred thousand. The first was called the *Haunted House*, and had a small mention of a true occurrence in his boyhood which is not included in the bitter record on a former page. "I was taken home, and there was debt i. 52. "at home as well as death, and we had a sale "there. My own little bed was so superciliously "looked upon by a power unknown to me hazily "called The Trade, that a brass coal-scuttle, a True Incident. "roasting jack, and a bird cage were obliged to "be put into it to make a lot of it, and then it "went for a song. So I heard mentioned, and I "wondered what song, and thought what a dis-"mal song it must have been to sing!" The other subjects will have mention in another chapter.

His tales were not his only important work in Detached papers. *All the Year Round*. The detached papers written by him there had a character and completeness derived from their plan, and from the personal tone, as well as frequent individual confessions, by which their interest is enhanced, and which will always make them specially attractive. Their title expressed a personal liking. Of all the societies, charitable or self-assisting, which his tact

"produced; in whose loss every man among us feels that he has lost a "friend and an instructor." Temple-Hatton, 10th of June 1870.

London
1859-61.

and eloquence in the "chair" so often helped,
none had interested him by the character of its
service to its members, and the perfection of its
management, so much as that of the Commercial
Travellers. His admiration of their schools introduced him to one who then acted as their
treasurer, and whom, of all the men he had known,
I think he rated highest for the union of business
qualities in an incomparable measure to a nature
comprehensive enough to deal with masses of
men, however differing in creed or opinion,
humanely and justly. He never afterwards wanted
support for any good work that he did not think
first of Mr. George Moore, * and appeal was never
made to him in vain. "Integrity, enterprise,
"public spirit, and benevolence," he told the
Commercial Travellers on one occasion, "had
"their synonym in Mr. Moore's name;" and it
was another form of the same liking when he
took to himself the character and title of a
Traveller *Un*commercial. "I am both a town
"traveller and a country traveller, and am always
"on the road. Figuratively speaking, I travel for
"the great house of Human-interest Brothers, and
"have rather a large connection in the fancy

Commercial
Travellers'
schools.

Mr. George
Moore.

A traveller
for Human-
interest
Brothers.

Children
and Bishop.

---

* If space were available here, his letters would supply many proofs
of his interest in Mr. George Moore's admirable projects : but I can only
make exception for his characteristic allusion to an incident that tickled
his fancy very much at the time. "I hope" (20th of Aug. 1863) "you
"have been as much amused as I am by the account of the Bishop of
"Carlisle at (my very particular friend's) Mr. George Moore's schools?
"It strikes me as the funniest piece of weakness I ever saw, his address-
"ing those unfortunate children concerning Colenso. I cannot get over
"the ridiculous image I have erected in my mind, of the shovel-hat and
"apron holding forth, at that safe distance, to that safe audience. There
"is nothing so extravagant in Rabelais, or so satirically humorous in
"Swift or Voltaire."

"goods way.. Literally speaking, I am always "wandering here and there from my rooms in "Covent-garden, London: now about the city "streets; now about the country by-roads: seeing "many little things, and some great things, which, "because they interest me, I think may interest "others." In a few words that was the plan and drift of the papers which he began in 1860, and continued to write from time to time until the last autumn of his life.

LONDON: 1859-61.

Many of them, such as "Travelling Abroad," "City Churches," "Dullborough," "Nurses' Stories," and "Birthday Celebrations," have supplied traits, chiefly of his younger days, to portions of this memoir; and parts of his later life receive illustration from others, such as "Tramps," "Night Walks," "Shy Neighbourhoods," "The Italian Prisoner," and "Chatham Dockyard." Indeed hardly any is without its personal interest or illustration. One may learn from them, among other things, what kind of treatment he resorted to for the disorder of sleeplessness from which he had often suffered amid his late anxieties. Experimenting upon it in bed, he found to be too slow and doubtful a process for him; but he very soon defeated his enemy by the brisker treatment, of getting up directly after lying down, going out, and coming home tired at sunrise. "My last special feat was "turning out of bed at two, after a hard day "pedestrian and otherwise, and walking thirty "miles into the country to breakfast." One description he did not give in his paper, but I recollect his saying that he had seldom seen any-

Personal references.

Remedy for sleeplessness.

thing so striking as the way in which the wonders of an equinoctial dawn (it was the 15th of
October 1857) presented themselves during that
walk. He had never before happened to see
night so completely at odds with morning, "which

"was which." Another experience of his night
ramblings used to be given in vivid sketches of
the restlessness of a great city, and the manner
in which *it* also tumbles and tosses before it can
get to sleep. Nor should anyone curious about
his habits and ways omit to accompany him with
his Tramps into Gadshill lanes; or to follow him
into his Shy Neighbourhoods of the Hackney-
road, Waterloo-road, Spitalfields, or Bethnal-green.
For delightful observation both of country and
town, for the wit that finds analogies between
remote and familiar things, and for humorous
personal sketches and experience, these are perfect
of their kind.

"I have my eye upon a piece of Kentish
"road, bordered on either side by a wood, and
"having on one hand, between the road-dust and
"the trees, a skirting patch of grass. Wild flowers
"grow in abundance on this spot, and it lies high
"and airy, with a distant river stealing steadily
"away to the ocean, like a man's life. To gain
"the milestone here, which the moss, primroses,
"violets, blue-bells, and wild roses, would soon
"render illegible but for peering travellers pushing
"them aside with their sticks, you must come up
"a steep hill, come which way you may. So, all

"the tramps with carts or caravans—the Gipsy-
"tramp, the Show-tramp, the Cheap Jack—find it

"impossible to resist the temptations of the place;
"and all turn the horse loose when they come to
"it and boil the pot. Bless the place, I love the
"ashes of the vagabond fires that have scorched
"its grass!" It was there he found Dr. Marigold,
and Chops the dwarf, and the White-haired Lady
with the pink eyes eating meat-pie with the Giant.
So, too, in his Shy Neighbourhoods, when he relates his experiences of the bad company that
birds are fond of, and of the effect upon domestic fowls of living in low districts, his method of
handling the subject has all the charm of a discovery. "That anything born of an egg and in-
"vested with wings should have got to the pass
"that it hops contentedly down a ladder into a
"cellar, and calls *that* going home, is a circum-
"stance so amazing as to leave one nothing more
"in this connexion to wonder at." One of his
illustrations is a reduced Bantam family in the
Hackney-road deriving their sole enjoyment from
crowding together in a pawnbroker's side entry;
but seeming as if only newly come down in the
world, and always in a feeble flutter of fear that
they may be found out. He contrasts them with
others. "I know a low fellow, originally of a
"good family from Dorking, who takes his whole
"establishment of wives, in single file, in at the
"door of the Jug Department of a disorderly
"tavern near the Haymarket, manoeuvres them
"among the company's legs, emerges with them
"at the Bottle Entrance, and so passes his life:
"seldom, in the season, going to bed before two
"in the morning. . . . But, the family I am best

London:
1859-61.
Bethnal-
green fowls.
"acquainted with, reside in the densest part of "Bethnal-green. Their abstraction from the ob-"jects among which they live, or rather their con-"viction that those objects have all come into "existence in express subservience to fowls, has "so enchanted me, that I have made them the "subject of many journeys at divers hours. After "careful observation of the two lords and the ten "ladies of whom this family consists, I have come "to the conclusion that their opinions are re-"presented by the leading lord and leading lady: Aged hen. "the latter, as I judge, an aged personage, "afflicted with a paucity of feather and visibility "of quill that gives her the appearance of a "bundle of office pens. When a railway goods-"van that would crush an elephant comes round "the corner, tearing over these fowls, they emerge "unharmed from under the horses, perfectly satis-"fied that the whole rush was a passing property "in the air, which may have left something to "eat behind it. They look upon old shoes, wrecks "of kettles and saucepans, and fragments of bon-"nets, as a kind of meteoric discharge, for fowls to "peck at. . . . Gaslight comes quite as natural to "them as any other light; and I have more than "a suspicion that, in the minds of the two lords, "the early public-house at the corner has super-"seded the sun. They always begin to crow "when the public-house shutters begin to be taken "down, and they salute the Potboy, the instant he "appears to perform that duty, as if he were Potboy Phoebus. "Phœbus in person." For the truth of the per-sonal adventure in the same essay, which he tells

in proof of a propensity to bad company in more LONDON:
1859-61.
refined members of the feathered race, I am myself in a position to vouch. Walking by a dirty
court in Spitalfields one day, the quick little
busy intelligence of a goldfinch, drawing water
for himself in his cage, so attracted him that he
bought the bird, which had other accomplishments;
but not one of them would the little creature An incident
of Doughty-
street.
show off in his new abode in Doughty-street, and
he drew no water but by stealth or under the
cloak of night. "After an interval of futile and
"at length hopeless expectation, the merchant
"who had educated him was appealed to. The
"merchant was a bow-legged character, with a
"flat and cushiony nose, like the last new straw-
"berry. He wore a fur cap, and shorts, and was The goldfinch
and his
friend.
"of the velveteen race, velveteeny. He sent word
"that he would 'look round.' He looked round,
"appeared in the doorway of the room, and
"slightly cocked up his evil eye at the goldfinch.
"Instantly a raging thirst beset that bird; and
"when it was appeased, he still drew several un-
"necessary buckets of water, leaping about his
"perch and sharpening his bill with irrepressible
"satisfaction."

The Uncommercial Traveller papers, his two
serial stories, and his Christmas tales, were all the
contributions of any importance made by Dickens
to *All the Year Round;* but he reprinted in it, on
the completion of his first story, a short tale
called "Hunted Down," written for a newspaper "Hunted
"Down."
in America called the *New York Ledger*. Its subject had been taken from the life of a notorious
criminal already named, and its principal claim I. 230.
IV. 103.

to notice was the price paid for it.   For a story not longer than half of one of the numbers of *Chuzzlewit* or *Copperfield*, he had received a thousand pounds.*   It was one of the indications of the eager desire which his entry on the career of a public reader had aroused in America to induce him again to visit that continent; and at the very time he had this magnificent offer from the New York journal, Mr. Fields of Boston, who was then on a visit to Europe, was pressing him so much to go that his resolution was almost shaken.   "I am now," he wrote to me from Gadshill on the 9th of July 1859, "getting the *Tale* "*of Two Cities* into that state that IF I should "decide to go to America late in September, I "could turn to, at any time, and write on with

"great vigour.   Mr. Fields has been down here for "a day, and with the strongest intensity urges "that there is no drawback, no commercial ex-"citement or crisis, no political agitation; and "that so favourable an opportunity, in all respects, "might not occur again for years and years.   I "should be one of the most unhappy of men if "I were to go, and yet I cannot help being much "stirred and influenced by the golden prospect "held before me."

He yielded nevertheless to other persuasion, and for that time the visit was not to be.   In six months more the Civil War began, and America was closed to any such enterprise for nearly five years.

---

* Eight years later he wrote "Holiday Romance" for a Child's Magazine published by Mr. Fields, and "George Silverman's Explanation"—of the same length, and for the same price.   There are no other such instances, I suppose, in the history of literature.

CHAPTER LV.

SECOND SERIES OF READINGS.

1861-1863.

At the end of the first year of residence at Gadshill it was the remark of Dickens that nothing had gratified him so much as the confidence with which his poorer neighbours treated him. He had tested generally their worth and good conduct, and they had been encouraged in illness or trouble to resort to him for help. There was pleasant indication of the feeling thus awakened, when, in the summer of 1860, his younger daughter Kate was married to Charles Alston Collins, brother of the novelist, and younger son of the painter and academician, who might have found, if spared to witness that summer-morning scene, subjects not unworthy of his delightful pencil in many a rustic group near Gadshill. All the villagers had turned out in honour of Dickens, and the carriages could hardly get to and from the little church for the succession of triumphal arches they had to pass through. It was quite unexpected by him; and when the feu de joie of the blacksmith in the lane, whose enthusiasm had smuggled a couple of small cannon into his forge, exploded upon him at the return, I doubt if the shyest of men was ever so taken aback at an ovation.

[margin: Gadshill: 1860.]

[margin: Daughter Kate's marriage.]

To name the principal persons present that day will indicate the faces that (with addition of Miss Mary Boyle, Miss Marguerite Power, Mr. Fechter, Mr. Charles Kent, Mr. Edmund Yates, Mr. Percy Fitzgerald, and members of the family of Mr. Frank Stone, whose sudden death* in the preceding year had been a great grief to Dickens) were most familiar at Gadshill in these later years. Mr. Frederic Lehmann was there with his wife, whose sister, Miss Chambers, was one of the
bridesmaids; Mr. and Mrs. Wills were there, and Dickens's old fast friend Mr. Thomas Beard; the two nearest country neighbours with whom the family had become very intimate, Mr. Hulkes and Mr. Malleson, with their wives, joined the party; among the others were Henry Chorley, Chauncy Townshend, and Wilkie Collins; and, for friend special to the occasion, the bridegroom had brought his old fellow-student in art, Mr. Holman Hunt. Mr. Charles Collins had himself been bred as a painter, for success in which line he had some rare gifts; but inclination and capacity led him also to literature, and, after much indecision between the two callings, he took finally to letters.
His contributions to *All the Year Round* were among the most charming of its detached papers,

---

* "You will be grieved," he wrote (Saturday 19th of Nov. 1859) " to " hear of poor Stone. On Sunday he was not well. On Monday, went "to Dr. Todd, who told him he had aneurism of the heart. On Tues-"day, went to Dr. Walsh, who told him he hadn't. On Wednesday I "met him in a cab in the Square here, and he got out to talk to me. I "walked about with him a little while at a snail's pace, cheering him up; "but when I came home, I told them that I thought him much changed, "and in danger. Yesterday at 2 o'clock he died of spasm of the heart. "I am going up to Highgate to look for a grave for him."

and two stories published independently showed strength of wing for higher flights. But his health broke down, and his taste was too fastidious for his failing power. It is possible however that he may live by two small books of description, the *New Sentimental Journey* and the *Cruise on Wheels*, which have in them unusual delicacy and refinement of humour; and if those volumes should make any readers in another generation curious about the writer, they will learn, if correct reply is given to their inquiries, that no man disappointed so many reasonable hopes with so little fault or failure of his own, that his difficulty always was to please himself, and that an inferior mind would have been more successful in both the arts he followed. He died in 1873 in his forty-fifth year; and until then it was not known, even by those nearest to him, how great must have been the suffering which he had borne, through many trying years, with uncomplaining patience.

His daughter's marriage was the chief event that had crossed the even tenor of Dickens's life since his first paid readings closed; and it was followed by the sale of Tavistock House, with the resolve to make his future home at Gadshill. In the brief interval (29th of July) he wrote to me of his brother Alfred's death. "I was tele-"graphed for to Manchester on Friday night. "Arrived there at a quarter past ten, but he had "been dead three hours, poor fellow! He is to be "buried at Highgate on Wednesday. I brought "the poor young widow back with me yesterday."

All that this death involved,* the troubles of his
change of home, and some difficulties in working
out his story, gave him more than sufficient occupation till the following spring; and as the time
arrived for the new Readings, the change was a
not unwelcome one.

The first portion of this second series was
planned by Mr. Arthur Smith, but he only super-
intended the six readings in London which opened
it. These were the first at St. James's Hall (St.
Martin's Hall having been burnt since the last
readings there) and were given in March and
April 1861. "We are all well here and flourish-
"ing," he wrote to me from Gadshill on the 28th
of April. "On the 18th I finished the readings
"as I purposed. We had between seventy and
"eighty pounds *in the stalls*, which, at four shillings
"apiece, is something quite unprecedented in these
"times. . . The result of the six was, that, after
"paying a large staff of men and all other charges,
"and Arthur Smith's ten per cent. on the receipts,
"and replacing everything destroyed in the fire at
"St. Martin's Hall (including all our tickets,
"country-baggage, cheque-boxes, books, and a
"quantity of gas-fittings and what not), I got up-

* He was now hard at work on his story; and a note written from
Gadshill after the funeral shows, what so frequently was incident to his
pursuits, the hard conditions under which sorrow, and its claim on his
exertion, often came to him. "To-morrow I have to work against time
"and tide and everything else, to fill up a No. keeping open for me,
"and the stereotype plates of which must go to America on Friday.
"But indeed the enquiry into poor Alfred's affairs; the necessity of
"putting the widow and children somewhere; the difficulty of knowing
"what to do for the best; and the need I feel under of being as com-
"posed and deliberate as I can be, and yet of not shirking or putting
"off the occasion that there is for doing a duty; would have brought me
"back here to be quiet, under any circumstances."

"wards of £500. A very great result. We cer-
"tainly might have gone on through the season,
"but I am heartily glad to be concentrated on
"my story."

It had been part of his plan that the Provincial Readings should not begin until a certain
interval after the close of his story of *Great Expectations*. They were delayed accordingly until
the 28th of October, from which date, when they
opened at Norwich, they went on with the Christmas intervals to be presently named to the 30th
of January 1862, when they closed at Chester.
Kept within England and Scotland, they took in
the border town of Berwick, and, besides the
Scotch cities, comprised the contrasts and varieties
of Norwich and Lancaster, Bury St. Edmunds and
Cheltenham, Carlisle and Hastings, Plymouth and
Birmingham, Canterbury and Torquay, Preston
and Ipswich, Manchester and Brighton, Colchester
and Dover, Newcastle and Chester. They were
followed by ten readings at the St. James's Hall,
between the 13th of March and the 27th of June
1862; and by four at Paris in January 1863, given
at the Embassy in aid of the British Charitable
Fund. The second series had thus in the number
of the readings nearly equalled the first, when it
closed at London in June 1863 with thirteen
readings in the Hanover Square Rooms; and it
is exclusively the subject of such illustrations or
references as this chapter will supply.

On *Great Expectations* closing in June 1861,
Bulwer Lytton, at Dickens's earnest wish, took
his place in *All the Year Round* with the "Strange

London
1861.

Good of
doing no-
thing.

Preparing
readings.

Now subjects
for readings.

Illness of
manager.

"Story;" and he then indulged himself in idleness
for a little while. "The subsidence of those dis-
"tressing pains in my face the moment I had done
"my work, made me resolve to do nothing in that
"way for some time if I could help it."* But his
"doing nothing" was seldom more than a figure
of speech, and what it meant in this case was
soon told. "Every day for two or three hours, I
"practise my new readings, and (except in my of-
"fice work) do nothing else. With great pains I
"have made a continuous narrative out of *Cop-
"perfield*, that I think will reward the exertion it
"is likely to cost me. Unless I am much mis-
"taken, it will be very valuable in London. I have
"also done *Nicholas Nickleby* at the Yorkshire
"school, and hope I have got something droll out
"of Squeers, John Browdie, & Co. Also, the Ba-
"stille prisoner from the *Tale of Two Cities*. Also,
"the Dwarf from one of our Christmas numbers."
Only the first two were added to the list for the
present circuit.

It was in the midst of these active preparations
that painful news reached him. An illness under
which Mr. Arthur Smith had been some time
suffering took unexpectedly a dangerous turn,
and there came to be but small chance of his recovery. A distressing interview on the 28th of
September gave Dickens little hope. "And yet
"his wakings and wanderings so perpetually turn
"on his arrangements for the Readings, and he is

---

* The same letter adds: "The fourth edition of *Great Expecta-
"tions* is now going to press; the third being nearly out. Bulwer's story
"keeps us up bravely. As well as we can make out, we have even risen
"fifteen hundred."

"so desperately unwilling to relinquish the idea LONDON: 1861.
"of 'going on with the business' to-morrow and
"to-morrow and to-morrow, that I had not the
"heart to press him for the papers. He told me
"that he believed he had by him '70 or 80 letters
"'unanswered.' You may imagine how anxious it
"makes me, and at what a deadstop I stand."
Another week passed, and with it the time fixed
at the places where his work was to have opened;
but he could not bring himself to act as if all
hope had gone. "With a sick man who has been
"so zealous and faithful, I feel bound to be very
"tender and patient. When I told him the other
"day about my having engaged Headland — 'to
"'do all the personally bustling and fatiguing part
"'of your work,' I said — he nodded his heavy
"head with great satisfaction, and faintly got out Mr. Arthur
"of himself the words, 'Of course I pay him, and Smith's death.
"'not you.'" The poor fellow died in October;
and on the day after attending the funeral, *
Dickens heard of the death of his brother-in-law
and friend, Mr. Henry Austin, whose abilities and
character he respected as much as he liked the Brother-in-law's death.
man. He lost much in losing the judicious and Ante, 242.
safe counsel which had guided him on many

* "There was a very touching thing in the Chapel" (at Brompton).
"When the body was to be taken up and carried to the grave, there
"stepped out, instead of the undertaker's men with their hideous para-
"phernalia, the men who had always been with the two brothers at the Funeral of
"Egyptian Hall; and they, in their plain, decent, own mourning clothes, Mr. Arthur
"carried the poor fellow away. Also, standing about among the grave- Smith.
"stones, dressed in black, I noticed every kind of person who had ever
"had to do with him — from our own gas man and doorkeepers and bill-
"stickers, up to Johnson the printer and that class of man. The father
"and Albert and he now lie together, and the grave, I suppose, will
"be no more disturbed. I wrote a little inscription for the stone, and it
"is quite full."

public questions in which he took lively interest, and it was with a heavy heart he set out at last upon his second circuit. "With what difficulty I "get myself back to the readings after all this loss "and trouble, or with what unwillingness I work "myself up to the mark of looking them in the "face, I can hardly say. As for poor Arthur Smith "at this time, it is as if my right arm were gone. "It is only just now that I am able to open one "of the books, and screw the text out of myself "in a flat dull way. Enclosed is the list of what "I have to do. You will see that I have left ten "days in November for the Christmas number, and "also a good Christmas margin for our meeting "at Gadshill. I shall be very glad to have the "money that I expect to get; but it will be earned." That November interval was also the date of the marriage of his eldest son to the daughter of Mr. Evans, so long, in connection with Mr. Bradbury, his publisher and printer.

The start of the readings at Norwich was not good, so many changes of vexation having been incident to the opening announcements as to leave some doubt of their fulfilment. But the second night, when trial was made of the *Nickleby* scenes, "we had a splendid hall, and I think "*Nickleby* will top all the readings. Somehow it "seems to have got in it, by accident, exactly the "qualities best suited to the purpose; and it went "last night, not only with roars, but with a general "hilarity and pleasure that I have never seen sur- "passed." * From this night onward, the success

.* Of his former manager he writes in the same letter: " I miss him

was uninterrupted, and here was his report to PROVINCES:
1861. me from Brighton on the 8th of November. "We ──────── "turned away half Dover and half Hastings and "half Colchester; and, if you can believe such a "thing, I may tell you that in round numbers "we find 1000 stalls already taken here in Brighton! "I left Colchester in a heavy snow-storm. To-day "it is so warm here that I can hardly bear the "fire, and am writing with the window open down "to the ground. Last night I had a most charm- "ing audience for *Copperfield*, with a delicacy of Audience at
Brighton. "perception that really made the work delightful. "It is very pretty to see the girls and women "generally, in the matter of Dora; and everywhere "I have found that peculiar personal relation be- "tween my audience and myself on which I counted "most when I entered on this enterprise. *Nickleby* "continues to go in the wildest manner."

A storm was at this time sweeping round the coast, and while at Dover he had written of it to his sister-in-law (7th of November): "The bad "weather has not in the least touched us, and the "storm was most magnificent at Dover. All the "great side of the Lord Warden next the sea had A storm. "to be emptied, the break of the waves was so "prodigious, and the noise so utterly confounding. "The sea came in like a great sky of immense "clouds, for ever breaking suddenly into furious

"dreadfully. The sense I used to have of compactness and comfort "about me while I was reading, is quite gone; and on my coming out "for the ten minutes, when I used to find him always ready for me with "something cheerful to say, it is forlorn... Besides which, H. and all "the rest of them are always somewhere, and he was always every- "where."

"rain; all kinds of wreck were washed in; among "other things, a very pretty brass-bound chest "being thrown about like a feather . . . The un-"happy Ostend packet, unable to get in or go "back, beat about the Channel all Tuesday night, "and until noon yesterday; when I saw her come "in, with five men at the wheel, a picture of "misery inconceivable . . . The effect of the read-"ings at Hastings and Dover really seems to have "outdone the best usual impression; and at Dover "they wouldn't go, but sat applauding like mad.

"The most delicate audience I have seen in any "provincial place, is Canterbury" ("an intelligent "and delightful response in them," he wrote to his daughter, "like the touch of a beautiful in-"strument"); "but the audience with the greatest "sense of humour certainly is Dover. The people "in the stalls set the example of laughing, in the "most curiously unreserved way; and they laughed "with such really cordial enjoyment, when Squeers "read the boys' letters, that the contagion ex-"tended to me. For, one couldn't hear them "without laughing too . . . So, I am thankful to "say, all goes well, and the recompense for the "trouble is in every way Great."

From the opposite quarter of Berwick-on-Tweed he wrote again in the midst of storm. But first his mention of Newcastle, which he had also taken on his way to Edinburgh, reading two nights there, should be given. "At Newcastle, "against the very heavy expenses, I made more "than a hundred guineas profit. A finer audience "there is not in England, and I suppose them to

"be a specially earnest people; for, while they
"can laugh till they shake the roof, they have a ————
"very unusual sympathy with what is pathetic or
"passionate. An extraordinary thing occurred on Alarming
"the second night. The room was tremendously scene.
"crowded and my gas-apparatus fell down. There
"was a terrible wave among the people for an
"instant, and God knows what destruction of life
"a rush to the stairs would have caused. For-
"tunately a lady in the front of the stalls ran out
"towards me, exactly in a place where I knew
"that the whole hall could see her. So I addressed
"her, laughing, and half-asked and half-ordered
"her to sit down again; and, in a moment, it was
"all over. But the men in attendance had such
"a fearful sense of what might have happened
"(besides the real danger of Fire) that they
"positively shook the boards I stood on, with
"their trembling, when they came up to put things
"right. I am proud to record that the gas-man's Gas-man's
"sentiment, as delivered afterwards, was, 'The compliment to his master.
"'more you want of the master, the more you'll
"'find in him.' With which complimentary homage,
"and with the wind blowing so that I can hardly
"hear myself write, I conclude." *

---

* The more detailed account of the scene which he wrote to his
daughter is also well worth giving. "A most tremendous hall here last
"night. Something almost terrible in the cram. A fearful thing might
"have happened. Suddenly, when they were all very still over Smike, More of the
"my Gas Batten came down, and it looked as if the room were falling. alarm at
"There were three great galleries crammed to the roof, and a high steep Newcastle.
"flight of stairs; and a panic must have destroyed numbers of people.
"A lady in the front row of stalls screamed, and ran out wildly towards
"me, and for one instant there was a terrible wave in the crowd. I ad-
"dressed that lady, laughing (for I knew she was in sight of everybody
"there), and called out as if it happened every night—' There's nothing
"'the matter I assure you; don't be alarmed; pray sit down——' and

Berwick-
on-Tweed:
1861.
It was still blowing, in shape of a gale from the sea, when, an hour before the reading, he wrote from the King's Arms at Berwick-on-Tweed. "As odd and out of the way a place to be at, it "appears to me, as ever was seen! And such a "ridiculous room designed for me to read in! An "immense Corn Exchange, made of glass and "iron, round, dome-topp'd, lofty, utterly absurd "for any such purpose, and full of thundering "echoes; with a little lofty crow's nest of a stone "gallery, breast high, deep in the wall, into which "it was designed to put——*me!* I instantly struck, "of course; and said *I* would either read in a "room attached to this house (a very snug one, "capable of holding 500 people), or not at all. "Terrified local agents glowered, but fell prostrate, "and my men took the primitive accommodation "in hand. Ever since, I am alarmed to add, the "people (who besought the honour of the visit) "have been coming in numbers quite irrecon- "cileable with the appearance of the place, and "what is to be the end I do not know. It was "poor Arthur Smith's principle that a town on "the way paid the expenses of a long through- "journey, and therefore I came." The Reading paid more than those expenses.

Impromptu
reading-hall.

Scotland.
Enthusiastic greeting awaited him in Edin-

"she sat down directly, and there was a thunder of applause. It took "some five minutes to mend, and I looked on with my hands in my "pockets; for I think if I had turned my back for a moment, there "might still have been a move. My people were dreadfully alarmed— "Boycott" (the gas-man) "in particular, who I suppose had some notion "that the whole place might have taken fire—'but there stood the "'master,' he did me the honour to say afterwards, in addressing the "rest, 'as cool as ever I see him a lounging at a Railway Station.'"

burgh. "We had in the hall exactly double what SCOTLAND:
1861.
"we had on the first night last time. The success ————
"of *Copperfield* was perfectly unexampled. Four *Ante*, 231.
"great rounds of applause with a burst of cheer-
"ing at the end, and every point taken in the
"finest manner." But this was nothing to what
befell on the second night, when, by some mis-
take of the local agents, the tickets issued were Over-issue
of tickets.
out of proportion to the space available. Writing
from Glasgow next day (3rd of December) he
described the scene. "Such a pouring of hun-
"dreds into a place already full to the throat,
"such indescribable confusion, such a rending
"and tearing of dresses, and yet such a scene of
"good humour on the whole, I never saw the
"faintest approach to. While I addressed the
"crowd in the room, G addressed the crowd in
"the street. Fifty frantic men got up in all parts
"of the hall and addressed me all at once. Other
"frantic men made speeches to the walls. The
"whole B family were borne in on the top of a Confusion
and good-
"wave, and landed with their faces against the humour.
"front of the platform. I read with the platform
"crammed with people. I got them to lie down
"upon it, and it was like some impossible tableau
"or gigantic pic-nic—one pretty girl in full dress,
"lying on her side all night, holding on to one
"of the legs of my table! It was the most extra-
"ordinary sight. And yet, from the moment I
"began to the moment of my leaving off, they
"never missed a point, and they ended with a
"burst of cheers. ... The expenditure of lungs
"and spirits was (as you may suppose) rather

"great; and to sleep well was out of the question. "I am therefore rather fagged to-day; and as the "hall in which I read to-night is a large one, I "must make my letter a short one. . . . My people "were torn to ribbons last night. They have not "a hat among them—and scarcely a coat." He came home for his Christmas rest by way of Manchester, and thus spoke of the reading there on the 14th of December. "*Copperfield* in the "Free Trade Hall last Saturday was really a "grand scene."

He was in southern latitudes after Christmas, and on the 8th of January wrote from Torquay: "We are now in the region of small rooms, and "therefore this trip will not be as profitable as "the long one. I imagine the room here to be "very small. Exeter I know, and that is small "too. I am very much used up on the whole, "for I cannot bear this moist warm climate. It "would kill me very soon. And I have now got "to the point of taking so much out of myself "with *Copperfield* that I might as well do Richard "Wardour . . . This is a very pretty place—a "compound of Hastings, Tunbridge Wells, and "little bits of the hills about Naples; but I met "four respirators as I came up from the station, "and three pale curates without them who seemed "in a bad way." They had been not bad omens, however. The success was good, at both Torquay and Exeter; and he closed the month, and this series of the country readings, at the great towns of Liverpool and Chester. "The beautiful St. "George's Hall crowded to excess last night"

(28th of January 1862) "and numbers turned
"away. Brilliant to see when lighted up, and for
"a reading simply perfect. You remember that
"a Liverpool audience is usually dull; but they
"put me on my mettle last night, for I never saw
"such an audience—no, not even in Edinburgh!
"The agents (alone, and of course without any
"reference to ready money at the doors), had
"taken for the two readings two hundred pounds."
But as the end approached the fatigues had told
severely on him. He described himself sleeping
horribly, and with head dazed and worn by gas
and heat. Rest, before he could resume at the
St. James's Hall in March, was become an absolute
necessity.

Two brief extracts from letters of the dates
respectively of the 8th of April * and the 28th of
June will sufficiently describe the London readings. "The money returns have been quite
"astounding. Think of £190 a night! The effect
"of *Copperfield* exceeds all the expectations which
"its success in the country led me to form. It
"seems to take people entirely by surprise. If this
"is not new to you, I have not a word of news.
"The rain that raineth every day seems to have
"washed news away or got it under water." That

* The letter referred also to the death of his American friend Professor Felton. "Your mention of poor Felton's death is a shock of sur-
"prise as well as grief to me, for I had not heard a word about it. Mr.
"Fields told me when he was here that the effect of that hotel disaster
"of had drinking water had not passed away; so I suppose, as you do,
"that he sank under it. Poor dear Felton! It is so years since I told
"you of the delight my first knowledge of him gave me, and it is as
"strongly upon me to this hour. I wish our ways had crossed a little
"oftener, but that would not have made it better for us now. Alas! alas!
"all ways have the same finger-post at the head of them, and at every
"turning in them."

was in April. In June he wrote: "I finished my "readings on Friday night to an enormous hall "—nearly £200. The success has been throughout "complete. It seems almost suicidal to leave off "with the town so full, but I don't like to depart "from my public pledge. A man from Australia
"is in London ready to pay £10,000 for eight "months there. If——" It was an If that troubled him for some time, and led to agitating discussion. The civil war having closed America, an increase made upon the just-named offer tempted him to Australia. He tried to familiarize himself with the fancy that he should thus also get new material for observation, and he went so far as to plan an Uncommercial Traveller Upside Down.* It is however very doubtful if such a

---

* I give the letter in which he put the scheme formally before me, after the renewed and larger offers had been submitted. "If there were "reasonable hope and promise, I could make up my mind to go to Au-"stralia and get money. I would not accept the Australian people's "offer. I would take no money from them: would bind myself to nothing "with them: but would merely make them my agents at such and such "a per centage, and go and read there. I would take some man of "literary pretensions as a secretary (Charles Collins? What think you?) "and with his aid" (he afterwards made the proposal to his old friend Mr. Thomas Beard) "would do, for *All the Year Round* while I was "away, The Uncommercial Traveller Upside Down. If the notion of "these speculators be anything like accurate, I should come back rich. "I should have seen a great deal of novelty to boot. I should have been
"very miserable too. . . Of course one cannot possibly count upon the "money to be realized by a six months' absence, but £12,000 is supposed "to be a low estimate. Mr. S. brought me letters from members of the "legislature, newspaper editors, and the like, exhorting me to come, "saying how much the people talk of me, and dwelling on the kind of "reception that would await me. No doubt this is so, and of course a "great deal of curious experience for after use would be gained over "and above the money. Being my own master too, I could 'work' my-"self more delicately than if I bound myself for money beforehand. A "few years hence, if all other circumstances were the same, I might not "be so well fitted for the excessive wear and tear. This is about the "whole case. But pray do not suppose that I am in my own mind "favourable to going, or that I have any fancy for going." That was late in October. From Paris in November (1862), he wrote: "I men-

scheme would have been entertained for a moment, but for the unwonted difficulties of invention that were now found to beset a twenty-number story. Such a story had lately been in his mind, and he had just chosen the title for it (*Our Mutual Friend*); but still he halted and hesitated sorely. "If it was not" (he wrote on the 5th of October 1862) "for the hope of a gain "that would make me more independent of the "worst, I could not look the travel and absence "and exertion in the face. I know perfectly well "beforehand how unspeakably wretched I should "be. But these renewed and larger offers tempt "me. I can force myself to go aboard a ship, "and I can force myself to do at that reading-"desk what I have done a hundred times; but "whether, with all this unsettled fluctuating dis-"tress in my mind, I could force an original book "out of it, is another question." On the 22nd, still striving hard to find reasons to cope with the all but irresistible arguments against any such adventure, which indeed, with everything that then surrounded him, would have been little short of madness, he thus stated his experience of his two circuits of public reading. "Remember that "at home here the thing has never missed fire, "but invariably does more the second time than "it did the first; and also that I have got so used

Margin notes:
LONDON: 1862.
Writing not always possible.
Reading always possible.
Experiences.

"tioned the question to Bulwer when he dined with us here last Sunday, "and he was all for going. He said that not only did he think the whole "population would go to the Readings, but that the country would "strike me in some quite new aspect for a Book; and that wonders "might be done with such book in the way of profit, over there as well "as here."

LONDON:
1862.
"to it, and have worked so hard at it, as to get
"out of it more than I ever thought was in it for
"that purpose. I think all the probabilities for
"such a country as Australia are immense." The
Home argu-
ment Against terrible difficulty was that the home argument
struck both ways. "If I were to go it would be a
"penance and a misery, and I dread the thought
"more than I can possibly express. The domestic
"life of the Readings is all but intolerable to me
"when I am away for a few weeks at a time
"merely, and what would it be——." On the
other hand it was also a thought of home, far beyond the mere personal loss or gain of it, that
made him willing still to risk even so much
misery and penance; and he had a fancy that it
might be possible to take his eldest daughter
with him. "It is useless and needless for me to
"say what the conflict in my own mind is. How
Home
argument For. "painfully unwilling I am to go, and yet how
"painfully sensible that perhaps I ought to go—
"with all the hands upon my skirts that I cannot
"fail to feel and see there, whenever I look round.
"It is a struggle of no common sort, as you will
"suppose, you who know the circumstances of the
"struggler." It closed at once when he clearly saw
that to take any of his family with him, and make
satisfactory arrangement for the rest during such
an absence, would be impossible. By this time
also he began to find his way to the new story,
and better hopes and spirits had returned.

FRANCE:
1863.
Readings
in Paris.   In January 1863 he had taken his daughter
and his sister-in-law to Paris, and he read twice
at the Embassy in behalf of the British Charitable

Fund, the success being such that he consented
to read twice again.* He passed his birthday of
that year (the 7th of the following month) at Ar-
ras. "You will remember me to-day, I know.
"Thanks for it. An odd birthday, but I am as
"little out of heart as you would have me be—
"floored now and then, but coming up again at
"the call of Time. I wanted to see this town,
"birthplace of our amiable Sea Green" (Robes-
pierre); "and I find a Grande Place so very re-
"markable and picturesque that it is astonishing
"how people miss it. Here too I found, in a bye-
"country place just near, a Fair going on, with a
"Religious Richardson's in it—THÉÂTRE RELIGIEUX
"—'donnant six fois par jour, l'histoire de la Croix
"'en tableaux vivants, depuis la naissance de
"'notre Seigneur jusqu'à sa sépulture. Aussi
"'l'immolation d'Isaac, par son père Abraham.'
"It was just before nightfall when I came upon
"it; and one of the three wise men was up to his
"eyes in lamp oil, hanging the moderators. A
"woman in blue and fleshings (whether an angel
"or Joseph's wife I don't know) was addressing
"the crowd through an enormous speaking-trumpet;
"and a very small boy with a property lamb (I
"leave you to judge who *he* was) was standing
"on his head on a barrel-organ." Returning to
England by Boulogne in the same year, as he
stepped into the Folkestone boat he encountered

* A person present thus described (1st of February 1863) the second At British
night to Miss Dickens. "No one can imagine the scene of last Friday Embassy.
"night at the Embassy . . a two hours' storm of excitement and pleasure.
"They actually murmured and applauded right away into their carriages
"and down the street."

a friend, Mr. Charles Manby (for, in recording a trait of character so pleasing and honourable, it is not necessary that I should suppress the name), also passing over to England. "Taking leave of

"Manby was a shabby man of whom I had some "remembrance, but whom I could not get into "his place in my mind. Noticing when we stood "out of the harbour that he was on the brink of "the pier, waving his hat in a desolate manner, I "said to Manby, 'Surely I know that man.'——— "'I should think you did,' said he; 'Hudson!' "He is living—just living—at Paris, and Manby "had brought him on. He said to Manby at "parting, 'I shall not have a good dinner again, "'till you come back.' I asked Manby why he "stuck to him? He said, Because he (Hudson) "had so many people in his power, and had held

"his peace; and because he (Manby) saw so "many Notabilities grand with him now, who "were always grovelling for 'shares' in the days "of his grandeur."

Upon Dickens's arrival in London the second series of his readings was brought to a close; and opportunity may be taken, before describing the third, to speak of the manuscript volume found among his papers, containing Memoranda for use in his writings.

CHAPTER LVI.

HINTS FOR BOOKS WRITTEN AND UNWRITTEN.

1855-1865.

DICKENS began the Book of Memoranda for possible use in his work, to which occasional reference has been made, in January 1855, six months before the first page of *Little Dorrit* was written; and I find no allusion leading me to suppose, except in one very doubtful instance, that he had made addition to its entries, or been in the habit of resorting to them, after the date of *Our Mutual Friend*. It seems to comprise that interval of ten years in his life.

In it were put down any hints or suggestions that occurred to him. A mere piece of imagery or fancy, it might be at one time; at another the outline of a subject or a character; then a bit of description or dialogue; no order or sequence being observed in any. Titles for stories were set down too, and groups of names for the actors in them; not the least curious of the memoranda belonging to this class. More rarely, entry is made of some oddity of speech; and he has thus preserved in it, *verbatim et literatim*, what he declared to have been as startling a message as he ever received. A confidential servant at Tavis-

London: 1855-65.

Book of MS. Memoranda.

tock House, having conferred on some proposed changes in his bed-room with the party that was to do the work, delivered this ultimatum to her master. "The gas-fitter says, sir, that he can't "alter the fitting of your gas in your bed-room "without taking up almost the ole of your bed-"room floor, and pulling your room to pieces.

"He says, of course you can have it done if you "wish, and he'll do it for you and make a good "job of it, but he would have to destroy your "room first, and go entirely under the jistes."*

It is very interesting in this book, last legacy as it is of the literary remains of such a writer, to compare the way in which fancies were worked out with their beginnings entered in its pages. Those therefore will first be taken that in some form or other appeared afterwards in his writings, with such reference to the latter as may enable the reader to make comparison for himself.

"Our House. Whatever it is, it is in a first-"rate situation, and a fashionable neighbourhood. "(Auctioneer called it 'a gentlemanly residence.') "A series of little closets squeezed up into the "corner of a dark street—but a Duke's Mansion "round the corner. The whole house just large "enough to hold a vile smell. The air breathed "in it, at the best of times, a kind of Distillation "of Mews." He made it the home of the Barnacles in *Little Dorrit.*

What originally he meant to express by Mrs.

* From the same authority proceeded, in answer to a casual question one day, a description of the condition of his wardrobe of which he has also made note in the Memoranda. "Well, sir, your clothes is all "shabby, and your boots is all burst."

Clennam in the same story has narrower limits, LONDON: 1853-65.
and a character less repellent, in the Memoranda Original of
than it assumed in the book. "Bed-ridden (or Mrs. Clennam.
"room-ridden) twenty — five-and-twenty — years;
"any length of time. As to most things, kept at
"a standstill all the while. Thinking of altered
"streets as the old streets—changed things as the Fancies used.
"unchanged things—the youth or girl I quarrelled
"with all those years ago, as the same youth or
"girl now. Brought out of doors by an unex-
"pected exercise of my latent strength of cha-
"racter, and then how strange!"

One of the people of the same story who becomes a prominent actor in it, Henry Gowan, a
creation on which he prided himself as forcible
and new, seems to have risen to his mind in this
way. "I affect to believe that I would do any-
"thing myself for a ten-pound note, and that
"anybody else would. I affect to be always
"book-keeping in every man's case, and post-
"ing up a little account of good and evil
"with every one. Thus the greatest rascal be- Too much impartiality
"comes 'the dearest old fellow,' and there is between evil
"much less difference than you would be inclined and good.
"to suppose between an honest man and a
"scoundrel. While I affect to be finding good
"in most men, I am in reality decrying it where
"it really is, and setting it up where it is not.
"Might not a presentation of this far from un-
"common class of character, if I could put it
"strongly enough, be likely to lead some men to
"reflect, and change a little? I think it has never
"been done."

LONDON:
1855-65.
River and
ferryman.
In *Little Dorrit* also will be found a picture which seems to live with a more touching effect in his first pleasing fancy of it. "The ferryman "on a peaceful river, who has been there from "youth, who lives, who grows old, who does well, who "does ill, who changes, who dies—the river runs six "hours up and six hours down, the current sets off "that point, the same allowance must be made for "the drifting of the boat, the same tune is always "played by the rippling water against the prow."

Notions for
Little Dorrit.
Here was an entry made when the thought occurred to him of the close of old Dorrit's life. "First sign of the father failing and break-"ing down. Cancels long interval. Begins to "talk about the turnkey who first called him the "Father of the Marshalsea—as if he were still "living. 'Tell Bob I want to speak to him. See "'if he is on the Lock, my dear.'" And here was the first notion of Clennam's reverse of for-tune. "His falling into difficulty, and himself "imprisoned in the Marshalsea. Then she, out "of all her wealth and changed station, comes "back in her old dress, and devotes herself in "the old way."

My lord and
his followers.
He seems to have designed, for the sketches of society in the same tale, a "Full-length por-"trait of his lordship, surrounded by worshippers;" of which, beside that brief memorandum, only his first draft of the general outline was worked at. "Sensible men enough, agreeable men "enough, independent men enough in a certain "way;—but the moment they begin to circle "round my lord, and to shine with a borrowed

"light from his lordship, heaven and earth how London: 1855-65.
"mean and subservient! What a competition and
"outbidding of each other in servility."

The last of the Memoranda hints which were
used in the story whose difficulties at its opening
seem first to have suggested them, ran thus:
"The unwieldy ship taken in tow by the
"snorting little steam tug"—by which was pre-
figured the patriarch Casby and his agent Panks.

In a few lines are the germ of the tale called
Hunted Down: "Devoted to the Destruction of a Original of *Hunted Down.*
"man. Revenge built up on love. The secretary
"in the Wainewright case, who had fallen in love
"(or supposed he had) with the murdered girl."
—The hint on which he worked in his description
of the villain of that story, is also in the Memoranda. "The man with his hair parted straight
"up the front of his head, like an aggravating
"gravel-walk. Always presenting it to you. 'Up
"'here, if you please. Neither to the right
"'nor left. Take me exactly in this direction.
"'Straight up here. Come off the grass—'"

His first intention as to the *Tale of Two Cities*
was to write it upon a plan proposed in this manu-
script book. "How as to a story in two periods
"—with a lapse of time between, like a French
"Drama? Titles for such a notion. TIME! THE Titles for *Tale of Two Cities.*
"LEAVES OF THE FOREST. SCATTERED LEAVES.
"THE GREAT WHEEL. ROUND AND ROUND. OLD
"LEAVES. LONG AGO. FAR APART. FALLEN
"LEAVES. FIVE AND TWENTY YEARS. YEARS
"AND YEARS. ROLLING YEARS. DAY AFTER DAY.
"FELLED TREES. MEMORY CARTON. ROLLING

LONDON:
1855-65.
First germ
of Carton.
"STONES. TWO GENERATIONS." That special title
of *Memory Carton* shows that what led to the
greatest success of the book as written was always in his mind; and another of the memoranda
is this rough hint of the character itself. "The
"drunken?—dissipated?—What?—LION—and his
"JACKALL and Primer, stealing down to him at
"unwonted hours."

Hints for
Mutual Friend.
The studies of Silas Wegg and his patron as
they exist in *Our Mutual Friend*, are hardly such
good comedy as in the form which the first
notion of them seems to have intended. "Gib-
"bon's Decline and Fall. The two characters.
Wegg and
Boffin.
"One reporting to the other as he reads. Both
"getting confused as to whether it is not all
"going on now." In the same story may be
traced, more or less clearly, other fancies which
had found their first expression in the Memoranda. A touch for Bella Wilfer is here. "Buy-
Bella Wilfer.
"ing poor shabby—FATHER?—a new hat. So in-
"congruous that it makes him like African King
"Boy, or King George; who is usually full dressed
"when he has nothing upon him but a cocked
"hat or a waistcoat." Here undoubtedly is the
voice of Podsnap. "I stand by my friends and
"acquaintances;—not for their sakes, but be-
"cause they are *my* friends and acquaintances. *I*
"know them, *I* have licensed them, they have
"taken out *my* certificate. Ergo, I champion them
Podsnap.
"as myself." To the same redoubtable person
another trait clearly belongs. "And by denying a
"thing, supposes that he altogether puts it out of
"existence." A third very perfectly expresses the

boy, ready for mischief, who does all the work *London:*
there is to be done in Eugene Wrayburn's place *1855-65.*
of business. "The office boy for ever looking out *Office boy.*
"of window who never has anything to do."

The poor wayward purposeless good-hearted
master of the boy, Eugene himself, is as evidently
in this: "If they were great things, I, the untrust-
"worthy man in little things, would do them
"earnestly—But O No, I wouldn't!" What fol- *Eugene.*
lows has a more direct reference; being indeed
almost literally copied in the story. "As to the
"question whether I, Eugene, lying ill and sick
"even unto death, may be consoled by the repre-
"sentation that coming through this illness, I shall
"begin a new life, and have energy and purpose
"and all I have yet wanted: '*I hope* I should, but
"'*I know* I shouldn't. Let me die, my dear.'"

In connection with the same book, the last in
that form which he lived to complete, another
fancy may be copied from which, though not
otherwise worked out in the tale, the relation of
Lizzie Hexham to her brother was taken. "A
"man, and his wife—or daughter—or niece. The *Reprobate's*
"man, a reprobate and ruffian; the woman (or *notion of Duty.*
"girl) with good in her, and with compunctions.
"He believes nothing, and defies everything; yet
"has suspicions always, that she is 'praying
"'against' his evil schemes, and making them go .
"wrong. He is very much opposed to this, and
"is always angrily harping on it. 'If she *must*
"'pray, why can't she pray in their favour, in-
"'stead of going against 'em? She's always ruin-
"'ing me—she always is—and calls that, Duty!

"'There's a religious person! Calls it Duty to fly
"'in my face!   Calls it Duty to go sneaking
"'against me!'"

Other fancies preserved in his Memoranda
were left wholly unemployed, receiving from him
no more permanent form of any kind than that
which they have in this touching record; and
what most people would probably think the most
attractive and original of all the thoughts he had
thus set down for future use, are those that were
never used.

Here were his first rough notes for the opening of a story. "Beginning with the breaking up
"of a large party of guests at a country house:
"house left lonely with the shrunken family in
"it: guests spoken of, and introduced to the
"reader that way.—OR, beginning with a house
"abandoned by a family fallen into reduced cir-
"cumstances. Their old furniture there, and num-
"berless tokens of their old comforts. Inscrip-

"tions under the bells downstairs—'Mr. John's
"'Room,' 'Miss Caroline's Room.' Great gardens
"trimly kept to attract a tenant: but no one in
"them. A landscape without figures. Billiard
"room: table covered up, like a body. Great
"stables without horses, and great coach-houses
"without carriages: Grass growing in the chinks
"of the stone-paving, this bright cold winter day.
"*Downhills*." Another opening had also suggested itself to him. "Open a story by bringing
"two strongly contrasted places and strongly con-
"trasted sets of people, into the connexion neces-
"sary for the story, by means of an electric mes-

"sage. Describe the message—*be* the message— London: 1855-65.
"flashing along through space, over the earth, and Uses for an electric message.
"under the sea."* Connected with which in some
way would seem to be this other notion, following
it in the Memoranda. "Representing London—or
"Paris, or any other great place—in the new light Great cities under new aspects.
"of being actually unknown to all the people in
"the story, and only taking the colour of their
"fears and fancies and opinions. So getting a
"new aspect, and being unlike itself. An *odd*
"unlikeness of itself."

The subjects for stories are various, and some
are striking. There was one he clung to much,
and thought of frequently as in a special degree
available for a series of papers in his periodical;
but when he came to close quarters with it the
difficulties were found to be too great. "English England first seen by an Englishman.
"landscape. The beautiful prospect, trim fields,
"clipped hedges, everything so neat and orderly
"—gardens, houses, roads. Where are the people
"who do all this? There must be a great many
"of them, to do it. Where are they all? And
"are *they*, too, so well kept and so fair to see?
"Suppose the foregoing to be wrought out by an
"Englishman: say from China: who knows no-
"thing about his native country." To which may

* The date when this fancy dropped into his Memoranda is fixed by
the following passage in a letter to me of the 25th of August 1862. "I
"am trying to coerce my thoughts into hammering out the Christmas Idea for a book.
"number. And I have an idea of opening a book (not the Christmas
"number—a book) by bringing together two strongly contrasted places
"and two strongly contrasted sets of people, with which and with whom
"the story is to rest, through the agency of an electric message. I think
"a fine thing might be made of the message itself shooting over the land
"and under the sea, and it would be a curious way of sounding the key
"note."

LONDON:
1855-65.
Insects and
men.
be added a fancy that savours of the same mood of discontent, political and social. "How do I "know that I, a man, am to learn from insects— "unless it is to learn how little my littlenesses "are? All that botheration in the hive about the "queen bee, may be, in little, me and the court "circular."

A domestic story he had met with in the State Trials struck him greatly by its capabilities, and I may preface it by mentioning another subject, not entered in the Memoranda, which for a long time impressed him as capable of attractive Touching
fancy. treatment. It was after reading one of the witch-trials that this occurred to him; and the heroine was to be a girl who for a special purpose had taken a witch's disguise, and whose trick was not discovered until she was actually at the stake. Here is the State Trials story as told by Dickens. "There is a case in the State Trials, where a cer-Miser's
daughter."tain officer made love to a (supposed) miser's "daughter, and ultimately induced her to give her "father slow poison, while nursing him in sickness. "Her father discovered it, told her so, forgave "her, and said 'Be patient my dear—I shall not " 'live long, even if I recover: and then you shall " 'have all my wealth.' Though penitent then, "she afterwards poisoned him again (under the Story from
State Trials."same influence), and successfully. Whereupon it "appeared that the old man had no money at all, "and had lived on a small annuity which died "with him, though always feigning to be rich. "He had loved this daughter with great affection."

A theme touching closely on ground that

some might think dangerous, is sketched in the
following fancy. "The father (married young)
"who, in perfect innocence, venerates his son's
"young wife, as the realization of his ideal of
"woman. (He not happy in his own choice.) The
"son slights her, and knows nothing of her worth.
"The father watches her, protects her, labours for *Father and*
"her, endures for her,—is for ever divided be- *son's wife.*
"tween his strong natural affection for his son as
"his son, and his resentment against him as this
"young creature's husband." Here is another,
less dangerous, which he took from an actual
occurrence made known to him when he was at
Bonchurch. "The idea of my being brought up
"by my mother (me the narrator), my father being *Daughter and*
"dead; and growing up in this belief until I find *unknown father.*
"that my father is the gentleman I have some-
"times seen, and oftener heard of, who has the
"handsome young wife, and the dog I once took
"notice of when I was a little child, and who
"lives in the great house and drives about."

Very admirable is this. "The girl separating
"herself from the lover who has shewn himself un-
"worthy—loving him still—living single for his
"sake—but never more renewing their old rela-
"tions. Coming to him when they are both
"grown old, and nursing him in his last illness." Nor
is the following less so. "Two girls *mis-marrying* *Girls mis-*
"two men. The man who has evil in him, dragging *marrying.*
"the superior woman down. The man who has
"good in him, raising the inferior woman up."
Dickens would have been at his best in working
out both fancies.

London:
1855-65.
Over-in-
teresting.

In some of the most amusing of his sketches of character, women also take the lead. "The "lady un peu passée, who is determined to be "interesting. No matter how much I love that "person—nay, the more so for that very reason— "I MUST flatter, and bother, and be weak and "apprehensive and nervous, and what not. If I "were well and strong, agreeable and self-denying, "my friend might forget me." Another not re- motely belonging to the same family is as neatly

Sentimen-
talist and
her Fate.

hit off. "The sentimental woman feels that the "comic, undesigning, unconscious· man, is 'Her "'Fate.'—I her fate? God bless my soul, it puts "me into a cold perspiration to think of it. *I* her "fate? How can *I* be her fate? I don't mean "to be. I don't want to have anything to do "with her.—Sentimental woman perceives never- "theless that Destiny must be accomplished."

Other portions of a female group are as humorously sketched and hardly less entertaining. "The enthusiastically complimentary person, who "forgets you in her own flowery prosiness: as—

Compli-
mentary.

"'I have no need to say to a person of your "'genius and feeling, and wide range of ex- "'perience'—and then, being shortsighted, puts "up her glass to remember who you are."—"Two "sisters" (these were real people known to him). "One going in for being generally beloved (which "she is not by any means); and the other for "being generally hated (which she needn't be)."— "The bequeathed maid-servant, or friend. Left "as a legacy. And a devil of a legacy too."—

Female
groups.

"The woman who is never on any account to

"hear of anything shocking. For whom the world London: 1855-65.
"is to be of barley-sugar."—"The lady who lives
"on her enthusiasm; and hasn't a jot."—"Bright-
"eyed creature selling jewels. The stones and
"the eyes." Much significance is in the last few
words. One may see to what uses Dickens would
have turned them.

A more troubled note is sounded in another
of these female characters. "I am a common
"woman—fallen. Is it devilry in me—is it a
"wicked comfort—what is it—that induces me to
"be always tempting other women down, while I
"hate myself!" This next, with as much truth in
it, goes deeper than the last. "The prostitute who
"will not let one certain youth approach her.
"'O let there be some one in the world, who hav- Fallen
"'ing an inclination towards me has not gratified women.
"'it, and has not known me in my degradation!'
"She almost loving him.—Suppose, too, this touch
"in her could not be believed in by his mother
"or mistress: by some handsome and proudly
"virtuous woman, always revolting from her." A
more agreeable sketch than either follows, though
it would not please M. Taine so well. "The
"little baby-like married woman—so strange in Baby-wife.
"her new dignity, and talking with tears in her
"eyes, of her sisters 'and all of them' at home.
"Never from home before, and never going back
"again." Another from the same manuscript
volume not less attractive, which was sketched in
his own home, I gave upon a former page.   III. 47, 48.

The female character in its relations with the
opposite sex has lively illustration in the Mc-

moranda. "The man who is governed by his
"wife, and is heartily despised in consequence by
"all other wives; who still want to govern *their*
"husbands, notwithstanding." An alarming family
pair follows that. "The playful—and scratching
"—family. Father and daughter." And here
is another. "The agreeable (and wicked) young-
"mature man, and his devoted sister." What next
was set down he had himself partly seen; and,
by enquiry at the hospital named, had ascertained
the truth of the rest. "The two people in the
"Incurable Hospital.—The poor incurable girl
"lying on a water-bed, and the incurable man
"who has a strange flirtation with her; comes and
"makes confidences to her; snips and arranges
"her plants; and rehearses to her the comic songs (!)
"by writing which he materially helps out his
"living." *

Two lighter figures are very pleasantly touched.
"Set of circumstances which suddenly bring an
"easy, airy fellow into near relations with people
"he knows nothing about, and has never even
"seen. This, through his being thrown in the

* Following this in the "Memoranda" is an advertisement cut
from the *Times:* of a kind that always expressed to Dickens a child-
farming that deserved the gallows quite as much as the worst kind of
starving, by way of farming, babies. The fourteen guineas a-year,
"tender" age of the "dear" ones, maternal care, and no vacations or
extras, to him had only one meaning.

EDUCATION FOR LITTLE CHILDREN.—
Terms 14 to 18 guineas per annum; no extras or
vacations. The system of education embraces the wide
range of each useful and ornamental study suited to
the tender age of the dear children. Maternal care
and kindness may be relied on.—X., Heald's Library,
Fulham-road.

"way of the innocent young personage of the
"story. 'Then there is Uncle Sam to be con-
"'sidered.' says she. 'Aye to be, sure,' says he,
"'so there is! By Jupiter, I forgot Uncle Sam.
"'He's a rock ahead, is Uncle Sam.' He must
"'be considered, of course; he must be smoothed
"'down; he must be cleared out of the way. To
"'be sure. I never thought of Uncle Sam.—
"'By the bye, who *is* Uncle Sam!'"

There are several such sketches as that, to
set against the groups of women; and some have
Dickens's favourite vein of satire in them. "The
"man whose vista is always stopped up by the
"image of Himself. Looks down a long walk,
"and can't see round himself, or over himself, or
"beyond himself. Is always blocking up his own
"way. Would be such a good thing for him, if
"he could knock himself down." Another picture
of selfishness is touched with greater delicacy.
"'Too good' to be grateful to, or dutiful to, or
"anything else that ought to be. 'I won't thank
"'you: you are too good.'—'Don't ask me to
"'marry you: you are too good.'—In short, I
"don't particularly mind ill-using you, and being
"selfish with you: for you are *so* good. Virtue
"its own reward!" A third, which seems to reverse the dial, is but another face of it: frankly
avowing faults, which are virtues. "In effect—I
"admit I am generous, amiable, gentle, magna-
"nimous. Reproach me—I deserve it—I know
"my faults—I have striven in vain to get the
"better of them." Dickens would have made
much, too, of the working out of the next. "The

LONDON:
1855-65.
Self-
knowledge.
"knowing man in distress, who borrows a round
"sum of a generous friend. Comes, in depression
"and tears, dines, gets the money, and gradually
"cheers up over his wine, as he obviously enter-
"tains himself with the reflection that his friend
"is an egregious fool to have lent it to him, and
"that *he* would have known better." And so of
this other. "The man who invariably says ap-
"posite things (in the way of reproof or sarcasm)
"THAT HE DON'T MEAN. Astonished when they
"are explained to him."

Here is a fancy that I remember him to have
been more than once bent upon making use of:
but the opportunity never came. "The two men
"to be guarded against, as to their revenge. One,
Danger not
on the sur-
face.
"whom I openly hold in some serious animosity,
"whom I am at the pains to wound and defy,
"and whom I estimate as worth wounding and
"defying;—the other, whom I treat as a sort of
"insect, and contemptuously and pleasantly flick
"aside with my glove. But, it turns out to be
"the latter who is the really dangerous man; and,
"when I expect the blow from the other, it comes
"from *him.*"

We have the master hand in the following bit
of dialogue, which takes wider application than
that for which it appears to have been intended.

"'There is some virtue in him too.'

How to get
good out of
a man.
"'Virtue! Yes. So there is in any grain of
"'seed in a seedsman's shop—but you must put
"'it in the ground, before you can get any good
"'out of it.'

"'Do you mean that *he* must be put in the LONDON:
1855-65.
"'ground before any good comes of *him?*' ˙

"'Indeed I do. You may call it burying him,
"'or you may call it sowing him, as you like.
"'You must set him in the earth, before you get
"'any good of him.'"

One of the entries is a list of persons and Subjects for
description.
places meant to have been made subjects for
special description, and it will awaken regret that
only as to one of them (the Mugby Refreshments)
his intention was fulfilled. "A Vestryman. A Unused
subjects.
"Briber. A Station Waiting-Room. Refreshments
"at Mugby. A Physician's Waiting-Room. The
"Royal Academy. An Antiquary's house. A Sale
"Room. A Picture Gallery (for sale). A Waste-
"paper Shop. A Post-Office. A Theatre."

All will have been given that have particular
interest or value, from this remarkable volume,
when the thoughts and fancies I proceed to tran-
scribe have been put before the reader.

"The man who is incapable of his own happi- Fancies not
worked
upon.
"ness. Or who is always in pursuit of happi-
"ness. Result, Where is happiness to be found
"then? Surely not Everywhere? Can that be so,
"after all? Is *this* my experience?"

"The people who persist in de 'ning and
"analysing their (and everybody else's) moral
"qualities, motives and what not, at once in the
"narrowest spirit and the most lumbering man-

London:
1855-65.
"ner;—as if one should put up an enormous
"scaffolding for the building of a pigstye."

"The house-full of Toadies and Humbugs.
"They all know and despise one another; but—
"partly to keep their hands in, and partly to make
"out their own individual cases—pretend not to
"detect one another."

"People realising immense sums of money,
"imaginatively — speculatively — counting their
"chickens before hatched. Inflaming each other's
"imaginations about great gains of money, and
"entering into a sort of intangible, impossible,
"competition as to who is the richer."

Unused
characters.
"The advertising sage, philosopher, and friend:
"who educates 'for the bar, the pulpit, or the
"'stage.'"

"The character of the real refugee—not the
"conventional; the real."

"The mysterious character, or characters, inter-
"changing confidences. 'Necessary to be very
"'careful in that direction.'—'In what direction?'
"—'B'—'You don't say so. What, do you mean
"'that C——?'—'Is aware of D. Exactly.'"

"The father and boy, as I dramatically see London:
"them. Opening with the wild dance I have in —————— 1865-65.
"my mind."

_____

"The old child. That is to say, born of Old children.
"parents advanced in life, and observing the
"parents of other children to be young. Taking
"an old tone accordingly."

_____

"A thoroughly sulky character — perverting
"everything. Making the good, bad—and the
"bad, good."

_____

"The people who lay all their sins, negligences
"and ignorances, on Providence."

_____

"The man who marries his cook at last, after
"being so desperately knowing about the sex."

_____

"The swell establishment, frightfully mean and Showy and
"miserable in all but the 'reception rooms.' Those mean.
"very showy."

_____

"B. tells M. what my opinion is of his work,
"&c. Quoting the man you have once spoken
"to, as if he had talked a life's talk in two
"minutes."

_____

19*

London:
1855-65.
Hide and
seek.

"A misplaced and mis-married man; always, as
"it were, playing hide and seek with the world;
"and never finding what Fortune seems to have
"hidden when he was born."

Dead
children.

"Certain women in Africa who have lost
"children, carry little wooden images of children
"on their heads, and always put their food to
"the lips of those images, before tasting it them-
"selves.   This is in a part of Africa where the
"mortality among children (judging from the num-
"ber of these little memorials) is very great."

Available
names.

Two more entries are the last which he made.
"AVAILABLE NAMES" introduces a wonderful list
in the exact following classes and order; as to
which the reader may be left to his own memory
for selection of such as found their way into the
several stories from *Little Dorrit* to the end.
The rest, not lifted into that higher notice by
. such favour of their creator, must remain like
any other undistinguished crowd.   But among
them may perhaps be detected, by those who
have special insight for the physiognomy of a
name, some few with so great promise in them
of fun and character as will make the "mute in-
"glorious" fate which has befallen them a subject
for special regret; and much ingenious speculation
will probably wait upon all. Dickens has generally
been thought, by the curious, to display not a

few of his most characteristic traits in this par- LONDON: 1855-65.
ticular field of invention.

First there are titles for books; and from the
list subjoined were taken two for Christmas
numbers and two for stories, though *Nobody's
Fault* had ultimately to give way to *Little Dorrit.*

> "THE LUMBER ROOM.   *Titles for books.*
> "SOMEBODY'S LUGGAGE.
> "TO BE LEFT TILL CALLED FOR.
> "SOMETHING WANTED.
> "EXTREMES MEET.
> "NOBODY'S FAULT.
> "THE GRINDSTONE.
> "ROKESMITH'S FORGE.
> "OUR MUTUAL FRIEND.
> "THE CINDER HEAP.
> "TWO GENERATIONS.
> "BROKEN CROCKERY.
> "DUST.
> "THE HOME DEPARTMENT.
> "THE YOUNG PERSON.
> "NOW OR NEVER.
> "MY NEIGHBOURS.
> "THE CHILDREN OF THE FATHERS,
> "NO THOROUGHFARE."

Then comes a batch of "Christian names":
Girls and Boys: which stand thus, with mention
of the source from which he obtained them.
These therefore can hardly be called pure invention. Some would have been reckoned too
extravagant for anything but reality.

"Girls from Privy Council Education lists.

"LELIA.	ETTY.	DORIS.
"MENELLA.	REBINAH.	BALZINA.
"RUBINA.	SEBA.	PLEASANT.
"IRIS.	PERSIA.	GENTILLA.
"REBECCA.	ARAMANDA.	

"Boys from Privy Council Education lists.

"DOCTOR.	ZERUBBABEL.	PICKLES.
"HOMER.	MAXIMILIAN.	ORANGE.
"ODEN.	URBIN.	FEATHER.
"BRADLEY.	SAMILLAS.	

"Girls and Boys from Ditto.

"AMANDA, ETHLYNIDA; BOETIUS, BOLTIUS."

To which he adds supplementary lists that appear to be his own.

"More Boys.

"ROBERT LADLE.	WALTER ASHES.
"JOLY STICK.	ZEPHANIAH FERRY (or
"BILL MARIGOLD.	FURY).
"STEPHEN MARQUICK.	WILLIAM WHY.
"JONATHAN KNOTWELL.	ROBERT GOSPEL.
"PHILIP BROWNDRESS.	THOMAS FATHERLY.
"HENRY GHOST.	ROBIN SCUBBAM.
"GEORGE MUZZLE.	

"More Girls.

"SARAH GOLDSACKS.	ALICE THORNEYWORK.
"ROSETTA DUST.	SALLY GIMBLET.
"SUSAN GOLDRING.	VERITY HAWKYARD.
"CATHERINE TWO.	BIRDIE NASH.
"MATILDA RAINBIRD.	AMBROSINA EVENTS.
"MIRIAM DENIAL.	APAULINA VERNON.
"SOPHIA DOOMSDAY.	NELTIE ASHFORD."

And then come the mass of his "available LONDON: 1855-65. "names," which stand thus, without other introduction or comment:

"TOWNDLING.   HIGDEN.
"MOOD.   MORFIT.
"GUFF.   GOLDSTRAW.
"TREBLE.   BARREL.
"CHILBY.   INGE.
"SPESSIFER.   JUMP.
"WODDER.   JIGGINS.
"WHELPFORD.   BONES.
"FENNERCK.   COY.
"GANNERSON.   DAWN.
"CHINKERBLE.   TATKIN.
"BINTREY.   DROWVEY.
"FLEDSON.   PUDSEY.
"HIRLL.   PEDSEY.   Available names.
"BRAYLE.   DUNCALF.
"MULLENDER.   TRICKLEBANK.
"TRESLINGHAM.   SAPSEA.
"BRANKLE.   READYHUFF.
"SITTERN.   DUFTY.
"DOSTONE.   FOGGY.
"CAY-LON.   TWINN.
"SLYANT.   BROWNSWORD.
"QUEEDY.   PEARTREE.
"BESSELTHUR.   SUDDS.
"MUSTY.   SILVERMAN.
"GROUT.   KIMBER.
"TERTIUS JOBBER.   LAUGHLEY.
"AMON HEADSTON.   LESSOCK.
"STRAYSHOTT.   TIPPINS.

London:
1855-65.

Available
names.

"MINNITT.	SANLORN.
"RADLOWE.	LIGHTWORD.
"PRATCHET.	TITBULL.
"MAWDETT.	BANGHAM.
"WOZENHAM.	KYLE—NYLE.
"SNOWELL.	PEMBLE.
"LOTTRUM.	MAXEY.
"LAMMLE.	ROKESMITH.
"FROSER.	CHIVERY.
"HOLBLACK.	WABBLER.
"MULLEY.	PEEX—SPEEX.
"REDWORTH.	GANNAWAY.
"REDFOOT.	MRS. FLINKS.
"TARBOX (B)	FLINX.
"TINKLING.	JEE.
"DUDDLE.	HARDEN.
"JEBUS.	MERDLE.
"POWDERHILL.	MURDEN.
"GRIMMER.	TOPWASH.
"SKUSE.	PORDAGE.
"TITCOOMBE.	DORRET—DORRIT.
"CRABBLE.	CARTON.
"SWANNOCK.	MINIFIE.
"TUZZEN.	SLINGO.
"TWEMLOW.	JOAD.
"SQUAB.	KINCH.
"JACKMAN.	MAG.
"SUGG.	CHELLYSON.
"BREMMIDGE.	BLENNAM—CL.
"SILAS BLODGET.	BARDOCK.
"MELVIN BEAL.	SNIGSWORTH.
"BUTTRICK.	SWENTON.
"EDSON.	CASBY—BEACH.

"LOWLEIGH—LOWELY.	DIBTON.	LONDON: 1855-65.
"PIGRIN.	WILFER.	
"YERBURY.	GLIBBERY.	
"PLORNISH.	MULVEY.	
"MAROON.	HORLICK.	
"BANDY-NANDY.	DOOLGE.	
"STONEBURY.	GANNERY.	
"MAGWITCH.	GARGERY.	
"MEAGLES.	WILLSHARD.	
"PANCKS.	RIDERHOOD.	
"HAGGAGE.	PRATTERSTONE.	
"PROVIS.	CHINKIBLE.	Available
"STILTINGTON.	WOPSELL.	names.
"STILTWALK.	WOPSLE.	
"STILTINGSTALK.	WHELPINGTON.	
"STILTSTALKING.	WHELPFORD.	
"RAVENDER.	GAYVERY.	
"PODSNAP.	WEGG.	
"CLARRIKER.	HUBBLE.	
"COMPERY.	URRY.	
"STRIVER—STRYVER.	KIBBLE.	
"PUMBLECHOOK.	SKIFFINS.	
"WANGLER.	WODDER.	
"BOFFIN.	ETSER.	
"BANTINCK.	AKERSHEM."	

The last of the Memoranda, and the last words
written by Dickens in the blank paper book containing them, are these. "'Then I'll give up snuff.'
"Brobity.—An alarming sacrifice. Mr. Brobity's
"snuff-box. The Pawnbroker's account of it!"
What was proposed by this must be left to con-
jecture; but "Brobity" is the name of one of the

people in his unfinished story, and the suggestion may have been meant for some incident in it. If so, it is the only passage in the volume which can be in any way connected with the piece of writing on which he was last engaged. Some names were taken for it from the lists, but there is otherwise nothing to recall *Edwin Drood*.

CHAPTER LVII.

THIRD SERIES OF READINGS.

1864-1867.

THE sudden death of Thackeray on the Christmas eve of 1863 was a painful shock to Dickens.
It would not become me to speak, when he has
himself spoken, of his relations with so great a
writer and so old a friend.

"I saw him first, nearly twenty-eight years ago,
"when he proposed to become the illustrator of
"my earliest book. I saw him last,* shortly be-
"fore Christmas, at the Athenæum Club, when
"he told me that he had been in bed three days
" . . . and that he had it in his mind to try a new
"remedy which he laughingly described. He was
"cheerful, and looked very bright. In the night
"of that day week, he died. The long interval
"between these two periods is marked in my
"remembrance of him by many occasions when

London:
1864.

Death of
Thackeray.

---

* There had been some estrangement between them since the
autumn of 1858, hardly now worth mention even in a note. Thackeray,
justly indignant at a published description of himself by the member of
a club to which both he and Dickens belonged, referred it to the Committee, who decided to expel the writer. Dickens, thinking expulsion
too harsh a penalty for an offence thoughtlessly given, and, as far as
might be, manfully atoned for by withdrawal and regret, interposed to
avert that extremity. Thackeray resented the interference, and Dickens
was justly hurt by the manner in which he did so. Neither was wholly
right, nor was either altogether in the wrong.

Estrange-
ment.

LONDON:
1861.

"he was extremely humorous, when he was irre-
"sistibly extravagant, when he was softened and
"serious, when he was charming with children. . .
"No one can be surer than I, of the greatness
"and goodness of his heart. . . In no place should
"I take it upon myself at this time to discourse
"of his books, of his refined knowledge of cha-
"racter, of his subtle acquaintance with the weak-
"nesses of human nature, of his delightful play-
"fulness as an essayist, of his quaint and touch-
"ing ballads, of his mastery over the English
"language. . . But before me lies all that he had

Dickens on
Thackeray.

"written of his latest story . . . and the pain I
"have felt in perusing it has not been deeper
"than the conviction that he was in the healthiest
"vigour of his powers when he worked on this
"last labour. . . The last words he corrected in
"print were 'And my heart throbbed with an ex-
"'quisite bliss.' God grant that on that Christmas
"Eve when he laid his head back on his pillow
"and threw up his arms as he had been wont to
"do when very weary, some consciousness of duty
"done, and of Christian hope throughout life

Cornhill
Magazine for
February
1861.

"humbly cherished, may have caused his own
"heart so to throb, when he passed away to his
"Redeemer's rest. He was found peacefully lying
"as above described, composed, undisturbed, and
"to all appearance asleep."

Other griefs were with Dickens at this time,
and close upon them came the too certain evidence that his own health was yielding to the
overstrain which had been placed upon it by the
occurrences and anxieties of the few preceding

years. His mother, whose infirm health had been
tending for more than two years to the close,
died in September 1863; and on his own birthday in the following February he had tidings of
the death of his second son Walter, on the last
day of the old year, in the officers' hospital at
Calcutta; to which he had been sent up invalided
from his station, on his way home. He was a
lieutenant in the 26th Native Infantry regiment,
and had been doing duty with the 42nd High-
landers. In 1853 his father had thus written to
the youth's godfather, Walter Savage Landor:
"Walter is a very good boy, and comes home
"from school with honorable commendation and
"a prize into the bargain. He never gets into
"trouble, for he is a great favourite with the whole
"house and one of the most amiable boys in the
"boy-world. He comes out on birthdays in a
"blaze of shirt pin." The pin was a present from
Landor; to whom three years later, when the boy
had obtained his cadetship through the kindness
of Miss Coutts, Dickens wrote again. "Walter
"has done extremely well at school; has brought
"home a prize in triumph; and will be eligible
"to 'go up' for his India examination soon after
"next, Easter. Having a direct appointment he
"will probably be sent out soon after he has
"passed, and so will fall into that strange life
"'up the country' before he well knows he is
"alive, or what life is—which indeed seems to
"be rather an advanced state of knowledge." If
he had lived another month he would have reached
his twenty-third year, and perhaps not then the

advanced state of knowledge his father speaks of. But, never forfeiting his claim to those kindly paternal words, he had the goodness and simplicity of boyhood to the last.

Dickens had at this time begun his last story in twenty numbers, and my next chapter will show through what unwonted troubles, in this and the following year, he had to fight his way. What otherwise during its progress chiefly interested him, was the enterprise of Mr. Fechter at the Lyceum, of which he had become the lessee; and Dickens was moved to this quite as much by generous sympathy with the difficulties of such a position to an artist who was not an Englishman, as by genuine admiration of Mr.

Fechter's acting. He became his helper in disputes, adviser on literary points, referee in matters of management; and for some years no face was more familiar than the French comedian's at Gadshill or in the office of his journal. But theatres and their affairs are things of a season,

and even Dickens's whim and humour will not revive for us any interest in these. No bad example, however, of the difficulties in which a French actor may find himself with English playwrights, will appear in a few amusing words from one of his letters about a piece played at the Princess's before the Lyceum management was taken in hand.

"I have been cautioning Fechter about the "play whereof he gave the plot and scenes to "B; and out of which I have struck some enor- "mities, my account of which will (I think) amuse

"you. It has one of the best first acts I ever LONDON:
"saw; but if he can do much with the last two, —— 1864.
"not to say three, there are resources in his art
"that *I* know nothing about. When I went over
"the play this day week, he was at least 20
"minutes, *in a boat, in the last scene*, discussing
"with another gentleman (also in the boat)
"whether he should kill him or not; after which Ticklish
"the gentleman dived overboard and swam for points.
"it. Also, in the most important and dangerous
"parts of the play, there was a young person of
"the name of Pickles who was constantly being
"mentioned by name, in conjunction with the
"powers of light or darkness; as, 'Great Heaven!
"'Pickles?'—'By Hell, 'tis Pickles!'—'Pickles? a
"'thousand Devils!'—'Distraction! Pickles?'" *

* As I have thus fallen on theatrical subjects, I may add one or
two practical experiences which befell Dickens at theatres in the autumn
of 1864, when he sallied forth from his office upon these night wanderings to "cool" a boiling head. "I went the other night" (8th of October) "to see the *Streets of London* at the Princess's. A piece that is *Streets of*
"really drawing all the town, and filling the house with nightly overflows. *London* at
"It is the most depressing instance, without exception, of an utterly Princess's.
"degraded and debased theatrical taste that has ever come under my
"writhing notice. For not only do the audiences—of all classes—go,
"but they are unquestionably delighted. At Astley's there has been
"much puffing at great cost of a certain Miss Ada Isaacs Menkin, who
"is to be seen bound on the horse in *Mazeppa* 'ascending the fearful *Mazeppa*
"'precipices not as hitherto done by a dummy.' Last night, having a at Astley's.
"boiling head, I went out from here to cool myself on Waterloo Bridge,
"and I thought I would go and see this heroine. Applied at the box-
"door for a stall. 'None left sir.' For a box-ticket. 'Only standing-
"'room sir.' Then the man (busy in counting great heaps of veritable
"checks) recognizes me and says—'Mr. Smith will be very much con-
"cerned when he hears that you went away sir'—'Never mind; I'll
"'come again.' 'You never go behind I think sir, or—?' 'No thank
"'you, I never go behind.' 'Mr. Smith's box, sir—' 'No thank you,
"'I'll come again.' Now who do you think the lady is? If you don't
"already know, ask that question of the highest Irish mountains that
"look eternal, and they'll never tell you—*Mrs. Heenan!*" This lady, A poetical
who turned out to be one of Dickens's greatest admirers, addressed him admirer.
at great length on hearing of this occurrence, and afterwards dedicated

London:
1865.
Sorrowful
New Year.

The old year ended and the new one opened sadly enough. The death of Leech in November affected Dickens very much,* and a severe attack of illness in February put a broad mark between his past life and what remained to him of

Lameness.
VI. 211-12.

the future. The lameness now began in his left foot which never afterwards wholly left him, which was attended by great suffering, and which baffled experienced physicians. He had persisted in his ordinary exercise during heavy snow-storms, and to the last he had the fancy that his illness was merely local. But that this was an error is now certain; and it is more than probable that if the nervous danger and disturbance it implied had been correctly appreciated at the time, its warning might have been of priceless value to

Over-con-
fidence.

Dickens. Unhappily he never thought of husbanding his strength except for the purpose of making fresh demands upon it, and it was for this he took a brief holyday in France during

---

a volume of poems to him! There was a pleasanter close to his letter. "Contrariwise I assisted another night at the Adelphi (where I couldn't,

Mr. Toole.
Ante, 49.

"with careful calculation, get the house up to Nine Pounds), and saw "quite an admirable performance of Mr. Toole and Mrs. Mellon—she, "an old servant, wonderfully like Anne—he, showing a power of passion "very unusual indeed in a comic actor, as such things go, and of a "quite remarkable kind."

* Writing to me three months before, he spoke of the death of one whom he had known from his boyhood (ante, i. 55-6) and with whom he had fought unsuccessfully for some years against the management of the Literary Fund. "Poor Dilke! I am very sorry that the capital old

Charles
Wentworth
Dilke.

"stout-hearted man is dead." Sorrow may also be expressed that no adequate record should remain of a career which for steadfast purpose, conscientious maintenance of opinion, and pursuit of public objects with disregard of self, was one of very high example. So averse was Mr. Dilke to every kind of display that his name appears to none of the literary investigations which were conducted by him with an acuteness wonderful as his industry, and it was in accordance with his express instructions that the literary journal which his energy and self-denial had established kept silence respecting him at his death.

the summer. "Before I went away," he wrote to LONDON: 1865.
his daughter, "I had certainly worked myself into
"a damaged state. But the moment I got away,
"I began, thank God, to get well. I hope to
"profit by this experience, and to make future
"dashes from my desk before I want them." At
his return he was in the terrible railway accident
at Staplehurst, on a day * which proved after- Fatal anniversary.
wards more fatal to him; and it was with shaken
nerves but unsubdued energy he resumed the
labour to be presently described. His foot troubled
him more or less throughout the autumn; ** he
was beset by nervous apprehensions which the
accident had caused to himself, not lessened by
his generous anxiety to assuage the severer suf- Staplehurst
sufferers.
ferings inflicted by it on others; *** and that he

---

* One day before, the 8th of June 1865, his old friend Sir Joseph
Paxton had breathed his last.
** Here are allusions to it at that time. "I have got a boot on to-
"day,—made on an Otranto scale, but really not very discernible from
"its ordinary sized companion." After a few days' holiday: "I began
"to feel my foot stronger the moment I breathed the sea air. Still,
"during the ten days I have been away, I have never been able to wear
"a boot after four or five in the afternoon, but have passed all the
"evenings with the foot up, and nothing on it. I am burnt brown and Attack in his
"have walked by the sea perpetually, yet I feel certain that if I wore a foot.
"knot this evening, I should be taken with those torments again before See VI.211-12.
"the night was out." This last letter ended thus: "As a relief to my
"late dismal letters, I send you the newest American story. Backwoods
"Doctor is called in to the little boy of a woman-settler. Stares at the
"child some time through a pair of spectacles. Ultimately takes them
"off, and says to the mother: 'Wa'al Marm, this is small-pox. 'Tis
"'Marm, small-pox. But I am not posted up in Pustuls, and I do not American
"'know as I could bring him along slick through it. But I'll tell you story.
"'wa'at I can do Marm:—I can send him a draft as will certainly put
"'him into a most eternal Fit, and I am almighty smart at Fits, and we
"'might git round Old Grizly that way.'"
*** I give one such instance; "The railway people have offered, in The accident.
"the case of the young man whom I got out of the carriage just alive,
"all the expenses and a thousand pounds down. The father declines
"to accept the offer. It seems unlikely that the young man, whose des-
"tination is India, would ever be passed for the Army now by the Medi-

should nevertheless have determined, on the close of his book, to undertake a series of readings involving greater strain and fatigue than any hitherto, was a startling circumstance. He had perhaps become conscious, without owning it even to himself, that for exertion of this kind the time left him was short; but, whatever pressed him on, his task of the next three years, self-imposed, was to make the most money in the shortest time without any regard to the physical labour to be undergone. The very letter announcing his new engagement shows how entirely unfit he was to enter upon it.

"For some time," he wrote at the end of February 1866, "I have been very unwell. F. B. "wrote me word that with such a pulse as I de-"scribed, an examination of the heart was ab-"solutely necessary. 'Want of muscular power "'in the heart,' B said. 'Only remarkable irri-"'tability of the heart,' said Doctor Brinton of "Brook-street, who had been called in to con-"sultation. I was not disconcerted; for I knew "well beforehand that the effect could not pos-"sibly be without the one cause at the bottom of "it, of some degeneration of some function of "the heart. Of course I am not so foolish as to "suppose that all my work can have been achieved "without *some* penalty, and I have noticed for "some time a decided change in my buoyancy "and hopefulness—in other words, in my usual "'tone.' But tonics have already brought me

"cal heard. The question is, how far will that contingency tell, under " Lord Campbell's Act?"

"round. So I have accepted an offer from Chap-
"pells of Bond-street, of £50 a night for thirty
"nights to read 'in England, Ireland, Scotland, or
"'Paris;' they undertaking all the business, paying
"all personal expenses, travelling and otherwise,
"of myself, John" (his office servant), "and my
"gasman; and making what they can of it. I
"begin, I believe, in Liverpool on the Thursday
"in Easter week, and then come to London. I
"am going to read at Cheltenham (on my own
"account) on the 23rd and 24th of this month,
"staying with Macready of course."

The arrangement of this series of Readings
differed from those of its predecessors in relieving Dickens from every anxiety except of the
reading itself; but, by such rapid and repeated
change of nights at distant places as kept him
almost wholly in a railway carriage when not at
the reading-desk or in bed, it added enormously
to the physical fatigue. He would read at St.
James's Hall in London one night, and at Bradford the next. He would read in Edinburgh, go
on to Glasgow and to Aberdeen, then come
back to Glasgow, read again in Edinburgh, strike
off to Manchester, come back to St. James's Hall
once more, and begin the same round again. It
was labour that must in time have broken down
the strongest man, and what Dickens was when
he assumed it we have seen.

He did not himself admit a shadow of misgiving. "As to the readings" (11th of March),
"all I have to do is, to take in my book and
"read, at the appointed place and hour, and

"come out again. All the business of every kind,
"is done by Chappells. They take John and my
"other man, merely for my convenience. I have
"no more to do with any detail whatever, than

No mis-
givings.

"you have. They transact all the business at
"their own cost, and on their own responsibility.
"I think they are disposed to do it in a very
"good spirit, because, whereas the original pro-
"position was for thirty readings 'in England,
"'Ireland, Scotland, or Paris,' they wrote out their
"agreement 'in London, the Provinces, or else-
"'where, *as you and we may agree.*' For this
"they pay £1500 in three sums: £500 on be-
"ginning, £500 on the fifteenth Reading, £500
"at the close. Every charge of every kind, they
"pay besides. I rely for mere curiosity on *Doc-
"tor Marigold* (I am going to begin with him in

Faith in
Marigold.

"Liverpool, and at St. James's Hall). I have got
"him up with immense pains, and should like
"to give you a notion what I am going to do
"with him."

The success everywhere went far beyond even
the former successes. A single night at Manchester, when eight hundred stalls were let, two
thousand five hundred und sixty-five people admitted, and the receipts amounted to more than
three hundred pounds, was followed in nearly
the same proportion by all the greater towns;

Success be-
yond hope.

and on the 20th of April the outlay for the entire venture was paid, leaving all that remained,
to the middle of the month of June, sheer profit.
"I came back last Sunday," he wrote on the
30th of May, "with my last country piece of work

"for this time done. Everywhere the success has LONDON: 1866.
"been the same. St. James's Hall last night was
"quite a splendid spectacle. Two more Tues-
"days there, and I shall retire into private life.
"I have only been able to get to Gadshill once
"since I left it, and that was the day before
"yesterday."

One memorable evening he had passed at A memorable evening. 2nd April.
my house in the interval, when he saw Mrs. I. 139, 188.
Carlyle for the last time. Her sudden death followed shortly after, and near the close of April
he had thus written to me from Liverpool. "It
"was a terrible shock to me, and poor dear
"Carlyle has been in my mind ever since. How
"often I have thought of the unfinished novel.
"No one now to finish it. None of the writing
"women come near her at all." This was an
allusion to what had passed at their meeting. It
was on the second of April, the day when Mr.
Carlyle had delivered his inaugural address as Carlyle Lord Rector.
Lord Rector of Edinburgh University, and a
couple of ardent words from Professor Tyndall
had told her of the triumph just before dinner.
She came to us flourishing the telegram in her
hand, and the radiance of her enjoyment of it
was upon her all the night. Among other things
she gave Dickens the subject for a novel, from Subject for a novel.
what she had herself observed at the outside of
a house in her street; of which the various incidents were drawn from the condition of its
blinds and curtains, the costumes visible at its
windows, the cabs at its door, its visitors admitted or rejected, its articles of furniture de-

livered or carried away; and the subtle serious
humour of it all, the truth in trifling bits of character, and the gradual progress into a half-
romantic interest, had enchanted the skilled
novelist. She was well into the second volume
of her small romance before she left, being as far
as her observation then had taken her; but in a
few days' exciting incidents were expected, the
denouement could not be far off, and Dickens
was to have it when they met again. Yet it was
to something far other than this amusing little
fancy his thoughts had carried him, when he
wrote of no one being capable to finish what she
might have begun. In greater things this was
still more true. No one could doubt it who had
come within the fascinating influence of that
sweet and noble nature. With some of the
highest gifts of intellect, and the charm of a most
varied knowledge of books and things, there was
something "beyond, beyond." No one who knew
Mrs. Carlyle could replace her loss when she had
passed away.

The same letter which told of his uninterrupted success to the last, told me also that he
had a heavy cold upon him and was "very tired
and depressed." Some weeks before the first batch
of readings closed, Messrs. Chappell had already
tempted him with an offer for fifty more nights
to begin at Christmas, for which he meant, as he
then said, to ask them seventy pounds a night.
"It would be unreasonable to ask anything now
"on the ground of the extent of the late success,
"but I am bound to look to myself for the future.

"The Chappells are speculators, though of the LONDON: 1866.
"worthiest and most honourable kind. They make
"some bad speculations, and have made a very
"good one in this case, and will set this against
"those. I told them when we agreed: 'I offer
"'these thirty Readings to you at fifty pounds a
"'night, because I know perfectly well before-
"'hand that no one in your business has the least
"'idea of their real worth, and I wish to prove it.'
"The sum taken is £4720." The result of the Result of the last.
fresh negotiation, though not completed until the
beginning of August, may be at once described.
"Chappell instantly accepts my proposal of forty
"nights at sixty pounds a night, and every con-
"ceivable and inconceivable expense paid. To
"make an even sum, I have made it forty-two
"nights for £2500. So I shall now try to dis-
"cover a Christmas number" (he means the subject for one), "and shall, please Heaven, be quit
"of the whole series of readings so as to get to What was designed to be done.
"work on a new story for the new series of *All* VI. 157.
"*the Year Round* early in the spring. The read-
"ings begin probably with the New Year." These
were fair designs, but the fairest are the sport of
circumstance, and though the subject for Christmas was found, the new series of *All the Year
Round* never had a new story from its founder.
With whatever consequence to himself, the strong What was done.
tide of the Readings was to sweep on to its full.
The American war had ceased, and the first renewed
offers from the States had been made and rejected.
Hovering over all, too, were other sterner disposi-
tions. "I think," he wrote in September, "there

"is some strange influence in the atmosphere.
"Twice last week I was seized in a most distress-
"ing manner—apparently in the heart; but, I am
"persuaded, only in the nervous system."

In the midst of his ovations such checks had
not been wanting. "The police reported offi-
"cially," he wrote to his daughter from Liverpool
on the 14th of April, "that three thousand people
"were turned away from the hall last night. . .

"Except that I can *not* sleep, I really think myself
"in very much better training than I had antici-
"pated. A dozen oysters and a little champagne
"between the parts every night, seem to constitute
"the best restorative I have ever yet tried." "Such
"a prodigious demonstration last night at Man-
"chester," he wrote to the same correspondent
twelve days later, "that I was obliged (contrary
"to my principle in such cases) to go back. I am

"very tired to-day; for it would be of itself very
"hard work in that immense place, if there were
"not to be added eighty miles of railway and late
"hours to boot." "It has been very heavy work,"
he wrote to his sister-in-law on the 11th of May
from Clifton, "getting up at 6.30 each morning
"after a heavy night, and I am not at all well to-

"day. We had a tremendous hall at Birmingham
"last night, £230 odd, 2100 people; and I made
"a most ridiculous mistake. Had *Nickleby* on my
"list to finish with, instead of *Trial*. Read *Nickle-*
"*by* with great go, *and the people remained.* Went

"back again at 10 o'clock, and explained the ac-
"cident: but said if they liked I would give them
"the *Trial*. They *did* like;—and I had another

"half hour of it, in that enormous place. . . I have PROVINCES:
1866.
"so severe a pain in the ball of my left eye that ————
"it makes it hard for me to do anything after 100
"miles shaking since breakfast. My cold is no
"better, nor my hand either." It was his left eye,
it will be noted, as it was his left foot and hand;
the irritability or faintness of heart was also of
course on the left side; and it was on the same
left side he felt most of the effect of the railway See VI. 67.
accident.

Everything was done to make easier the labour
of travel, but nothing could materially abate either SCOTLAND.
the absolute physical exhaustion, or the nervous
strain. "We arrived here," he wrote from Aberdeen (16th of May), "safe and sound between At Aberdeen.
"3 and 4 this morning. There was a compart-
"ment for the men, and a charming room for
"ourselves furnished with sofas and easy chairs.
"We had also a pantry and washing-stand. This
"carriage is to go about with us." Two days
later he wrote from Glasgow: "We halted at
"Perth yesterday, and got a lovely walk there. At Perth.
"Until then I had been in a condition the reverse
"of flourishing; half strangled with my cold, and
"dyspeptically gloomy and dull; but, as I feel
"much more like myself this morning, we are
"going to get some fresh air aboard a steamer on
"the Clyde." The last letter during his country On the Clyde.
travel was from Portsmouth on the 24th of May,
and contained these words: "You need have no
"fear about America." The readings closed in
June.

The readings of the new year began with

even increased enthusiasm, but not otherwise with happier omen. Here was his first outline of plan: "I start on Wednesday afternoon (the "15th of January) for Liverpool, and then go on "to Chester, Derby, Leicester, and Wolverhamp-"ton. On Tuesday the 29th I read in London "again, and in February I read at Manchester "and then go on into Scotland." From Liverpool he wrote on the 21st: "The enthusiasm has been "unbounded. On Friday might I quite astonished "myself; but I was taken so faint afterwards that "they laid me on a sofa at the hall for half an "hour. I attribute it to my distressing inability "to sleep at night, and to nothing worse. Every-"thing is made as easy to me as it possibly can "be. Dolby would do anything to lighten the "work, and *does* everything." The weather was sorely against him. "At Chester," he wrote on the 24th from Birmingham, "we read in a snow-"storm and a fall of ice. I think it was the worst "weather I ever saw . . . At Wolverhampton last "night the thaw had thoroughly set in, and it "rained furiously, and I was again heavily beaten. "We came on here after the reading (it is only "a ride of forty miles), and it was as much as I "could do to hold out the journey. But I was "not faint, as at Liverpool. I was only ex-"hausted." Five days later he had returned for his Reading in London, and thus replied to a summons to dine with Macready at my house: "I am very tired; cannot sleep; have been severely "shaken on an atrocious railway; read to-night, "and have to read at Leeds on Thursday. But I

"have settled with Dolby to put off our going to
"Leeds on Wednesday, in the hope of coming to ————
"dine with you, and seeing our dear old friend.
"I say 'in the hope,' because if I should be a
"little more used-up to-morrow than I am to-day,
"I should be constrained, in spite of myself, to
"take to the sofa and stick there."

On the 15th of February he wrote to his
sister-in-law from Liverpool that they had had "an
"enormous turn-away" the previous night. "The
"day has been very fine, and I have turned it to
"the wholesomest account by walking on the
"sands at New Brighton all the morning. I am
"not quite right within, but believe it to be an
"effect of the railway shaking. There is no doubt
"of the fact that, after the Staplehurst experience,
"it tells more and more (railway shaking, that is)
"instead of, as one might have expected, less and
"less." The last remark is a strange one, from a
man of his sagacity; but it was part of the too-
willing self-deception which he practised, to justify
him in his professed belief that these continued
excesses of labour and excitement were really
doing him no harm. The day after that last
letter he pushed on to Scotland, and on the 17th
wrote to his daughter from Glasgow. The closing night at Manchester had been enormous.
"They cheered to that extent after it was over
"that I was obliged to huddle on my clothes (for
"I was undressing to prepare for the journey) and
"go back again. After so heavy a week, it *was*
"rather stiff to start on this long journey at a
"quarter to two in the morning; but I got more

Scotland:
1867.
"sleep than I ever got in a railway-carriage be-
"fore . . . I have, as I had in the last series of
"readings, a curious feeling of soreness all round
"the body—which I suppose to arise from the
"great exertion of voice . . ." Two days later he
wrote. to his sister-in-law from the Bridge of
Allan, which he had reached from Glasgow that

An old
malady,
II. 110.
morning. "Yesterday I was so unwell with an
"internal malady that occasionally at long inter-
"vals troubles me a little, and it was attended
"with the sudden loss of so much blood, that I
"wrote to F. B. from whom I shall doubtless hear
"to-morrow . , . I felt it a little more exertion to
"read, afterwards, and I passed a sleepless night
"after that again; but otherwise I am in good
"force and spirits to-day: I may say, in the best
"force . . . The quiet of this little place is sure
"to do me good." He rallied again from this attack, and, though he still complained of sleeplessness, wrote cheerfully from Glasgow on the 21st,
describing himself indeed as confined to his room,

In close
"hiding."
but only because "in close hiding from a local
"poet who has christened his infant son in my
"name, and consequently haunts the building."
On getting back to Edinburgh he wrote to me,
with intimation that many troubles ·had beset
him; but that the pleasure of his audiences, and
the providence and forethought of Messrs. Chappell, had borne him through. "Everything is done

What bore
him through.
"for me with the utmost liberality and considera-
"tion. Every want I can have on these journeys
"is anticipated, and not the faintest spark of the
"tradesman spirit ever peeps out. I have three

"men in constant attendance on me; besides NEWCASTLE: 1867.
"Dolby, who is an agreeable companion, an ex-
"cellent manager, and a good fellow."

On the 4th of March he wrote from New- Audiences at Newcastle.
castle: "The readings have made an immense
"effect in this place, and it is remarkable that al-
"though the people are individually rough, col-
"lectively they are an unusually tender and sym-
"pathetic audience; while their comic perception
"is quite up to the high London standard. The
"atmosphere is so very heavy that yesterday we
"escaped to Tynemouth for a two hours' sea walk.
"There was a high north wind blowing, and a
"magnificent sea running. Large vessels were
"being towed in and out over the stormy bar,
"with prodigious waves breaking on it; and,
"spanning the restless uproar of the waters, was
"a quiet rainbow of transcendent beauty. The
"scene was quite wonderful. We were in the full Scene at Tynemouth.
"enjoyment of it when a heavy sea caught us,
"knocked us over, and in a moment drenched us
"and filled even our pockets. We had nothing
"for it but to shake ourselves together (like
"Doctor Marigold), and dry ourselves as well as
"we could by hard walking in the wind and sun-
"shine. But we were wet through for all that,
"when we came back here to dinner after half-
"an-hour's railway drive. I am wonderfully well,
"and quite fresh and strong." Three days later
he was at Leeds; from which he was to work
himself round through the most important neighbouring places to another reading in London,
before again visiting Ireland.

IRELAND: 1867. Fenian excitements.

This was the time of the Fenian excitements; — it was with great reluctance he consented to go;* and he told us all at his first arrival that he should have a complete breakdown. More than 300 stalls were gone at Belfast two days before the reading, but on the afternoon of the reading in Dublin not 50 were taken. Strange to say however a great crowd pressed in at night, he had a tumultuous greeting, and on the 22nd of March I had this announcement from him: "You "will be surprised to be told that we have done "WONDERS! Enthusiastic crowds have filled the "halls to the roof each night, and hundreds have "been turned away. At Belfast the night before "last we had £246 5s. In Dublin to-night every-"thing is sold out, and people are besieging

In Dublin.

Unexpected crowds.

* He wrote to me on the 15th of March from Dublin: "So pro-"foundly discouraging were the accounts from here in London last "Tuesday that I held several councils with Chappell about coming at "all; had actually drawn up a bill announcing (indefinitely) the post-"ponement of the readings; and had meant to give him a reading to "cover the charges incurred—but yielded at last to his representations "the other way. We ran through a snow storm nearly the whole way, "and in Wales got snowed up, came to a stoppage, and had to dig the "engine out. . . We got to Dublin at last, found it snowing and rain-"ing, and heard that it had been snowing and raining since the first day "of the year . . . As to outward signs of trouble or preparation, they "are very few. At Kingstown our boat was waited for by four armed "policemen, and some stragglers in various dresses who were clearly "detectives. But there was no show of soldiery. My people carry a "long heavy box containing gas-fittings. This was immediately laid "hold of; but one of the stragglers instantly interposed on seeing my "name, and came to me in the carriage and apologised . . . The worst "looking young fellow I ever saw, turned up at Holyhead before we "went to bed there, and sat glooming and glowering by the coffee-room "fire while we warmed ourselves. He said he had been snowed up with "us (which we didn't believe), and was horribly disconcerted by some "box of his having gone to Dublin without him. We said to one another "'Fenian:' and certainly he disappeared in the morning, and let his "box go where it would." What Dickens heard and saw in Dublin, during this visit, convinced him that Fenianism and disaffection had found their way into several regiments.

Reluctance to go to Ireland.

Attentions of police.

"Fenian."

"Dolby to put chairs anywhere, in doorways, on
"my platform, in any sort of hole or corner. In
"short the Readings are a perfect rage at a time
"when everything else is beaten down." He took
the Eastern Counties at his return, and this
brought the series to a close. "The reception
"at Cambridge was something to be proud of in
"such a place. The colleges mustered in full
"force, from the biggest guns to the smallest; and
"went beyond even Manchester in the roars of
"welcome and rounds of cheers. The place was
"crammed, and all through the reading everything
"was taken with the utmost heartiness of enjoy-
"ment." The temptation of offers from America
had meanwhile again been presented to him so
strongly, and in such unlucky connection with
immediate family claims threatening excess of expenditure even beyond the income he was making, that he was fain to write to his sister-in-law:
"I begin to feel myself drawn towards America
"as Darnay in the *Tale of Two Cities* was at-
"tracted to Paris. It is my Loadstone Rock." Too
surely it was to be so; and Dickens was not to
be saved from the consequence of yielding to the
temptation, by any such sacrifice as had rescued
Darnay.

The letter which told me of the close of his
English readings had in it no word of the farther
enterprise, yet it seemed to be in some sort a
preparation for it. "Last Monday evening" (14th
May) "I finished the 50 Readings with great
"success. You have no idea how I have worked
"at them. Feeling it necessary, as their reputa-

"tion widened, that they should be better than at "first, I have *learnt them all*, so as to have no "mechanical drawback in looking after the words.

"I have tested all the serious passion in them by "everything I know; made the humorous points "much more humorous; corrected my utterance "of certain words; cultivated a self-possession not "to be disturbed; and made myself master of the "situation.   Finishing with *Dombey* (which I had "not read for a long time) I learnt that, like the "rest; and did it to myself, often twice a day, "with exactly the same pains as at night, over and "over and over again.".. Six days later brought his reply to a remark that no degree of excellence to which. he might have brought his readings could reconcile me to what there was little doubt would soon be pressed upon him. "It is curious" (20th May) "that you should touch the American sub- "ject, because I must confess that my mind is in "a most disturbed state about it. That the people "there have set themselves on having the read-

"ings, there is no question.   Every mail brings "me proposals, and the number of Americans at "St. James's Hall has been surprising.   A certain "Mr. Grau, who took Ristori out, and is highly "responsible, wrote to me by the last mail (for "the second time) saying that if I would give "him a word of encouragement he would come "over immediately and arrange on the boldest "terms for any number I chose, and would de- "posit a large sum of money at Coutts's.   Mr. "Fields writes to me on behalf of a committee of "private gentlemen at Boston who wished for the

"credit of getting me out, who desired to hear
"the readings and did not want profit, and would
"put down as a guarantee £10,000—also to be
"banked here. Every American speculator who
"comes to London repairs straight to Dolby, with *Offers.*
"similar proposals. And, thus excited, Chappells,
"the moment this last series was over, proposed
"to treat for America!" Upon the mere question
of these various offers he had little difficulty in
making up his mind. If he went at all, he would *Will go on his*
go on his own account, making no compact with *own account only.*
any one. Whether he should go at all, was what
he had to determine.

One thing with his usual sagacity he saw
clearly enough. He must make up his mind
quickly. "The Presidential election would be in
"the autumn of next year. They are a people
"whom a fancy does not hold long. They are
"bent upon my reading there, and they believe
"(on no foundation whatever) that I am going to
"read there. If I ever go, the time would be
"when the Christmas number goes to press.
"Early in this next November." Every sort of
enquiry he accordingly set on foot; and so far *Will go*
came to the immediate decision, that, if the an- *quickly if at all.*
swers left him no room to doubt that a certain
sum might be realized, he would go. "Have no
"fear that anything will induce me to make the
"experiment, if I do not see the most forcible
"reasons for believing that what I could get by
"it, added to what I have got, would leave me
"with a sufficient fortune. I should be wretched
"beyond expression there. My small powers of de-

LONDON:
1867.
Sole motive
in going.

At bay at
last.

Sends agent
to America.

VI. 70.

Warning
unheeded.

"scription cannot describe the state of mind in
"which I should drag on from day to day." At
the end of May he wrote: "Poor dear Stanfield!"
(our excellent friend had passed away the week
before). "I cannot think even of him, and of our
"great loss, for this spectre of doubt and indeci-
"sion that sits at the board with me and stands
"at the bedside. I am in a tempest-tossed con-
"dition, and can hardly believe that I stand at
"bay at last on the American question. The
"difficulty of determining amid the variety of
"statements made to me is enormous, and you
"have no idea how heavily the anxiety of it sits
"upon my soul. But the prize looks so large!"
One way at last seemed to open by which it was
possible to get at some settled opinion. "Dolby
"sails for America" (2nd of July) "on Saturday
"the 3rd of August. It is impossible to come to
"any reasonable conclusion, without sending eyes
"and ears on the actual ground. He will take
"out my MS. for the *Children's Magazine.* I hope
"it is droll, and very child-like; though the joke
"is a grown-up one besides. You must try to
"like the pirate story, for I am very fond of it."
The allusion is to his pleasant *Holiday Romance*
which he had written for Mr. Fields.

Hardly had Mr. Dolby gone when there came
that which should have availed to dissuade, far
more than any of the arguments which continued
to express my objection to the enterprise. "I am
"laid up," he wrote on the 6th of August, "with
"another attack in my foot, and was on the sofa
"all last night in tortures. I cannot bear to have

"the fomentations taken off for a moment. I was LONDON: 1867.
"so ill with it on Sunday, and it looked so fierce,
"that I came up to Henry Thompson. He has
"gone into the case heartily, and says that there
"is no doubt the complaint originates in the ac-
"tion of the shoe, in walking, on an enlargement
"in the nature of a bunion. Erysipelas has su-
"pervened upon the injury; and the object is to
"avoid a gathering, and to stay the erysipelas
"where it is. Meantime I am on my back, and Chafing.
"chafing. . . I didn't improve my foot by going
"down to Liverpool to see Dolby off, but I have
"little doubt of its yielding to treatment, and re-
"pose." A few days later he was chafing still; the accomplished physician he consulted having dropped Sir Henry
other hints that somewhat troubled him. "I could Thompson's opinion.
"not walk a quarter of a mile to-night for £500.
"I make out so many reasons against supposing
"it to be gouty that I really do not think it is."

So momentous in my judgment were the con-
sequences of the American journey to him that
it seemed right to preface thus much of the in-
ducements and temptations that led to it. My
own part in the discussion was that of steady Discussion
dissuasion throughout: though this might perhaps useless.
have been less persistent if I could have recon-
ciled myself to the belief, which I never at any
time did, that Public Readings were a worthy
employment for a man of his genius. But it had
by this time become clear to me that nothing
could stay the enterprise. The result of Mr.
Dolby's visit to America—drawn up by Dickens
himself in a paper possessing still the interest of

having given to the Readings when he crossed the Atlantic much of the form they then assumed*—reached me when I was staying at

---

* This renders it worth preservation in a note. He called it

"THE CASE IN A NUTSHELL.

" 1. I think it may be taken as proved, that general enthusiasm and "excitement are awakened in America on the subject of the "Readings, and that the people are prepared to give me a "great reception. *The New York Herald*, indeed, is of opinion "that 'Dickens must apologise first'; and where a *New York* "*Herald* is possible, any thing is possible. But the prevailing "tone, both of the press and of people of all conditions, is highly "favourable. I have an opinion myself that the Irish element "in New York is dangerous; for the reason that the Fenians "would be glad to damage a conspicuous Englishman. This is "merely an opinion of my own.

" 2. All our original calculations were based on 100 Readings. But "an unexpected result of careful enquiry on the spot, is the "discovery that the month of May is generally considered (in "the large cities) bad for such a purpose. Admitting that "what governs an ordinary case in this wise, governs mine, "this reduces the Readings to 80, and consequently at a blow "makes a reduction of 20 per cent. in the means of making "money within the half year—unless the objection should not "apply in my exceptional instance.

" 3. I dismiss the consideration that the great towns of America "could not possibly be exhausted—or even visited—within 6 "months, and that a large harvest would be left unreaped. Be-"cause I hold a second series of Readings in America is to be "set down as out of the question: whether regarded as involv-"ing two more voyages across the Atlantic, or a vacation of five "months in Canada.

" 4. The narrowed calculation we have made, is this: What is the "largest amount of clear profit derivable, under the most ad-"vantageous circumstances possible, as to their public recep-"tion, from 80 Readings and no more? In making this calcula-"tion, the expenses have been throughout taken on the New "York scale—which is the dearest; as much as 20 per cent. "has been deducted for management, including Mr. Dolby's "commission; and no credit has been taken for any extra pay-"ment on reserved seats, though a good deal of money is con-"fidently expected from this source. But on the other hand "it is to be observed that four Readings (and a fraction over) "are supposed to take place every week, and that the "estimate of receipts is based on the assumption that the au-"diences are, on all occasions, as large as the rooms will reason-"ably hold.

" 5. So considering 80 Readings, we bring out the nett profit of that "number, remaining to me after payment of all charges what-"ever, as £15,500.

" 6. But it yet remains to be noted that the calculation assumes

Ross; and upon it was founded my last argument against the scheme. This he received in
London on the 28th of September, on which day
he thus wrote to his eldest daughter: "As I tele-
"graphed after I saw you, I am off to Ross to
"consult with Mr. Forster and Dolby together.
"You shall hear, either on Monday, or by Mon- Final con-
"day's post from London, how I decide finally." sultation.
The result he wrote to her three days later: "You
"will have had my telegram that I go to America.
"After a long discussion with Forster, and con-
"sideration of what is to be said on both sides, I
"have decided to go through with it. We have
"telegraphed 'Yes' to Boston." Seven days later Decision
he wrote to me: "The Scotia being full, I do not to go.
"sail until lord mayor's day; for which glorious
"anniversary I have engaged an officer's cabin on
"deck in the Cuba. I am not in very brilliant
"spirits at the prospect before me, and am deeply
"sensible of your motive and reasons for the line
"you have taken; but I am not in the least shaken
"in the conviction that I could never quite have
"given up the idea."

"New York City, and the State of New York, to be good for
"a very large proportion of the 80 Readings; and that the cal-
"culation also assumes the necessary travelling not to extend
"beyond Boston and adjacent places, New York City and ad-
"jacent places, Philadelphia, Washington, and Baltimore.
"But, if the calculation should prove too sanguine on this
"head, and if these places should *not* be good for so many
"Readings, then it may prove impracticable to get through
"80 within the time: by reason of other places that would come
"into the list, lying wide asunder, and necessitating long and
"fatiguing journeys.
"7. The loss consequent on the conversion of paper money into
"gold (with gold at the present ruling premium) is al-
"lowed for in the calculation. It counts seven dollars to the
"pound."

The remaining time was given to preparations; on the 2nd of November there was a Farewell Banquet in the Freemasons' Hall over which Lord Lytton presided; and on the 9th Dickens sailed for Boston. Before he left he had contributed his part to the last of his Christmas Numbers; all the writings he lived to complete were done; and the interval of his voyage may be occupied by a general review of the literary labour of his life.

END OF VOL. V.